Aeschylus, Edward Hayes Plumptre

The Tragedies of Aeschylos

Aeschylus, Edward Hayes Plumptre

The Tragedies of Aeschylos

ISBN/EAN: 9783337075033

Printed in Europe, USA, Canada, Australia, Japan

Cover: Foto ©Andreas Hilbeck / pixelio.de

More available books at **www.hansebooks.com**

THE TRAGEDIES OF
ÆSCHYLOS

A New Translation

WITH A BIOGRAPHICAL ESSAY, AND AN APPENDIX OF
RHYMED CHORAL ODES

BY THE LATE VERY REV. E. H. PLUMPTRE, D.D.

DEAN OF WELLS

NEW AND CHEAP EDITION

LONDON
ISBISTER AND COMPANY, LIMITED
15 & 16, TAVISTOCK STREET, COVENT GARDEN
1891

RICHARD CHENEVIX TRENCH, D.D.,

ARCHBISHOP OF DUBLIN.

DEAR friend, of old true guide of pilgrims known,
    Leading their steps where Wisdom's fair pearls lie
    With orient gems, in Truth's rich treasury,
On to the altar-stairs and sapphire Throne,
Now reaping harvest which thou hadst not sown,
    The heaped-up debt of far ancestral crimes,
    Bearing the brunt of these our troublous times,
While mists are thick, and loud the night-winds moan·
Scant leisure thine to look with studious eyes
    On these poor transcripts of a glorious page,
The heathen's dim, 'unconscious prophecies,'
    The dreams of Hellas in her golden age:
Nay, gird thee to thy task, come good, come ill,
And so 'mid storms and fears thy Master's hest fulfil

October 14, 1863.

PREFACE.

I HAVE been led by the interest which I found in the work of translating Sophocles, and in part also by the reception which my translation met with, to enter on another, and, in some respects, more difficult task, in which I have had predecessors at once more numerous and of higher mark. I leave it to others to compare the merits and defects of my work with theirs.

I have adhered in it to the plan of using for the Choral Odes such unrhymed metres, observing the strophic and antistrophic arrangement, as seemed to me most analogous in their general rhythmical effect to those of the original; while, for the sake of those who cannot abandon their preference for the form with which they are more familiar, I have added, in an Appendix, a rhymed version of the chief Odes of the Oresteian trilogy. Those in the other dramas did not seem to me of equal interest, or to lend themselves with equal facility to a like attempt.

I have for the most part followed the text of Mr. Paley's edition of 1861, and, in common with all students of Æschylos, I have to acknowledge a large debt of gratitude to him both for his textual criticism and for the varied amount of illustrative material which he has brought together in his notes. It is right to name Professor Conington also as at once among the most distinguished of those with whose labours my own will have to be compared, and as one who has done for Æschylos at Oxford what Mr. Paley has done at Cambridge, bringing to bear on the study of his dramas at once the accuracy of a critic and the insight of a poet. Had his work as a translator been carried further, had the late Dean of St. Paul's left us more than the single tragedy of the *Agamemnon*, or my friend, Miss Swanwick, been able to complete what she began so well in her version of the Oresteian trilogy, I should probably not have undertaken the work which I have now brought to a conclusion. I have felt, however, that it was desirable for the large mass of readers to whom the culture which comes through the study of Greek literature in the inimitable completeness of the originals is more or less inaccessible, that there should be a translation within their reach, embracing all that has been left to us by one who takes all but the highest place among the tragic poets of Athens, and making it, as far as was possible, intelligible and interesting in its connexion with the history of Greek thought, political and theological.

I have indicated by an asterisk (*) passages where

the reading or the rendering is more or less conjectural, and in which therefore the student would do
well to consult the notes of commentators. Passages
which are regarded as spurious by editors of authority
are placed between brackets [ ].

It only remains that I should once again acknowledge my obligations to my friend the Rev. Charles
Hole, for much help kindly given in the progress of
my work through the press.

6th October, 1868.

NOTE TO THE SECOND EDITION.—The whole work
has been subjected to revision. Additional notes have
been added where they seemed necessary. I have
thought it best to arrange the plays in their chronological order.

29th December, 1872.

CONTENTS.

LIFE OF ÆSCHYLOS.

THE materials for a life of Æschylos are like in kind
and quantity to those which we possess for a life of
Sophocles. A brief anonymous memoir, written probably some four or five hundred years after his death,[1]
a few scattered facts in scholia and lexicons, a few
anecdotes or allusions in contemporary, or all but contemporary, authors; this is all we have to deal with.[2]
My purpose in this essay is to do for the older as I
have done for the younger dramatist, to put these *dis-
jecta membra* together in such an order as may best
show what the man himself was, to illustrate them
from the poet's own works, to throw light on them
from the history of the period in which he lived.

The birth of Æschylos[3] is fixed partly by dates
given by Suidas and in the Arundel Inscriptions, partly
by a conjectural emendation of the text of the anony-

---

(1) The memoir in question is prefixed to the Medicean MS. of the
plays, and is to be found in most editions. It is the authority for all
statements in the text for which no special reference is given.

(2) In some respects, indeed, the earlier dramatist has fared worse than
the later. Even Germany supplies but two monographs, *De Vitâ Æschyli*,
one by Dahm, the other by Petersen, and these are meagre and unin-
teresting as compared with those by Lessing and Schöll on the life of
Sophocles.

(3) The name, a diminutive of αἰσχρὸς, and so meaning "little and
ugly," is of an unusual type, and might almost seem to imply some personal deformity in the child to whom it was given. May we connect
this with the passionate, irascible temper by which the poet was charac-
terised ?

mous biographer, at B.C. <u>525</u>. Both his parentage and
his place of birth may be thought of as having influenced
his poetry. He was an Eupatrid, one of the old noble
families of Attica, born at a time when the separation
between them and the other citizens was far more
strongly marked than at a later period, and we find
the feelings of his class clinging to him through life.
He delights to dwell on the nobler character, the more
generous treatment even of slaves, to be found in the
" heirs of ancient wealth " than in the *nouveaux riches*,
who rose into prominence and power under Pericles,
(*Agam.* ver. 1010-12.) He utters his protest through
the lips of Athena against defiling the " clear stream "
of the old nobility with the " foul mire " of aliens and
traders,[1] (*Eumen.* v. 665.) With this as the dominant
feeling in his mind, he attached himself to the cause
of Kimon as against Pericles, and, as we shall see
hereafter, defended the Areiopagos against the attacks
that threatened its authority. Something of the same
temper—as of one who places noble blood above
wealth, because it more often goes together with
nobleness of nature—is seen in his scorn for " gold-
decked " houses where the hands of those who dwell
in them are soiled, (*Agam.* v. 748,) while he maintains
that there is no inevitable connexion between greatness
and the fall that so often follows on it, that there are
families in which prosperity and honour pass on from
generation to generation, (*Agam.* v. 736.)

Nor can the fact that he was born at Eleusis be

---

(1) One may note the parallelism of Dante's vehement protest against
" *la gente nuova*," " *le bestie Fiesolane*," that had been received into Flo-
rence from neighbouring cities, or made their way to power by " *i subiti
guadagni*."—*Infern.* **xv.** 62, xvi. 73.

considered as of less importance. Initiation into the Mysteries that were connected with that spot, may have been postponed, indeed, (if he was ever actually initiated,)[1] to mature age. But the local influence must have been round him from the first. Men came there to pass through the rites of probation, counted it the blessedness of their life to be admitted by the hierophant, spoke of it as unfolding the secrets of immortality. Theories as to the nature and teacher of these and other mysteries, have indeed varied very widely.[2] Some have seen in them the channels by which a primitive religion was kept from perishing utterly, and faith in the providence, perhaps in the unity, of God, and in a future retribution, transmitted to fit recipients. Others have discerned nothing more than a Phallic symbolism of the reproductive powers of nature, the attractions of which lay in the debasing character of the symbols and the stimulus they supplied to a prurient imagination. Others have found in them symbols, indeed, but symbols no longer understood, the story which had once clothed a thought being dramatised for its own sake, till the thought

(1) The question remains *sub judice*. On the one side there is the statement preserved by Clement of Alexandria in his *Stromata*, (ii. 166,) that when accused before the Areiopagos of having brought the mysteries on the stage, he defended himself by pleading that he had never been initiated. On the other, we have the fact that Aristophanes, in the *Frogs*, (v. 886,) represents him as invoking Demêter,

> "Who hast trained my soul
> To meetness for thy holy mysteries."

The latter testimony, as being nearly contemporary, seems to have greatest weight. Aristotle, however, in referring to the case as illustrating his doctrine of sins of ignorance, (*Eth. Nicom.* iii. 2,) may be thrown into the other scale, as corroborating the tradition given by Clement.

(2) Warburton, in his *Divine Legation of Moses*, has brought together most of the ancient authorities on the subject. Lobeck, in a treatise bearing the title of *Aglaophamus*, has treated the question with a more exhaustive scholarship. St. Croix's *Recherches sur les Mystères du Paganisme* may also be consulted.

itself was forgotten in the interest of the fantastic
mythos that embodied it. With views so divergent
before us, we cannot safely build much on any estimate of the influence which the mysteries of Eleusis
may have exercised upon the mind of Æschylos. It
may be suggested, perhaps, that they, like all other
symbolic rites, degenerated as they grew older ; that
whatever of obscenity or triviality was in them, was
of later growth ; that if they were parables of Nature
and her life-giving power, they also helped men to
think of that life as extending into a more distant
future. Like the secrets of Freemasonry, they may
have had a religious meaning at first, which afterwards
degenerated into a mere conventional mystery, and a
fantastic triviality which a later age strove in vain to
re-clothe with a religious significance. The language
in which Sophocles and Pindar speak of them[1] forbids
us to think of them as in his time other than witnesses
to a loftier truth than that held by the uninitiated
many. The stress laid by Æschylos on the righteous
government of God, on the immortality of the spirits
of the dead, may possibly be traceable to that witness.
His reverence for the Goddess of Eleusis was at all
events thought of as so characteristic, that he is represented, in the Aristophanic caricature already quoted,
as swearing by her name and no other.

(1) Sophocles, *Fragm.* 719—

"Thrice happy they who having seen these rites
Then pass to Hades : there to these alone
Is granted life ; all others evil find."

Pindar, *Thren. Fragm.* 8—

" Blessed is he who having looked on them,
Passes below the hollow earth, for he
Knows life's true end, and Zeus-given sov'reignty."

The education of Æschylos would, in its main outlines, be such as has been described in my life of
Sophocles. It would want, indeed, that which the
latter found as he grew to manhood in the dramas of
Æschylos himself. It would want also the poetry of
Pindar.[1] But the music, and the athletic training, and
the poetry of Homer, were already there to form the
character and develop its nascent powers. The care
taken by Peisistratos to collect and arrange the so-
called Homeric poems, and the formation of a library
at Athens by his sons Hippias and Hipparchos, were
at once symptoms and causes of the intellectual life
which was about to bud and blossom and bear fruit
with such unexampled rapidity. The education of the
young men of Athens was based thenceforward upon
Homer. The cycle of the *Iliad* supplied nearly the
whole material which was to be worked up by the
coming dramatists. Æschylos himself spoke of his
tragedies as being but "made-up dishes" ($\tau\epsilon\mu\alpha\chi\bar{\eta}$)
from the great Homeric banquet, (*Athen.* viii. p. 347.)
Nor can we forget that the name which has stamped
itself upon dramatic art was then beginning to be
known, and that the works of Thespis began, ten
years before the birth of Æschylos, to give a new
character to the festival of the Dionysia. Concurrently
with the influence of the heroic, there must also have
been that of the early gnomic poetry of Greece. The
sententious morality of Theognis appears to have impressed itself on a mind which loved to reproduce
even the earlier, simpler proverbs that entered into

(1) Pindar and Simonides were, however, contemporaries of the great
dramatist, and might easily exercise some influence on the growth of his
genius.

the common speech of men, those which bade them
not to " kick against the pricks," or taught them that
' out of a little seed may spring a mighty tree," that
" pain is gain," that " wisdom comes by sorrow," that
" the highest wisdom is self-knowledge," and the like.
And, accordingly, the parallelisms between the two
writers are striking enough to exclude the notion of
mere coincidence.[1]

The resemblance is, however, in mind and teaching
much more than in words and images. There is the
same dread of the evils of over-prosperous fortune,
the same reverence for the rights of the suppliant and

(1) I owe the references to these passages to a note of Mr. Paley's.
Comp. (1) Theognis. vv. 41-9—

> " In all my deeds thou'lt find me like pure gold,
> Still glowing red, though tried by touchstone's test,
> And the black stain not e'en the surface mars."

Agam. v. 381—

> " And like to worthless bronze,
> By friction tried and tests,
> It turns to tarnished blackness in its hue."

(2) Theogn. v. 151—

> " But full-flushed Lust begetteth Recklessness,
> When prosperous fortune comes to villain soul.

Agam. v. 738—

> " But Recklessness of old
> Is wont to breed another Recklessness ;
>
> That in its youth, in turn
> Doth full-flushed Lust beget,
> Begets Satiety."

(3) Theogn. v. 961—

> " Many there are with false mood counterfeit,
> Who hide their lies with show of short-lived zeal."

Agam. v. 760—

> " Men there are who right transgressing,
> Honour semblance more than being ;
> O'er the sufferer all are ready
> Wail of bitter grief to utter,
> Though the biting pang of sorrow
> Never to their heart approaches ;
> So with counterfeit rejoicing
> Men strain faces that are smileless."

the guest, the same belief in a Nemesis working at times slowly and secretly, but sure to manifest itself at last as the avenger of outrage, and turbulence, and wrong. Even the tone in which the ethical poet speaks of the chastisement which the Gods had sent upon the haughty Medes is in the same key as that which pervades the *Persians* (vv. 744 and 775) of the dramatist. Both are intensely national; both are also intensely the poets of an aristocracy. Theognis complains (vv. 53-58)—

> "This State is still a State, but men are changed;
> Those who erewhile knew nought of Right and Law,
> And clad in goatskin lived outside the gates,
> These are now known as nobles, and the men
> Who once were noble, now as cowards live.
> Men honour wealth, and wealth corrupts the blood,
> Bad marrying good, and good with villains wed."

Just as Æschylos makes Athena warn her people—

> "But if with streams defiled and tainted soil
> Clear river thou pollute, no drink thou'lt find."
> *—Eumen.* v. 665.

and utters his complaint that—

> "Now Success
> Is man's sole God and more."
> *—Lib. Pourers,* v. 50.

The chronological relation of the two poets to each other was just such as to bring the younger poet under the influence of the older. Theognis lived to witness the overthrow of the Persians, and died just as Æschylos was rising into fame.

The reference in *Fragm.* 123 to the story of the eagle shot with one of its own feathers, as taken from the *Libyan Fables*, seems to indicate an acquaintance also with that form of composition which, about this time, was travelling from Asia and Africa into the literature of Greece.

The legend which has come down to us through Pausanias, (*Att.* i. 21, § 3,) though too remote in time to claim a place among the elements of a biography, may yet be received as the expression of the influence exercised on Æschylos by the new art which Thespis had introduced, and its religious associations. "He was set," so the story runs, "to watch grapes as they were ripening for the vintage, and fell asleep : And lo ! as he slept, Dionysos appeared to him, and bade him give himself to write tragedies for the great festival of the God. And when he awoke, he found himself invested with new powers of thought and utterance, and the work was as easy to him as if he had been trained to it for many years." The parable shadows forth, as I have said elsewhere, the chief characteristics both of the excellence and the faults of Æschylos, —the presence of a creative power flaming as with a divine light, striking out lofty thoughts, and clothing them in words of singular felicity, yet wanting in the supreme refinement and equilibrium of a deliberate and conscious art.

Of the dramatic poets who preceded him we know the names, and little more. The date assigned to the first exhibition of tragedies at Athens by Thespis is B.C. 535. So far as we can judge amid conflicting statements of the precise nature of the changes introduced by him, they consisted—(1.) In the introduction of new subjects, still, however, confined to the Dionysiac cycle; (2.) in the addition of dialogue to the choral songs which had previously made up, as it were, the *libretto* of the Dionysian opera; and (3.) in the use of 'masks, or pigments, to make personation of characters more life-like. Groups of satyrs, following the chariot of the God, singing his adventures, and representing some of these adventures in rude mimetic action, seem to have furnished the starting-point of Greek drama. Then came, at Sikyon or elsewhere, (Herod. v. 67,) the celebration of the deeds of other gods, or of the heroes of the Homeric cycle, but still confined to odes, and with a satyr chorus as the chief or only actors.[1] The recitation of the Homeric poems by the travelling minstrels known as Rhapsodists, would naturally tend to enlarge the range of the subjects in which spectators were interested. Thespis had the credit of seizing on the opening thus given, and introducing an actor on the stage conversing with the chorus. Possessed of the versatile mimetic power which has in our own times led men like Charles Mathews and Albert Smith to sustain many characters, and so to be the one actor in a drama which yet had something of a plot, he appeared now in one dress, now in another; now, *e.g.*, as Dionysos, now as Pentheus, now as Agave; and so on, representing the whole story which we find in the *Bacchæ* of Euripides. At first, apparently, the change was in the mode rather than in the subjects. When these, too, were altered, and when the people came to the vintage festival, and found, as in the plays of Phrynichos and Æschylos,

(1) The people of Sikyon, the historian tells us, honoured the hero Adrastos, the son of Talaos, with "tragic choruses" which celebrated his adventures, and which were transferred by Cleisthenes to Dionysos.

nothing that reminded them of the vintage God, they missed the rough, coarse mirth in which they had revelled, and asked in words which passed into a proverb, "What has this to do with Dionysos?"[1] The change from one cycle of subjects to the whole range of the legends of the heroic age was analogous to that which passed over the English drama when *Ferrex and Porrex* and *Gorboduc* took the place of the "mysteries" and "miracle plays" of an earlier period. The later arrangement, which made a satyric drama the necessary completion of a tragic trilogy, (as the Christmas pantomime comes, in the modern drama, after the five-act tragedy,) was probably of the nature of a compromise between the tastes of the men of culture and those of the people, who still craved for something of the old rough sport, and frolicsome, rampant humour.

Phrynichos, whose name thus meets us in conjunction with that of Æschylos, (he gained his first prize B.C. 511, and his last B.C. 476,) went further in the development of the new art. The impulse given to the study of Homer by the influence of Peisistratos, supplied him, as it afterwards supplied his successors, not only, as has been said, with an almost inexhaustible material, loftier and nobler than the subjects of the old Dionysian mimes or the earlier dramas of Thespis, but also with a higher culture generally. The choral odes of his dramas were long remembered as at once exquisitely sweet, and pure and lofty in their tone. With Aristophanes, he is the type of the older and better style of poetry and music, as com-

---

(1) Plutarch, *Sympos.* ii. p. 1092.

pared with later and more artificial refinements. His songs are "sweet as the honey of the bee." He himself is the "master of all singers."[1] The introduction of masks for the female characters, and of solemn measures for the rhythmical movements of the chorus, was also ascribed to him. Perhaps the most striking fact in connexion with him is, that he was the first to seize on the facts of contemporary history as subjects for his dramas, and in B.C. 494, brought on the stage the capture of Miletos, which had just fallen into the hands of the Persians. With a just perception of the true purpose of the drama, the Athenians, though moved to tears by the sorrows which were thus brought before them, felt that the sufferings of a city so nearly related to them should not be displayed for the amusement of the people. They fined the poet a thousand drachmæ, and forbade the reproduction of the drama. Taught by this experience, at a later period, with the victorious Themistocles as his *choragos*, he dramatised, not the disasters, but the successes of the Athenians; and in a drama which bore the title of the *Phœnikians*, represented, probably in B.C. 476, the defeat of Xerxes, and so set the example which Æschylos followed in his *Persians*. Phrynichos, however, did not stand alone. The intellectual activity of the time threw itself at Athens into this line of work, and little as we know of Chœrilos, Pratinas, and other contemporaries, we must bear in mind that they were there, stimulating the mind of Æschylos to emulation, and contributing, each of them, some new improvement to the progress of the art.

(1) Athen. viii. p. 348; Aristoph., *Birds*, v. 748; *Wasps*, vv. 219-209 *Frogs*, vv. 911-1294; *Thesm.* v. 164.

But before we enter on the dramatic career of him who was to surpass them all, it will be well to note some other influences to which he must, in the nature of things, have been exposed, and the operation of which we can actually trace in his writings.

(1.) Foremost among these must be noted the spirit of enterprise which was leading the Greeks to voyages of discovery and to settlements in remote lands. The temper, of which the *Odyssey*, and the legend of the Argonauts, were the first-fruits, had rapidly developed itself in them. They had begun to establish themselves in Egypt in the time of Psammitichos, and the wonders which the land of the Nile presented to their view, drew travellers who, like Herodotos a little later, gazed round them in astonishment, and sought to discover affinities between the myths of Egypt and those of Hellas. Others pressed on, as Herodotos also did, to the land of the two great rivers, to the cities on the shores of the Euphrates and the Tigris, to those of the Medes and Persians. The invasion of Syria and the seaboard of the Euxine by the Skythians, had brought them also into prominence, increased, of course, by the stories of the expedition of Dareios against them. In the West also, colonies of Greeks had settled in the south of Italy and Sicily. The marvels of Skylla and Charybdis, of Ætna and the Kyclops, of Atlas and the pillars of Heracles, and the Islands of the Blessed, and the mysterious Atlantis, had impressed themselves on their imagination. Æschylos himself, there is some reason to believe, shared in some of these adventurous voyages, and visited Sicily before he had reached the age of twenty-six,

before **his success as a** dramatist began.[1] When he
dwells on **the** wonders which travellers had told, he
may have reproduced what he had thus heard himself.
When he went to the court of Hieron after his defeat
by Sophocles, it was not as a stranger, but as one who
had already made friends there, **and** was sure of
patronage. He at any rate shared in the spirit which
delighted in these reports from far-off lands. In pro-
portion to the distance, the tales of travellers were
stranger and more fantastic. What the Spanish Main
and El Dorado, and the " still vexed Bermoothes "
and Prester John, were to the Elizabethan dramatists,
that the one-eyed Arimaspi, and the long-lived, happy
Hyperborei, and the Gorgons, and the Kyclops, **were**
to the dramatic poets of Athens. And in Æschylos
the position which they occupy is obviously a prominent one. In the *Prometheus* the wanderings **of** Io
are brought in, if in part for deeper mythological
reasons, **yet** in part also to enable the tale of these
marvels to be told fully. In it and in the *Suppliants*
he yields to the fascination of the mysterious legends
of Io and the " touch-born " Epaphos, and claims a
common origin for the Argives and the Egyptians. He
revels, and his hearers must have revelled, (some of
them remembering their own adventures,) in **the**
uncouth names and wild imagery into which he thus
plunges. He delights, as Milton delighted, **in the**
rhythmic grandeur of semi-barbaric names, each with
its associations of mystery and wonder.

(1) The question lies more or less in the region of conjecture. His
migration to Sicily is assigned by different writers now to this, now to
that cause, and is placed by some before, by some after, the death of
Gelon. I follow Hermann (*Opusc.* ii., *De Choro Eumen.*) in the hypothesis that the accounts may be reconciled by assuming three cr more
distinct journeys.

(2.) As the Greeks were thus stimulated in their
intellectual life by the spirit of discovery, so also were
they by their struggle for political freedom against the
" tyranny " of Peisistratos and his sons, and by the
contest—imminent as Æschylos was growing up to
manhood, and over before any of his extant tragedies
were composed—with the non-Hellenic races gathered
under the command, first of Dareios and then of
Xerxes. What Spain was to the poets of England
under Elizabeth, (to return to the analogy already
suggested,) Persia was to those of Greece, and the
victory of Salamis had its analogue in the overthrow
of the Armada. It was the lot of Sophocles, then a
mere stripling, to lead the choral band that celebrated
that victory. It was the work of Æschylos, in the
Persians, (probably the earliest of his extant plays,) to
give it a yet more illustrious and lasting monument ;
to bring before an Athenian audience the strange
dresses, and the servile prostrations, and the wild
wailings, and the strange-sounding names of the defeated invaders. But beyond the limits of that play
we find traces of the same feeling. The pride and
pomp of the " barbarian " are instanced in the embroidered tapestry which Clytæmnestra spreads for the
march of Agamemnon, in order that he may bring
upon himself the wrath of the Hellenic Gods, (*Agam.*
892.)

(3.) I am disposed to assign a larger share of influence upon the character and poetry of Æschylos than
is commonly recognised, to that strange mysterious
personage who appeared for a short moment on the
stage of Athenian history about seventy years before

his birth, (B.C. 596,) Epimenides, the prophet of Crete.
Scanty as are the materials for any history of the man
or of his teaching, it is clear that at the time his fame
was like in kind and almost equal in degree to that of
Pythagoras.[1] The ascetic life, (it was said that no
man ever saw him eat;) the ecstatic state which issued
in prophetic utterances, and led men to think that he
was communing with the Gods; the sleep, prolonged
through fifty years, out of which he woke with a new
and heaven-taught wisdom;—all this invested him in
the eyes of the Greeks with a mysterious, supernatural
character.[2] Like Balaam the son of Beor, he was sent
for from far countries to bless or to curse, to teach
men how to purify their land from the guilt of blood,
to appease their dread of the unseen Powers. His
arrival at Athens in obedience to the summons which
called him to their help, when pestilence and discord
seemed to proclaim the wrath of the Gods against the
guilt which the " bloody house " of the Alcmæonidæ
had brought upon the land by their treacherous murder
of Kylon and his adherents, must have left a deep
impression. Echoes of his teaching (so far as that
teaching has come down to us in fragmentary notices)
are found in Æschylos.

(a.) The prophet refers all his power to predict to
the wisdom which he had gained in his long slumber,

---

(1) It has been often said, as by Cicero, (*Tusc. Disp.* ii. 10,) that
Æschylos was "non poeta solum, sed etiam Pythagoreus;" and Mr.
Paley, in his Preface, has enlarged on the thought, and pointed out many
interesting coincidences between the poet and the philosopher. For the
most part, however, they belong to tenets characteristic of both Pythagoras and Epimenides, and the derivation is more easily traceable in the
case of the latter than of the former.

(2) Comp. Heinrich's elaborate monograph, *Epimenides aus Kreta*,
where all that is known about him is brought together and discussed,
and Hoeck's *Kreta*, iii. 2, s. 11.

and which was renewed in visions of the night.[1]   The
poet proclaims—

> " And slowly dropping on the heart in sleep,
>   Comes woe-recording care,
>   And makes the unwilling yield to wiser thoughts."
>   —*Agam.* v. 173.

(*b.*) The idea of a transmitted pollution cleaving to
a family from generation to generation, sin becoming
the penalty of sin, until some one comes who, by
penitence and prayer, and rites of expiation, obtains
pardon and deliverance, was that which had brought
Epimenides to Athens.   He is pre-eminently the
" purifier," the " prophet-healer," the servant of
Apollo in the work of cleansing and clearing the guilty,
as that god is brought before us in the *Eumenides.*   It
is needless to point out that this is throughout the
key-note of the Oresteian trilogy.   We meet it in
Clytæmnestra's reference to the Alastor, the avenging
fiend, with whom she identifies herself (*Agam.* v. 1478)
in her hope that her crime will—

> " At last have freed my house
> From madness that sets each man's hand 'gainst each,"
>   —(*Agam.* v. 1552 ;)

in the stress which Orestes lays on the rites of purification that have cleansed him, (*Eumen.* v. 423.)   The
more generalised teaching,

> " But how to blot the guilt of kindred blood,
>   This needs a great atonement, *many victims
>   falling to many Gods*, to heal the woe,"
>   —(*Suppl.* v. 444,)

---

(1) Maximus Tyr. xxxviii. 3.

almost reproduces the process by which Epimenides is
said to have purified Athens by turning loose a flock
of sheep, black and white mingled, and sacrificing them
to the Gods at whose altars they fell, erecting an altar,
if they rested where none existed previously, to the
UNKNOWN or to an unnamed GOD.   Even the sacrifice
of Iphigeneia has a parallel in the story preserved by
Athenæos (xiii. 8), that a noble youth, Cratinos, had
immolated himself, with the sanction of the Cretan
prophet, to appease the wrath of the Gods.

(c.) Epimenides, it is said, on leaving Athens, told
its inhabitants to erect on the Areiopagos[1] two unhewn
stones as altars to Outrage (ὕβρις) and Shamelessness.
They were to look on those personified attributes as
the demons who had vexed their city, and whom they
must entreat never again to trouble them.   It is impossible, I think, not to recognise an echo of that
teaching, (1) in the reverence which Æschylos shows
in the last play of the Oresteian trilogy for the court
of the Areiopagos ; and (2) in the like personification
of the self-same evil Powers—

"But Outrage (ὕβρις) done of old,
Is wont to breed another Outrage still,
Sporting its youth in human miseries,
At once, or whensoe'er the fixed time comes."
—*Agam.*, 738.

(d.) The Cretan prophet is said to have done much
to naturalise at Athens the worship of the Chthonian
Goddesses, (dwelling, *i.e.*, in the thick darkness below
the Earth,) known as the Erinnyes or Eumenides, who

---

(1) Clem. Alex., *Protrept.*, p. 22; Cicero, *De Legibus*, ii. 11.

are so prominent in the poetry of Æschylos.[1] The temple to them, which stood on the Areiopagos, and which is glorified in the closing scene of the trilogy, was said to have been built under the direction of **Epimenides.**

(*e*.) The seer is said to have been at one time on the point of dedicating a temple to the Muses, when a voice from heaven bade him stop, and be for the future a worshipper of Zeus only.[2] Whatever view we may take of this, as indicating a step upwards to a mono-theistic creed, we cannot fail to see a close parallel to it in the words of the dramatist—

> " O Zeus—whate'er He be,
> If that name please him well,
> By that on him I call,
> Weighing all other names, I fail to guess
> Aught else but Zeus."—*Agam.*, v. 155.

(*f*.) Lastly, Epimenides is said to have restrained the unmeasured barbaric wailing over the dead to which the women of Athens had till then been accustomed.[3] And here, too, his teaching is echoed by Æschylos. He brings that kind of wailing forward in the *Persians* as characteristic of barbarian manners; he hardly ever speaks of it but in connection with some barbaric name, Mariandynian, Kissian, or the like; he puts into the mouth of Eteocles a vehement protest against it, (*Seven ag. Thebes*, vv. 169-190.)

With a genius so formed and fashioned, Æschylos followed the leading of the time, and entered on his

(1) Diog. Laert., i. 12; **Plutarch.**, *Solon.*, c. **12.**
(2) Diog. Laert., i. 10.
(3) Plutarch., *Solon.*, c. **12.**

work as a dramatic writer. He resembled Phrynichos, as we have seen, in his choice of heroic legends or contemporary history, instead of the revel mimes of the older Dionysia. And the language in which the tales were clothed rose also far above the earlier level. He was the first of the Greeks to " build the lofty rhyme,"[1] to bring out the strange compound words, " neck-breaking," " cumbrous," " pegged and wedged and dove-tailed," as Aristophanes called them, coined in the mint of his own brain; to startle the eyes as well as the ears of his audience with figures of monstrous forms of animals, winged dragons, beasts half-cock and half-horse, half-goat and half-stag, like those that draw the chariots of Okeanos in the *Prometheus*, of Athena in the *Eumenides ;* to array his actors in stately robes, so gorgeous that they were afterwards copied by priests in temples and by the hierophants of mysteries;[2] to trust to the " sensation " caused by the presence of actors who were prominent through the whole action of a play, but never opened their lips, or spoke but a single sentence.[3] If we would appreciate his dramas as we read them, without the accessories which accompanied them as they were performed, we must remember that they were in a high degree *spectacles* rather than poems,—with but few speakers, but with all the scenic effect of dresses, processions, and decorations.

---

(1) Aristoph., *Frogs*, 943.   (2) Athen., i. p. 21.
(3) Aristoph., *Frogs*, vv. 906-912. In this apparently he followed Phrynichos. It probably belonged to his earlier manner. No instance of it occurs in the seven extant tragedies. Aristophanes refers to Achilles and Niobe as the characters thus represented. In the *Libation-Pourers*, however, Pylades, though present throughout the greater part of the action of the play, speaks but once.

The personal temperament of the man seems to have been in harmony with these characteristics of his genius. Vehement, passionate, irascible; writing his tragedies (as later critics judged) as if half-drunk, doing (as Sophocles said of him) what was right in his art without knowing why;[1] following the impulses that led him to strange themes and dark problems, rather than aiming at the perfection of a complete, all-sided culture; frowning with shaggy brows, like a wild bull, glaring fiercely, and bursting into a storm of wrath when annoyed by critics or rival poets; a Marlow rather than a Shakspeare: this is the portrait sketched by one who must have painted a figure still fresh in the minds of the Athenians.[2] Such a man, both by birth and disposition, was likely to attach himself to the aristocratic party, and to look with scorn on the claims of the *demos* to a larger share of power. His ancestors had fought against Peisistratos, and he too entered his protest against that form of government which the Greeks called a *tyranny*, the despotism of a political adventurer, self-raised to sovereign power, without the divine sanction which attached to the old hereditary kings who traced their descent from Zeus himself.[3] Through his whole life, he was faithful to his early creed. There is hardly a play in which some political bias in that direction may not be distinctly traced. The time of his greatest popularity was during the ascendancy first of Aristeides and then of Kimon. When his star waned before the clearer, calmer, less fitful light of Sophocles, the change syn-

(1) Athen., x. p. 428.   (2) Aristoph., *Frogs*, vv. 802-855.
              (3) See the passages quoted in p. lii.

chronised with the rise of Pericles to political supremacy. It was natural with such a character that his
career as a dramatist and a man should be somewhat
more chequered than that of his great successor.
Sophocles was from first to last the favourite of the
Athenians,— easy, genial, contented.   Æschylos —
quick to take offence, quick also to give it ; startling
men by strange *tours de force* ; coming into direct collision with their feelings, moral, political, and religious ;
wounding them where they were most susceptible—
experienced the mutability of popular favour in a more
than ordinary degree. The incidents of his life, so
far as they are known to us, seem to point to a series
of irritations, misunderstandings, and temporary aliena-
tions between him and his countrymen.

The date B.C. 499 is fixed for his first dramatic contest with Pratinas and Chœrilos.[1] He was not successful ; but the excitement of the competition drew
so great a crowd of spectators, that the wooden
scaffolding on which they sat gave way.[2] Partly hurt
at his defeat, partly urged by the spirit of adventure,
he went, as has been said, in the same year to Sicily.
His absence did not last long. He was at Athens
when the expedition of Datis and Artaphernes threatened the liberties of Greece, and he and his brother
Kynægeiros fought at Marathon. Like all who took
part in that first great battle in Athenian history, he

(1) The chronology depends on a combination of the two notices in
Suidas under the headings *Æschylos* and *Pratinas.*
(2) Pausan. *Att.* i. 4 ; Suidas, *l.c.* It is interesting to note that this
disaster led the Athenians to build their first stone theatre for the
Dionysiac festivals, and so prepared the way for the stately buskin, and
the gorgeous dresses, and the other stage effects which Æschylos and his
contemporaries were not slow to introduce.

c

looked back on it as the great glory of his life. When
he wrote his own epitaph, in advanced age and in a
distant land, it was to record, not that he had been a
poet and had won thirteen prizes from the Athenian
people, but that the " plain of Marathon and the long-
haired Mede " could attest his well-tried valour.[1]

The glory of Marathon was, however, probably followed by the mortification of another defeat. The
Athenians (already pushing forward to intellectual as
well as military excellence) wanted for those who had
fallen in the battle an elegy that should be worthy of their
fame, and when the prize was awarded to Simonides,
Æschylos, it is said, was irritated at his failure, and
again took his departure for Sicily in B.C. 488.[2]   Gelon
was at that time rising to power, and with him, almost
sharing his authority, was his brother Hieron. In that
prince, the patron of poets and philosophers, the friend

---

(1) The epitaph is given, p. xlvii.
(2) The two epitaphs are given in the *Anthologia Graca*, and may be
rendered as follows :—

SIMONIDES.

Farewell, ye heroes, warriors famed in fight,
Ye youth of Athens, horsemen strong in might,
Who for your goodly country gave your prime,
And in the sight of all of Hellas' clime,
Fought against myriads with a faith sublime!

ÆSCHYLOS.

These valiant swordsmen gloomy Fate laid low,
  In act to free the plains where roam the sheep,
But still for those who yielded to the blow
  Lives glory, though in Ossa's dust they sleep.

The two elegiac poems here given are identified with the Marathonian
epitaphs by Stanley, in his notes on the Life of Æschylos, with a "facile
crederem," (ii. p. 172) ; by Droysen, (ii. p. 302) ; and by Bunsen, (*God in
History*, ii. p. 153), without any qualification. I agree, however, with
Bode (*Geschichte des Hellenischen Dichtkunst*, ii. p. 262; iii. p. 215,) in looking on the conjecture as very uncertain in either case. That ascribed
to Æschylos seems to refer to some unrecorded act of heroism on the part
of the Thessalians, and is indeed described in some MSS. as written
for their warriors.—See Jacobs' *Antholog. Graca*, notes on Book vii.
254, 255.

of Pindar and Simonides,—immortalised by the former as victor at Olympic games,—he found a liberal patron. Sicily became almost a second home to him, a place of refuge after any trouble or disappointment in his own city. This time, however, his absence was not of long duration, and in the interval between Marathon and Salamis, in B.C. 484, he was for the first time successful in his competition with those who had been the leading dramatic poets, Pratinas, Phrynichos, and Chœrilos. It was the beginning of a series of thirteen like successes.[1] Most, if not all, the prizes awarded to him were obtained between that date and B.C. 470. It was the period when the policy of Kimon and Aristeides was in the ascendant, when the Eupatrids were yet able to resist the encroachments of the democracy. With that policy then, as afterwards, Æschylos identified himself. He was the poet of the conservative party, as Sophocles was afterwards the representative poet of the cultivated liberalism of that of Pericles.

Of the plays now extant, the *Persians* stands first in order of time. Written, as it was, within eight years of the battle of Salamis, it appealed to those in whose memories every incident of the battle was yet fresh. The vividness and minuteness of the account there given of the engagement seems to indicate that he himself, like his brother Ameinias, had a large share in the glory of the day.[2] It has accordingly the in-

---

(1) The total number of dramas ascribed to him is stated by Suidas as ninety, by the anonymous biographer as seventy. We have the titles of seventy-eight.

(2) To Ameinias the Athenians awarded the *aristeia*, or prize of valour, as to the man who, of all the Greeks that fought at Salamis, had done the worthiest deeds. Some years afterwards, when Æschylos was accused of impiety, as having divulged the mysteries, and was on the point of being stoned, Ameinias was said to have shown the arm, the hand of which had

terest of being a contemporary record by an eye-
witness, and represented before eye-witnesses, and
gives, we may well believe, a truer account than that
which we find forty years later in Herodotos, when
there had been time for the growth of numerous em-
bellishments, approaching in some instances almost to
the character of legends. The drama itself is for us,
perhaps, apart from this fact, one of the least interesting of the seven extant plays. At the time, it was
probably accepted as worthy of the triumph which it
celebrated. To understand the *Persians*, we must
think of it as a spectacle, performed before thousands
of those who had fought themselves, or had had
brothers or fathers in the battle, exulting over the
thought that the Gods had fought for them, and that
their enemies had been defeated. The nearest analogue in literature, in spite of the difference in form, is
found in the Song of Deborah. The close of that
hymn, picturing, as it does, the mother of Sisera looking out of her lattice, anticipating tidings of victory
when she is about to hear those of utter failure, suggests a theme which, with a nation of greater dramatic
power than the Hebrews, might have been developed
as Æschylos does the like emotions in the mother of
Xerxes. In each case the poem supplies facts which
the history, compiled at a later period, omits or
colours.[1] In both there is the same fiery glow, the

been lost at Salamis, and with that to have pleaded his brother's cause.
The judges yielded to the appeal, and gave a verdict of acquittal. This
apparently was the trial of which Clement of Alexandria, in the passage
already quoted, gives so different an account.—Ælian. V.H. v. 19.

(1) Comp., *e.g.*, the account of the disaster which befell the Persians as
they crossed the frozen Strymon, (*Pers.* vv. 500—510,) and that of the
destruction of the hosts of Jabin as they crossed the swollen torrent of
the Kishon (Judg. v. 21, 22).

same sense of a victory over aliens. In the work of
the Athenian, we must not forget that what seems to
us as we read it, the monstrous iteration of interjec-
tions, cries, lamentations, must have been, as it was
performed, one of its most striking features. It was
because these wailings, and tearing of hair, and beating of breasts, and rending of robes, were regarded as
especially Asiatic and barbarous, that the Athenians
loved to listen to, and to look on them, when they
were associated with the defeat and disgrace of their
foes. Their own civilisation had raised them above
these violent displays of grief, and from the time of
Solon, who had legislated against them, even wives
and mothers had learnt to bear the deaths of those
they loved with a more decent and tranquil sorrow.

   The success which had attended this treatment of a
naval engagement, led Æschylos, in his next trilogy,
probably in the following year, (B.C. 471,) to take
another equally warlike, ("full of Ares," as Aristophanes calls it,) and to represent in *The Seven who
fought against Thebes* the incidents of a siege, the warriors heading the storming-party, each bearing his
shield, the leaders with some device and motto painted
on it in bright colours, the women of the besieged city
going in procession to offer their prayers at the shrines
of the Gods, the scouts looking out from the ramparts,
and bringing back word of the disposition of the
enemy's forces, and the issue of the conflict. The fact
that he was writing of a mythical, not of an actual war
in which living men had taken part, robs *The Seven
against Thebes*, indeed, of the interest which attaches
to the *Persians*. But here also there was a political

purpose mingling with the poet's work. The bearing of the play was directed against the policy of aiming at the supremacy of Athens by attacking other Greek states. It brought before men the horrors that attend the capture of a city, and led them to ask whether these horrors should be perpetrated on a Hellenic city by those who spoke the same Hellenic speech, (*Seven ag. Thebes*, vv. 78-168.) It maintained, that is, the policy of Aristeides as against that of Themistocles, and when the words were uttered which described a statesman and a general "who sought to be *just* in deed as well as name,"[1] (v. 588,) the enthusiasm which burst out from an audience raised to the highest pitch of excitement, showed that the skill of the poet had not been wasted.

Within a few years, (in B.C. 468,) the career of success was interrupted by the rising genius of a poet of higher culture, and the first prize at the Dionysian festival was awarded to Sophocles, then in his twenty-ninth year. The defeat was, perhaps, the more mortifying as occurring under the direction of Kimon, the leader of the party to which Æschylos had attached himself.[2] It led him to leave Athens for a time, and to visit Sicily. Other causes may have contributed to that decision. He had incurred, it is said, at some period the date of which it is not easy to fix, the displeasure of the Athenians by introducing in his drama some of the mystic rites which were confined to the initiated few. The spectators, seeing on the stage what many among them knew to belong to the mysteries of Eleu-

---

(1) Plutarch, *Arist.* c. 3.
(2) Plutarch, *Kim.* Comp. the account in my *Life of Sophocles*.

sis, were roused to a wild frenzy, and rushed upon the poet, who, as himself acting, was on the stage. His life was in danger, and he only escaped by fleeing to the altar of Dionysos as to the privilege of sanctuary. By the intercession of members of the court of Areiopagos, he was rescued, brought to a more formal trial, and acquitted.[1] If the *Prometheus*, the date of which is uncertain, had been performed before this time, it may well have contributed to shock the feelings of the Athenians. He had probably, as has been before stated, been previously acquainted with the country, and had already come within the attraction of the patronage extended by Hieron to artists and men of letters. Here, it is said, he composed dramas, the subject-matter of which was taken from local legends, —*The Women of Ætna*, and the like; and, at the request of Hieron, reproduced the *Persians* on the stage of Syracuse. Here too he may have heard of the ravages of the great volcanic eruption of B.C. 477, to which he refers in his *Prometheus*, (vv. 370-380,) even if he had not been one of the actual spectators during his previous visit.

The date assigned to the *Suppliants* rests upon the assumption that it is connected with the alliance be-

---

(1) The account is given by Eustratius (p. 40) in a passage quoted by Lobeck, (*Aglaoph.* i. 12.) The trilogy which gave occasion to the suspicion is said to have included the plays of Sisyphos, Iphigeneia, and Œdipus. Lobeck inclines to the belief, not that there was any disclosure of the secret *doctrines* of the mysteries, (if indeed there were any such,) but that some solemn stage procession, like that which we find at the close of the *Eumenides*, startled the Athenians by its resemblance to that with which the initiated were familiar. It is in connexion with this charge that we meet with the two versions of the story given respectively by Ælian and Clement of Alexandria—(1.) That his brother Ameinias pleaded for him with his handless arm; (2.) That he defended himself by asserting that he had never been initiated in the mysteries, and therefore could not divulge them.

tween Argos and Athens, which was entered on in
B.C. 461, and the war with the Persian forces in
Egypt, upon which the Athenians had entered as
allies of the Libyan prince Inaros and a section of the
Egyptian population.[1] That connexion accounts for
the popularity of a tragedy in which, as in the *Persians*, we find more of the excellence of a spectacle
than a poem. The object was to represent the enemies of another race with whom they were in conflict,
as more barbarous and insolent than the Persians
themselves. The allusions to the wolves of Hellas
as stronger than the dogs of Egypt ; to the barley-
bread and wine of the Hellenes as better than the
byblos fruit and beer of the Egyptians, (*Suppl.*, vv.
740-930 ;) the implied reminder that there might be
found affinities of race and religion among some of the
Egyptians, in spite of diversities of dress and complexion ;—all these had, we may well believe, a significance at the time which it is difficult for us now to
estimate.

The date of the trilogy of which the *Prometheus
Bound* forms a part, is more a matter of conjecture
than that of any other of the plays of Æschylos.
Some, on the strength of the reference to Ætna,
(v. 374,) have supposed it to have been written shortly
after the eruption took place B.C. 477 ; others have
referred it to B.C. 470. In the absence of more direct
evidence, it is open to maintain as probable that it
belongs to the period after he had returned from Sicily,
when allusions to its phænomena would be natural,
and after the attention of the Athenians had been

(1) Thuc., i. 102-104.

drawn, by the force of circumstances, to the legends of Egypt. The prominence given to the episode of Io and Epaphos is hardly intelligible, unless it is taken in connexion with the position which that legend occupies in the *Suppliants*. The pervading unity of thought in the two plays, so far as they both deal with the seeming caprice and cruelty of Zeus, and yet imply an ultimate prevalence of his compassion, belongs to another region of inquiry. It may be touched on here as at least strengthening the circumstantial evidence of the probable nearness of the two plays as to the date of their composition. It is possible that the lines in which Prometheus generalises his experience as to the ingratitude of princes—

> " For somehow this disease in sovereignty
> Inheres, of never trusting to one's friends,"
> —*(Prom.*, 230)—

may have had their origin in some slight which the irascible poet may have thought he had received at the hands of Hieron.

The date of the Oresteian trilogy is fixed, both by external and internal evidence, at B.C. 458. In the ten years which had passed since the first success of Sophocles, the greater part of which had been spent by Æschylos abroad, the principles to which the latter were most opposed had made rapid progress. He found on his return new men, new measures, a new philosophy, a new taste in poetry. The old order of the days of Marathon was passing away. Men who could claim no connexion with Eupatrid descent were pressing forward to the foremost place of power. The

institutions which were held most sacred as the safeguard of Athenian religion were criticised and attacked.
The court of Areiopagos, which had exercised an awful
and undefined authority in all matters connected,
directly or indirectly, with the religious life of the
state, was covertly attacked under the plea of reforming its administration.   Oracles and divinations no
longer commanded men's reverence and trust.   There
were whispers that men were beginning to say that
there was no God, or that the old name of Zeus was
to pass away before those of a Supreme Intelligence,
or a measureless Vortex. And the leader of the movement in all its bearings upon religion, politics, art, and
thought, was one who inherited the curse of the Alcmæonidæ, against whom the aristocratic party had
revived the memory of that curse, who had been suspected himself of sacrilege and scepticism on account
of his connexion with Anaxagoras.

It is impossible to mistake the bearing of the whole
trilogy upon the state of things thus described.   We
hear the protest of the poet of conservatism against
the coming changes, and his praise of the old Eupatrids, in the words which proclaim,—

> " Great gain it is to meet with lords who own
>   Ancestral wealth.   But whoso reap full crops
>   They never dared to hope for, these in all,
>   And beyond measure, to their slaves are harsh."
>   —*Agam.*, 1010-13.

The excellence of a constitutional government, such
as the Athenians had inherited, and the necessity of
reverence as its safeguard, is urged in the speech of
Athena :

> " I give my counsel to you, citizens,
>   To reverence and guard well that form of state
> Which is nor lawless nor tyrannical,
>   And not to cast all fear from out the city."
>   —*Eumen.*, 666-9.

The scepticism of those who could not trace a divine order in the mingled course of human life and its events, meet with his rebuke in terms which must have suggested a direct application to some well-known individual teacher like Anaxagoras :

> " Yea, *one* there was who said
> The Gods deign not to care for mortal men,
> By whom the grace of things inviolable
>   Is trampled under foot :
>   No fear of God had he."—*Agam.*, 360-4.

The idea of a curse hanging over the doers of guilt to the third and fourth generation, was dwelt upon as illustrated at every stage by the history of the sons of Atreus : while the poet at once saved himself from the charge of making God the author of man's evil, and sharpened the edge of his attack upon the democratic leader, by declaring that the curse was transmitted because each generation accepted and reproduced the deeds of its fathers :

> " There lives an old saw, framed in ancient days,
>   In memories of men, that high estate,
>   Full grown, brings forth its young, nor childless dies,
>   But that from good success
>   Springs to the race a woe insatiable.
>   But I, apart from all,
>   Hold this my creed alone :
>   For impious act it is that offspring breeds
>   Like to their parent stock."

He proclaims, as the burden of his prophecy, that—

"Recklessness of old
Is wont to breed another Recklessness."—*Agam.*, 731-38.

The natural exultation of Pericles and his party, such
as we find later in the Funeral Oration of Thuc. ii.
35-46, in the material prosperity and political greatness
of Athens, is met with the warning that all such prosperity is hollow **and uncertain:**

"But **Justice** shineth bright
In dwellings that are dark and dim with smoke,
          And honours life law-ruled,
While gold-decked homes conjoined with hands **defiled**
          She with averted eyes
          Hath left, and draweth near
To holier things, nor worships might of wealth,
          If counterfeit its praise."—*Agam.*, 750.

"Of high, o'erflowing health
There is no limit fixed that satisfies;
For evermore disease, as neighbour close,
          Whom but a wall divides,
Upon it presses, and man's prosperous state
Moves on its course, and strikes
          Upon an unseen rock."—*Agam.*, 971.

All tendencies to new and more philosophical thoughts
of the Gods than those of the Greek people, are re-
pressed by the protest already quoted:

"Weighing all other names, I fail to guess
Aught else but Zeus, if I would cast aside
          Clearly, in very deed,
From off my soul this weight of vaguest care."
                              —*Agam.*, 154.

The belief that man receives counsel and guidance
from oracles and prophets, and in visions of the night,
is again and again asserted. Loxias is the prophet of
his father Zeus, (*Eumen.* 19,) and the poet turns to—

> "Zeus, who leadeth men in wisdom's way,
>   And fixeth fast the law,
>   That pain is gain."—*Agam.*, 170.

The belief that men incurred a guilt by deeds of violence and wrong, and yet could be cleansed from that guilt by rites of expiation, such as Epimenides had taught and practised, is the key-note, as has been already shown, **both of the** *Libation-Pourers* **and the** *Eumenides.* The very ceremonies of purification are dwelt on, like those of supplication, with a manifest delight. And, lastly, the whole scheme and interest of the trilogy culminates in the assertion, in the last play, of the divine authority of the Areiopagos. Personal gratitude for the help which the leading members of that court had given to the poet-prophet of their party in his hour of peril may have combined with his religious convictions to lead him to rush to the rescue when it too was imperilled. It is represented as instituted by the guardian Goddess of the State :

> " This council I establish pure from bribe,
>   Reverend, and keen to act, for those that sleep
>   An ever-watchful sentry of the land."—*Eumen.*, 674.

Even the Argive alliance, as part of the policy of those who defended the jurisdiction of the Areiopagos, is dwelt on as that which shall—

> " Last as law for evermore."—*Eumen.*, 643.

It was, in part, owing to the earnestness which made the Oresteian trilogy the channel through which to utter the deepest convictions of his heart, that it rises to

such a high pre-eminence over all the other works of
Æschylos. But in part, also, that pre-eminence is due
to the gradual ripening of powers that had at first
been spasmodic and irregular in their action. The
poet had profited even by the discipline of defeat, and
had learnt some lessons from the higher finish and
more conscious art of his younger rival.[1] Written at
the age of sixty, and but three years before his death,
the trilogy exhibits all his powers in their full perfection. There is a far deeper human interest, a fuller
unfolding of human passions, than we find in the *Persians*, the *Suppliants*, or the *Seven against Thebes*.
While the "spectacle" element was not wanting, it was
no longer the chief source of interest. Of all the earlier
plays, the *Prometheus* is the only one which at all
approaches to it in greatness, and that is but a fragment of a whole, requiring the two lost companion
plays to enable us to judge fairly of its excellence. No
character in any other can be compared with that of
Clytæmnestra.

The actual result of the representation as a political
movement was disappointing. It did not stop the
action of the reforming party. The schemes of Ephialtes and Pericles were carried into effect, and the
Areiopagos, though not abolished, lost something of its
old power and more of its old glory. The introduction
in the *Eumenides* of a chorus of the avenging Erinnyes,
fifty in number, with masks of unequalled and horrible
ugliness,—serpents twisted in their hair, blood dropping

---

(1) Such, *e.g.*, as the introduction of a third actor in the dialogues, more
elaborate and expressive dances, the "pantomime" which told a tale
without words, the buskin, and the masks which increased the volume
of the voice.

from their eyes, a red tongue projecting between their lips,—so startled the spectators that it was said to have sent children into fits and frightened women into miscarriage. Popular feeling was once more excited against him. The old charges were probably raked up. The poet of a failing party could not live harmoniously with the Athenian *demos*. He left Athens soon after the date of the trilogy, never to return, and settled once more at Gela under the patronage of Hieron.

The three years that followed were spent in the fullest activity as a writer. To this period some have referred the repetition of the *Persians* and the composition of the *Women of Ætna*, which have been assigned here to an earlier visit. He was, at all events, a welcome and an honoured guest. His death, if the account given be not mythical, was the result of a strange casualty. An eagle seized a tortoise and carried it off, dropped it that it might break the shell and get at the flesh, and it fell upon the head of Æschylos, as he was in the act of writing, and killed him on the spot. He was buried at Gela, and on his monument was placed an epitaph which, it was said, he had composed for himself, and which, in the absence of all mention of what the Sicilians most honoured in him, and the prominence given to what the poet looked on as the great glory of his life, has at least a strong internal presumption in favour of its genuineness :

> " This tomb the dust of Æschylos doth hide,
>   Euphorion's son, and fruitful Gela's pride ;
>   How tried his valour Marathon may tell,
>   And long-haired Medes who knew it all too well."

The Athenians showed their reverence for his

memory by a decree, that any one who would under-
take to represent his dramas should be supplied with a
grant from the public treasury to defray the cost.[1]

II.—THE THEOLOGY OF ÆSCHYLOS.

The question, " What did this or that poet believe
as to the will of God, the government of the universe,
the destinies of mankind ?" seems to a large school of
critics an almost idle inquiry. " We are concerned,"
they say, " with the elements of perfection in his work,
not with his opinions or beliefs. The function of the
poet is that of the supreme artist, capable of sympathising with all fixed moods and passing impulses of
man's nature, so far as to gain the power of repro-
ducing them, and therefore with his religious affections
among others. His own religious affections, if he have
any, are nought to us. He is called to

> ' Sit apart, holding no form of creed,
>   And contemplating all ;'

to be many-sided, myriad-minded, as Shakspeare and
Goethe were. Strong convictions, a definite creed,
may have their value, in the formation of character or
in various forms of action upon men ; but as regards
the poet's work, they are simply detrimental ; tending,
at the best, to a second-rate excellence, marring the
fair bloom and exquisite beauty of the artist's work-
manship, bringing it down to the level of hymns, or
sermons in verse, or didactic morality."

---

(1) It is argued, however, by Dahm, in his *De Vitâ Æschyli*, that this
rather implies that the dramas were not popular enough to be performed
without some such legislative protection.

The question thus raised is a wider one than can be adequately discussed now. It may be conceded that the power of entering into other forms of character, and therefore into other forms of religious belief than his own, is essential to the highest work of the poet, an indispensable condition of the drama or the dramatic idyll. But the critics who infer from this that the excellence of the poet varies inversely as the strength of his religious convictions, seem to forget—(1.) That this contemplation of many creeds, this power of dramatising the inner life of each, is only possible when the poet is the heir of many ages, and has himself lived through a manifold experience. It belongs to the latest period of national culture. One might almost speak of it as a symptom of national decay. It comes, when firm faith and strong emotion, bounding joy and passionate hope, have died out; and it is not easy to strike the balance of what has been lost and gained since the earlier days, when men sang and wrote because "their heart was hot within them," and at last the "fire kindled" and so they "spake with their tongue." If there be in the history of most nations a still earlier period, when their literature is more simply objective, when, as yet, their minds are not vexed with questions, it must be remembered that the second stage is the fruit of a progress upwards, of thoughts widening with the years; and that, if there be a third and higher stage of excellence, it must be found in a combination of what was good in each, not by a mere return, or effort to return, to the first. (2.) They forget that many of the poems which have fixed themselves in men's hearts and memories—psalms, hymns, battle-songs—have been of the kind which they despise, the utterance of strong emotion having its root in very definite religious convictions. (3.) It is true that even of those who are most many-sided, and seem most creedless, that they preach a creed, that they are then at their highest point when they cease to bring before us the *dramatis personæ* of their ideal world, and utter something which they have felt intensely, and therefore speak strongly. Even of Goethe, Browning, and Tennyson, we may say that the words of theirs which dwell most with men, are those which bring some message to them, offering, truly or falsely, some new apocalypse. If this is not true of the " *sovrano poeta* " of Greece, it is because he lived in that earliest stage of progress when the problems of life are hardly more felt by men than they are by a vigorous and healthy child, when even the widest sympathy could only bring him into contact with human passions, and could not draw within the range of his art, materials that were then non-existent. And of Shakspeare it is only true in part. If there is no utterance of religious conviction, there is, as has been often shown, a pervading reverence for the Christian life of England in the form which made it most conspicuously national.[1] And of some poets, whom no critic will venture to place on the lower level of the second class,—of the unknown author of the book of Job, of Lucretius, and Dante, and Milton,—it is conspicuously true, that their belief is part of their poetry ; that they wrote poems to give utterance to it; that unless we understand it, the

---

(1) Comp. especially Archbishop Trench's *Sermon at the Stratford Festival*, and Bishop Wordsworth's *Shakspeare and the Bible*.

poems themselves are as a dead letter to us. Would those who bid us look only to the artistic perfection of the works of Sophocles and Æschylos, regard an inquiry into the teaching of the book of Job as to the divine government of the world, as beyond the province of true criticism ?

And if we have already learnt to see, as we have seen in the case of Æschylos, that any given poet throws himself, with all the intensity of his nature, into the cause of one party against another in a great political controversy, if that controversy were inextricably blended with all the movements of thought, feeling, taste, that affect men's inner as well as outer life, then we may well believe that his poetry would be pervaded by his religious convictions also. Even if they be regarded as a disturbing force, they must yet be taken into account, if we wish to understand the special excellences and the special defects of his genius. If authority were needed for such an inquiry into the theology of Æschylos, it might be found in the copious and interesting literature which has gathered round it.[1]

What we have seen then of this political action on the part of Æschylos will help us to estimate his position in relation to the religious history of Greece. We cannot place him with the great thinkers, who,

[1] The mere titles would fill a page. I name, (1.) as most accessible to the English reader, Müller's *Dissertation on the Eumenides*; the chapters on the Greek Dramatists in Bunsen's *God in History*; Mr. B. F. Westcott's masterly article on "Æschylos as a Religious Teacher," in th' *Contemporary Review* for Nov. 1866; a paper by Mr. Paley on "Chthonian Worship," in the *Journal of Philology* for June, 1868; the sections bearing on this subject in A. W. Schlegel's *History of Dramatic Literature*, in Grote's and Thirlwall's *Histories of Greece*, in Müller and Donaldson's *History of Greek Literature*; and (2.) as worth consulting by those who have the opportunity, Klausen's *Theologumena Æschyli*; Dronke's *Die religiosen und sittlichen Vorstellungen des Æschylos und Sophokles*, and Nägelsbach's *Nachhomerische Theologie des Griechischen Volksglaubens*.

like Socrates and Plato, recognised the corrupting character of much of the current mythology, and would fain have banished it from their polity, who, in part at least, seem to stand forth as witnesses to the Divine unity, whose conformity with popular worship is but a tolerance of that which is imperfect, because the perfect is not yet come. His belief does not stand on the same level as the Theism of Anaxagoras, or the Pantheism or Atheism of Diagoras. When he speaks of the Gods, it is neither with the serenity of Sophocles, as looking to eternal laws that belong altogether to a different region of thought, nor with the ill-concealed Voltairian irony of Euripides. He is the Calderon, not the Goethe of Greek literature. He takes his thoughts of the Gods from Homer and Hesiod—from the latter even more than the former—and (with some notable exceptions) abides by them. He is conservative in religion as in politics; looks with real alarm on the decay of reverence in the *demos* of Athens and among the young men of culture; would have sympathised, we may believe, with Aristophanes in his attack on Socrates as unsettling their minds; with Nikias in his respect for omens, his reverence for the dead, his shrinking from over-much prosperity; with the alarm and irritation caused by the mutilation of the Hermæ-busts, and the alleged profanation of the Mysteries;[1] perhaps even with those who condemned the " preacher of righteousness" who had dwelt among them to drink the hemlock.

(1) The fact that he had been himself charged with a like offence would not have made him less tolerant of an offence, the *animus* of which was, or seemed to him, so different from that which had actuated him.

He starts then with a belief that the myths of Greece represent the facts of the Divine history, and is not troubled by questions and doubts about them. Zeus reigns supreme, after having deposed Cronos, as Cronos had deposed Uranos:

> " Nor He who erst was great,
> Full of the might to war,
> Avails now : He is gone,
> And He who next came hath departed too,
> His victor meeting."—*Agam.*, 162-166.

The Titans rose against him in support of the old order, and he hurled them down to Tartaros, or buried them beneath volcanoes. The Olympian deities who reign under him with a limited jurisdiction, are his sons and daughters. He governs with inexorable severity ; just, but with little sympathy for the sufferings of mankind. Their progress towards knowledge and power and culture under the teaching of Prometheus is displeasing to him. He punishes the "philanthropy" of the more benevolent Titan by a penalty that is to last for ages. All this lay, however, in the remote past. In the age in which the Hellénes lived and acted, the deliverer of the Titan had come; a vicarious death had freed him from his agony ;[1] there had been a solution of what seemed harsh and unjust in the government of Zeus. He looked on man with a more benignant eye. The worshipper could think of Him as no longer arbitrary in his chastisement. It is obvious that this recognition of a Supreme Ruler over

---

(1) This is implied in the fact that the *Prometheus Unbound* was the third play of the trilogy, and that the mode of deliverance was found in the readiness of Cheiron to bear the penalty of death in Prometheus' stead, and so to work out a redemption for him.

many Gods might clothe itself in lofty words, simu-
lating almost the language of a monotheistic creed :

> "Safe, by no fall tripped-up
> The full-wrought deed decreed by brow of Zeus:
> For dark and shadowed o'er
> The pathways of the counsels of His heart,
> And difficult to see.
> And from high-towering hopes He hurleth down
> To utter doom the heir of mortal birth ;
> Yet sets He in array
> No forces violent:
> All that God works is effortless and calm :[1]
> Seated on loftiest throne,
> Thence, though we know not how,
> He works His perfect will."—*Suppl.*, 85-95.

Or this,—

> "O King of kings, and blest
> Above all blessed ones,
> And power most mighty of the mightiest;
> O Zeus of high estate,
> Hear this our prayer."—*Ibid.*, 518-521.

Or this,—

> "He is our Father, author of our life,
> The King whose right hand worketh all His will,
> Our line's great Author, in His counsels deep
> Recording things of old,
> Directing all His plans, the great Work-master, Zeus.
> For not, as suppliant sitting at the beck
> Of strength above his own,
> Reigns He subordinate to mightier powers,

---

(1) Comp. the recurrence of the same thought in the words of Apollo
in *Eumen.*, ver. 620—

> "But all things else He turneth up and down,
> And orders without toil or weariness."

> Nor does He pay His homage from below
> While one sits throned in majesty above :
>   Act is for Him as speech
> To hasten what His teeming mind resolves."
>
> —*Ibid.*, 584-590.

If *Fragm.* 293 be genuine, we have a yet clearer pantheistic, if not monotheistic creed :

> " The air is Zeus, Zeus earth, and Zeus the heaven,
> Zeus all that is, and what transcends them all."

But with all this, the believing polytheist is still there. Artemis, Apollo, Hera, are to him real, not imaginary beings, each with a region of activity and a delegated sovereignty, as much as they were to Homer. The primary meaning of the myths of Hellas, as we explain them, as symbols of the changes of day and night, dawn and sunset, has for him passed away into the dim distance, and he sees it not. Attributes have become persons ; men's wandering fancies have crystallised and hardened. A change had come, however, over the religion of Greece since the Homeric age. It is inherent in the nature of Polytheism that a prominence is given to the worship, now of this deity, and now of that ; that new rites, symbols, mysteries, confraternities, rise up to meet the ever-restless fears or fancies of men's hearts ; that these come more or less into collision with each other. The story of the migration of Apollo from Delos to Delphi, of Orpheus and the mysteries which he founded, indicates a transition from the Homeric thought of the Sun, as slaying men with its arrows of pestilence, to that of the Giver of light, the Revealer of secrets, the Prophet of his father Zeus, (*Eumen.*, v. 19.) That of the travels of

Dionysos, of the throng of Mænads who followed him, of the fate of Pentheus, and of Orpheus himself, indicates a struggle between the calmer and the more violent *cultus*,—between the inspiration which issues in wisdom and poetry, and that which shows itself in the abdication, by man's reason, of its sovereignty over his brute nature. And in this conflict, Æschylos, true to the influence of Epimenides,[1] is clearly on the side of the former. Frequent as are the appeals to Zeus, Apollo, Athena, it is noticeable that no single invocation of Dionysos is found in the extant plays. In the lost tetralogy of the *Lycurgeia*, which had the adventures of Dionysos for its subject, he seems to have brought in the death of Orpheus as the servant of Apollo, a martyr in the cause of sun-worship.[2] Whether in that stage of his religious development the issue of the whole drama was a reconciliation of the conflicting powers, like that which we see in the *Eumenides*, and must assume in the *Prometheus Unbound*, is a question which we have not *data* to answer. In either case, the absence of the name of Dionysos from Æschylos, as compared with its prominence in Sophocles and Euripides, is striking and significant.[3]

(1) The Cretan prophet is described by Epiphanius, following some old tradition, as having been a priest of Mithras, the Persian analogue of Apollo.

(2) I take the following account of the play from an extract from Eratosthenes, given by Ahrens in his dissertation on the *Fragments* of Æschylos, (Didot., 1842.)

"But Orpheus paid no honour to Dionysos, holding the Sun, whom also he called Apollo, to be the greatest of the Gods. And rising up by night, before the earliest dawn, he was wont to go to the mountain called Pangæos, and there to wait for the Sun, that he might look on him as he first rose. Wherefore Dionysos was wroth, and sent the Bassarid women against him," (analogous to the Mænads and Thyiads, which are more familiar names to us,) "as Æschylos the poet says, and they tore him in pieces, and cast out his limbs one by one. And the Muses gathered them together, and buried them in the place called Leibethra."

(3) Petersen, in an interesting monograph on *Die Delphische Festeyclus.*

With the same tendency in his choice among the "Gods many and Lords many" of the Greek Pantheon, we may note the prominence which he gives to the Chthonian as distinguished from the Olympian Gods, to those who dwell in darkness as contrasted with those who dwell in light. He turns to the worship of Demêter, as initiated, it may be, in the mysteries which had their local habitation in his native *deme*.[1] He dwells, with devoutest reverence on the thought, (speaking of Hades where the Chthonian Gods had their dwelling,) that—

> ". . . There, as men relate, a second Zeus
> Judges men's evil deeds, and to the dead
> Assigns their last great penalties."—*Suppl.*, 226, 227.

So in like tone he speaks in the same play of—

> "The Avenger terrible,
> God that destroyeth, who not e'en in Hades
> Gives freedom to the dead."—*Ibid.*, 409, 410.

The same feeling leads him to dwell on the office of Hermes as the escort of the souls of the dead, and to introduce the spectres of the dead, as in the *Persians*

---

pp. 24, 25, urges that in the inner theology of Delphi, the contending claims had been reconciled mainly through the teaching of the Orphic confraternities, and that Zeus, Hades, Apollo, and Dionysos were all recognised for one and the self-same Power, manifesting itself in many ways. He refers especially to the strange treatise of Plutarch, *De 'EI apud Delphos*, as showing that Dionysos, Zagreus, Phœbos, Apollo, Aidoneus, were all manifestations of the Divine Unity, of which that mystic word was, as he interprets it, the symbol. With this we may compare the remarkable verse quoted by Justin Martyr, (*Cohort. ad Græc.*, c. 15,) as from Orpheus.

> " There is one Zeus, one Hades, and one Sun,
> One Dionysos, yea, one God in all."

In all such passages, however, there is the risk of our transferring to an earlier age the Pantheistic speculations which were specially characteristic of the later periods of Greek thought.

(1) Comp. note on p. xv

and *Eumenides*, as actors in his plays. But above all other deities of darkness, he fastens on the Erinnyes as the ministers of divine vengeance,[1] at first terrible and wrathful, seeking nothing less than the life-blood of their victim, in conflict with Apollo as the God of light, cast out by Zeus, having no share in the banquet of Olympian Gods, but at last confining their work within the limits of what is required by the law of retribution, or is enough to deter others from crime, or to bring the offender to repentance. In some sense they are older and more venerable than Zeus himself:

> " This lot the all-pervading Destiny
>   Hath spun to hold its ground for evermore,
>   That we should still attend
>   On him on whom there rests the guilt of blood
>   Of kin shed causelessly."
>
>   .   .   .   .   —*Eumen.*, 320-21.

It is their task to do the work which would interfere with the calm bliss of the Olympian Gods. At first their office seems simply terrible. The sins of the father are visited on the children to the third and fourth generation. An Atè cleaves to the house, thirsting for blood, breeding new evils, making sin at once the punishment of past and the parent of future sin, until at last the entail of curses is cut off by the purification of one on whom the inherited curse has fallen, and by the favour of the propitiated Gods. The Erinnyes become the Eumenides—gentle, benignant,

---

(1) On this subject Müller's Treatise *On the Eumenides* is of special interest. The Erinnyes are, as he interprets them, the personification of the passionate impulses of righteous wrath, which first burst out in curses, then work in acts of vengeance, then are tempered down into moral indignation against Evil.

blessing. Panic terror passes into the awe and reverence without which there is no safety for the individual
or the state. The law of retribution still remains,

> " For unto them the lot is given
> All things human still to order,"
> —(*Eumen.*, 890,)

but there is no longer any rivalry or antagonism :

> " Dread and mighty,
> With the Undying is Erinnys,
> And with Those beneath the earth too."
> —*Eumen.*, 910.

The prominence thus given to the representatives
and agents of divine Vengeance shows the kind of
questions which lay deepest in the poet's heart, and
the answer which he had found for them. Was there
a righteous government? Was the ruler of Gods and
men capricious like the kings of earth? Was He
enslaved by some higher law of destiny, which moved
on its way in a darkness that none could penetrate,
and to which even He was subject?[1] It has often
been said that this was the theory of the universe
which Æschylos embraced, that the underlying thought
in all Greek tragedy, and pre-eminently in his, is that

---

(1) The language in the *Prometheus*, vv. 519, 530, is apparently at
variance with the sovereignty of Zeus. Necessity seems supreme over
Zeus himself. He too cannot escape his destiny. What that destiny is,
the Titan boasts that he knows, but will not utter. On the other hand,
when questioned

> " Who then directs Necessity's career ?"

His answer is,

> " Fates triple-formed, Erinnyes unforgetting."

And so far as we may think of this as not merely the boast of defiance
put into the lips of the rebel, but expressing the poet's own thoughts, we
are thrown back upon his teaching as to the functions of those Erinnyes
in the Oresteian trilogy, in which they appear as subordinate to, or at
least in harmony with, the mind of Zeus.

of a curse cleaving causelessly to a given race, generation after generation, against which man struggles
vainly, each effort to escape only riveting the chains
more firmly. If any explanation is at hand of the
dark mystery of evil, it is that prosperity, as such,
makes men obnoxious to the jealous wrath of the Gods
or of their ruler.

It would be far truer, I believe, to say that this is
precisely the theory of the divine government which
Æschylos lived to denounce and protest against. That
it was one of the natural solutions of the problems
presented by the strange chances and changes of life,
that men who had come to think of God as even such
an one as themselves might be led to accept it, is clear
enough. It is the key-note of the theology of Herodotus.[1] " God is a jealous God," not in the Hebrew
sense, as demanding all man's heart, but as envious of
man's success, afraid of his independence, aiming his
thunderbolts at the loftiest trees simply because they
are the loftiest. Against such a theory the heart of
Æschylos revolted. He craved for a *theodikæa*, and
came forward in the spirit, one might almost say, of an
Athanasius contra mundum, to attack the prevailing
creed.

" There lives an old saw, framed in ancient days
   In memories of men, that high estate
   Full grown brings forth its young, nor childless dies,
      But that from good success
   Springs to the race a woe insatiable.
      But I, *apart from all,*
      Hold this my creed, alone :
   For impious act it is that offspring breeds,

---

(1) Compare Herod. i. 32 ; iii. 40 ; vii. 10, 46, 1??.

> Like to their parent stock :
> For still in every house
> That loves the right, their fate for evermore
> Hath issue good and fair."—*Agam.*, 727-737.

If prosperity seemed to be followed by disaster, it was because men yielded to the temptations which it brought with it, and became wanton, haughty, reckless. The sequence of evils might always be traced to the fountain-head of some sin which might have been avoided, but which, once committed, went on with accelerating force. At every stage each evil act received its just recompense of reward, but that very recompense was brought about through the instrumentality of a fresh transgression waiting in its turn its punishment. The woes of Atreus' line, the curse that rested on the house of Œdipus, the misery of Troïa, are all referred to a root-sin which remained unrepented and unatoned for. And the sins which presented themselves to the poet's mind as certain to be most fruitful in these transmitted curses, are those which offend against the primary relations of human fellowship. Murder, especially when the blood which has been shed is that of kindred ; lust, especially when it works regardless of the obligations that bind host to guest, and guest to host ; defiance of the Gods, as seen in impious speech or act, in surrendering suppliants or plundering temples,—these are the crimes for which the Erinnyes come as avengers. Zeus is, in a special sense, the God of the stranger, the God of host and guest, the protector of those who flee to him for succour. At times we seem to be hearing the very echoes of a higher apocalypse of the truth. Æschylos proclaims in Greece, as Ezekiel had done on the banks of Chebar, that " the soul that sinneth, it shall die ;" that men have no right to extend the law of retribution beyond the limits of justice, or to impute their own evil to the sins of their ancestors, or to the irresistible decrees of God. He too protests against the doctrine that " the fathers have eaten sour grapes, and that the children's teeth are set on edge" (Ezek. xviii. 2-4).

It was indeed the defect of the teaching of Æschylos that it generalised too hastily, that he seemed to himself to have discovered the solution of all problems in the tangled web of human life. Like the friends of Job, he pressed his theory of retribution to the conclusion that all suffering implied guilt ; that where prosperity ceased to smile on men, it was because they had forfeited their right to it. It was characteristic of Sophocles that, with a clearer appreciation of the truth, he brought into prominence the fact that there are phenomena which the theory does not explain, evils which seem to originate altogether in sins of ignorance, strange chances and changes which the theory of Nemesis, no less than that of the jealousy of the Gods, fails to help us to explain. Not losing his faith in the Divine Righteousness, maintaining the eternal authority of the laws of Truth and Right, he is yet compelled to confess that there is much in the actual order of the world that is altogether incomprehensible. He balances the retributive theory of Æschylos as the teaching of *Ecclesiastes*, or the closing chapters of the *Book of Job* itself, balance that of Eliphaz the Temanite.

What is indicated with more or less distinctness in the change of name from the Erinnyes to Eumenides is brought out explicitly as one of the great laws of the divine government. The evils which follow on guilt may, rightly accepted, be an education. In the discipline of suffering, in the "reproof of life," in the παθήματα which are also μαθήματα, men may find that which raises them out of recklessness, insolence, outrage, to "self-reverence, self-knowledge, self-control," to all that the Hebrew meant by "wisdom," all that the Greek meant by σωφροσύνη. And this comes of God:

> "'Tis Zeus who leadeth men in wisdom's way,
>   And fixeth fast the law,
>   That pain is gain;
>   And slowly dropping on the heart in sleep
>   Comes woe-recording care,
>   And makes the unwilling yield to wiser thoughts."
>   —*Agam.*, 170-74.

>   " Justice turns the scale
>   For those to whom through pain
>   At last comes wisdom's gain."
>   .   .   .   —*Ibid.*, 241.

>   " There are with whom 'tis well
>   That awe should still abide
>   As watchman o'er their souls :
>   Calm wisdom gained by sorrow profits much."
>   —*Eumen.*, 491-94.

But with this recognition of a moral discipline by which men—

>   " May rise on stepping-stones
>   Of their dead selves to higher things,"

there is also a consciousness, dim and dark, as of one groping after a truth which he feels rather than sees, that this is not enough. Whether the phænomenon be one of that parallelism in religious feeling which often meets us in races that have had no contact with each other, or be due to the influence of Semitic thought passing from Phœnikia to the "isles of Chittim," and so through Epimenides to Greece, we need not now discuss. It is enough to note the fact that in the theology of Æschylos, as in the ritual which the Cretan prophet had introduced, and which was propagated by the Orphic and other mystic brotherhoods, the sufferer who groans under the burden of guilt needs, over and above the discipline of suffering and a life ruled by law, purification and atonement; that the purification must be wrought by blood poured or sprinkled on the man who sought it; that he needs the mediation of another in order that the purification may be accomplished; that to render this office is the greatest kindness which friend can show to friend, or host to suppliant guest; that when this is done he may once more draw near, "with contrite heart," "harmless and pure," to the temples of the Gods.

One who took this belief of the world's history as manifesting God's righteous judgment—a belief every way analogous to that which is dominant in the Old Testament—would not be likely to look forward to a life after death as redressing the anomalies of the present, or compensating for its imperfections. But the consciousness of immortality was as strong in him as in the Hellenic race generally; stronger, it may be, than it was among the great body of the Jews. And with this conviction he can but look forward to that future 'as continuing and completing the retribution. There, in that other world, sits the "second Zeus," who awards to each man's deeds their final doom.

(*Suppl.* v. 227.)   There the kings and the great ones of the earth still retain something of their old prerogatives.   Still they hold some fellowship with the living, feel shame and ignominy when funeral honours are refused to them, can pass out of Hades where they dwell, to haunt and vex those who have wronged them, (as in the case of Clytæmnestra,) or be summoned by prayers and incantations (as are Agamemnon and Dareios) to help those whom they have loved.

And there, too, in that world of the dead, are the Erinnyes still carrying on their appointed task.   There is no sleep of death for the doer of evil.   They are—

"A terror of the living and the dead."—*Eumen.*, **312.**

"Death sets not **free** from their attacks."—*Ibid.*, **322.**

> " With **the** Undying is Erinnys,
> And with **Those** beneath **the earth** too ;
> And full clearly and completely
> Work they **all things** out for mortals,
> Giving these the **songs** of gladness,
> Those a life bedimmed with weeping."
> —*Ibid.*, **910-15.**

Does the law of continuity hold good there also ? Were **the Erinnyes, as** they did their work in the world of the dead, recognised even there **as the** Eumenides ?   Is the connexion between suffering **and** education, between "pain" and "gain," projected into that other life ?   These questions lay then, as they **lie now,** behind **the** veil, shrouded **in a** mist and darkness which men seek in **vain to penetrate. It** may be that Æschylos felt that it would be ill to lose either the vague terror or the wider hope.   **To** them he gives **no** answer.

There remains yet one other of the problems of the
world's history on which it is interesting to note what
we find in the teaching of Æschylos. We ask the
" whence?" as well as the " whither?" of the human
race. How has it come to be as it is? Has it fallen
from some paradise state, some Golden Age, each
generation becoming feebler and more corrupt than its
predecessors, or made its way onwards, through a long
succession of ages, to its present culture, giving in
that progress the pledge of yet further advancement?
The former was the dominant idea in Greek legend. It
was adopted by Hesiod (*Works and Days*, vv. 106-171,)
it took form in the mythos of Pandora, from whose
fatal gifts all man's ills had come. But here, as in his
theory of the divine law of retribution, Æschylos seems
to strike out a new path for himself, and to anticipate,
by a bold conjecture, conclusions that have been
arrived at slowly, and after a long induction, by
modern palæontologists :—

> " Like forms
> Of phantom-dreams, through all their length of life,
> They muddled all at random ; did not know
> Houses of brick that catch the sunlight's warmth,
> Nor yet the work of carpentry. They dwelt
> In hollowed holes like swarms of tiny ants,
> In sunless depths of cavern; and they had
> No certain signs of winter, nor of spring
> Flower-laden, nor of summer with her fruits ;
> But without counsel fared their whole life long."
> —*Prom.*, 455-465.

It may be questioned whether Sir Charles Lyell or
Sir John Lubbock could have given a better picture of
the state of mankind in the so-called "stone period."

And out of this they were raised by Prometheus, as the representative of a divine Wisdom sympathising with man's infirmities, becoming the "light that lighteth every man," at first in seeming antagonism to the Ruler of Heaven, but at last brought into entire harmony with that Supreme Will. The gift of fire came, and with it new capacities and new thoughts, a strange mastery over brute creatures and the brute elements of nature, like that on which Sophocles dwells in the memorable chorus of the *Antigone*—

> "Many the things that strange and wondrous are,
> None stranger and more wonderful than man."
> —*Antig.*, v. 332.

In representing this as bringing down the wrath of Zeus on the beneficent Titan, Æschylos did but unconsciously embody on the one hand the law of sacrifice, which has made all the great benefactors and teachers of mankind achieve their task, and win their victory, through suffering ; and on the other, the truth, that the first result of the possession and the consciousness of enlarged powers is a new self-assertion, the spirit of independence and rebellion against the control of a divine order, the " many inventions" that tend to evil, an outburst of impiety and lawlessness, needing the discipline of punishment before it can be brought round again into a nobler harmony. Men " become as Gods," and " their eyes are opened to discern good and evil," but it is to " know that they are naked," and to " eat bread in the sweat of their brow." During this process the government under which men live appears stern, arbitrary, tyrannical.

The eagle's fangs rend the heart of the hero Titan who represents the intellect of mankind as a race, the mind that belongs to all, in its defiant self-assertion. The struggle and the agony must last till Cheiron comes of his own free will to bear the pains of death, and so deliver him.

With this, as being, as all thinkers have felt, among the noblest of the " unconscious prophecies of heathendom," among the profoundest anticipations of an eternal truth, in the form of a *mythos*, of which the writer felt rather than discerned the meaning, I close this present essay. Far as it has been from an exhaustive treatment of a subject which might well claim a volume to itself, it may yet revive, I trust, in those who know Æschylos already, some recollections of what most interested them as they read, and answer some questions which that perusal raised ; and help those who enter on the study of his dramas for the first time, to do so with a better prospect of understanding and appreciating him.

THE PERSIANS.

B

ARGUMENT.

When Xerxes came to the throne of Persia, remembering how his
father Dareios had sought to subdue the land of the Hellenes,
and seeking to avenge the defeat of Datis and Artaphernes on
the field of Marathon, he gathered together a mighty host of all
nations under his dominion, and led them against Hellas.
And at first he prospered and prevailed, crossed the Hellespont,
and defeated the Spartans at Thermopylæ, and took the city of
Athens, from which the greater part of its citizens had fled.
But at last he and his armament met with utter overthrow at
Salamis. Meanwhile Atossa, the mother of Xerxes, with her
handmaids and the elders of the Persians, waited anxiously at
Susa, where was the palace of the great king, for tidings of h r
son.

Note.—Within two years after the battle of Salamis, the feeling of
national exultation was met by Phrynichos in a tragedy bearing the title
of *The Phœnikians*, and having for its subject the defeat of Xerxes. As
he had come under the displeasure of the Athenian *demos* for having
brought on the stage the sufferings of their Ionian kinsmen in his *Capture of Miletos*, he was apparently anxious to regain his popularity by a
'sensation' drama of another kind; and his success seems to have
prompted Æschylos to a like attempt five years later, B.C. 473. The
Tetralogy to which the play belonged, and which gained the first prize on
its representation, included the two tragedies (unconnected in subject)
of *Phineus* and *Glaucos*, and the satiric drama of *Prometheus the Firestealer*.
The play has, therefore, the interest of being strictly a contemporary
narrative of the battle of Salamis and its immediate consequences, by one
who may himself have been present at it, and whose brother Ameinias
(Herod. viii. 93) had distinguished himself in it by a special act of heroism.
As such, making all allowance for the influence of dramatic exigencies,
and the tendency to colour history so as to meet the tastes of patriotic
Athenians, it may claim, where it differs from the story told by Herodotos, to be a more trustworthy record. And it has, we must remember,
the interest of being the only extant drama of its class, the only tragedy
the subject of which is not taken from the cycle of heroic myths, but
from the national history of the time. Far below the Oresteian Trilogy,
as it may seem to us, as a work of art, having more the character of a
spectacle than a poem, it was, we may well believe, unusually successful
at the time, and it is said to have been chosen by Hiero for reproduction
at Syracuse after Æschylos had settled there under his patronage.

Dramatis Personæ.

ATOSSA.

Messenger.

Ghost of DAREIOS.

XERXES.

Chorus of Persian Elders.

THE PERSIANS.

SCENE.—Susa, *in front of the palace of* Xerxes, *the Tomb of* Dareios *occupying the position of the thymele.*

Enter Chorus of Persian Elders.

We the title bear of Faithful, [1]
Friends of Persians gone to Hellas,
Watchers left of treasure city, [2]
Gold-abounding, whom, as oldest,
Xerxes hath himself appointed,
He, the offspring of Dareios,
As the warders of his country.
And about our king's returning,
And our army's, gold-abounding,
Over-much, and boding evil,
Does my mind within me shudder   10
(For our whole force, Asia's offspring,
Now is gone), and for our young chief
Sorely frets: nor courier cometh,
Nor any horseman, bringing tidings
To the city of the Persians.
From Ecbatana departing,
Susa, or the Kissian fortress, [3]

(1) "The Faithful," or "trusty," seems to have been a special title of honour given to the veteran councillors of the king, (Xenoph. *Anab.* i. 15), just as that of the "Immortals" was chosen for his body-guard. (Herod. vii. 83.)

(2) Susa was pre-eminently the treasury of the Persian kings (Herod. v. 49 ; Strabo, xv. p. 731), their favourite residence in spring, as Ecbatana in Media was in summer and Babylon in winter.

(3) Kissia was properly the name of the district in which Susa stood ; but here, and in v. 123, it is treated as if it belonged to a separate city. Throughout the play there is, indeed, a lavish use of Persian barbaric names of persons and places, without a very minute regard to historical accuracy.

Forth they sped upon their journey,
Some in ships, and some on horses,
Some on foot, still onward marching,
In their close array presenting
Squadrons duly armed for battle :   20
Then Amistres, Artaphernes,
Megabazes, and Astaspes,
Mighty leaders of the Persians,
Kings, and of the great King servants,[1]
March, the chiefs of mighty army.
Archers they and mounted horsemen.
Dread to look on, fierce in battle,
Artembares proud, on horseback,
And Masistres, and Imæos,   30
Archer famed, and Pharandakes,
And the charioteer Sosthanes.
Neilos mighty and prolific
Sent forth others, Susikanes,
Pegastagon, Egypt's offspring,
And the chief of sacred Memphis ;
Great Arsames, Ariomardos,
Ruler of primeval Thebæ,
And the marshmen,[2] and the rowers,
Dread, and in their number countless.   40
And there follow crowds of Lydians,
Very delicate and stately,[3]

(1) Here, as in Herodotos and Greek writers generally, the title, "the
King," or "the great King," was enough. It could be understood only
of the Persian. The latter name had been borne by the kings of Assyria.
(2 Kings xviii. 28.) A little later it passed into the fuller, more boastful
form of "the King of kings."

(2) The inhabitants of the Delta of the Nile, especially those of the
marshy districts near the Heracleotic mouth, were famed as supplying
the best and bravest soldiers of any part of Egypt.—Comp. Thucyd. i.
110.

(3) The epithet was applied probably by Æschylos to the Lydians properly so called, the barbaric race with whom the Hellenes had little or
nothing in common. They, in dress, diet, mode of life, their distaste for
the contests of the arena, seemed to the Greeks the very type of effeminacy. The Ionian Greeks, however, were brought under the same
influence, and gradually acquired the same character. The suppression
of the name of the Ionians in the list of the Persian forces may be noticed
as characteristic. The Athenian poet would not bring before an Athenian
audience the shame of their Asiatic kinsmen.

Who the people of the mainland
Rule throughout,—whom Mitragathes
And brave Arkteus, kingly chieftains,
Led, from Sardis, gold-abounding,
Riding on their many chariots,
Three or four a-breast their horses,
Sight to look upon all dreadful.
And the men of sacred Tmôlos [1]
Rush to place the yoke of bondage
On the neck of conquered Hellas.   50
Mardon, Tharabis, spear-anvils, [2]
And the Mysians, javelin-darting; [3]
Babylôn too, gold-abounding,
Sends a mingled cloud, swept onward,
Both the troops who man the vessels,
And the skilled and trustful bowmen;
And the race the sword that beareth,
Follows from each clime of Asia,
At the great King's dread commandment.
These, the bloom of Persia's greatness,
Now are gone forth to the battle;   60
And for these, their mother country,
Asia, mourns with mighty yearning;
Wives and mothers faint with trembling
Through the hours that slowly linger,
Counting each day as it passes.

STROPH. I.

The king's great host, destroying cities mighty,
Hath to the land beyond the sea passed over,
Crossing the straits of Athamantid Helle, [4]   70
    On raft by ropes secured,

(1) Tmôlos, sacred as being the mythical birth-place of Dionysos.
(2) "Spear-anvils," sc., meeting the spear of their foes as the anvils
would meet it, turning its point, themselves steadfast and immovable.
(3) So Herodotos (vii. 74) in his account of the army of Xerxes describes the Mysians as using for their weapons those darts or "javelins"
made by hardening the ends in the fire.
(4) Helle the daughter of Athamas, from whom the Hellespont took its
name. For the description of the pontoons formed by boats, which were
moored together with cables and finally covered with faggots, comp.
Herod. vii. 36.

And thrown his path, compact of many a vessel,
As yoke upon the neck of mighty ocean.

ANTISTROPH. I.

Of populous Asia thus the mighty ruler
'Gainst all the land his God-sent host directeth
In two divisions, both by land and water,
    Trusting the chieftains stern,
The men who drive the host to fight, relentless—
He, sprung from gold-born race, a hero god-like.[1]   80

STROPH. II.

Glancing with darkling look, and eyes as of ravening
    dragon,
With many a hand, and many a ship, and Syrian chariot
    driving,[2]
He upon spearmen renowned brings battle of conquering
    arrows.[3]

ANTISTROPH. II.

Yea, there is none so tried as, withstanding the flood of
    the mighty,   90
To keep within steadfast bounds that wave of ocean re-
    sistless;
Hard to fight is the host of the Persians, the people stout-
    hearted.

MESODE.

Yet ah! what mortal can ward the craft of the God
    all-deceiving?
Who, with a nimble foot, of one leap is easily sovereign?

---

(1) " Gold-born," *sc.*, descended from Perseus, the child of Danaë.
(2) Syrian, either in the vague sense in which it became almost synonymous with Assyrian, or else showing that Syria, properly so called,
retained the fame for chariots which it had had at a period as early as
the time of the Hebrew Judges, (Judg. v. 3.) Herodotos (vii. 140) gives
an Oracle of Delphi in which the same epithet appears.
(3) The description, though put into the mouth of Persians, is meant
to flatter Hellenic pride. The Persians and their army were for the most
part light-armed troops only, barbarians equipped with javelins or bows.
In the sculptures of Persepolis, as in those of Nineveh and Khorsabad,
this mode of warfare is throughout the most conspicuous. They, the
Hellenes, were the *hoplites*, warriors of the spear and the shield, the
cuirass and the greaves.

For Atè, fawning and kind, at first a mortal be-
    traying,   100
    Then in snares and meshes decoys him,
Whence one who is but man in vain doth struggle to
    'scape from.

STROPH. III.

For Fate of old, by the high Gods' decree,
Prevailed, and on the Persians laid this task,
    Wars with the crash of towers,
And set the surge of horsemen in array,
And the fierce sack that lays a city low.   110

ANTISTROPH. III.

But now they learnt to look on ocean plains,[1]
The wide sea hoary with the violent blast,
    Waxing o'er confident
In cables formed of many a slender strand,
And rare device of transport for the host.

STROPH. IV.

    So now my soul is torn,
As clad in mourning, in its sore affright,
Ah me! ah me! for all the Persian host!   120
    Lest soon our country learn
That Susa's mighty fort is void of men.

ANTISTROPH. IV.

    And through the Kissians' town
Shall echo heavy thud of hands on breast.
Woe! woe! when all the crowd of women speak
    This utterance of great grief,
And byssine robes are rent in agony.

STROPH. V.

    For all the horses strong,
    And host that march on foot,

(1) A touch of Athenian exultation in their life as seamen. To them
the sea was almost a home. They were familiar with it from childhood.
To the Persians it was new and untried. They had a new lesson to
learn, late in the history of the nation, late in the lives of individual
soldiers.

Like swarm of bees, have gone with him who led   130
    The vanguard of the host.
Crossing the sea-washed, bridge-built promontory
That joins the shores of either continent.[1]

ANTISTROPH. V.

    And beds with tears are wet
    In grief for husbands gone,
And Persian wives are delicate in grief,
    Each yearning for her lord;
And each who sent her warrior-spouse to battle   140
Now mourns at home in dreary solitude.
    But come, ye Persians now,
And sitting in this ancient hall of ours,
Let us take thought deep-counselling and wise,
    (Sore need is there of that,)
How fareth now the great king Xerxes, he
    Who calls Dareios sire,
Bearing the name our father bore of old?
Is it the archer's bow that wins the day?
    Or does the strength prevail   150
Of iron point that heads the spear's strong shaft?
But lo! in glory like the face of gods,
The mother of my king, my queen, appears:
Let us do reverent homage at her feet;
    Yea, it is meet that all
Should speak to her with words of greeting kind.

Enter ATOSSA *in a chariot of state.*

  Chor. O sovereign queen of Persian wives deep-zoned,
Mother of Xerxes, reverend in thine age,
    Wife of Dareios! hail!
'Twas thine to join in wedlock with a spouse
    Whom Persians owned as God,[2]

---

(1) The bridge of boats, with the embankment raised upon it, is
thought of as a new headland putting out from the one shore and reaching to the other.

(2) Stress is laid by the Hellenic poet, as in the *Agamemnon*, (v. 895,)
and in v. 707 of this Play, on the tendency of the East to give to its kings
the names and the signs of homage which were due only to the Gods.

And of a God thou art the mother too,
Unless its ancient Fortune fails our host.   160
   Atoss. Yes, thus I come, our gold-decked palace
      leaving,
The bridal bower Dareios with me slept in.
Care gnaws my heart, but now I tell you plainly
A tale, my friends, which may not leave me fearless,
Lest boastful wealth should stumble at the threshold,
And with his foot o'erturn the prosperous fortune
That great Dareios raised with Heaven's high blessing.
And twofold care untold my bosom haunteth:
We may not honour wealth that has no warriors,
Nor on the poor shines light to strength proportioned;
Wealth without stint we have, yet for our eye we
      tremble;   170
For as the eye of home I deem a master's presence.
Wherefore, ye Persians, aid me now in counsel;
Trusty and old, in you lies hope of wisdom.
   Chor. Queen of our land! be sure thou need'st not
      utter
Or thing or word twice o'er, which power may point to;
Thou bid'st us counsel give who fain would serve thee.
   Atoss. Ever with many visions of the night[1]
Am I encompassed, since my son went forth,
Leading a mighty host, with aim to sack
The land of the Ionians.   But ne'er yet   180
Have I beheld a dream so manifest
As in the night just past.   And this I'll tell thee:
There stood by me two women in fair robes;
And this in Persian garments was arrayed,
And that in Dorian came before mine eyes;
In stature both of tallest, comeliest size;
And both of faultless beauty, sisters twain

The Hellenes might deify a dead hero, but not a living sovereign. On
different grounds the Jews shrank, as in the stories of Nebuchadnezzar
and Dareios, (Dan. iii. 6,) from all such acts.
   (1) In the Greek, as in the translation, there is a change of metre, intended apparently to represent the transition from the tone of eager
excitement to the ordinary level of discourse.

Of the same stock.[1]   And they twain had their homes,
One in the Hellenic, one in alien land.
And these two, as I dreamt I saw, were set   190
At variance with each other.   And my son
Learnt it, and checked and mollified their wrath,
And yokes them to his chariots, and his collar
He places on their necks.   And one was proud
Of that equipment,[2] and in harness gave
Her mouth obedient; but the other kicked,
And tears the chariot's trappings with her hands,
And rushes off uncurbed, and breaks its yoke
Asunder.   And my son falls low, and then
His father comes, Dareios, pitying him.
And lo! when Xerxes sees him, he his clothes   200
Rends round his limbs.   These things I say I saw
In visions of the night; and when I rose,
And dipped my hands in fountain flowing clear,[3]
I at the altar stood with hand that bore
Sweet incense, wishing holy chrism to pour
To the averting Gods whom thus men worship.
And I beheld an eagle in full flight
To Phœbos' altar-hearth; and then, my friends,   210
I stood, struck dumb with fear; and next I saw
A kite pursuing, in her wingèd course,
And with his claws tearing the eagle's head,
Which did nought else but crouch and yield itself.
Such terrors it has been my lot to see,
And yours to hear: For be ye sure, my son,
If he succeed, will wonder-worthy prove;

(1) With reference either to the *mythos* that Asia and Europa were both
daughters of Okeanos, or to the historical fact that the Asiatic Ionians
and the Dorians of Europe were both of the same Hellenic stock. The contrast between the long flowing robes of the Asiatic women, and the short,
scanty kilt-like dress of those of Sparta must be borne in mind if we
would see the picture in its completeness.
(2) Athenian pride is flattered with the thought that they had resisted
while the Ionian Greeks had submitted all too willingly to the yoke of the
Barbarian.
(3) Lustrations of this kind, besides their general significance in
cleansing from defilement, had a special force as charms to turn aside
dangers threatened by foreboding dreams.—Comp. Aristoph. *Frogs*, v.
1264; Persius, *Sat.* ii. 16.

But if he fail, still irresponsible
He to the people, and in either case,
He, should he but return, is sovereign still.[1]

 Chor. We neither wish, O Lady, thee to frighten
O'ermuch with what we say, nor yet encourage:
But thou, the Gods adoring with entreaties,
If thou hast seen aught ill, bid them avert it,
And that all good things may receive fulfilment
For thee, thy children, and thy friends and country.   **221**
And next 'tis meet libations due to offer
To Earth and to the dead. And ask thy husband,
Dareios, whom thou say'st by night thou sawest,
With kindly mood from 'neath the Earth to send thee
Good things to light for thee and for thine offspring,
While adverse things shall fade away in darkness.
Such things do I, a self-taught seer, advise thee
In kindly mood, and any way we reckon
That good will come to thee from out these omens.

 Atoss. Well, with kind heart, hast thou, as first
   expounder,
Out of my dreams brought out a welcome meaning
For me, and for my sons; and thy good wishes,
May they receive fulfilment! And this also,
As thou dost bid, we to the Gods will offer   **230**
And to our friends below, when we go homeward.
But first, my friends, I wish to hear of Athens,
Where in the world do men report it standeth?[2]

 Chor. Far to the West, where sets our king the Sun-God.

 Atoss. Was it this city my son wished to capture?

 Chor. Aye, then would Hellas to our king be subject.

 Atoss. And have they any multitude of soldiers?

 Chor. A mighty host, that wrought the Medes much
   mischief.

(1) The political bearing of the passage as contrasting this characteristic
of the despotism of Persia with the strict account to which all Athenian
generals were subject, is, of course, unmistakable.

(2) The question, which seems to have rankled in the minds of the
Athenians, is recorded as an historical fact, and put into the mouth of
Dareios by Herodotos, (v. 101.) He had asked it on hearing that Sardis
had been attacked and burnt by them.

Atoss. And what besides? Have they too wealth
    sufficing?

Chor. A fount of silver have they, their land's trea-
    sure.[1]   240

Atoss. Have they a host in archers' skill excelling?

Chor. Not so, they wield the spear and shield and
    bucklers.[2]

Atoss. What shepherd rules and lords it o'er their
    people?

Chor. Of no man are they called the slaves or subjects.

Atoss. How then can they sustain a foe invading?

Chor. So that they spoiled Dareios' goodly army.

Atoss. Dread news is thine for sires of those who 're
    marching.

Chor. Nay, but I think thou soon wilt know the whole
    truth;

This running one may know is that of Persian:[3]

For good or evil some clear news he bringeth.   250

Enter Messenger.

Mess. O cities of the whole wide land of Asia!

O soil of Persia, haven of great wealth!

How at one stroke is brought to nothingness

Our great prosperity, and all the flower

Of Persia's strength is fallen! Woe is me!

'Tis ill to be the first to bring ill news;

Yet needs must I the whole woe tell, ye Persians:

All our barbaric mighty host is lost.[4]

---

(1) The words point to the silver mines of Laureion, which had been worked under Peisistratos, and of which this is the first mention in Greek literature.

(2) Once more the contrast between the Greek *hoplite* and the light-armed archers of the invaders is dwelt upon. The next answer of the Chorus dwells upon the deeper contrast, then prominent in the minds of all Athenians, between their democratic freedom and the despotism of Persia. Comp. Herod. v. 78.

(3) The system of postal communications by means of couriers which Dareios had organized had made their speed in running proverbial, (Herod. viii. 97.)

(4) With the characteristic contempt of a Greek for other races, Æschylos makes the Persians speak of themselves throughout as 'barbarians,' 'barbaric.'

Strophe. I.

Chor. O piteous, piteous woe!
 O strange and dread event!
Weep, O ye Persians, hearing this great grief!
 Mess. Yea, all things there are ruined utterly;
And I myself beyond all hope behold
 The light of day at home.

Antistroph. I.

Chor. O'er-long doth life appear
 To me, bowed down with years,
On hearing this unlooked-for misery.
 Mess. And I, indeed, being present and not hearing
The tales of others, can report, ye Persians,
 What ills were brought to pass.

Stroph. II.

Chor. Alas, alas! in vain
The many-weaponed and commingled host
Went from the land of Asia to invade
 The soil divine of Hellas.
 Mess. Full of the dead, slain foully, are the coasts
Of Salamis, and all the neighbouring shore.

270

Antistroph. II.

Chor. Alas, alas! sea-tossed
The bodies of our friends, and much disstained:
Thou say'st that they are drifted to and fro
 *In far out-floating garments.[1]
 Mess. E'en so; our bows availed not, but the host
Has perished, conquered by the clash of ships.

Stroph. III.

Chor. Wail, raise a bitter cry
And full of woe, for those who died in fight.
How every way the Gods have wrought out ill,
Ah me! ah me, our army all destroyed.
 Mess. O name of Salamis that most I loathe!
Ah, how I groan, remembering Athens too!

280

(1) Perhaps— "On planks that floated onward,"
   or— "Onl and and sea far spreading."

ANTISTROPH. III.

Chor. Yea, to her enemies
Athens may well be hateful, and our minds
Remember how full many a Persian wife   &c.
She, for no cause, made widows and bereaved.

   Atoss. Long time I have been silent in my woe,
Crushed down with grief; for this calamity
Exceeds all power to tell the woe, or ask.
Yet still we mortals needs must bear the griefs
The Gods send on us.   Clearly tell thy tale,
Unfolding the whole mischief, even though
Thou groan'st at evils, who there is not dead,
And which of our chief captains we must mourn,
And who, being set in office o'er the host,
Left by their death that office desolate.   &c.

   Mess. Xerxes still lives and sees the light of day.

   Atoss. To my house, then, great light thy words have
               brought,
Bright dawn of morning after murky night.

   Mess. Artembares, the lord of myriad horse,
On the hard flinty coasts of the Sileni
Is now being dashed; and valiant Dadakes,
Captain of thousands, smitten with the spear,
Leapt wildly from his ship.   And Tenagon,
Best of the true old Bactrians, haunts the soil
Of Aias' isle; Lilaios, Arsames,   310
And with them too Argestes, there defeated,
Hard by the island where the doves abound,[1]
Beat here and there upon the rocky shore.
[And from the springs of Neilos, Ægypt's stream,
Arkteus, Adeues, Pheresseues too,
These with Pharnuchos in one ship were lost;]
Matallos, Chrysa-born, the captain bold
Of myriads, leader he of swarthy horse

_____

(1) Possibly Salamis itself, as famed for the doves which were reared
there as sacred to Aphrodite, but possibly also one of the smaller islands
in the Saronic gulf, which the epithet would be enough to designate for
an Athenian audience. The " coasts of the Sileni " in v. 305 are identified
by scholiasts with Salamis.

Some thrice ten thousand strong, has fallen low,
His red beard, hanging all its shaggy length,
Deep dyed with blood, and purpled all his skin.　　　320
Arabian Magos, Bactrian Artames,
They perished, settlers in a land full rough.
[Amistris and Amphistreus, guiding well
The spear of many a conflict, and the noble
Ariomardos, leaving bitter grief
For Sardis; and the Mysian Seisames.]
With twelve score ships and ten came Tharybis;
Lyrnœan he in birth, once fair in form,
He lies, poor wretch, a death inglorious dying:
And, first in valour proved, Syennesis,
Kilikian satrap, who, for one man, gave　　　330
Most trouble to his foes, and nobly died.
Of leaders such as these I mention make,
And out of many evils tell but few.

　　Atoss. Woe, woe! I hear the very worst of ills,
Shame to the Persians, cause of bitter wail;
But tell me, going o'er the ground again,
How great the number of the Hellenes' navy,
That they presumed with Persia's armament
To wage their warfare in the clash of ships.

　　Mess. As far as numbers went, be sure the ships
Of Persia had the better, for the Hellenes　　　340
Had, as their total, ships but fifteen score,
And other ten selected as reserve.[1]
And Xerxes (well I know it) had a thousand
Which he commanded—those that most excelled [2]
In speed were twice five score and seven in number;
So stands the account. Deem'st thou our forces less
In that encounter? Nay, some Power above
Destroyed our host, and pressed the balance down
With most unequal fortune, and the Gods
Preserve the city of the Goddess Pallas.

(1) Perhaps— "And ten of these selected as reserve."
(2) As regards the number of the Persian ships, 1000 of average, and
207 of special swiftness. Æschylos agrees with Herodotus, who gives the
total of 1207. The latter, however, reckons the Greek ships not at 310,
but 378 (vii. 89, viii. 48).

C

Atoss. Is the Athenians' city then unsacked ?   250
Mess. Their men are left, and that is bulwark strong.[1]
Atoss. Next tell me how the fight of ships began.
Who led the attack ?   Were those Hellenes the first,
Or was't my son, exulting in his strength ?
Mess. The author of the mischief, O my mistress,
Was some foul fiend or Power on evil bent ;
For lo ! a Hellene from the Athenian host[2]
Came to thy son, to Xerxes, and spake thus,
That should the shadow of the dark night come,
The Hellenes would not wait him, but would leap   300
Into their rowers' benches, here and there,
And save their lives in secret, hasty flight.
And he forthwith, this hearing, knowing not
The Hellene's guile, nor yet the Gods' great wrath,
Gives this command to all his admirals,
Soon as the sun should cease to burn the earth
With his bright rays, and darkness thick invade
The firmament of heaven, to set their ships
In three-fold lines, to hinder all escape,
And guard the billowy straits, and others place   370
In circuit round about the isle of Aias :
For if the Hellenes 'scaped an evil doom,
And found a way of secret, hasty flight,
It was ordained that all should lose their heads.[3]
Such things he spake from soul o'erwrought with pride,
For he knew not what fate the Gods would send ;
And they, not mutinous, but prompt to serve,
Then made their supper ready, and each sailor
Fastened his oar around true-fitting thole

(1) **The** fact that Athens had actually been taken, **and** its chief buildings plundered and laid waste, was, of course, not a pleasant one for the
poet to dwell on.   It could hardly, however, be entirely passed over, and
this is the one allusion to it.   In the truest sense it was still "unsacked : " it had not lost its most effective defence, its most precious
treasure.
(2) As the story is told by Herodotos, (viii. 75,) this was Sikinnos, the
slave of Themistocles, and the stratagem was the device of that com-
mander to save the Greeks from the disgrace and ruin of a *sauve qui peut*
flight in all directions.
(3) **The** Greeks never beheaded their criminals, and the punishment is
mentioned as being specially characteristic of the barbaric Persians.

And when the sunlight vanished, and the night
Had come, then each man, master of an oar,   380
Went to his ship, and all men bearing arms,
And through the long ships rank cheered loud to rank;
And so they sail, as 'twas appointed each,
And all night long the captains of the fleet
Kept their men working, rowing to and fro;
Night then came on, and the Hellenic host
In no wise sought to take to secret flight.
And when day, bright to look on with white steeds,
O'erspread the earth, then rose from the Hellenes   390
Loud chant of cry of battle, and forthwith
Echo gave answer from each island rock;
And terror then on all the Persians fell,
Of fond hopes disappointed.   Not in flight
The Hellenes then their solemn pæans sang:
But with brave spirit hasting on to battle.
With martial sound the trumpet fired those ranks;
And straight with sweep of oars that flew through foam,
They smote the loud waves at the boatswain's call;
And swiftly all were manifest to sight.   400
Then first their right wing moved in order meet;[1]
Next the whole line its forward course began,
And all at once we heard a mighty shout,—
" O sons of Hellenes, forward, free your country;
Free too your wives, your children, and the shrines
Built to your fathers' Gods, and holy tombs
Your ancestors now rest in.   Now the fight
Is for our all."   And on our side indeed
Arose in answer din of Persian speech,
And time to wait was over; ship on ship   410
Dashed its bronze-pointed beak, and first a barque
Of Hellas did the encounter fierce begin,[2]
And from Phœnikian vessel crashes off

(1) The Æginetans and Megarians, according to the account preserved by Diodoros, (xi. 18,) or the Lacedæmonians, according to Herodotos, (viii. 65.)
(2) This may be meant to refer to the achievements of Ameinias of
Pallene, who appears in the traditional life of Æschylos as his youngest
brother.

Her carved prow.   And each against his neighbour
Steers his own ship : and first the mighty flood
Of Persian host held out.   But when the ships
Were crowded in the straits,[1] nor could they give
Help to each other, they with mutual shocks,
With beaks of bronze went crushing each the other,
Shivering their rowers' benches.   And the ships
Of Hellas, with manœuvring not unskilful,
Charged circling round them.   And the hulls of ships   420
Floated capsized, nor could the sea be seen,
Strown, as it was, with wrecks and carcases ;
And all the shores and rocks were full of corpses.
And every ship was wildly rowed in fight,
All that composed the Persian armament.
And they, as men spear tunnies,[2] or a haul
Of other fishes, with the shafts of oars,
Or spars of wrecks went smiting, cleaving down ;
And bitter groans and wailings overspread
The wide sea-waves, till eye of swarthy night   430
Bade it all cease : and for the mass of ills,
Not, though my tale should run for ten full days,
Could I in full recount them.   Be assured
That never yet so great a multitude
Died in a single day as died in this.

   Atoss. Ah, me !   Great then the sea of ills that breaks
On Persia and the whole barbaric host.

   Mess. Be sure our evil fate is but half o'er :
On this has supervened such bulk of woe,
As more than twice to outweigh what I've told.   440

   Atoss. And yet what fortune could be worse than this ?
Say, what is this disaster which thou tell'st,
That turns the scale to greater evils still ?

   Mess. Those Persians that were in the bloom of life,

---

(1) *Sc.*, in Herod. viii. 60, the strait between Salamis and the mainland.
(2) Tunny-fishing has always been prominent in the occupations of the
Mediterranean coasts, and the sailors who formed so large a part of
every Athenian audience would be familiar with the process here described, of striking or harpooning them. Aristophanes (*Wasps*, 1087)
coins (or uses) the word "to tunny" ($\theta\upsilon\nu\nu\acute{\alpha}\zeta\omega$) to express the act.
Comp. Herod. 1. 62.

Bravest in heart and noblest in their blood,
And by the king himself deemed worthiest trust,
Basely and by most shameful death have died.

Atoss. Ah! woe is me, my friends, for our ill fate!
What was the death by which thou say'st they perished?

Mess. There is an isle that lies off Salamis,[1]
Small, with bad anchorage for ships, where Pan,   450
Pan the dance-loving, haunts the sea-washed coast.
There Xerxes sends these men, that when their foes,
Being wrecked, should to the islands safely swim,
They might with ease destroy th' Hellenic host,
And save their friends from out the deep sea's paths;
But ill the future guessing: for when God
Gave the Hellenes the glory of the battle,
In that same hour, with arms well wrought in bronze
Shielding their bodies, from their ships they leapt,
And the whole isle encircled, so that we   460
Were sore distressed,[2] and knew not where to turn;
For here men's hands hurled many a stone at them;
And there the arrows from the archer's bow
Smote and destroyed them; and with one great rush,
At last advancing, they upon them dash
And smite, and hew the limbs of these poor wretches,
Till they each foe had utterly destroyed.
[And Xerxes when he saw how deep the ill,[3]
Groaned out aloud, for he had ta'en his seat,
With clear, wide view of all the army round,
On a high cliff hard by the open sea;
And tearing then his robes with bitter cry,   470
And giving orders to his troops on shore,

(1) *Sc.*, Psyttaleia, lying between Salamis and the mainland. Pausanias
(i. 36-82) describes it in his time as having no artistic shrine or statue,
but full everywhere of roughly-carved images of Pan, to whom the island
was sacred. It lay just opposite the entrance to the Peiræos. The connexion of Pan with Salamis and its adjacent islands seems implied in
Sophocles, *Aias.* 695.
(2) The manœuvre was, we learn from Herodotos (viii. 95), the work of
Aristeides, the personal friend of Æschylos, and the statesman with
whose policy he had most sympathy.
(3) The lines are noted as probably a spurious addition, by a weaker
hand, to the text, as introducing surplusage, as inconsistent with Herodotos, and as faulty in their metrical structure.

He sends them off in foul retreat.   This grief
'Tis thine to mourn besides the former ills.]
   Atoss. O hateful Power, how thou of all their hopes
Hast robbed the Persians ! Bitter doom my son
Devised for glorious Athens, nor did they,
The invading host who fell at Marathon,
Suffice ; but my son, counting it his task
To exact requital for it, brought on him
So great a crowd of sorrows.   But I pray,
As to those ships that have this fate escaped,   484
Where did'st thou leave them ? Can'st thou clearly tell ?
   Mess. The captains of the vessels that were left,
With a fair wind, but not in meet array,
Took flight : and all the remnant of the army
Fell in Bœotia—some for stress of thirst
About the fountain clear, and some of us,
Panting for breath, cross to the Phokians' land,
The soil of Doris, and the Melian gulf,
Where fair Spercheios waters all the plains
With kindly flood, and then the Achæan fields   490
And city of the Thessali received us,
Famished for lack of food ;[1] and many died
Of thirst and hunger, for both ills we bore ;
And then to the Magnetian land we came,
And that of Macedonians, to the stream
Of Axios, and Bolbe's reed-grown marsh,
And Mount Pangaios and the Edonian land.
And on that night God sent a mighty frost,
Unwonted at that season, sealing up
The whole course of the Strymon's pure, clear flood ;[2]
And they who erst had deemed the Gods as nought,   500
Then prayed with hot entreaties, worshipping
Both earth and heaven.   And after that the host

---

(1) So Herodotos (viii. 115) describes them as driven by hunger to eat
even grass and leaves.
   (2) No trace of this passage over the frozen Strymon appears in Herodotos, who leaves the reader to imagine that it was crossed, as before, by
a bridge.   It is hardly, indeed, consistent with dramatic probability
that the courier should have remained to watch the whole retreat of the
defeated army ; and on this and other grounds, the latter part of the
speech has been rejected by some critics as a later addition.

Ceased from its instant calling on the Gods,
It crosses o'er the glassy, frozen stream;
And whosoe'er set forth before the rays
Of the bright God were shed abroad, was saved;
For soon the glorious sun with burning blaze
Reached the mid-stream and warmed it with its flame,
And they, confused, each on the other fell.
Blest then was he whose soul most speedily
Breathed out its life.   And those who yet survived
And gained deliverance, crossing with great toil   510
And many a pang through Thrakè, now are come,
Escaped from perils, no great number they,
To this our sacred land, and so it groans,
This city of the Persians, missing much
Our country's dear-loved youth.   Too true my tale,
And many things I from my speech omit,
Ills which the Persians suffer at God's hand.
   Chor. O Power resistless, with what weight of woe
On all the Persian race have thy feet leapt!
   Atoss. Ah! woe is me for that our army lost!   520
O vision of the night that cam'st in dreams,
Too clearly did'st thou shew me of these ills!
But ye (*to Chorus*) did judge them far too carelessly;
Yet since your counsel pointed to that course,
I to the Gods will first my prayer address.
And then with gifts to Earth and to the Dead,
Bringing the chrism from my store, I'll come.
For our past ills, I know, 'tis all too late,
But for the future, I may hope, will dawn
A better fortune!   But 'tis now your part
In these our present ills, in counsel faithful
To commune with the Faithful; and my son,   530
Should he come here before me, comfort him,
And home escort him, lest he add fresh ill
To all these evils that we suffer now.   [*Exit.*
   Chor. Zeus our king, who now to nothing
     Bring'st the army of the Persians,
     Multitudinous, much boasting;

And with gloomy woe hast shrouded
Both Ecbatana and Susa;
Many maidens now are tearing
With their tender hands their mantles,   540
And with tear-floods wet their bosoms,
In the common grief partaking;
And the brides of Persian warriors,
Dainty even in their wailing,
Longing for their new-wed husbands,
Reft of bridal couch luxurious,
With its coverlet so dainty,
Losing joy of wanton youth-time,
Mourn in never-sated wailings.
And I too in fullest measure
Raise again meet cry of sorrow,
Weeping for the loved and lost ones.

STROPH. I.

For now the land of Asia mourneth sore,   650
        Left desolate of men,
    'Twas Xerxes led them forth, woe! woe!
    'Twas Xerxes lost them all, woe! woe!
'Twas Xerxes who with evil counsels sped
        Their course in sea-borne barques.
Why was Dareios erst so free from harm,
        First bowman of the state,
The leader whom the men of Susa loved,

ANTISTROPH. I.

While those who fought as soldiers or at sea,   660
        These ships, dark-hulled, well-rowed,
    Their own ships bore them on, woe! woe!
    Their own ships lost them all, woe! woe!
Their own ships, in the crash of ruin urged,
        And by Ionian hands?[1]
The king himself, we hear, but hardly 'scapes,
        Through Thrakè's wide-spread steppes,
And paths o'er which the tempests wildly sweep.

(1) The Ionians, not of the Asiatic Ionia, but of Attica.

STROPH. II.

And they who perished first, ah me!   570
Perforce unburied left, alas!
Are scattered round Kychreia's shore,[1] woe! woe!
Lament, mourn sore, and raise a bitter cry,
   Grievous, the sky to pierce, woe! woe!
And let thy mourning voice uplift its strain
   Of loud and full lament.

ANTISTROPH. II.

Torn by the whirling flood, ah me!
Their carcases are gnawed, alas!
By the dumb brood of stainless sea, woe! woe!   580
And each house mourneth for its vanished lord;
   And childless sires, woe! woe!
Mourning in age o'er griefs the Gods have sent,
   Now hear their utter loss.

STROPH. III.

And throughout all Asia's borders
None now own the sway of Persia,
Nor bring any more their tribute,
Owning sway of sovereign master.
Low upon the Earth, laid prostrate,   590
Is the strength of our great monarch.

ANTISTROPH. III.

No more need men keep in silence
Tongues fast bound: for now the people
May with freedom speak at pleasure;
For the yoke of power is broken;
And blood-stained in all its meadows
Holds the sea-washed isle of Aias
What was once the host of Persia.

Re-enter ATOSSA.

Atoss. Whoe'er, my friends, is vexed in troublous
   times,   600

(1) Kychreia, the archaic name of Salamis.

Knows that when once a tide of woe sets in,
A man is wont to fear in everything;
But when Fate flows on smoothly, then to trust
That the same Fate will ever send fair gales.
So now all these disasters from the Gods
Seem in mine eyes filled full of fear and dread,
And in mine ears rings cry unpæanlike,
So great a dread of all has seized my soul:
And therefore now, without or chariot's state
Or wonted pomp, have I thus issued forth   610
From out my palace, to my son's sire bringing .
Libations loving, gifts propitiatory,
Meet for the dead; milk pure and white from cow
Unblemished, and bright honey that distils
From the flower-working bee, and water drawn
From virgin fountain, and the draught unmarred
From mother wild, bright child of ancient vine;
And here too of the tree that evermore
Keeps its fresh life in foliage, the pale olive,
Is the sweet-smelling fruit, and twinèd wreaths
Of flowers, the children of all-bearing earth.[1]   620
But ye, my friends, o'er these libations poured
In honour of the dead, chant forth your hymns,
And call upon Dareios as a God:
While I will send unto the Gods below
These votive offerings which the earth shall drink.

> [*Goes to the tomb of* DAREIOS *in the centre
> of the stage.*

   Chor. O royal lady, honoured of the Persians,
      Do thou libations pour
To the dark chambers of the dead below;
      And we with hymns will pray
The Powers that act as escorts of the dead
To give us kindly help beneath the earth.
But oh, ye holy Ones in darkness dwelling,   630

---

(1) The ritual described is Hellenic rather than Persian, and takes its
place (Soph. *Electr.* 836; Eurip. *Iphig. Taur.* 583; Homer, *Il.* xxiii. 219)
as showing what offerings were employed to soothe or call up the spirits
of the dead. Comp. Pliny, *Hist. Nat.* xxx.

Hermes and Earth, and thou, the Lord of Hell,
    Send from beneath, a soul
    Up to the light of earth;
For should he know a cure for these our ills,
He, he alone of men, their end may tell.

Stroph. I.

Doth he, the blest one hear,
The king, like Gods in power,
Hear me, as I send forth
My cries in barbarous speech,
Yet very clear to him,—
Sad, varied, broken cries
So as to tell aloud
Our troubles terrible?
Ah, doth he hear below?

640

Antistroph. I.

But thou, O Earth, and ye,
The other Lords of those
Beneath the grave that dwell;
Grant that the godlike one
May come from out your home,
The Persians' mighty God,
In Susa's palace born;
Send him, I pray you, up,
The like of whom the soil
Of Persia never hid.

Stroph. II.

Dear was our chief, and dear to us his tomb,
    For dear the life it hides;
Aidoneus, O Aidoneus, send him forth,
Thou who dost lead the dead to Earth again,
*Yea, send Dareios. . . What a king was he!

650

Antistroph. II.

For never did he in war's bloody woe
    Lose all his warrior-host,
But Heaven-taught Counsellor the Persians called him,

And Heaven-taught Counsellor in truth he proved,
Since he still ruled his hosts of subjects well.

STROPH. III.

Monarch, O ancient monarch, come, oh, come,
Come to the summit of sepulchral mound,
       Lifting thy foot encased
       In slipper saffron-dyed,
       And giving to our view
       Thy royal tiara's crest:[1]
Speak, O Dareios, faultless father, speak.

ANTISTROPH. III.

Yea, come, that thou, O Lord, may'st hear the woes,
Woes new and strange, our lord has now endured;
       For on us now has fallen
       A dark and Stygian mist,
       Since all the armed youth
       Has perished utterly;
Speak, O Dareios, faultless father, speak.

EPODE.

     O thou, whose death thy friends
     Bewail with many tears,
     *Why thus, O Lord of lords,
*In double error of wild frenzy born,
       Have all our triremes good
       Been lost to this our land,
Ships that are ships no more, yea, ships no more?

The Ghost *of* DAREIOS *appears on the summit of the mound.*

     Dar. O faithful of the Faithful, ye who were
Companions of my youth, ye Persian elders,
What troubles is 't my country toils beneath?
The whole plain groans, cut up and furrowed o'er,[2]

---

(1) The description obviously gives the state dress of the Persian kings.
They alone wore the tiara erect.—Xen. *Kyrop.* viii. 3, 13.
(2) Either that he has felt the measured tread of the mourners round
his tomb, as they went wailing round and round, or that he has heard

And I, beholding now my queen beloved
Standing hard by my sepulchre, feared **much**,   680
And her libations graciously received;
But ye wail loud near this my sepulchre,
And shouting shrill with cries that raise the dead,
Ye call me with your plaints. No easy task
Is it to come, for this **cause above all**,
That the great **Gods** who reign below are apter
To seize men than release : yet natheless I,
Being great **in power** among them, now am come.
Be quick then, that none blame me as too late ; [1]
What new dire evils on the Persians weigh ?

   Chor. I fear to look on **thee**,   690
      Fear before **thee to speak**,
With all the awe **of thee I felt** of old.
   Dar. But since I came by thy complaints persuaded,
From below rising, spin no lengthened tale ;
But shortly, clearly speak, and tell thy story,
And leave awhile thine awe and fear of me.
   Chor. I dread thy **wish to grant**,
      *I dread to say thee nay,[2]
Saying things that it is hard for friends to speak.
   Dar. Nay, then, since that old dread of thine prevents
      thee,
Do thou [*to* ATOSSA], the ancient partner of my bed,   700
My **noble** queen, from these thy plaints and moanings
Cease, and **say something** clearly. Human sorrows
May well on mortals fall; for many evils,
Some on the sea, and some on dry land **also**,
Happen to men if life be far prolongèd.
   Atoss. O thou, who in the fate of fair **good fortune**
Excelled'st all men, who, while yet thou sawest
The sun's bright rays, did'st lead a life all blessed,
Admired, yea, worshipped as a God by Persians,

the rush of armies, and seen the plain tracked by chariot-wheels, **and**
comes, not knowing all these things, to learn what it means.
   (1) The words point to the widespread belief that when the souls of
the dead were permitted to return to earth, it was with strict limitations
as to the time of their leave of absence.
   (2) Perhaps—   " I dread to speak the truth."

Now, too, I count thee blest in that thou died'st
Before thou saw'st the depth of these our evils.
For now, Dareios, thou shalt hear a story
Full, yet in briefest moment. Utter ruin,
To sum up all, is come upon the Persians.   710

 Dar. How so? Hath plague or discord seized my
  country?

 Atoss. Not so, but all the host is lost near Athens.

 Dar. What son of mine led that host thither, tell me?[1]

 Atoss. Xerxes o'er-hasty, emptying all the mainland.

 Dar. Made he this mad attempt by land or water?

 Atoss. By both; two lines there were of two great
  armies.

 Dar. How did so great a host effect its passage?

 Atoss. He bridged the straits of Helle, and found
  transit.

 Dar. Did he prevail to close the mighty Bosporos?

 Atoss. So was it; yet some God, it may be, helped
  him.   720

 Dar. Alas! some great God came and stole his wisdom.

 Atoss. Yea, the end shows what evil he accomplished.

 Dar. And how have they fared, that ye thus bewail
  them?

 Atoss. The naval host, o'ercome, wrecked all the land-
  force.

 Dar. What! is the whole host by the spear laid prostrate?

 Atoss. For this doth Susa's city mourn her losses.

 Dar. Alas, for that brave force and mighty army!

 Atoss. The Bactrians all are lost, not old men merely.

 Dar. Poor fool! how he hath lost his host's fresh vigour!

 Atoss. Xerxes, they say, alone, with but few
  others   730

 Dar. What is his end, and where? Is there no safety?

 Atoss. Was glad to gain the bridge that joins two
  mainlands.

(1) According to Herodotos (vii. 225) two brothers of Xerxes fell at
Thermopylæ.

Dar. And has he reached this mainland? Is that
    certain?

Atoss. Yea, the report holds good. Here is no discord.[1]

Dar. Ah me! Full swift the oracles' fulfilment!
And on my son hath Zeus their end directed.
I hoped the Gods would work them out more slowly;
But when man hastens, God too with him worketh.
And now for all my friends a fount of evils
Seems to be found. And this my son, not knowing,   740
In youth's rash mood, hath wrought; for he did purpose
To curb the sacred Hellespont with fetters,
As though it were his slave, and sought to alter
The stream of God, the Bosporos, full-flowing,
And his well-hammered chains around it casting,
Prevailed to make his mighty host a highway;
And though a mortal, thought, with no good counsel,
To master all the Gods, yea, e'en Poseidon.
Nay, was not my poor son oppressed with madness?
And much I fear lest all my heaped-up treasure
Become the spoil and prey of the first comer.

   Atoss. Such things the o'er-hasty Xerxes learns from
    others,   750
By intercourse with men of evil counsel;[2]
Who say that thou great wealth for thy son gained'st
By thy spear's might, while he with coward spirit
Does his spear-work indoors, and nothing addeth
Unto his father's glory. Such reproaches
Hearing full oft from men of evil counsel,
He planned this expedition against Hellas.

   Dar. Thus then a deed portentous hath been wrought,
Ever to be remembered, such as ne'er
Falling on Susa made it desolate,
Since Zeus our king ordained this dignity,
That one man should be lord of Asia's plains.

---

(1) As Herodotos (viii. 117) tells the story, the bridge had been broken
by tempest before Xerxes reached it.

(2) Probably Mardonios and Onomacritos the Athenian soothsayer are
referred to, who, according to Herodotos (vii. 6, viii. 99) were the chief
instigators of the expedition.

Where feed her thousand flocks, and hold the rod 760
Of sovran guidance : for the Median first [1]
Ruled o'er the host, and then his son in turn
Finished the work, for reason steered his soul ;
And Kyros came as third, full richly blest,
And ruled, and gained great peace for all his friends ;
And he won o'er the Lydians and the Phrygians,
And conquered all the wide Ionian land ; [2]
For such his wisdom, he provoked not God.
And Kyros' son came fourth, and ruled the host ;
And Mardos fifth held sway, his country's shame, [3] 770
Shame to the ancient throne ; and him with guile
Artaphrenes [4] the brave smote down, close leagued
With men, his friends, to whom the work was given.
[Sixth, Maraphis and seventh Artaphrenes,]
And I obtained this post that I desired,
And with a mighty host great victories won.
Yet no such evil brought I on the state ;
But my son Xerxes, young, thinks like a youth,
And all my solemn charge remembers not ;
For know this well, my old companions true, 780
That none of us who swayed the realm of old,
Did e'er appear as working ills like these.
   Chor. What then, O King Dareios ? To what end
Lead'st thou thy speech ? And how, in this our plight,
Could we, the Persian people, prosper best ?
   Dar. If ye no more attack the Hellenes' land,

---

(1) Astyages, the father-in-law of Kyaxares and grandfather of Kyros.
In this case Æschylos must be supposed to accept Xenophon's statement
that Kyaxares succeeded Astyages. Possibly, however, the Median may
be Kyaxares I., the father of Astyages, and so the succession here would
harmonise with that of Herodotos. The whole succession must be
looked on as embodying the loose, floating notions of the Athenians as
to the history of their great enemy, rather than as the result of inquiry.
  (2) Stress is laid on the violence to which the Asiatic Ionians had suc-
cumbed, and their resistance to which distinguished them from the
Lydians or Phrygians, whose submission had been voluntary.
  (3) Mardos. Under this name we recognise the Pseudo-Smerdis of
Herodotos, (iii. 67,) who, by restoring the dominion of the Median Magi,
the caste to which he himself belonged, brought shame upon the
Persians.
  (4) Possibly another form of Intaphernes, who appears in Herodotos
(iii. 70) as one of the seven conspirators against the Magian Pseudo-
Smerdis.

E'en though the Median host outnumber theirs.
To them the very land is true ally.

> *Chor.* What meanest thou? How fights the land for
> them?

  Dar. *It slays with famine those vast multitudes.   790

  Chor. We then a host, select, compact, will raise.

  Dar. Nay, e'en the host which now in Hellas stays [1]

Will ne'er return in peace and safety home.

> *Chor.* How say'st thou? Does not all the barbarous
> host

Cross from Europa o'er the straits of Hellè?

  Dar. But few of many; if 'tis meet for one

Who looks upon the things already done

To trust the oracles of Gods; for they,

Not these or those, but all, are brought to pass:

If this be so, then, resting on vain hopes, [2]   800

He leaves a chosen portion of his host:

And they abide where, watering all the plain,

Asòpos pours his fertilising stream

Dear to Bœotian land; and there of ills

The topmost crown awaits them, penalty

Of wanton outrage and of godless thoughts;

For they to Hellas coming, held not back

In awe from plundering sculptured forms of Gods [3]

And burning down their temples; and laid low

Are altars, and the shrines of Gods o'erthrown,

E'en from their base. They therefore having wrought

Deeds evil, now are suffering, and will suffer

Evil not less, and not as yet is seen   810

*E'en the bare groundwork of the ills, but still

---

(1) The force of 300,000 men left in Greece under Mardonios, (Herod.
viii. 113,) afterwards defeated at Platæa.

(2) Comp. the speech of Mardonios urging his plan on Xerxes, (Herod.
viii. 100.)

(3) This was of course a popular topic with the Athenians, whose own
temples had been outraged. But other sanctuaries also, the temples at
Delphi and Abæ had shared the same fate, and these sins against the
Gods of Hellas were naturally connected in the thoughts of the Greeks
with the subsequent disasters of the Persians. In Egypt these outrages
had an iconoclastic character. In Athens they were a retaliation for the
destruction of the temple at Sardis, (Herod. v. 102.)

They grow up to completeness.   Such a stream
Of blood and slaughter soon shall flow from them
By Dorian spear upon Platæan ground,[1]
And heaps of corpses shall to children's children,
Though speechless, witness to the eyes of men
That mortal man should not wax overproud ;
For wanton pride from blossom grows to fruit,
The full corn in the ear, of utter woe,
And reaps a tear-fraught harvest.   Seeing then,
Such recompense of these things, cherish well
The memory of Athens and of Hellas ;   820
Let no man in his scorn of present fortune,
And thirst for other, mar his good estate ;
Zeus is the avenger of o'erlofty thoughts,
A terrible controller.   Therefore now,
Since voice of God bids him be wise of heart,
Admonish him with counsel true and good
To cease his daring sacrilegious pride ;
And thou, O Xerxes' mother, old and dear,
Go to thy home, and taking what apparel
Is fitting, go to meet thy son ; for all   830
The costly robes around his limbs are torn
To rags and shreds in grief's wild agony.
But do thou gently soothe his soul with words ;
For he to thee alone will deign to hearken ;
But I must leave the earth for darkness deep :
And ye, old men, farewell, although in woe,
And give your soul its daily bread of joy ;
For to the dead no profit bringeth wealth.
          [*Exit, disappearing in the earth.*
      Chor. I shudder as I hear the many woes
Both past and present that on Persians fall.   840
      Atoss. [O God, how many evils fall on me ![2]
And yet this one woe biteth more than all,

----

(1) The reference to the prominent part taken by the Peloponnesian
forces in the battle of Platœæ is probably due to the political sympathies
of the dramatist.
   (2) The speech of Atossa is rejected by Paley, on internal grounds, as
spurious.

Hearing my son's shame in the rags of robes
That clothe his limbs. But I will go and take
A fit adornment from my house, and try
To meet my son. We will not in his troubles
Basely abandon him whom most we love.]

Stroph. I.

Chor. Ah me ! a glorious and a blessed life
　　Had we as subjects once,
When our old king, Dareios, ruled the land,   850
Meeting all wants, dispassionate, supreme,
　　A monarch like a God.

Antistroph. I.

For first we showed the world our noble hosts;
　　And laws of tower-like strength
Directed all things; and our backward march
After our wars unhurt, unsuffering led
　　Our prospering armies home.

Stroph. II.

　　How many towns he took,
　　Not crossing Halys' stream [1]   860
　　Nor issuing from his home,
　　There where in Strymon's sea,
　　The Acheloian Isles [2]
Lie near the coasts of Thrakian colonies.

Antistroph. II.

And those that lie outside the Ægæan main,
　　The cities girt with towers,
　　They hearkened to our king ;
　　And those who boast their site
　　By Hellè's full, wide stream,
Propontis with its bays, and mouth of Pontos broad.   870

(1) Apparently an allusion to the oracle given to Crœsos, that he, if he
crossed the Halys, should destroy a great kingdom.
(2) The name originally given to the Echinades, a group of islands at
the mouth of the Acheloös, was applied generically to all islands lying
near the mouth of great rivers, and here, probably, includes Imbros,
Thasos, and Samothrakè.

STROPH. III.

And all the isles that lie
Facing the headland jutting in the sea,[1]
 Close bound to this our coast ;
Lesbos, and Samos with its olive groves ;
 Chios and Paros too ;
Naxos and Myconos, and Andros too
 On Tenos bordering.

ANTISTROPH. III.

And so he ruled the isles
That lie midway between the continents,
 Lemnos, and Icaros,
Rhodos and Cnidos and the Kyprian towns,
 Paphos and Soli famed,
 And with them Salamis,
Whose parent city now our groans doth cause ;[2]

EPODE.

And many a wealthy town and populous,
Of Hellenes in the Ionian region dwelling,
 He by his counsel ruled ;
His was the unconquered strength of warrior host,
 Allies of mingled race.
 And now, beyond all doubt,
In strife of war defeated utterly,
 We find this high estate
 Through wrath of God o'erturned,
 And we are smitten low,
 By bitter loss at sea.

Enter XERXES *in kingly apparel, but with his robes rent,
with* Attendants.

 Xer. Oh, miserable me !
  Who this dark hateful doom
  That I expected least

(1) The geography is somewhat obscure, but the words seem to refer to
the portion of the islands that are named as opposite (in a southerly direction) to the promontory of the Troad.
(2) Salamis in Kypros had been colonised by Teukros, the son of Aias,
and had received its name in remembrance of the island in the Saronic
Gulf.

Have met with as my lot,
With what stern mood and fierce
Towards the Persian race
Is God's hand laid on us!
What woe will come on me?
Gone is my strength of limb,
As I these elders see.
Ah, would to Heaven, O Zeus,
That with the men who fell
Death's doom had covered me!

Chor. Ah, woe, O king, woe! woe!
For the army brave in fight,
And our goodly Persian name,
And the fair array of men,
Whom God hath now cut off!
And the land bewails its youth
Who for our Xerxes fell,
For him whose deeds have filled
*Hades with Persian souls;
For many heroes now
*Are Hades-travellers,
Our country's chosen flower,
Mighty with darts and bow;
*For lo! the myriad mass
Of men has perished quite.
Woe, woe for our fair fame!
And Asia's land, O King,
Is terribly, most terribly, o'erthrown.

Xer. I then, oh misery!
Have to my curse been proved
Sore evil to my country and my race.

Chor. Yea, and on thy return
I will lift up my voice in wailing loud,
Cry of sore-troubled thought,
As of a mourner born
In Mariandynian land,[1]
Lament of many tears.

Paphlagonian tribe, conspicuous for their

ANTISTROPH. I.

Xer. Yea, utter ye a wail
        Dreary and full of grief;
        For lo! the face of Fate
        Against me now is turned.

Chor. Yea, I will raise a cry
         Dreary and full of grief,
         Giving this tribute due
         To all the people's woes,
         And all our loss at sea,
         Troubles of this our State
         That mourneth for her sons;
         Yea, I will wail full sore,
         With flood of bitter tears.

STROPH. II.

Xer. For Ares, he whose might
        Was in our ships' array,
        Giving victory to our foes,   920
        Has in Ionians, yea,
        Ionians, found his match,
        And from the dark sea's plain,
        And that ill-omened shore,
        Has a fell harvest reaped.

Chor. Yea, wail, search out the whole;
         Where are our other friends?
         Where thy companions true,
         Such as Pharandakes,
         Susas, Pelagon, Psammis, Dotamas,
         Agdabatas, Susiskanes,
         From Ecbatana who started?   940

ANTISTROPH. II.

Xer. I left them low in death,
        Falling from Tyrian ship,
        On Salaminian shores,
        Beating now here, now there,
        On the hard rock-girt coast.

orgiastic worship of Adonis, had become proverbial for the wildness of
their plaintive dirges.

Chor. Ah, where Pharnuchos then,
And Ariomardos brave ?
And where Sevalkes king,
Lilæos proud of race,
Memphis and Tharybis,
Masistras, and Artembares,
Hystæchmas ? This I ask.

Strophe. III.

Xer. Woe! woe is me!
They have looked on at Athens' ancient towers,
Her hated towers, ah me!
All, as by one fell stroke,
Unhappy in their fate
Lie gasping on the shore.
Chor. And he, thy faithful Eye,[1]
Who told the Persian host,
Myriads on myriads o'er,[2]
Alpistos, son and heir
Of Batanôchos old

*   *   *   *   *

And the son of brave Sesames,
Son himself of Megabates.
Parthos, and the great Œbares,
Did'st thou leave them, did'st thou leave them ?
Ah, woe! ah, woe is me,
For those unhappy ones !
Thou to the Persians brave
Tellest of ills on ills.

Antistrophe. III.

Xer. Ah, thou dost wake in me
The memory of the spell of yearning love
For comrades brave and true,

(1) The name seems to have been an official title for some Inspector-General of the Army. Comp. Aristoph. *Acharn.* v. 92.
(2) As in the account which Herodotos gives (vii. 60) of the way in which the army of Xerxes was numbered, sc., by enclosing 10,000 men in a given space, and then filling it again and again till the whole army had passed through.

Telling of cursed ills,
Yea, cursed, hateful doom ;
And lo, within my frame
My heart cries out, cries out.
Chor. Yea, another too we long for,
Xanthes, captain of ten thousand
Mardian warriors, and Anchares
Arian born, and great Arsakes
And Diæxis, lords of horsemen,
Kigdagatas and Lythimnas,
Tolmos, longing for the battle :
*Much I marvel, much I marvel,[1]
For they come not, as the rear-guard
Of thy tent on chariot mounted.[2]

STROPH. IV.

Xer. Gone those rulers of the army.
Chor. Gone are they in death inglorious.
Xer. Ah woe ! ah woe ! Alas ! alas !
Chor. Ah ! the Gods have sent upon us
Ill we never thought to look on,
Eminent above all others ;
Ne'er hath Atè seen its equal.

ANTISTROPH. IV.

Smitten we by many sorrows,
Such as come on men but seldom.
Chor. Smitten we, 'tis all too certain. . .
Xer. Fresh woes ! fresh woes ! ah me !
Chor. Now with adverse turn of fortune,
With Ionian seamen meeting,
Fails in war the race of Persians.

STROPH. V.

Xer. Too true. Yea I and that vast host of mine
Are smitten down.

(1) Another reading gives—
    "They are buried, they are buried."
(2) Perhaps referring to the waggon-chariots in which the rider reclined at ease, either protected by a canopy, or, as in the Assyrian sculptures and perhaps in the East generally, overshadowed by a large umbrella
which an eunuch holds over him.

Chor. Too true—the Persians' majesty and might
    Have perished utterly.
Xer. Sees't thou this remnant of my armament?
Chor. I see it, yea, I see.   1000
Xer. (*pointing to his quiver.*) Dost see thou that which
    arrows wont to hold ?. . .
Chor. What speak'st thou of as saved?
Xer. This treasure-store for darts.
Chor. Few, few of many left !
Xer. Thus we all helpers lack.
Chor. Ionian soldiers flee not from the spear.

Antistroph. V.

Xer. Yea, very brave are they, and I have seen
    Unlooked-for woe.
Chor. Wilt tell of squadron of our sea-borne ships
    Defeated utterly ?
Xer. I tore my robes at this calamity.
Chor. Ah me, ah me, ah me !   1010
Xer. Ay, more than all ' ah me's' !
Chor. Two-fold and three-fold ills !
Xer. Grievous to us—but joy,
    Great joy, to all our foes !
Chor. Lopped off is all our strength.
Xer. Stripped bare of escort I !
Chor. Yea, by sore loss at sea
    Disastrous to thy friends.

Stroph. VI.

Xer. Weep for our sorrow, weep,
    Yea, go ye to the house.
Chor Woe for our griefs, woe, woe !
Xer. Cry out an echoing cry.
Chor. Ill gift of ills on ills.   1055
Xer. Weep on in wailing chant.
Chor. Oh! ah! Oh! ah!
Xer. Grievous our bitter woes.
Chor Ah me, I mourn them sore.

ANTISTROPH. VI.

Xer. Ply, ply your hands and groan ;
    Yea, for my sake bewail
Chor. I weep in bitter grief.
Xer. Cry out an echoing cry.
Chor. Yea, we may raise our voice,
    O Lord and King, in wail.
Xer. Raise now shrill cry of woe.
Chor. Ah me! Ah! Woe is me!   1030
Xer. Yea, with it mingle dark. . . . .
Chor. And bitter, grievous blows.

STROPH. VII.

Xer. Yea, beat thy breast, and cry
    After the Mysian type.
Chor. Oh, misery! oh, misery!
Xer. Yea, tear the white hair off thy flowing beard.
Chor. Yea; with clenched hands, with clenchèd hands,
    I say,
    In very piteous guise.
Xer. Cry out, cry out aloud.
Chor. That also will I do.

ANTISTROPH. VII.

Xer. And with thy fingers tear
    Thy bosom's folded robe.
Chor. Oh, misery! oh, misery!   1040
Xer. Yea, tear thy hair in wailing for our host.
Chor. Yea, with clenched hands, I say, with clenchèd
    hands,
    In very piteous guise.
Xer. Be thine eyes wet with tears.
Chor. Behold the tears stream down.

EPODE.

Xer. Raise a re-echoing cry.
Chor. Ah woe! ah woe!
Xer. Go to thy home with wailing loud and long.
Chor. O land of Persia, full of lamentations !

Xer. Through the town raise your cries.
Chor. We raise them, yea, we raise.   1060
Xer. Wail, wail, ye men that walked so daintily.
Chor. O land of Persia, full of lamentations!
     Woe; woe!
Xer. Alas for those who in the triremes perished!
Chor. With broken cries of woe will I escort thee.

            *[Exeunt in procession, wailing, and
                 rending their robes.*

THE SEVEN WHO FOUGHT AGAINST THEBES.

ARGUMENT.

When Œdipus king of Thebes discovered that he had unknowingly been the murderer of his father, and had lived in incest with his mother, he blinded himself. And his two sons, Eteocles and Polyneikes, wishing to banish the remembrance of these horrors from the eyes of men, at first kept him in confinement. And he, being wroth with them, prayed that they might divide their inheritance with the sword. And they, in fear lest the prayer should be accomplished, agreed to reign in turn, each for a year, and Eteocles, as the elder of the two, took the first turn. But when at the end of the year Polyneikes came to ask for the kingdom, Eteocles refused to give way, and sent him away empty. So Polyneikes went to Argos and married the daughter of Adrastos the king of that country, and gathered together a great army under six great captains, himself coming as the seventh, and led it against Thebes. And so they compassed it about, and at each of the seven gates of the city was stationed one of the divisions of the army.

Note.—The Seven against Thebes appears to have been produced B.C. 47 the year after The Persians.

Dramatis Personæ.

ETEOCLES.

Scout.

ISMENE.

ANTIGONE.

Herald.

Chorus of Theban Maidens.

THE SEVEN WHO FOUGHT AGAINST THEBES.

SCENE.—Thebes *in front of the Acropolis.*

Enter ETEOCLES, *and crowd of* Theban Citizens.

Eteoc. Ye citizens of Cadmos, it behoves
That one who standeth at the stern of State
Guiding the helm, with eyes unclosed in sleep,
Should speak the things that meet occasion's need.
For should we prosper, God gets all the praise :
But if (which God forbid !) disaster falls,
Eteocles, much blame on one head falling,
Would find his name the by-word of the State,[1]
Sung in the slanderous ballads of the town ;
Yes, and with groanings, which may Zeus the Averter,
True to his name, from us Cadmeians turn !
But now 'tis meet for all, both him who fails
Of full-grown age, and him advanced in years,
Yet boasting still a stalwart strength of frame,
And each in life's full prime, as it is fit,
The State to succour and the altars here
Of these our country's Gods, that never more
Their votive honours cease,—to help our sons,
And Earth, our dearest mother and kind nurse ;
For she, when young ye crept her kindly plain,
Bearing the whole charge of your nourishment,
Reared you as denizens that bear the shield,

(1) Probably directed against the tendency of the Athenians, as
shown in their treatment of Miltiades, and later in that of Thukydides,
to punish their unsuccessful generals, "*pour encourager les autres.*"

That ye should trusty prove in this her need.   20
And now thus far God turns the scale for us;
For unto us, beleaguered these long days,
War doth in most things with God's help speed well,
But now, as saith the seer, the augur skilled,[1]
Watching with ear and mind, apart from fire,
The birds oracular with mind unerring,
He, lord and master of these prophet-arts,
Says that the great attack of the Achæans
This very night is talked of, and their plots
Devised against the town.   But ye, haste all   30
Unto the walls and gateways of the forts;
Rush ye full-armed, and fill the outer space,
And stand upon the platforms of the towers,
And at the entrance of the gates abiding
Be of good cheer, nor fear ye overmuch
The host of aliens.   Well will God work all.
And I have sent my scouts and watchers forth,
And trust their errand is no fruitless one.
I shall not, hearing them, be caught with guile.
                              [*Exeunt* Citizens.

Enter one of the Scouts.

Mess. King of Cadmeians, great Eteocles,
I from the army come with tidings clear,   40
And am myself eye-witness of its acts;
For seven brave warriors, leading armèd bands,
Cutting a bull's throat o'er a black-rimmed shield,
And dipping in the bull's blood with their hands,
Swore before Ares, Enyo,[2] murderous Fear,
That they would bring destruction on our town,
And trample under foot the tower of Cadmos,
Or dying, with their own blood stain our soil;
And they memorials for their sires at home
Placed with their hands upon Adrastos' car,[3]   50

(1) Teiresias, as in Sophocles, (*Antig.* v. 1005,) sitting, though blind,
and listening, as the birds flit by him, and the flames burn steadily or
fitfully; a various reading gives "apart from sight."
(2) Enyo, the goddess of war, and companion of Ares.
(3) Amphiaraos **the seer** had prophesied that Adrastos alone should

Weeping, but no wail uttering with their lips,
For courage iron-hearted breathed out fire
In manliness unconquered, as when lions
Flash battle from their eyeballs. And report
Of these things does not linger on the way.
I left them casting lots, **that each might take,**
As the lot fell, his station at the gate.
Wherefore do thou our city's **chosen ones**
Array with speed at entrance of the gates;
For near already is the Argive host,
Marching through clouds of dust, and whitening foam ⁶⁰
Spots **all the** plain with drops from horses' mouths.
And thou, as prudent helmsman of the ship,
Guard thou our fortress ere the blasts of Ares
Swoop on it wildly; for there comes the roar
Of the land-wave of armies. And do thou
Seize for these things the swiftest tide and time;
And I, in all that comes, will keep my eye
As faithful sentry; so through speech full clear,
Thou, knowing all things yonder, shalt be safe.

[*Exit.*

Eteoc. O Zeus and Earth, and all ye guardian Gods!
Thou Curse and strong Erinnys of my sire!   ⁷⁰
Destroy ye not my city root and branch,
With sore destruction smitten, one whose voice
Is that of Hellas, nor our hearths and homes; ¹
Grant that they never hold in yoke of bondage
Our country free, and town of Cadmos named;
But be ye our defence. I deem I speak
Of what concerns us both; for still 'tis true,
A prosperous city honours well the Gods.   [*Exit.*

Enter Chorus of Theban Maidens *in solemn procession as
suppliants.*

Chor. I in wild terror utter cries of woe;

return home in safety. On his car, therefore, the other chieftains hung
the clasps, or locks of hair, or other memorials which in the event of
their death were to be taken to their parents.
(1) The Hellenic feeling, such as the Platæans appealed to in the

An army leaves its camp and is let loose :
Hither the vanguard of the horsemen flows,   90
    And the thick cloud of dust,
    That suddenly is seen,
    . Dumb herald, yet full clear,
    Constrains me to believe ;
And smitten with the horses' hoofs, the plain
Of this my country rings with noise of war ;
    It floats and echoes round,
Like voice of mountain torrent dashing down
    Resistless in its might.
    Ah Gods ! Ah Goddesses !
    Ward off the coming woe.
With battle-shout that rises o'er the walls,
    The host whose shields are white [1]   95
Marches in full array against our city.
    Who then, of all the Gods
Or Goddesses, will come to help and save ?
Say, shall I fall before the shrines of Gods ?
    O blessed Ones firm fixed !
'Tis time to clasp your sacred images.
Why linger we in wailing overmuch ?
Hear ye, or hear ye not, the din of shields ?
    When, if not now, shall we
Engage in prayer with peplos and with boughs ? [2]
I hear a mighty sound ; it is the din   100
    Not of a single spear.
O Ares ! ancient guardian of our land !
What wilt thou do ? Wilt thou betray thy land ?
    O God of golden casque,

Peloponnesian war, (Thuc. iii. 58, 59,) that it was noble and right for Hellenes to destroy a city of the barbarians, but that they should spare one belonging to a people of their own stock.

(1) The characteristic feature of the Argive soldiers was, that they bore a shield painted white, (comp. Sophocles, *Antig.* v. 114.) The leaders alone appear to have embellished this with devices and mottoes.

(2) In solemn supplications, the litanies of the ancient world, especially in those to Pallas, the suppliants carried with them in procession the shawl or *peplos* of the Goddess, and with it enwrapt her statue. To carry boughs of trees in the hands was one of the uniform, probably indispensable, accompaniments of such processions.

Look on our city, yea, with favour look,
    The city thou did'st love.
And ye, ye Gods who o'er the city rule,
    Come all of you, come all.
Behold the band of maidens suppliant,
    In fear of bondage foul;
    For now around the town
The wave of warriors bearing slopèd crests,
With blasts of Ares rushing, hoarsely sounds: 110
But thou, O Zeus! true father of us all,
Ward off, ward off our capture by the foe.

Stroph. I.

For Argives now surround the town of Cadmos,
And dread of Ares' weapons falls on us;
    And, bound to horses' mouths,
The bits and curbs ring music as of death;
And seven chief rulers of the mighty host,
With warriors' arms, at each of seven tall gates,
    Spear-armed and harnessed all,
    Stand, having cast their lots.

        *   *   *   *   *

Mesode.

And thou, O Zeus-born power in war delighting,   120
O Pallas! be our city's saviour now:
    And Thou who curb'st the steed,
    Great King of Ocean's waves,
Poseidon, with thy trident fish-spear armed,[1]
Give respite from our troubles, respite give!
And Thou, O Ares, guard the town that takes
    Its name from Cadmos old,[2]
    Watch o'er it visibly.

(1) The words recall our thoughts to the original use of the trident,
which became afterwards a symbol of Poseidon, as employed by the sailors
of Hellas to spear or harpoon the larger fish of the Archipelago. Comp.
Pers. v. 426, where the slaughter of a defeated army is compared to tunny-
fishing.
(2) Cadmos, probably "the man from the East," the Phœnikian who
had founded Thebes, and sown the dragon's seed, and taught men a
Semitic alphabet for the non-Semitic speech of Hellas.

ANTISTROPH. I.

And thou, O Kypris, of our race the mother,
Ward off these ills, for we are thine by blood :
    To thee in many a prayer,   120
With voice that calls upon the Gods we cry,
And unto thee draw near as suppliants :
And Thou, Lykeian king, Lykeian be,[1]
    Foe of our hated foes,
    For this our wailing cry;
And Thou, O child of Leto, Artemis,
    Make ready now thy bow.

STROPH. II.

Ah! ah! I hear a din of chariot wheels
    Around the city walls;
    O Hera great and dread !
The heavy axles of the chariots groan,   144
    O Artemis beloved !
And the air maddens with the clash of spears;
    What must our city bear?
    What now shall come on us?
    When will God give the end?

ANTISTROPH. II.

Ah! ah! a voice of stones is falling fast
    On battlements attacked; [2]
    O Lord, Apollo loved,
A din of bronze-bound shields is in the gates;
    And oh! that Zeus may give   159
A faultless issue of this war we wage !
    And Thou, O blessed queen,
    As Guardian Onca known,[3]
    Save thy seven-gated seat.

---

(1) Worthy of his name as the Wolf-destroyer, mighty to destroy his foes.

(2) Possibly, "*from* battlements attacked." In the primitive sieges of Greek warfare stones were used as missiles alike by besieged and besiegers.

(3) The name of Onca belonged especially to the Theban worship of Pallas, and was said to have been of Phœnikian origin, introduced by Cadmos. There seems, however, to have been a town Onkæ in Bœotia, with which the name was doubtless connected.

Strophi. III.

And ye, all-working Gods,
Of either sex divine,
Protectors of our towers,
Give not our city, captured by the spear,
To host of alien speech.[1]
Hear ye our maidens; hear,
As is most meet, our prayers with outstretched hands.

160

Antistroph. III.

O all ye loving Powers,
Compass our State to save;
Show how that State ye love;
Think on our public votive offerings,
And as ye think, oh, help:
Be mindful ye, I pray,
Of all our city's rites of sacrifice.

Re-enter ETEOCLES.

Eteoc. (*to the Chorus.*) I ask you, O ye brood intoler-
able,
Is this course best and safest for our city?
Will it give heart to our beleaguered host,
That ye before the forms of guardian Gods
Should wail and howl, ye loathèd of the wise;[2]
Ne'er be it mine, in ill estate or good,
To dwell together with the race of women;
For when they rule, their daring bars approach,
And when they fear, alike to house and State
Comes greater ill: and now with these your rushings
Hither and thither, ye have troubled sore
Our subjects with a coward want of heart;

170

---

(1) "Alien," on account of the difference of dialect between the speech of Argos and that of Bœotia, though both were Hellenic.

(2) The vehemence with which Eteocles reproves the wild frenzied wailing of the Chorus may be taken as an element of the higher culture showing itself in Athenian life, which led Solon to restrain such lamentations by special laws, (Plutarch, *Solon*, c. 20.) Here, too, we note in Æschylos an echo of the teaching of Epimenides.

And do your best for those our foes without;   ₁₈₀
And we are harassed by ourselves within.
This comes to one who dwells with womankind.
And if there be that will not own my sway,
Or man or woman in their prime, or those
Who can be classed with neither, they shall take
Their trial for their life, nor shall they 'scape
The fate of stoning.   Things outdoors are still
The man's to look to : let not woman counsel.
Stay thou within, and do no mischief more.
Hear'st thou, or no ? or speak I to the deaf ?

STROPH. I.

Chor. Dear son of Œdipus,   190
I shuddered as I heard the din, the din
        Of many a chariot's noise,
When on the axles creaked the whirling wheels,
        *And when I heard the sound
*Of fire-wrought curbs within the horses' mouths.
    Eteoc. What then ?   Did ever yet the sailor flee
From stern to stem, and find deliverance so,
While his ship laboured in the ocean's wave ?[1]

ANTISTROPH. I.

Chor. Nay, to the ancient forms
Of mighty Powers I rushed, as trusting Gods ;
        And when behind the gates
Was heard the crash of fierce and pelting storm,   ₂₀₀
        Then was it, in my fear,
I prayed the Blessed Ones to guard our city.
    Eteoc. Pray that our towers hold out 'gainst spear of
            foes.[2]
    Chor. Do not the Gods grant these things ?

---

(1) As now the sailor of the Mediterranean turns to the image of his
patron saint, so of old he ran in his distress to the figure of his God upon
the prow of his ship, (often, as in Acts xxviii. 11, that of the *Dioscuri*,)
and called to it for deliverance, (comp. Jonah i. 8.)

(2) Eteocles seems to wish for a short, plain prayer for deliverance,
instead of the cries and supplications and vain repetitions of the Chorus.

Eteoc.   Nay, the Gods,
So say they, leave the captured city's walls.[1]

Stroph. II.

Chor. Ah! never in my life
May all this goodly company of Gods
        Depart; nor may I see
This city scene of rushings to and fro,
*And hostile army burning it with fire!
Eteoc. Nay, call not on the Gods with counsel base;
Obedience is the mother of success,
Child strong to save. 'Tis thus the saying runs.

Antistroph. II.

Chor. True is it; but the Gods
Have yet a mightier power, and oftentimes,
        In pressure of sore ill,
It raises one perplexed from direst woe,
When dark clouds gather thickly o'er his eyes.
Eteoc. 'Tis work of men to offer sacrifice
And victims to the Gods, when foes press hard;
Thine to be dumb and keep within the house.

Stroph. III.

Chor. 'Tis through the Gods we live
In city unsubdued, and that our towers
Ward off the multitude of jealous foes.
        What Power will grudge us this?
Eteoc. I grudge not your devotion to the Gods;
But lest you make my citizens faint-hearted
Be tranquil, nor to fear's excess give way.

---

(1) The thought thus expressed was, that the Gods, yielding to the mightier law of destiny, or in their wrath at the guilt of men, left the city before its capture. The feeling was all but universal. Its two representative instances are found in Virgil, *Æn.* 351—

> " Excessere omnes adytis arisque relictis
> Di quibus imperium hoc steterat;"

and the narrative given alike by Tacitus, (*Hist.* v. 13,) and Josephus (*Bell. Jud.* vi. 5, 3,) that the cry "Let us depart hence," was heard at midnight through the courts of the Temple, before the destruction of Jerusalem.

ANTISTROPH. III.

Chor. Hearing but now a din
Strange, wildly mingled, I with shrinking fear
Here to our city's high Acropolis,
    Time-hallowed spot, have come   234
Eteoc. Nay, if ye hear of wounded men or dying,
Bear them not swiftly off with wailing loud ;
*For blood of men is Ares' chosen food.[1]
   Chor. Hark ! now I hear the panting of the steeds.
   Eteoc. Clear though thou hear, yet hear not overmuch.
   Chor. Lo ! from its depths the fortress groans, be-
       leaguered.
   Eteoc. It is enough that I provide for this.
   Chor. I fear : the din increases at the gates.
   Eteoc. Be still, say nought of these things in the city.
   Chor. O holy Band ![2] desert ye not our towers.   240
   Eteoc. A curse fall on thee ! wilt thou not be still?
   Chor. Gods of my city, from the slave's lot save me !
   Eteoc. 'Tis thou enslav'st thyself and all thy city.
   Chor. Oh, turn thy darts, great Zeus, against our
       foes !
   Eteoc. Oh, Zeus, what race of women thou hast given
       us !
   Chor. A sorry race, like men whose city falls.
   Eteoc. What? Cling to these statues, yet speak words
       of ill ?
   Chor. Fear hurries on my tongue in want of courage.
   Eteoc. Could'st thou but grant one small boon at my
       prayer !   250
   Chor. Speak it out quickly, and I soon shall know.
   Eteoc. Be still, poor fool, and frighten not thy friends.
   Chor. Still am I, and with others bear our fate.
   Eteoc. These words of thine I much prefer to those :
And further, though no longer at the shrines,
Pray thou for victory, that the Gods fight with us .

---

(1) *Sc.,* Blood must be shed in war. Ares would not be Ares without
it. It is better to take it as it comes.
(2) *Sc.,* the company of Gods, Pallas, Hera and the others whom the
Chorus had invoked.

And when my prayers thou hearest, then do thou
Raise a loud, welcome, holy pæan-shout,
The Hellenes' wonted cry at sacrifice;
So cheer thy friends, and check their fear of foes;
And I unto our country's guardian Gods,   260
Who hold the plain or watch the agora,
The springs of Dirkè, and Ismenos' stream;—
If things go well, and this our city's saved,—
I vow that staining with the blood of sheep
The altar-hearths of Gods, or slaying bulls,
We'll fix our trophies, and our foemen's robes
On the spear's point on consecrated walls,
Before the shrines I'll hang.[1]   Pray thou this prayer,
Not weakly wailing, nor with vain wild sobs,
For no whit more thou'lt 'scape thy destined lot: 270
And I six warriors, with myself as seventh,
Against our foes in full state like their own,
Will station at the seven gates' entrances,
Ere hurrying heralds and swift-rushing words
Come and inflame them in the stress of need.   [*Exit.*

Stroph. I.

Chor. My heart is full of care and knows not sleep,
    By panic fear o'ercome;
    And troubles throng my soul,
    And set a-glow my dread
Of the great host encamped around our walls,
    As when a trembling dove
    Fears, for her callow brood,   260
The snakes that come, ill mates for her soft nest;
    For some upon our towers
March in full strength of mingled multitude;
    And what will me befall?
And others on our men on either hand
    Hurl rugged blocks of stone.

---

(1) Reference to this custom, which has passed from Pagan temples
into Christian churches, is found in the *Agamemnon*, v. 562. It was
connected, of course, with the general practice of offering as *ex votos*
any personal ornaments or clothing as a token of thanksgiving for special
mercies.

In every way, ye Zeus-born Gods, defend   294
    The city and the host
    That Cadmos claim as sire.

ANTISTROPH. I.

What better land will ye receive for this,
    If ye to foes resign
    This rich and fertile clime,
    And that Dirkœan stream,
Goodliest of founts by great Poseidon sent,
    Who circleth earth, or those
    Who Tethys parent call?[1]   300
And therefore, O ye Gods that guard our city,
    Sending on those without
Our towers a woe that robs men of their life,
    And makes them lose their shield,
Gain glory for these countrymen of mine;
    And take your standing-ground,
As saviours of the city, firm and true,
    In answer to our cry
    Of wailing and of prayer.

STROPH. II.

For sad it were to hurl to Hades dark
    A city of old fame,   51
    The spoil and prey of war,
With foulest shame in dust and ashes laid,
By an Achæan foe at God's decree;
And that our women, old and young alike,
    Be dragged away, ah me!
    Like horses, by their hair
    Their robes torn off from them.
And lo, the city wails, made desolate,
    While with confusèd cry   320
The wretched prisoners meet doom worse than death.
    Ah, at this grievous fate
    I shudder ere it comes.

(1) Rivers and streams as the children of Tethys and Okeanos.

Antistroph. II.

And piteous 'tis for those whose youth is fresh,
    Before the rites that cull
    Their fair and first-ripe fruit,
To take a hateful journey from their homes.
Nay, but I say the dead far better fare
Than these, for when a city is subdued
    It bears full many an ill.
    This man takes prisoner that,   330
    Or slays, or burns with fire;
And all the city is defiled with smoke,
    And Ares fans the flame
In wildest rage, and laying many low,
    Tramples with foot unclean
    On all men sacred hold.

Stroph. III.

And hollow din is heard throughout the town,
    Hemmed in by net of towers;
And man by man is slaughtered with the spear,
    And cries of bleeding babes,
    Of children at the breast,   340
    Are heard in piteous wail,
And rapine, sister of the plunderer's rush;
    Spoiler with spoiler meets,
And empty-handed empty-handed calls,
    Wishing for share of gain,
Both eager for a portion no whit less,
    For more than equal lot
With what they deem the others' hands have found.

Antistroph. III.

And all earth's fruits cast wildly on the ground,   350
    Meeting the cheerless eye
Of frugal housewives, give them pain of heart;
    And many a gift of earth
    In formless heaps is whirled
    In waves of nothingness;

And the young maidens know a sorrow new;
 For now the foe prevails,
And gains rich prize of wretched captive's bed;   360
 And now their only hope
Is that the night of death will come at last,
 Their truest, best ally,
To rescue them from sorrow fraught with tears.

  Enter ETEOCLES, *followed by his* Chief Captains,
    and by the Scout.

 Semi-Chor. A. The army scout, so deem I, brings to us,
Dear friends, some tidings new, with quickest speed
Plying the nimble axles of his feet.
 Semi-Chor. B. Yea, the king's self, the son of Œdipus,
Is nigh to hear the scout's exact report;
And haste denies him too an even step.
 Mess. I knowing well, will our foes' state report, 370
How each his lot hath stationed at the gates.
At those of Prœtos, Tydeus thunders loud,
And him the prophet suffers not to cross
Ismenos' fords, the victims boding ill.[1]
And Tydeus, raging eager for the fight,
Shouts like a serpent in its noon-tide scream,
And on the prophet, Œcleus' son, heaps shame, ·
That he, in coward fear, doth crouch and fawn
Before the doom and peril of the fight.
And with such speech he shakes his triple crest,
O'ershadowing all his helm, and 'neath his shield 380
Bells wrought in bronze ring out their chimes of fear;
And on his shield he bears this proud device,—
A firmament enchased, all bright with stars;[2]

---

(1) Here, as in v. 571, Tydeus appears as the real leader of the expedition, who had persuaded Adrastos and the other chiefs to join in it, and
Amphiaraos, the prophet, the son of Œcleus, as having all along foreseen
its disastrous issue. The account of the expedition in the *Œdipus at
Colonos* (1300—1330) may be compared with this.
(2) The legend of the Medusa's head on the shield of Athena shows the
practice of thus decorating shields to have been of remote date. In
Homer it does not appear as common, and the account given of the shield
of Achilles lays stress upon the work of the artist (Hephæstos) who

And in the **midst the full moon's** glittering **orb**,
Sovran of stars and eye of Night, shines forth.
And thus exulting in o'er boastful arms,
By the stream's bank **he** shouts in lust of war,
[E'en as a war-horse panting in his strength
Against the curb that galls him, who at sound
Of trumpet's **clang** chafes hotly.] Whom wilt thou
Set against him? Who is there strong enough
When the bolts yield, to guard the Proetan **gates?** · 390

   Eteoc. **No fear** have I **of any man's array;**
Devices have no power **to pierce or wound,**
And crest and bells bite **not without** a spear ;
And for this picture of the heavens at night,
Of which thou tellest, glittering on his shield,
*Perchance his madness may a prophet prove ;
For if night fall upon his dying eyes,
Then for the man who bears **that** boastful sign
It may right well be all too truly named,   400
And his own pride shall prophet be of **ill.**
And against Tydeus, to defend the **gates,**
I'll set this valiant son of Astacos ;
Noble is he, and honouring well **the throne**
Of Reverence, and hating vaunting speech,
Slow to all baseness, unattuned to ill :
And of the dragon-race that Ares spared [1]
He as a scion grows, a native true,
E'en Melanippos ; Ares soon will test
His valour in the hazard of the die :
And kindred Justice sends **him forth to** war,
For her that bore him foeman's spear to check.   410

            STROPH. I.
  Chor. May the Gods grant my champion good success !

wrought the shield in relief, not, **as** here, upon painted insignia. **They**
were obviously common in the time of Æschylos.
  (1) The older families of Thebes boasted that they sprang from the sur-
vivors of the Sparti, who, sprung from the Dragon's teeth, waged deadly
war against each other, till all but five were slain. The later settlers, who
were said to have come with Cadmos, stood to these as the " greater " to
the "lesser *gentes*" at Rome.

For justly he goes forth
For this our State to fight;
But yet I quake with fear
To see the deaths of those who die for friends.
  Mess. Yea, may the Gods give good success to him!
The Electran gates have fallen to Capaneus,
A second giant, taller far than he
Just named, with boast above a mortal's bounds;
And dread his threats against our towers (O Fortune,   420
Turn them aside!)—for whether God doth will,
Or willeth not, he says that he will sack [1]
The city, nor shall e'en the wrath of Zeus,
On the plain swooping, turn him from his will;
And the dread lightnings and hot thunderbolts
He likens to the heat of noon-day sun.
And his device, the naked form of one
Who bears a torch; and bright the blaze shines forth
And in gold characters he speaks the words,
" THE CITY I WILL BURN."   Against this man
Send forth . . . . but who will meet him in the fight? 430
Who, without fear, await this warrior proud?
  Eteoc. Herein, too, profit upon profit comes;
And 'gainst the vain and boastful thoughts of men,
Their tongue itself is found accuser true.
Threatening, equipped for work is Capaneus,
Scorning the Gods: and giving speech full play,
And in wild joy, though mortal, vents at Zeus,
High in the heavens, loud-spoken foaming words.
And well I trust on him shall rightly come
Fire-bearing thunder, nothing likened then
To heat of noon-day sun.   And so 'gainst him,   440
Though very bold of speech, a man is set
Of fiery temper, Polyphontes strong,
A trusty bulwark, by the loving grace
Of guardian Artemis [2] and other Gods.
Describe another, placed at other gates.

---

(1) So in the *Antigone* of Sophocles, (v. 134,) Capaneus apears as the special representative of boastful, reckless impiety.
(2) Artemis, as one of the special Deities to whom Thebes was consecrated.

ANTISTROPH. I.

Chor. A curse on him who 'gainst our city boasts!
    May thunder smite him down   450
    Before he force his way
    Into my home, and drive
Me from my maiden bower with haughty spear!
  Mess. And now I'll tell of him who by the gates
Stands next; for to Eteoclos, as third,
To march his cohort to Neïstian gates,
Leaped the third lot from upturned brazen helm:
And he his mares, in head-gear snorting, whirls,
Full eager at the gates to fall and die;
Their whistling nozzles of barbaric mode,
Are filled with loud blast of the panting nostrils.[1]
In no poor fashion is his shield devised;   460
A full-armed warrior climbs a ladder's rungs,
And mounts his foeman's towers as bent to sack;
And he too cries, in words of written speech,
That "NOT E'EN ARES FROM THE TOWERS SHALL DRIVE
    HIM."
Send thou against him some defender true,
To ward the yoke of bondage from our State.
  Eteoc. Such would I send now; by good luck indeed
He has been sent, his vaunting in his deeds,
Megareus, Creon's son, who claims descent
From those as Sparti known, and not by noise
Of neighings loud of warlike steeds dismayed,   470
Will he the gates abandon, but in death
Will pay our land his nurture's debt in full,[2]
Or taking two men, and a town to boot,
(That on the shield,) will deck his father's house
With those his trophies. Of another tell
The bragging tale, nor grudge thy words to me.

(1) Apparently an Asiatic invention, to increase the terror of an attack of war-chariots.
(2) The phrase and thought were almost proverbial in Athens. Men, as citizens, were thought of as fed at a common table, bound to contribute their gifts to the common stock. When they offered up their lives in battle, they were giving, as Pericles says, (Thucyd. ii. 43,) their noblest "contribution," paying in full their subscription to the society of which they were members.

F

STROPH. II.

Chor. Him I wish good success,
O guardian of my home, and for his foes
          All ill success I pray ;
And since against our land their haughty words
          With maddened soul they speak,
          May Zeus, the sovran judge,
With fiery, hot displeasure look on them !   470

Mess. Another stands as fourth at gates hard by,
Onca-Athenà's, with a shout of war,
Hippomedon's great form and massive limbs ;
And as he whirled his orb, his vast shield's disk,
I shuddered ; yea, no idle words I speak.
No cheap and common draughtsman sure was he
Who wrought this cunning ensign on his shield :
Typhon emitting from his lips hot blast
Of darkling smoke, the flickering twin of fire :
And round the belly of the hollow shield
A rim was made with wreaths of twisted snakes.   480
And he too shouts his war-cry, and in frenzy,
As man possessed by Ares, hastes to battle,
Like Thyiad, darting terror from his eyes.[1]
'Gainst such a hero's might we well may guard ;
Already at the gates men brag of rout.

Eteoc. First, the great Onca-Pallas, dwelling nigh
Our city's gates, and hating man's bold pride,
Shall ward him from her nestlings like a snake
Of venom dread ; and next Hyperbios,
The stalwart son of Œnops, has been chosen,   490
A hero 'gainst this hero, willing found
To try his destiny at Fortune's hest.
No fault has he in form, or heart, or arms ;
And Hermes with good reason pairs them off ;
For man with man will fight as enemy,
And on their shields they'll bring opposing Gods ;
For this man beareth Typhon, breathing fire,

---

(1) Thyiad, another name for the Mænads, the frenzied attendants on
Dionysos.

And on Hyperbios' shield sits father Zeus,
Full firm, with burning thunderbolt in hand;
And never yet has man seen Zeus, I trow,
O'ercome.   Such then the favour of the Gods,   510
We with the winners, they with losers are : [1]
Good reason then the rivals so should fare,
If Zeus than Typhon stronger be in fight,
And to Hyperbios Zeus will saviour prove,
As that device upon his shield presents him.

ANTISTROPH. II.

Chor. Now do I trust that he
Who bears upon his shield the hated form
    Of Power whom Earth doth shroud,
Antagonist to Zeus, unloved by men
    And by the ageless Gods,
    Before those gates of ours
To his own hurt may dash his haughty head.   520
  Mess. So may it be!   And now the fifth I tell,
Who the fifth gates, the Northern, occupies,
Hard by Amphion's tomb, the son of Zeus;
And by his spear he swears, (which he is bold
To honour more than God or his own eyes,)
That he will sack the fort of the Cadmeians
With that spear's might.   So speaks the offspring fair
Of mother mountain-bred, a stripling hero;
And the soft down is creeping o'er his cheeks,   530
Youth's growth, and hair that floweth full and thick;
And he with soul, not maiden's like his name, [2]
But stern, with flashing eye, is standing there.
Nor stands he at the gate without a vaunt;
For on his brass-wrought buckler, strong defence,
Full-orbed, his body guarding, he the shame
Of this our city bears, the ravenous Sphinx,
With rivets fixed, all burnished and embossed; [3]

---

(1) *Sc.*, in the legends of Typhon, not he, but Zeus, had proved the conqueror.   The warrior, therefore, who chose Typhon for his badge was identifying himself with the losing, not the winning side.
(2) The name, as we are told in v. 542, is Parthenopæos, the maiden-faced.
(3) The Sphinx, besides its general character as an emblem of terror,

And under her she holdeth a Cadmeian,
That so on him most arrows might be shot.
No chance that he will fight a peddling fight,   840
Nor shame the long, long journey he hath come,
Parthenopæos, in Arcadia born:
This man did Argos welcome as a guest,
And now he pays her for her goodly rearing,
And threatens these our towers with . . . God avert it!
      Eteoc Should the Gods give them what they plan
            'gainst us,
Then they, with those their godless boastings high,
Would perish shamefully and utterly.
And for this man of Arcady thou tell'st of,
We have a man who boasts not, but his hand
Sees the right thing to do;—Actôr, of him   850
I named but now the brother,—who no tongue
Divorced from deeds will ever let within
Our gates, to spread and multiply our ills,
Nor him who bears upon his foeman's shield
The image of the hateful venomed beast;
But she without shall blame him as he tries
To take her in, when she beneath our walls
Gets sorely bruised and battered.[1]   And herein,
If the Gods will, I prophet true shall prove.

Stroph. III.

Chor. Thy words thrill through my breast;
         My hair stands all on end,
         To hear the boastings great
         Of those who speak great things   860
         Unholy.   May the Gods
         Destroy them in our land!
Mess. A sixth I tell of, one of noblest mood,
Amphiaraos, seer and warrior famed;
He, stationed at the Homolôian gates,

had, of course, a special meaning as directed to the Thebans. The warrior
who bore it threatened to renew the old days when the monster whom
Œdipus had overcome had laid waste their city.
   (1) *Sc.*, the Sphinx on his shield will not be allowed to enter the city.
It will only serve as a mark, attracting men to attack both it and the
warrior who bears it.

Reproves the mighty Tydeus with sharp words
As 'murderer,' and 'troubler of the State,'[1]
'To Argos teacher of all direst ills,
  Erinnys' sumpnour,'[2] 'murder's minister,'   570
Whose counsels led Adrastos to these ills.
*And at thy brother Polyneikes glancing
With eyes uplifted for his father's fate,
And ending, twice he syllabled his name,[3]
And called him, and thus speaketh with his lips :—
"A goodly deed, and pleasant to the Gods,
Noble for after age to hear and tell,
Thy father's city and thy country's Gods
To waste through might of mercenary host!
And how shall Justice stay thy mother's tears?[4]   580
And how, when conquered, shall thy fatherland,
Laid waste, become a true ally to thee?
As for myself, I shall that land make rich,[5]
A prophet buried in a foeman's soil :
To arms! I look for no inglorious death."
So spake the prophet, bearing full-orbed shield
Wrought all of bronze, no ensign on that orb.
He wishes to be just, and not to seem,[6]

---

(1) The quarrel between Tydeus and the seer Amphiaraos had been already touched upon.

(2) I have used the old English word to express a term of like technical use in Athenian law processes. As the "sumpnour" called witnesses or parties to a suit into court, so Tydeus had summoned the Erinnys to do her work of destruction.

(3) Sc., so pronounced his name as to emphasize the significance of its two component parts, as indicating that he who bore it was a man of much contention.

(4) The words are obscure, but seem to refer to the badge of Polyneikes, the figure of Justice described in v. 643 as on his shield. How shall that Justice, the seer asks, console Jocasta for her son's death! Another rendering gives,

    "And how shall Justice quench a mother's life!"

the "mother" being the country against which Polyneikes wars.

(5) The words had a twofold fulfilment, (1) in the burial of Amphiaraos, in the Theban soil; and (2) in the honour which accrued to Thebes after his death, through the fame of the oracle at his shrine.

(6) The passage cannot be passed over without noticing the old tradition, (Plutarch, *Aristeid.* c. 3,) that when the actor uttered these words, he and the whole audience looked to Aristeides, surnamed the Just, as recognising that the words were true of him as they were of no one else. "Best," instead of "just," is, however, a very old various reading.

Reaping full harvest from his soul's deep furrows,
Whence ever new and noble counsels spring.   590
I bid thee send defenders wise and brave
Against him.   Dread is he who fears the Gods.
   Eteoc. Fie on the chance that brings the righteous man
Close-mated with the ungodly !   In all deeds
Nought is there worse than evil fellowship,
A crop men should not reap.   Death still is found
The harvest of the field of frenzied pride ;
For either hath the godly man embarked
With sailors hot in insolence and guile,[1]
And perished with the race the Gods did loathe ;   600
Or just himself, with citizens who wrong
The stranger and are heedless of the Gods,
Falling most justly in the self-same snare,
By God's scourge smitten, shares the common doom.
And thus this seer I speak of, Œcleus' son,
Righteous, and wise, and good, and reverent,
A mighty prophet, mingling with the godless
*And men full bold of speech in reason's spite,
Who take long march to reach a far-off city,[2]
If Zeus so will, shall be hurled down with them.   610
And he, I trow, shall not draw nigh the gates,
Not through faint-heart or any vice of mood,
But well he knows this war shall bring his death,
If any fruit is found in Loxias' words ;
And He or holds his speech or speaks in season.
Yet against him the hero Lasthenes,
A foe of strangers, at the gates we'll set ;
Old is his mind, his body in its prime,
His eye swift-footed, and his hand not slow
To grasp the spear from 'neath the shield laid bare :[3]   620
Yet 'tis by God's gift men must win success.

(1) If the former reference to Aristeides be admitted, we can scarcely
avoid seeing in this passage an allusion to Themistocles, as one with
whose reckless and democratic policy it was dangerous for the more conservative leader to associate himself.
   (2) The far-off city, not of Thebes, but Hades. In the legend of Thebes,
the earth opened and swallowed up Amphiaraos, as in 583.
   (3) The short spear was usually carried under the shelter of the shield ;
when brought into action, it was, of course, laid bare.

ANTISTROPH. III.

Chor. Hear, O ye Gods! our prayers,
  Our just entreaties grant,
  That so our State be blest.
  Turn ye the toils of war
  Upon the invading host.
  Outside the walls may Zeus
  With thunder smite them low!

Mess. The seventh chief then who at the seventh gate
  stands,
Thine own, own brother, I will speak of now,
What curses on our State he pours, and prays   630
That **he the** towers ascending, and proclaimed
By herald's voice to all the territory,
And shouting out the captor's pæan-cry,
May so fight with thee, slay, and with thee die;
Or driving thee alive, who did'st him wrong,
May on thee a vengeance wreak **like in** kind.
So clamours he, and bids his father's Gods,
His country's guardians, look upon his prayers,
[And grant them all. So Polyneikes prays.]
And he a new and well-wrought shield doth bear,
And twofold sign upon it riveted;   640
For there a woman with a stately tread
Leads one who seems a warrior wrought in gold:
Justice she calls herself, and thus she speaks:
" I WILL BRING BACK THIS MAN, AND HE SHALL HAVE
THE CITY AND HIS FATHER'S DWELLING-PLACE."
Such are **the signs and mottoes of those men;**
And thou, **know well whom thou dost mean to send :**
So **thou shalt** never **blame my heraldings;**
And thou thyself know how **to steer the** State.

Eteoc. **O** frenzy-stricken, hated sore of **Gods!**   650
O woe-fraught race (my race!) of Œdipus!
Ah me! my father's curse is now fulfilled;
But neither is it meet to weep or wail,
Lest cry more grievous on the issue come.
Of Polyneikes, name and omen true,

We soon shall know what way his badge shall end,
Whether his gold-wrought letters shall restore him,
His shield's great swelling words with frenzied soul.
Au if great Justice, Zeus's virgin child,
Ruled o'er his words and acts, this might have been;   860
But neither when he left his mother's womb,
Nor in his youth, nor yet in ripening age,
Nor when his beard was gathered on his chin,
Did Justice count him meet for fellowship;
Nor do I think that she befriends him now
In this great outrage on his father's land.
Yea, justly Justice would as falsely named
Be known, if she with one all-daring joined.
In this I trust, and I myself will face him:
Who else could claim a greater right than I?   870
Brother with brother fighting, king with king,
And foe with foe, I'll stand.   Come, quickly fetch
My greaves that guard against the spear and stones.
   Chor. Nay, dearest friend, thou son of Œdipus,
Be **ye** not like to him with that ill name.
It is enough Cadmeian men should fight
Against the Argives.   That blood may be cleansed;
But death so **murderous** of two brothers born,
This is pollution that will ne'er wax old.
   Eteoc. If a man must bear evil, let him still   880
Be without shame—sole profit that in death.
[No glory comes of base and evil deeds].
   Chor. What dost thou crave, my son?   Let no ill fate,
     Frenzied and hot for war,
     Carry thee headlong on;
Check the first onset of an evil lust.
   Eteoc. Since God so hotly urges on the matter,
Let all of Laios' race whom Phœbos hates,
Drift with the breeze upon Cokytos' wave.
   Chor. An over-fierce and passionate desire
     Stirs thee and pricks thee on
     To work an evil deed
Of guilt of blood thy hand should never shed.   890

Eteoc. Nay, my dear father's curse, in full-grown hate,
Dwells on dry eyes that cannot shed a tear,
And speaks of gain before the after-doom.
　　Chor. But be not thou urged on.　The coward's name
　　　　Shall not be thine, for thou
　　　　Hast ordered well thy life.
Dark-robed Erinnys enters not the house,
　　　　When at men's hands the Gods
　　　　Accept their sacrifice.
Eteoc. As for the Gods, they scorned us long ago,
And smile but on the offering of our deaths;　　　　　　700
What boots it then on death's doom still to fawn?
　　Chor. Nay do it now, while yet 'tis in thy power;[1]
　　　　Perchance may fortune shift
　　　　With tardy change of mood,
And come with spirit less implacable:
　　　　At present fierce and hot
　　　　She waxeth in her rage.
Eteoc. Yea, fierce and hot the Curse of Œdipus;
And all too true the visions of the night,
My father's treasured store distributing.
　　Chor. Yield to us women, though thou lov'st us not.
　　Eteoc. Speak then what may be done, and be not long. 710
　　Chor. Tread not the path that to the seventh gate leads.
　　Eteoc. Thou shalt not blunt my sharpened edge with
　　　　words.
　　Chor. And yet God loves the victory that submits.[2]
　　Eteoc. That word a warrior must not tolerate.
　　Chor. Dost thou then haste thy brother's blood to shed?
　　Eteoc. If the Gods grant it, he shall not 'scape harm.
　　　　　　[*Exeunt* ETEOCLES, Scout, *and* Captains.

STROPH. I.

　　Chor. I fear her might who doth this whole house wreck,

(1) Perhaps " since death is nigh at hand."
(2) The Chorus means that if Eteocles would allow himself to be overcome in this contest of his wishes with their prayers, the Gods would
honour that defeat as if it were indeed a victory. He makes answer that
the very thought of being overcome implied in the word "defeat" in
anything is one which the true warrior cannot bear.

The Goddess unlike Gods,
The prophetess of evil all too true,
The Erinnys of thy father's imprecations,   724
   Lest she fulfil the curse,
   O'er-wrathful, frenzy-fraught,
   The curse of Œdipus,
   Laying his children low.
   This Strife doth urge them on.

Antistroph. I.

And now a stranger doth divide the lots,
The Chalyb,[1] from the Skythians emigrant,
The stern distributor of heaped-up wealth,
The iron that hath assigned them just so much
   Of land as theirs, no more,
   As may suffice for them
   As grave when they shall fall,
   Without or part or lot
   In the broad-spreading plains.   730

Stroph. II.

And when the hands of each
The other's blood have shed,
And the earth's dust shall drink
   The black and clotted gore,
   Who then can purify?
   Who cleanse them from the guilt?
   Ah me! O sorrows new,
That mingle with the old woes of our house!

Antistroph. II.

I tell the ancient tale
Of sin that brought swift doom;   740
Till the third age it waits,
Since Laios, heeding not
Apollo's oracle,
(Though spoken thrice to him

---

(1) The 'Chalyb stranger' is the sword, thought of as taking its name from the Skythian tribe of the Chalybes, between Colchis and Armenia, and passing through the Thrakians into Greece.

In Pythia's central shrine,)
That dying childless, he should save the State.

Strophe. III.

But he by those he loved full rashly swayed,
    Doom for himself begat,
    His murderer Œdipus,   730
    Who dared to sow in field
    Unholy, whence he sprang,
    A root of blood-flecked woe.
    Madness together brought
    Bridegroom and bride accursed.

Antistroph. III.

And now the sea of evils pours its flood:
    This falling, others rise,
    As with a triple crest,
    Which round the State's stern roars:
    And but a bulwark slight,
    A tower's poor breadth, defends: 740
    And lest the city fall
    With its two kings I fear.

Strophe. IV.

*And that atonement of the ancient curse
    Receives fulfilment now; [1]
*And when they come, the evils pass not by.
E'en so the wealth of sea-adventurers,
    When heaped up in excess,
    Leads but to cargo from the stern thrown out.[2]

Antistroph. IV.

For whom of mortals did the Gods so praise,
    And fellow-worshippers,   770
*And race of those who feed their flocks and herds,[3]

(1) The two brothers, i.e., are set at one again, but it is not in the bonds
of friendship, but in those of death.
(2) The image meets us again in *Agam.* 980. Here the thought is, that
a man too prosperous is like a ship too heavily freighted. He must part
with a portion of his possession in order to save the rest. Not to part
with them leads, when the storm rages, to an enforced abandonment and
utter loss.
(3) Another reading gives—
    "And race of those who crowd the Agora."

As much as then they honoured Œdipus,
    Who from our country's bounds
Had driven the monster, murderess of men ?

Strophi. V.

    And when too late he knew,
Ah, miserable man ! his wedlock dire,
    Vexed sore with that dread shame,
    With heart to madness driven,
    He wrought a two-fold ill,
And with the hand that smote his father's life   780
*Blinded the eyes that might his sons have seen.

Antistrophi. V.

    And with a mind provoked
By nurture scant, he at his sons did hurl [1]
    His curses dire and dark,
    (Ah, bitter curses those !)
    That they with spear in hand ·
Should one day share their father's wealth ; and I
Fear now lest swift Erinnys should fulfil them.

Enter Messenger.

Mess. Be of good cheer, ye maidens, mother-reared ;
Our city has escaped the yoke of bondage,   790
The boasts of mighty men are fallen low,
And this our city in calm waters floats,
And, though by waves lashed, springs not any leak.
Our fortress still holds out, and we did guard
The gates with champions who redeemed their pledge.
In the six gateways almost all goes well ;
But the seventh gate did King Apollo choose,[2]

(1) This seems to have been one form of the legends as to the cause of
the curse which Œdipus had launched upon his sons. An alternative
rendering is—

    And with a mind enraged
At thought of what they were whom he had reared,
    He at his sons did hurl
    His curses dire and dark.

(2) *Sc.*, when Eteocles fell, Apollo took his place at the seventh gate,
and turned the tide of war in favour of the Thebans.

Seventh mighty chief, avenging Laios' want
Of counsel on the sons of Œdipus.

    Chor. What new disaster happens to our city?[1]   600

Mess. The city's saved, but both the royal brothers, . . .

Chor. Who? and what of them? I'm distraught with fear.

Mess. Be calm, and hear: the sons of Œdipus, ...

Chor. Oh wretched me! a prophet I of ill!

Mess. Slain by each other, earth has drunk their blood.

Chor. Came they to that? 'Tis dire; yet tell it me.

Mess. Too true, by brother's hand our chiefs are slain.

Chor. What, did the brother's hands the brother slay?

Mess. No doubt is there that they are laid in dust.

Chor. Thus was there then a common fate for both?

Mess. *Yea, it lays low the whole ill-fated race.

    Chor. These things give cause for gladness and for
        tears,   610

Seeing that our city prospers, and our lords,
The generals twain, with well-wrought Skythian steel,
Have shared between them all their store of goods,
And now shall have their portion in a grave,
Borne on, as spake their father's grievous curse.[2]

    Mess. [The city's saved, but of the brother-kings
The earth has drunk the blood, each slain by each.]

    Chor. Great Zeus! and ye, O Gods!
        Guardians of this our town,
        Who save in very deed
        The towers of Cadmos old,   620
        Shall I rejoice and shout
        Over the happy chance
        That frees our State from harm;
        Or weep that ill-starred pair,
The war-chiefs, childless and most miserable,
        Who, true to that ill name
Of Polyneikes, died in impious mood,
        Contending overmuch?

---

(1) I follow in this dialogue the arrangement which Paley adopts from
Hermann.

(2) There seems an intentional ambiguity. They are "borne on," but
it is as the corpses of the dead are borne to the sepulchre.

STROPH.

Oh dark, and all too true
That curse of Œdipus and all his race,[1]
An evil chill is falling on my heart,   838
        And, like a Thyiad wild,
Over his grave I sing a dirge of grief,
Hearing the dead have died by evil fate,
        Each in foul bloodshed steeped ;
Ah me !   Ill-omened is the spear's accord.[2]

ANTISTROPH.

It hath wrought out its end,
And hath not failed, that prayer the father poured ;
And Laios' reckless counsels work till now :
        I fear mè for the State ;
The oracles have not yet lost their edge ;   840
O men of many sorrows, ye have wrought
        This deed incredible ;
Not now in word come woes most lamentable.
        [*As the Chorus are speaking, the bodies of* ETEOCLES
        and POLYNEIKES *are brought in solemn procession by*
        Theban Citizens.

EPODE.

Yea, it is all too clear,
The herald's tale of woe comes full in sight ;
Twofold our cares, twin evils born of pride,
        Murderous, with double doom,
Wrought unto full completeness all these ills.
        What shall I say ?   What else
Are they than woes that make this house their home ?
But oh ! my friends, ply, ply with swift, strong gale,
That even stroke of hands upon your head,[3]   850

(1) **Not here** the **curse** uttered by Œdipus, but that which rested on
him and all his kin.   There is possibly an allusion to the curse which
Pelops is said to have uttered against Laios when he stole his son Chrysippos.   Comp. v. 837.
(2) **As in** v. 763, we read of the brothers as made one in death, so now
of the concord which is wrought out by conflict, the concord, *i.e.*, of the
grave.
(3) The Chorus **are called on** to change their character, and to pass

In funeral order, such as evermore
    O'er Acheron sends on
*That bark of State, dark-rigged, accursed its voyage,
Which nor Apollo visits nor the sun,[1]
    On to the shore unseen,
    The resting-place of all.
    [ISMENE *and* ANTIGONE *are seen approaching in mourn-
    ing garments, followed by a procession of women wail-
    ing and lamenting.*]
For see, **they come to bitter deed called forth,**
Ismene and **the** maid Antigone,
    To wail their brothers' fall;
    With little doubt I deem,
That they will pour from fond, deep-bosomed breasts
    A worthy strain of grief:
    But it is meet that we,
    Before we hear their cry,
Should utter the harsh hymn Erinnys loves,
    And sing to Hades dark
    The Pæan of distress.
O ye, most evil-fated in your kin,
Of all who gird their robes with maiden's band,
I weep and wail, and feigning know I none,
    That I should fail to speak
    My sorrow from my heart.

                STROPH. I.

Semi-Chor. A. Alas! alas!
Men of stern mood, who would not list to friends,
    Unwearied in all ills,   870

---

from the attitude of suppliants, with outstretched arms, to that of
mourners at a funeral, beating on their breasts. But, perhaps, the call
is addressed to the mourners who are seen approaching with Ismene and
Antigone.
    (1) The thought is drawn from the *theoris* or pilgrim-ship, which went
with snow-white sails, and accompanied by joyful pœans, on a solemn
mission from Athens to Delos. In contrast with this type of joy, Æschylos
draws the picture of the boat of Charon, which passes over the
gloomy pool accompanied by the sighs and gestures of bitter lamentation.
So, in the old Attic legend, the ship that annually carried seven youths
and maidens to the Minotaur of Crete was conspicuous for its black
sails.

Seizing your father's house, O wretched ones
       With the spear's murderous point.
   Semi-Chor. B. Yea, wretched they who found a
       wretched doom,
       With havoc of the house.

ANTISTROPHE. I.

Semi-Chor. A. Alas! alas!
Ye who laid low the ancient walls of home,
       On sovereignty, ill won,
Your eyes have looked, and ye at last are brought
       To concord by the sword.
   Semi-Chor. B. Yea, of a truth, the curse of Œdipus 880
       Erinnys dread fulfils.

STROPH. II.

Semi-Chor. A. Yea, smitten through the heart,
Smitten through sides where flowed the blood of brothers.
       Ah me! ye doomed of God!
       Ah me! the curses dire
Of deaths ye met with each at other's hands!
   Semi-Chor. B. Thou tell'st of men death-smitten
       through and through,
       Both in their homes and lives,
       With wrath beyond all speech,   890
       And doom of discord fell,
That sprang from out the curse their father spake.

ANTISTROPH. II.

Semi-Chor. A. Yea, through the city runs
A wailing cry. The high towers wail aloud;
Wails all the plain that loves her heroes well;
       And to their children's sons
       The wealth will go for which
The strife of those ill-starred ones brought forth death.
   Semi-Chor. B. Quick to resent, they shared their for-
       tune so,
       That each like portion won;
       *Nor can their friends regard

Their umpire without blame;
Nor is our voice in thanks to Ares raised.   900

STROPHE. III.

Semi-Chor. A. By the sword smitten low,
    Thus are they now;
    By the sword smitten low,
    There wait them . . . Nay,
    Doth one perchance ask what?
Shares in their old ancestral sepulchres.
Semi-Chor. B. * The sorrow of the house is borne to
    them
    By my heart-rending wail.
    Mine own the cries I pour;
    Mine own the woes I weep,
Bitter and joyless, shedding truest tears   910
From heart that faileth, even as they fall,
    For these two kingly chiefs.

ANTISTROPHE. III.

Semi-Chor. A. Yes; one may say of them,
    That wretched pair,
    That they much ill have wrought
    To their own host;
    Yea, and to alien ranks
Of many nations fallen in the fray.
Semi-Chor. B. Ah! miserable she who bare those twain,
    'Bove all of women born
    Who boast a mother's name!   920
    Taking her son, her own,
    As spouse, she bare these children, and they both,
By mutual slaughter and by brothers' hands,
    Have found their end in death.

STROPH. IV.

Semi-Chor. A . Yes; of the same womb born, and
    doomèd both,
    * Not as friends part, they fell,
    In strife to madness pushed
    In this their quarrel's end.

Semi-Chor. B. The quarrel now is hushed,
And in the ensanguined earth their lives are blent;   930
    Full near in blood are they.
    Stern umpire of their strifes
Has been the stranger from beyond the sea,[1]
Fresh from the furnace, keen and sharpened steel.
    Stern, too, is Ares found,
    Distributing their goods,
Making their father's curses all too true.

ANTISTROPH. IV.

Semi-Chor. A. At last they have their share, ah,
    wretched ones !
    Of burdens sent from God.   940
    And now, beneath them lies
    A boundless wealth of——earth.
Semi-Chor. B. O ye who your own race
Have made to burgeon out with many woes !
    Over the end at last
    The brood of Curses raise
Their shrill, sharp cry of lamentation loud,
The race being put to flight of utmost rout,
    And Atè's trophy stands,
    Where in the gates they fell ;
And Fate, now both are conquered, rests at last.   950

Enter ANTIGONE *and* ISMENE, *followed by mourning
maidens.*[2]

Ant. Thou wast smitten, and thou smotest.
Ism. Thou did'st slaughter, and wast slaughtered.

---

(1) The 'Chalyb,' or iron sword, which the Hellenes had imported from the Skythians. Comp. vv. 70, 86.

(2) The lyrical, operatic character of Greek tragedies has to be borne in mind as we read passages like that which follows. They were not meant to be *read.* Uttered in a passionate recitative, accompanied by expressive action, they probably formed a very effective element in the actual representation of the tragedy. We may look on it as the only extant specimen of the kind of wailing which was characteristic of Eastern burials, and which was slowly passing away in Greece under the influence of a higher culture. The early fondness of Æschylos for a *finale* of this nature is seen also in *The Persians,* and in a more solemn and subdued

Ant. Thou with spear to death did'st smite him.
Ism. Thou with spear to death wast smitten.
Ant. Oh, the woe of all your labours !
Ism. Oh, the woe of all ye suffered !
Ant. Pour the cry of lamentation.
Ism. Pour the tears of bitter weeping.
Ant. There in death thou liest prostrate.
Ism. Having wrought a great destruction.

STROPH.

Ant. Ah ! my mind is crazed with wailing.   968
Ism. Yea, my heart within me groaneth.
Ant. Thou for whom the city weepeth !
Ism. Thou too, doomed to all ill-fortune !
Ant. By a loved hand thou hast perished.
Ism. And a loved form thou hast slaughtered.
Ant. Double woes are ours to tell of.
Ism. Double woes too ours to look on.
Ant. * Twofold sorrows from near kindred.
Ism. * Sisters we by brothers standing.
Ant. Terrible are they to tell of.   976
Ism. Terrible are they to look on.
Chor. Ah me, thou Destiny,
Giver of evil gifts, and working woe,
And thou dread spectral form of Œdipus,
        And swarth Erinnys too,
        A mighty one art thou.

ANTISTROPH.

Ant. Ah me ! ah me ! woes dread to look on . . . .
Ism. Ye showed to me, returned from exile.
Ant. Not, when he had slain, returned he.
Ism. Nay, he, saved from exile, perished.   980
Ant. Yea, I trow too well, he perished.
Ism. And his brother, too, he murdered.
Ant. Woeful, piteous, are those brothers !

form, in the *Eumenides.* The feeling that there was something barbaric
in these outward displays of grief, showed itself alike in the legislation of
Solon, and the eloquence of Pericles.

Ism. Woeful, piteous, all they suffered!
Ant. Woes of kindred wrath enkindling!
Ism. Saturate with threefold horrors!
Ant. Terrible are they to tell of.
Ism. Terrible are they to look on.
  Chor. Ah me, thou Destiny,
Giver of evil gifts, and stern of soul,
And thou dread spectral form of Œdipus,   990
     And swarth Erinnys too,
     A mighty one art thou.

EPODE.

Ant. Thou, then, by full trial knowest . . .
Ism. Thou, too, no whit later learning. . . . .
Ant. When thou cam'st back to this city.[1] . . .
Ism. Rival to our chief in warfare.
Ant. Woe, alas! for all our troubles!
Ism. Woe, alas! for all our evils!
Ant. Evils fallen on our houses!
Ism. Evils fallen on our country!
Ant. And on me before all others. . . .
Ism. And to me the future waiting. . . .   1000
Ant. Woe for those two brothers luckless!
Ism. King Eteocles, our leader!
Ant. Oh, before all others wretched!
Ism. .   .   .   .   .   .
Ant. Ah, by Atè frenzy-stricken!
Ism. Ah, where now shall they be buried?
Ant. There where grave is highest honour.
Ism. Ah, the woe my father wedded!

Enter a Herald.

Her. 'Tis mine the judgment and decrees to publish
Of this Cadmeian city's counsellors:
It is decreed Eteocles to honour,
For his goodwill towards this land of ours,   1010

---

(1) Here, and perhaps throughout, we must think of Antigone as addressing and looking on the corpse of Polyneikes, Ismene on that of Eteocles.

With seemly burial, such as friend may claim ;
For warding off our foes he courted death ;
Pure as regards his country's holy things,
Blameless he died where death the young beseems ;
This then I'm ordered to proclaim of him.
But for his brother's, Polyneikes' corpse,
To cast it out unburied, prey for dogs,
As working havoc on Cadmeian land,
Unless some God had hindered by the spear
Of this our prince ;[1] and he, though dead, shall gain
The curse of all his father's Gods, whom he

            [*Pointing to* POLYNEIKES.

With alien host dishonouring, sought to take
Our city. Him by ravenous birds interred
Ingloriously, they sentence to receive
His full deserts ; and none may take in hand
To heap up there a tomb, nor honour him
With shrill-voiced wailings ; but he still must lie,
Without the meed of burial by his friends.
So do the high Cadmeian powers decree.

   Ant. And I those rulers of Cadmeians tell,[2]
That if no other care to bury him,
I will inter him, facing all the risk,
Burying my brother : nor am I ashamed
To thwart the State in rank disloyalty ;
Strange power there is in ties of blood, that we,
Born of woe-laden mother, sire ill-starred,
Are bound by : therefore of thy full free-will,
Share thou, my soul, in woes he did not will,
Thou living, he being dead, with sister's heart.
And this I say, no wolves with ravening maw,

----

(1) Perhaps—
    " Unless some God had stood against the spear
    This chief did wield."

(2) The speech of Antigone becomes the starting-point, in the hands of
Sophocles, of the noblest of his tragedies. The denial of burial, it will be
remembered, was looked on as not merely an indignity and outrage
against the feelings of the living, but as depriving the souls of the dead
of all rest and peace. As such it was the punishment of parricides and
traitors.

Shall tear his flesh—No! no! let none think that!
For tomb and burial I will scheme for him,   1040
Though I be but weak woman, bringing earth
Within my byssine raiment's fold, and so
Myself will bury him; let no man think
(I say't again) aught else.   Take heart, my soul!
There shall not fail the means effectual.

   Her. I bid thee not defy the State in this.
   Ant. I bid thee not proclaim vain words to me.
   Her. Stern is the people now, with victory flushed.
   Ant. Stern let them be, he shall not tombless lie.
   Her. And wilt thou honour whom the State doth
      loathe?
   Ant. * Yea, from the Gods he gets an honour due.[1] 1050
   Her. It was not so till he this land attacked.
   Ant. He, suffering evil, evil would repay.
   Her. Not against one his arms were turned, but all.
   Ant. Strife is the last of Gods to end disputes:
Him I will bury; talk no more of it.
   Her. Choose for thyself then, I forbid the deed.
   Chor. Alas! alas! alas!

     Ye haughty boasters, race-destroying,
     Now Fates and now Erinnyes, smiting
     The sons of Œdipus, ye slew them,
     With a root-and-branch destruction.   1060
     What shall I then do, what suffer?
     What shall I devise in counsel?
     How should I dare nor to weep thee,
     Nor escort thee to the burial?
     But I tremble and I shrink from
     All the terrors which they threatened,
     They who are my fellow-townsmen.

(1) The words are obscure enough, the point lying, it may be, in their
ambiguity. Antigone here, as in the tragedy of Sophocles, pleads that
the Gods have pardoned; they still command and love the reverence for
the dead, which she is about to show. The herald catches up her words
and takes them in another sense, as though all the honour he had met
with from the Gods had been defeat, and death, and shame, as the reward
of his sacrilege. Another rendering, however, gives—
   "Yes, so the Gods have done with honouring **him**."

Many mourners thou (*looking to the bier of*
    ETEOCLES) shalt meet with;
But he, lost one, unlamented,
With his sister's wailing only
Passeth.   Who with this complieth ?
Semi-Chor. A. Let the city doom or not doom
    Those who weep for Polyneikes;
    We will go, and we will bury,   107*
    Maidens we in sad procession;
    For the woe to all is common,
    And our State with voice uncertain,
    Of the claims of Right and Justice;
    Hither, thither, shifts its praises.
Semi-Chor. B. We will thus, our chief attending,
    Speak, as speaks the State, our praises:
    Of the claims of Right and Justice; [1]
    For next those the Blessed Rulers,
    And the strength of Zeus, he chiefly
    Saved the city of Cadmeians
    From the doom of fell destruction,
    From the doom of whelming utter,
    In the flood of alien warriors.
        [*Exeunt* ANTIGONE *and Semi-Chorus A., fol-
        lowing the corpse of* POLYNEIKES; ISMENE
        and Semi-Chorus B. that of ETEOCLES.

(1) The words are probably a protest against the changeableness of
the Athenian *demos,* as seen especially in their treatment of Aristeides.

PROMETHEUS BOUND.

ARGUMENT.

In the old time, when Cronos was sovereign of the Gods, Zeus, whom he had begotten, rose up against him, and the Gods were divided in their counsels, some, the Titans chiefly, siding with the father, and some with the son. And Prometheus, the son of Earth or Themis, though one of the Titans, supported Zeus, as did also Okeanos, and by his counsels Zeus obtained the victory, and Cronos was chained in Tartaros, and the Titans buried under mountains, or kept in bonds in Hades. And then Prometheus, seeing the miseries of the race of men, of whom Zeus took little heed, stole the fire which till then had belonged to none but Hephæstos and was used only for the Gods, and gave it to mankind, and taught them many arts whereby their wretchedness was lessened. But Zeus being wroth with Prometheus for this deed, sent Hephæstos, with his two helpers, Strength and Force, to fetter him to a rock on Caucasos.

And in yet another story was the cruelty of the Gods made known. For Zeus loved Io, the daughter of Inachos, king of Argos, and she was haunted by visions of the night, telling her of his passion, and she told her father thereof. And Inachos, sending to the God at Delphi, was told to drive Io forth from her home. And Zeus gave her the horns of a cow, and Hera, who hated her because she was dear to Zeus, sent with her a gadfly that stung her, and gave her no rest, and drove her over many lands.

Note.—The play is believed to have been the second of a Trilogy, of which the first was *Prometheus the Fire-giver*, and the third *Prometheus Unbound.*

Dramatis Personæ.

PROMETHEUS.

OKEANOS.

HEPHÆSTOS.

HERMES.

STRENGTH.

FORCE.

10

Chorus of Ocean Nymphs.

PROMETHEUS BOUND.

SCENE.—Skythia, *on the heights of Caucasos. The Euxine seen in the distance.*

Enter HEPHÆSTOS, STRENGTH, *and* FORCE, *leading* PROMETHEUS *in chains.*[1]

Strength. Lo! to a plain, earth's boundary remote,
We now are come,—the tract as Skythian known,
A desert inaccessible : and now,
Hephæstos, it is thine to do the hests
The Father gave thee, to these lofty crags
To bind this crafty trickster fast in chains
Of adamantine bonds that none can break ;
For he thy choice flower stealing, the bright glory
Of fire that all arts spring from, hath bestowed it
On mortal men. And so for fault like this
He now must pay the Gods due penalty,
That he may learn to bear the sovereign rule   10
Of Zeus, and cease from his philanthropy.
    Heph. O Strength, and thou, O Force, the hest of Zeus,
As far as touches you, attains its end,
And nothing hinders. Yet my courage fails

---

(1) The scene seems at first an exception to the early conventional rule, which forbade the introduction of a third actor on the Greek stage. But it has been noticed that (1) Force does not speak, and (2) Prometheus does not speak till Strength and Force have retired, and that it is there-fore probable that the whole work of nailing is done on a lay figure or effigy of some kind, and that one of the two who had before taken part in the dialogue then speaks behind it in the character of Prometheus. So the same actor must have appeared in succession as Okeanos, Io, and Hermes.

To bind a God of mine own kin by force
To this bare rock where tempests wildly sweep;
And yet I needs must muster courage for it:
'Tis no slight thing the Father's words to scorn.
O thou of Themis [to PROMETHEUS] wise in counsel son,
Full deep of purpose, lo! against my will,[1]
I fetter thee against thy will with bonds
Of bronze that none can loose, to this lone height,   20
Where thou shalt know nor voice nor face of man,
But scorching in the hot blaze of the sun,
Shalt lose thy skin's fair beauty. Thou shalt long
For starry-mantled night to hide day's sheen,
For sun to melt the rime of early dawn;
And evermore the weight of present ill
Shall wear thee down. Unborn as yet is he
Who shall release thee: this the fate thou gain'st
As due reward for thy philanthropy.
For thou, a God not fearing wrath of Gods,
In thy transgression gav'st their power to men;   33
And therefore on this rock of little ease
Thou still shalt keep thy watch, nor lying down,
Nor knowing sleep, nor ever bending knee;
And many groans and wailings profitless
Thy lips shall utter; for the mind of Zeus
Remains inexorable. Who holds a power
But newly gained[2] is ever stern of mood.
    Strength. Let be! Why linger in this idle pity?
Why dost not hate a God to Gods a foe,
Who gave thy choicest prize to mortal men?
    Heph. Strange is the power of kin and intercourse.[3]

---

(1) Prometheus (*Forethought*) is **the son of Themis** (*Right*) the second occupant of the Pythian Oracle (*Eumen.* v. 2.) His sympathy with man leads him to impart the gift which raised them out of savage animal life, and for this Zeus, who appears throughout the play as a hard taskmaster, sentences him to fetters. Hephæstos, from whom this fire had been stolen, has a touch of pity for him. Strength, who comes as the servant, not of Hephæstos, but of Zeus himself, acts, as such, with merciless cruelty.
(2) The generalised statement refers to Zeus, as having but recently expelled Cronos from his throne in Heaven.
(3) Hephæstos, as the great fire-worker, had taught Prometheus to use the fire which he afterwards bestowed on men.

Strength. I own it; yet to slight the Father's words, [40]
How may that be? Is not that fear the worse?

Heph. Still art thou ruthless, full of savagery.

Strength. There is no help in weeping over him:
Spend not thy toil on things that profit not.

Heph. O handicraft to me intolerable!

Strength. Why loath'st thou it? Of these thy present griefs
That craft of thine is not one whit the cause.

Heph. And yet I would some other had that skill.

Strength. *All things bring toil except for Gods to reign; [1]
For none but Zeus can boast of freedom true. [50]

Heph. Too well I see the proof, and gainsay not.

Strength. Wilt thou not speed to fix the chains on him,
Lest He, the Father, see thee loitering here?

Heph. Well, here the handcuffs thou may'st see prepared.

Strength. In thine hands take him. Then with all thy might
Strike with thine hammer; nail him to the rocks.

Heph. The work goes on, I ween, and not in vain.

Strength. Strike harder, rivet, give no whit of ease:
A wondrous knack has he to find resource,
Even where all might seem to baffle him.

Heph. Lo! this his arm is fixed inextricably. [60]

Strength. Now rivet thou this other fast, that he
May learn, though sharp, that he than Zeus is duller.

Heph. No one but he could justly blame my work.

Strength. Now drive the stern jaw of the adamant wedge
Right through his chest with all the strength thou hast.

Heph. Ah me! Prometheus, for thy woes I groan.

Strength. Again, thou'rt loth, and for the foes of Zeus
Thou groanest: take good heed to it lest thou
Ere long with cause thyself commiserate.

Heph. Thou see'st a sight unsightly to our eyes.

(1) Perhaps, "All might is ours except o'er Gods to rule."

Strength. I see this man obtaining his deserts :   70
Nay, cast thy breast-chains round about his ribs.
   Heph. I must needs do it.   Spare thine o'er much bid-
      ding ;
Go thou below and rivet both his legs.[1]
   Strength. Nay, I will bid thee, urge thee to thy work.
   Heph.   There, it is done, and that with no long toil.
   Strength. Now with thy full power fix the galling
      fetters :
Thou hast a stern o'erlooker of thy work.
   Heph. Thy tongue but utters words that match thy
      form.[2]
   Strength. Choose thou the melting mood ; but chide
      not me
For my self-will and wrath and ruthlessness.   80
   Heph. Now let us go, his limbs are bound in chains.
   Strength. Here then wax proud, and stealing what
      belongs
To the Gods, to mortals give it.   What can they
Avail to rescue thee from these thy woes ?
Falsely the Gods have given thee thy name,
Prometheus, Forethought ; forethought thou dost need
To free thyself from this rare handiwork.
      [*Exeunt* HEPHÆSTOS, STRENGTH, *and* FORCE,
        leaving PROMETHEUS *on the rock.*
   Prom.[3] Thou firmament of God, and swift-winged
      winds,
Ye springs of rivers, and of ocean waves
That smile innumerous !   Mother of us all,   90
O Earth, and Sun's all-seeing eye, behold,
I pray, what I a God from Gods endure.

   (1) The words indicate that the effigy of Prometheus, now nailed to the
rock, was, as being that of a Titan, of colossal size.
   (2) The touch is characteristic as showing that here, as in the *Eumenides,*
Æschylos relied on the horribleness of the masks, as part of the machinery
of his plays.
   (3) The silence of Prometheus up to this point was partly, as has been
said, consequent on the conventional laws of the Greek drama, but it is
also a touch of supreme insight into the heroic temper. In the presence
of his torturers, the Titan will not utter even a groan. When they are
gone, he appeals to the sympathy of Nature.

Behold in what foul case
I for ten thousand years
Shall struggle in my woe,
In these unseemly chains.
Such doom the new-made Monarch of the Blest
Hath now devised for me.
Woe, woe! The present and the oncoming pang
I wail, as I search out
The place and hour when end of all these ills
Shall dawn on me at last.
What say I? All too clearly I foresee
The things that come, and nought of pain shall be
By me unlooked-for; but I needs must bear
My destiny as best I may, knowing well
The might resistless of Necessity.
And neither may I speak of this my fate,
Nor hold my peace. For I, poor I, through giving
Great gifts to mortal men, am prisoner made
In these fast fetters; yea, in fennel stalk [1]
I snatched the hidden spring of stolen fire,
Which is to men a teacher of all arts,
Their chief resource. And now this penalty
Of that offence I pay, fast riveted
In chains beneath the open firmament.
          Ha! ha! What now?
What sound, what odour floats invisibly? [2]
Is it of God or man, or blending both?
And has one come to this remotest rock
To look upon my woes? Or what wills he?

100

110

(1) The legend is from Hesiod, (*Theogon.* v. 567.) The fennel, or *narthex*, seems to have been a large umbelliferous plant, with a large stem filled with a sort of pith, which was used when dry as tinder. Stalks were carried as wands (the *thyrsi*) by the men and women who joined in Bacchanalian processions. In modern botany, the name is given to the plant which produces Asafœtida, and the stem of which, from its resinous character, would burn freely, and so connect itself with the Promethean myth. On the other hand, the Narthex Asafœtida is found at present only in Persia, Affghanistan, and the Punjaub.
(2) The ocean nymphs, like other divine ones, would be anointed with ambrosial unguents, and the odour would be wafted before them by the rustling of their wings. This too we may think of as part of the "stage effects" of the play.

Behold me bound, a God to evil doomed,
    The foe of Zeus, and held
    In hatred by all Gods
    Who tread the courts of Zeus:
    And this for my great love,
    Too great, for mortal men.
    Ah me ! what rustling sounds
    Hear I of birds not far ?
    With the light whirr of wings
    The air re-echoeth :
All that draws nigh to me is cause of fear.[1]

   Enter Chorus of Ocean Nymphs, *with wings, floating
          in the air.*[2]

   Chor. Nay, fear thou nought : in love
    All our array of wings
    In eager race hath come
To this high peak, full hardly gaining o'er
    Our Father's mind and will ;
And the swift-rushing breezes bore me on :
For lo ! the echoing sound of blows on iron
Pierced to our cave's recess, and put to flight
    My shamefast modesty,
And I in unshod haste, on winged car,
    To thee rushed hitherward.
   Prom.   Ah me ! ah me !
Offspring of Tethys blest with many a child,
Daughters of Old Okeanos that rolls
Round all the earth with never-sleeping stream,
    Behold ye me, and see
    With what chains fettered fast,
I on the topmost crags of this ravine
Shall keep my sentry-post unenviable.
   Chor. I see it, O Prometheus, and a mist

---

   (1) The words are not those of a vague terror only. The sufferer knows
that his tormentor is to come to him before long on wings, and therefore
the sound as of the flight of birds is full of terrors.
   (2) By some stage mechanism the Chorus remains in the air till verse
280, when, at the request of Prometheus, they alight.

Of fear and full of tears comes o'er mine eyes,
    Thy frame beholding thus,
    Writhing on these high rocks   154
    In adamantine ills.
New pilots now o'er high Olympos rule,
    And with new-fashioned laws
    Zeus reigns, down-trampling right,
And all the ancient powers He sweeps away.
  Prom. Ah! would that 'neath the Earth, 'neath Hades
      too,
Home of the dead, far down to Tartaros   160
Unfathomable He in fetters fast
    In wrath had hurled me down:
    So neither had a God
Nor any other mocked at these my woes;
But now, the wretched plaything of the winds,
I suffer ills at which my foes rejoice.
  Chor. Nay, which of all the Gods
Is so hard-hearted as to joy in this?
Who, Zeus excepted, doth not pity thee
    In these thine ills? But He,
    Ruthless, with soul unbent,
Subdues the heavenly host, nor will He cease [1]   170
Until his heart be satiate with power,
Or some one seize with subtle stratagem
The sovran might that so resistless seemed.
  Prom. Nay, of a truth, though put to evil shame,
    In massive fetters bound,
    The Ruler of the Gods
Shall yet have need of me, yes, e'en of me,
    To tell the counsel new
    That seeks to strip from him
His sceptre and his might of sovereignty.

---

(1) Here, as throughout the play, the poet puts into the mouth of his *dramatis personæ* words which must have seemed to the devouter Athenians sacrilegious enough to call for an indictment before the Areiopagos. But the final play of the Trilogy came, we may believe, as the *Eumenides* did in its turn, as a reconciliation of the conflicting thoughts that rise in men's minds out of the seeming anomalies of the world.

In vain will He with words
Or suasion's honeyed charms
Sooth me, nor will I tell
Through fear of his stern threats,
Ere He shall set me free
From these my bonds, and make,
Of his own choice, amends
For all these outrages.

Chor. Full rash art thou, and yield'st
In not a jot to bitterest form of woe;
Thou art o'er-free and reckless in thy speech:
But piercing fear hath stirred
My inmost soul to strife;
For I fear greatly touching thy distress,
As to what haven of these woes of thine
Thou now must steer: the son of Cronos hath
A stubborn mood and heart inexorable.

Prom. I know that Zeus is hard,
And keeps the Right supremely to himself;
But then, I trow, He'll be
Full pliant in his will,
When He is thus crushed down.
Then, calming down his mood
Of hard and bitter wrath,
He'll hasten unto me,
As I to him shall haste,
For friendship and for peace.

Chor. Hide it not from us, tell us all the tale:
For what offence Zeus, having seized thee thus,
So wantonly and bitterly insults thee:
If the tale hurt thee not, inform thou us.

Prom. Painful are these things to me e'en to speak:
Painful is silence; everywhere is woe.
For when the high Gods fell on mood of wrath,
And hot debate of mutual strife was stirred,
Some wishing to hurl Cronos from his throne,
That Zeus, forsooth, might reign; while others strove,
Eager that Zeus might never rule the Gods:

Then I, full strongly seeking to persuade
The Titans, yea, the sons of Heaven and Earth,
Failed of my purpose.   Scorning subtle arts,
With counsels violent, they thought that they
By force would gain full easy mastery.
But then not once or twice my mother Themis
And Earth, one form though bearing many names,[1]
Had prophesied the future, how 'twould run,
That not by strength nor yet by violence,   220
But guile, should those who prospered gain the day.
And when in my words I this counsel gave,
They deigned not e'en to glance at it at all.
And then of all that offered, it seemed best
To join my mother, and of mine own will,
Not against his will, take my side with Zeus,
And by my counsels, mine, the dark deep pit
Of Tartaros the ancient Cronos holds,
Himself and his allies.   Thus profiting
By me, the mighty ruler of the Gods   230
Repays me with these evil penalties :
For somehow this disease in sovereignty
Inheres, of never trusting to one's friends.[2]
And since ye ask me under what pretence
He thus maltreats me, I will show it you :
For soon as He upon his father's throne
Had sat secure, forthwith to divers Gods
He divers gifts distributed, and his realm
Began to order.   But of mortal men
He took no heed, but purposed utterly   240
To crush their race and plant another new ;
And, I excepted, none dared cross his will ;
But I did dare, and mortal men I freed
From passing on to Hades thunder-stricken ;

(1) The words leave it uncertain whether Themis is identified with
Earth, or, as in the *Eumenides*, (v. 2,) distinguished from her. The Titans
as a class, then, children of Okeanos and Chthón, (another name for
Land or *Earth*,) are the kindred rather than the brothers of Prometheus.
(2) The generalising words here, as in v. 35, appeal to the Athenian
hatred of all that was represented by the words *tyrant* and *tyranny*.

And therefore am I bound beneath these woes,
Dreadful to suffer; pitiable to see :
And I, who in my pity thought of men
More than myself, have not been worthy deemed
To gain like favour, but all ruthlessly
I thus am chained, foul shame this sight to Zeus.

   Chor. Iron-hearted must he be and made of rock   250
Who is not moved, Prometheus, by thy woes :
Fain could I wish I ne'er had seen such things,
And, seeing them, am wounded to the heart.

    Prom. Yea, I am piteous for my friends to see.
    Chor. Did'st thou not go to farther lengths than this ?
    Prom. I made men cease from contemplating death.[1]
    Chor. What medicine did'st thou find for that disease ?
    Prom. Blind hopes I gave to live and dwell with
        them.
    Chor. Great service that thou did'st for mortal men !
    Prom. And more than that, I gave them fire, yes I.   260
    Chor. Do short-lived men the flaming fire possess ?
    Prom. Yea, and full many an art they'll learn from it.
    Chor. And is it then on charges such as these
That Zeus maltreats thee, and no respite gives
Of many woes ?   And has thy pain no end ?
    Prom. End there is none, except as pleases Him.
    Chor. How shall it please ?   What hope hast thou ?
        See'st not
That thou hast sinned ?   Yet to say how thou sinned'st
Gives me no pleasure, and is pain to thee.
Well ! let us leave these things, and, if we may,
Seek out some means to 'scape from this thy woe.   270
    Prom. 'Tis a light thing for one who has his foot
Beyond the reach of evil to exhort
And counsel him who suffers.   This to me
Was all well known.   Yea, willing, willingly

    (1) The state described is that of men who " through fear of death are
all their lifetime subject to bondage."   That state, the parent of all
superstition, fostered the slavish awe in which Zeus delighted.   Prometheus, representing the active intellect of man, bestows new powers, new
interests, new hopes, which at last divert them from that fear.

I sinned, nor will deny it. Helping men,
I for myself found trouble: yet I thought not
That I with such dread penalties as these
Should wither here on these high-towering crags,
Lighting on this lone hill and neighbourless.
Wherefore wail not for these my present woes,
But, drawing nigh, my coming fortunes hear, 280
That ye may learn the whole tale to the end.
Nay, hearken, hearken; show your sympathy
With him who suffers now. 'Tis thus that woe,
Wandering, now falls on this one, now on that.
 Chor. Not to unwilling hearers hast thou uttered,
   Prometheus, thy request,
And now with nimble foot abandoning
   My swiftly rushing car,
And the pure æther, path of birds of heaven, 290
I will draw near this rough and rocky land,
   For much do I desire
To hear this tale, full measure, of thy woes.

 Enter OKEANOS, *on a car drawn by a winged gryphon.*

 Okean. Lo, I come to thee, Prometheus,
   Reaching goal of distant journey,[1]
   Guiding this my winged courser
   By my will, without a bridle;
   And thy sorrows move my pity.
   Force, in part, I deem, of kindred
   Leads me on, nor know I any,
   Whom, apart from kin, I honour 300
   More than thee, in fuller measure.
   This thou shalt own true and earnest:
   I deal not in glozing speeches.
   Come then, tell me how to help thee:
   Ne'er shalt thou say that one more friendly
   Is found than unto thee is Okean.
 Prom. Let be. What boots it? Thou then too art come

(1) The home of Okeanos was in the far west, at the boundary of the
great stream surrounding the whole world, from which he took his
name.

To gaze upon my sufferings.   How did'st dare
Leaving the stream that bears thy name, and caves
Hewn in the living rock, this land to visit,
Mother of iron ?   What then, art thou come
To gaze upon my fall and offer pity ?   310
Behold this sight : see here the friend of Zeus,
Who helped to seat him in his sovereignty,
With what foul outrage I am crushed by him !

   Okean. I see, Prometheus, and I wish to give thee
My best advice, all subtle though thou be.
Know thou thyself,[1] and fit thy soul to moods
To thee full new.   New king the Gods have now;
But if thou utter words thus rough and sharp,
Perchance, though sitting far away on high,   320
Zeus yet may hear thee, and his present wrath
Seem to thee but as child's play of distress.
Nay, thou poor sufferer, quit the rage thou hast,
And seek a remedy for these thine ills.
A tale thrice-told, perchance, I seem to speak :
Lo ! this, Prometheus, is the punishment
Of thine o'er lofty speech, nor art thou yet
Humbled, nor yieldest to thy miseries,
And fain would'st add fresh evils unto these.
But thou, if thou wilt take me as thy teacher,   330
Wilt not kick out against the pricks;[2] seeing well
A monarch reigns who gives account to none.
And now I go, and will an effort make,
If I, perchance, may free thee from thy woes ;
Be still then, hush thy petulance of speech,
Or knowest thou not, o'er-clever as thou art,
That idle tongues must still their forfeit pay ?

   Prom. I envy thee, seeing thou art free from blame
Though thou shared'st all, and in my cause wast bold ;[3]

   (1) One of the sayings of the seven Sages, already recognised and
quoted as a familiar proverb.
   (2) See note on *Agam.* 1602.
   (3) In the mythos, Okeanos had given his daughter Hesione in marriage to Prometheus after the theft of fire, and thus had identified himself
w.th his transgression.

Nay, let me be, **nor** trouble thou thyself;   340
Thou wilt not, canst not soothe Him ; very hard
Is He of soothing.   Look to it thyself,
Lest thou some mischief meet with in the **way.**

   Okean. **It is thy wont thy neighbours'** minds to school
Far better than thine own.   From deeds, not words,
I draw my proof.   But do not draw me back
When I am hasting on, for lo, I deem,
I deem that Zeus will grant this boon to me,
That I should free thee from these woes of **thine.**

   Prom. I thank thee much, yea, ne'er will cease to
             thank ;
For thou no whit of zeal dost lack ; **yet take,**
I pray, no trouble for me ; all in vain
Thy trouble, nothing helping, **e'en if** thou   350
Should'st care to take the trouble.   Nay, be still ;
Keep out of harm's way ; sufferer though I **be,**
I would not therefore wish to give my **woes**
A wider range o'er others.   No, not so :
For lo! my mind is wearied with the grief
Of that my kinsman Atlas,[1] who doth stand
In the far West, supporting on his shoulders
The pillars of **the earth** and heaven, a burden
His arms can ill but hold : I pity too
The giant dweller of Kilikian caves,   360
Dread portent, with his hundred hands, subdued
By force, the mighty Typhon,[2] who arose

---

(1) In the *Theogony* of Hesiod, (v. 509,) Prometheus and Atlas appear as
the sons of two sisters. As other Titans were thought of as buried under
volcanoes, so this one was identified with the mountain which had been
seen by travellers to Western Africa, or in the seas beyond it, rising like
a column to support the vault of heaven. In Herodotos (iv. 174) and all
later writers, the name is given to the chain of mountains in Lybia, as
being the "pillar of the firmament;" but Humboldt and others identify
it with the lonely peak of Teneriffe, as seen by Phœnikian or Hellenic
voyagers. Teneriffe, too, like most of the other Titan mountains, was at
one time volcanic. Homer (*Odyss.* i. 53) represents him as holding the
pillars which separate heaven from earth; Hesiod (*Theogon.* v. 517) as
himself standing near the Hesperides, (this too points to Teneriffe) sus-
taining the heavens with his head and shoulders.

(2) The volcanic character of the whole of Asia Minor, and the liability
to earthquakes which has marked nearly every period of its history, led
men to connect it also with the traditions of the Titans, some accordingly

'Gainst all the Gods, with sharp and dreadful jaws
Hissing out slaughter, and from out his eyes
There flashed the terrible brightness as of one
Who would lay low the sovereignty of Zeus.
But the unsleeping dart of Zeus came on him,
Down-swooping thunderbolt that breathes out flame,
Which from his lofty boastings startled him,
For he i' the heart was struck, to ashes burnt,   370
His strength all thunder-shattered; and he lies
A helpless, powerless carcase, near the strait
Of the great sea, fast pressed beneath the roots
Of ancient Ætna, where on highest peak
Hephæstos sits and smites his iron red-hot,
From whence hereafter streams of fire shall burst,[1]
Devouring with fierce jaws the golden plains
Of fruitful, fair Sikelia.   Such the wrath
That Typhon shall belch forth with bursts of storm,
Hot, breathing fire, and unapproachable,
Though burnt and charred by thunderbolts of Zeus.   380
Not inexperienced art thou, nor dost need
My teaching : save thyself, as thou know'st how ;
And I will drink my fortune to the dregs,
Till from his wrath the mind of Zeus shall rest.[2]
     Okean. Know'st thou not this, Prometheus, even this,
Of wrath's disease wise words the healers are ?
     Prom. Yea, could one soothe the troubled heart in
               time,
Nor seek by force to tame the soul's proud flesh.
     Okean. But in due forethought with bold daring blent,
What mischief see'st thou lurking ? Tell me this.   390
     Prom. Toil bootless, and simplicity full fond.

placing the home of Typhon in Phrygia, some near Sardis, some, as here,
in Kilikia. Hesiod (*Theogon.* v. 820) describes Typhon (or Typhoeus) as
a serpent-monster hissing out fire ; Pindar (*Pyth.* i. 30, viii. 21) as lying
with his head and breast crushed beneath the weight of Ætna, and his
feet extending to Cumæ.
     (1) The words point probably to an eruption, then fresh in men's
memories, which had happened B.C. 476.
     (2) By some editors this speech from "No, not so," to "thou know'st
how," is assigned to Okeanos.

Okean. Let me, I pray, that sickness suffer, since
'Tis best being wise to have not wisdom's show.
  Prom. Nay, but this error shall be deemed as mine.
  Okean. Thy word then clearly sends me home at once.
  Prom. Yea, lest thy pity for me make a foe. . . .
  Okean. What! of that new king on his mighty throne?
  Prom. Look to it, lest his heart be vexed with thee.
  Okean. Thy fate, Prometheus, teaches me that lesson.
  Prom. Away, withdraw! keep thou the mind thou
        hast.   400
  Okean. Thou urgest me who am in act to haste;
For this my bird four-footed flaps with wings
The clear path of the æther; and full fain
Would he bend knee in his own stall at home.   [*Exit.*

STROPH. I.

  Chor. I grieve, Prometheus, for thy dreary fate,
        Shedding from tender eyes
        The dew of plenteous tears;
With streams, as when the watery south wind blows,
        My cheek is wet;   410
For lo! these things are all unenviable,
And Zeus, by his own laws his sway maintaining,
        Shows to the elder Gods
        A mood of haughtiness.

ANTISTROPH. I.

And all the country echoeth with the moan,
        And poureth many a tear
        For that magnific power
Of ancient days far-seen that thou did'st share
        With those of one blood sprung;
And all the mortal men who hold the plain   420
Of holy Asia as their land of sojourn,
        They grieve in sympathy
        For thy woes lamentable.

STROPH. II.

And they, the maiden band who find their home
        On distant Colchian coasts,

Fearless of fight,[1]
Or Skythian horde in earth's remotest clime,
        By far Mæotic lake ;[2]

ANTISTROPH. II.

*And warlike glory of Arabia's tribes,[3]
        Who nigh to Caucasos
        In rock-fort dwell,
An army fearful, with sharp-pointed spear
        Raging in war's array.

STROPH. III.

One other Titan only have I seen,
        One other of the Gods,
Thus bound in woes of adamantine strength—
        Atlas, who ever groans
Beneath the burden of a crushing might,
        The out-spread vault of heaven.

ANTISTROPH. III.

And lo ! the ocean billows murmur loud
        In one accord with him ;[4]
The sea-depths groan, and Hades' swarthy pit
        Re-echoeth the sound,
And fountains of clear rivers, as they flow,
        Bewail his bitter griefs.
    Prom. Think not it is through pride or stiff self-will
That I am silent.   But my heart is worn,
Self-contemplating, as I see myself
Thus outraged.   Yet what other hand than mine

---

(1) These are, of course, the Amazons, who were believed to have come
through Thrakè from the Tauric Chersonesos, and had left traces of their
name and habits in the Attic traditions of Theseus.
(2) Beyond the plains of Skythia, and the lake Mæotis (the sea of Azov)
there would be the great river Okeanos, which was believed to flow round
the earth.
(3) Sarmatia has been conjectured instead of Arabia. No Greek
author sanctions the extension of the latter name to so remote a region
as that north of the Caspian.
(4) The Greek leaves the object of the sympathy undefined, but it
seems better to refer it to that which Atlas receives from the waste of
waters around, and the dark world beneath, than to the pity shown to
Prometheus. This had already been dwelt on in line 421.

Gave these young Gods in fulness all their gifts?
But these I speak not of; for I should tell
To you that know them.   But those woes of men,[1]   450
List ye to them,—how they, before as babes,
By me were roused to reason, taught to think;
And this I say, not finding fault with men,
But showing my good-will in all I gave.
For first, though seeing, all in vain they saw,
And hearing, heard not rightly.   But, like forms
Of phantom-dreams, throughout their life's whole length
They muddled all at random; did not know
Houses of brick that catch the sunlight's warmth,
Nor yet the work of carpentry.   They dwelt
In hollowed holes, like swarms of tiny ants,   460
In sunless depths of caverns; and they had
No certain signs of winter, nor of spring
Flower-laden, nor of summer with her fruits;
But without counsel fared their whole life long,
Until I showed the risings of the stars,
And settings hard to recognise.[2]   And I
Found Number for them, chief device of all,
*Groupings of letters, Memory's handmaid that,
And mother of the Muses.[3]   And I first
Bound in the yoke wild steeds, submissive made   470
Or to the collar or men's limbs, that so
They might in man's place bear his greatest toils;
And horses trained to love the rein I yoked
To chariots, glory of wealth's pride of state;[4]
Nor was it any one but I that found

(1) The passage that follows has for modern palæontologists the interest of coinciding with their views as to the progress of human society, and the condition of mankind during what has been called the "Stone" period. Comp. Lucretius, v. 955-984.
(2) Comp. Mr. Blakesley's note on Herod. ii. 4, as showing that here there was the greater risk of faulty observation.
(3) Another reading gives perhaps a better sense—
"Memory, handmaid true
And mother of the Muses."
(4) In Greece, as throughout the East, the ox was used for all agricultural labours, the horse by the noble and the rich, either in war chariots, or stately processions, or in chariot races in the great games.

Sea-crossing, canvas-wingèd cars of ships:
Such rare designs inventing (wretched me!)
For mortal men, I yet have no device
By which to free myself from this my woe.[1]

    Chor. Foul shame thou sufferest: of thy sense be-
        reaved,   480
Thou errest greatly: and, like leech unskilled,
Thou losest heart when smitten with disease,
And know'st not how to find the remedies
Wherewith to heal thine own soul's sicknesses.

    Prom. Hearing what yet remains thou'lt wonder more,
What arts and what resources I devised:
And this the chief: if any one fell ill,
There was no help for him, nor healing food,
Nor unguent, nor yet potion; but for want
Of drugs they wasted, till I showed to them
The blendings of all mild medicaments,[2]   490
Wherewith they ward the attacks of sickness sore.
I gave them many modes of prophecy;[3]
And I first taught them what dreams needs must prove
True visions, and made known the ominous sounds
Full hard to know; and tokens by the way,
And flights of taloned birds I clearly marked,—
Those on the right propitious to mankind,
And those sinister,—and what form of life
They each maintain, and what their enmities
Each with the other, and their loves and friendships;   500
And of the inward parts the plumpness smooth,

---

(1) Compare with this **the account of the inventions of Palamedes in**
Sophocles, *Fragm.* 379.

(2) Here we can recognise the knowledge of one who had studied in
the schools of Pythagoras, or had at any rate picked up their terminology.
A more immediate connexion may perhaps be traced with the influence
of Epimenides, who was said to have spent many years in searching
out the healing virtues of plants, and to have written books about them.

(3) **The** lines that follow form almost a manual of the art of divination
as then practised. The "ominous sounds" include chance words,
strange cries, any unexpected utterance that connected itself with men's
fears for the future. The flights of birds were watched by the diviner
as he faced the north, and so the region on the right hand was that of the
sunrise, light, blessedness; on the left there were darkness and gloom
and death.

And with what colour they the Gods would please,
And the streaked comeliness of gall and liver:
And with burnt limbs enwrapt in fat, and chine,
I led men on to art full difficult:
And I gave eyes to omens drawn from fire,
Till then dim-visioned.   So far then for this.
And 'neath the earth the hidden boons for men,
Bronze, iron, silver, gold, who else could say   510
That he, ere I did, found them?   None, I know,
Unless he fain would babble idle words.
In one short word, then, learn the truth condensed,—
All arts of mortals from Prometheus spring.
   Chor. Nay, be not thou to men so over-kind,
While thou thyself art in sore evil case;
For I am sanguine that thou too, released
From bonds, shalt be as strong as Zeus himself.
   Prom. It is not thus that Fate's decree is fixed;
But I, long crushed with twice ten thousand woes   520
And bitter pains, shall then escape my bonds;
Art is far weaker than Necessity.
   Chor. Who guides the helm, then, of Necessity?
   Prom. Fates triple-formed, Erinnyes unforgetting.
   Chor. Is Zeus, then, weaker in his might than these?
   Prom. Not even He can 'scape the thing decreed.
   Chor. What is decreed for Zeus but still to reign?
   Prom. Thou may'st no further learn, ask thou no more.
   Chor. 'Tis doubtless some dread secret which thou
      hidest.
   Prom. Of other theme make mention, for the time   530
Is not yet come to utter this, but still
It must be hidden to the uttermost;
For by thus keeping it it is that I
Escape my bondage foul, and these my pains.

STROPH. I.

   Chor. Ah! ne'er may Zeus the Lord,
      Whose sovran sway rules all,
      His strength in conflict set

Against my feeble will!
Nor may I fail to serve
The Gods with holy feast
Of whole burnt-offerings,
Where the stream ever flows
That bears my father's name,
The great Okeanos!
Nor may I sin in speech!
May this grace more and more
Sink deep into my soul
And never fade away!

ANTISTROPH. I.

Sweet is it in strong hope
To spend long years of life,
With bright and cheering joy
Our heart's thoughts nourishing.
I shudder, seeing thee
Thus vexed and harassed sore
By twice ten thousand woes;
For thou in pride of heart,
Having no fear of Zeus,
In thine own obstinacy,
Dost show for mortal men,
Prometheus, love o'ermuch.

STROPH. II.

See how that boon, dear friends,
For thee is bootless found.
Say, where is any help?
What aid from mortals comes?
Hast thou not seen this brief and powerless life,
Fleeting as dreams, with which man's purblind race
Is fast in fetters bound?
Never shall counsels vain
Of mortal men break through
The harmony of Zeus.

ANTISTROPH. II.

This lesson have I learnt

Beholding thy sad fate,
Prometheus! Other strains
Come back upon my mind,
When I sang wedding hymns around thy bath,
And at thy bridal bed, when thou did'st take
In wedlock's holy bands
One of the same sire born,
Our own Hesione,   570
Persuading her with gifts
As wife to share thy couch.

Enter Io *in form like a fair woman with a heifer's horns,*[1]
followed by the Spectre of ARGOS.

Io. What land is this? What people? Whom
    shall I
Say that I see thus vexed
With bit and curb of rock?
For what offence dost thou
Bear fatal punishment?
Tell me to what far land
I've wandered here in woe.
    Ah me! ah me!
Again the gadfly stings me miserable.
    Spectre of Argos, thou, the earth-born one—
    Ah, keep him off, O Earth!
I fear to look upon that herdsman dread,   580
    Him with ten thousand eyes:
Ah lo! he cometh with his crafty look,
Whom Earth refuses even dead to hold;[2]

(1) So Io was represented, we are told, by Greek sculptors, (Herod. ii. 41,) as Isis was by those of Egypt. The points of contact between the myth of Io and that of Prometheus, as adopted, or perhaps developed, by Æschylos, are—(1) that from her the destined deliverer of the chained Titan is to come ; (2) that both were suffering from the cruelty of Zeus ; (3) that the wanderings of Io gave scope for the wild tales of far countries on which the imagination of the Athenians fed greedily. But, as the *Suppliants* may serve to show , the story itself had a strange fascination for him. In the birth of Epaphos, and Io's release from her frenzy, he saw, it may be, a reconciliation of what had seemed hard to reconcile, a solution of the problems of the world, like in kind to that which was shadowed forth in the lost *Prometheus Unbound.*

(2) Argos had been slain by Hermes, and his eyes transferred by Hera to the tail of the peacock, and that bird was thenceforth sacred to her.

I

But coming from beneath
He hunts me miserable,
And drives me famished o'er the sea-beach sand.

And still his waxened reed-pipe soundeth clear
A soft and slumberous strain ;
O heavens ! O ye Gods !   590
Whither do these long wanderings lead me on ?
For what offence, O son of Cronos, what,
Hast thou thus bound me fast
In these great miseries ?
Ah me ! ah me !
And why with terror of the gadfly's sting
Dost thou thus vex me, frenzied in my soul ?
Burn me with fire, or bury me in earth,
Or to wild sea-beasts give me as a prey :
Nay, grudge me not, O King,
An answer to my prayers :   600
Enough my many-wandered wanderings
Have exercised my soul,
Nor have I power to learn
How to avert the woe.
      (*To Prometheus*).   Hear'st thou the voice of maiden
                  crowned with horns ?
  Prom. Surely I heard the maid by gadfly driven,
Daughter of Inachos, who warmed the heart
Of Zeus with love, and now through Hera's hate
Is tried, perforce, with wanderings over-long ?

  Io. How is it that thou speak'st my father's name ?
            Tell me, the suffering one,   610
            Who art thou, who, poor wretch,
Who thus so truly nam'st me miserable,
            And tell'st the plague from Heaven,
            Which with its haunting stings
            Wears me to death ?   Ah woe !
And I with famished and unseemly bounds
Rush madly, driven by Hera's jealous craft.

Ah, who of all that suffer, born to woe,   620
Have trouble like the pain that I endure?
      But thou, make clear to me
      What yet for me remains,
What remedy, what healing for my pangs.
      Show me, if thou dost know:
      Speak out and tell to me,
      The maid by wanderings vexed.
  Prom. I will say plainly all thou seek'st to know;
Not in dark tangled riddles, but plain speech,
As it is meet that friends to friends should speak;
Thou see'st Prometheus who gave fire to men.   630
  Io. O thou to men as benefactor known,
Why, poor Prometheus, sufferest thou this pain?
  Prom. I have but now mine own woes ceased to wail.
  Io. Wilt thou not then bestow this boon on me?
  Prom. Say what thou seek'st, for I will tell thee all.
  Io. Tell me, who fettered thee in this ravine?
  Prom. The counsel was of Zeus, the hand Hephæstos'.
  Io. Of what offence dost thou the forfeit pay?
  Prom. Thus much alone am I content to tell.
  Io. Tell me, at least, besides, what end shall come   640
To my drear wanderings; when the time shall be.
  Prom. Not to know this is better than to know.
  Io. Nay, hide not from me what I have to bear.
  Prom. It is not that I grudge the boon to thee.
  Io. Why then delayest thou to tell the whole?
  Prom. Not from ill will, but loth to vex thy soul.
  Io. Nay, care thou not beyond what pleases me.
  Prom. If thou desire it I must speak. Hear then.
  Chor. Not yet though; grant me share of pleasure too.
Let us first ask the tale of her great woe,   650
While she unfolds her life's consuming chances;
Her future sufferings let her learn from thee.
  Prom. 'Tis thy work, Io, to grant these their wish,
On other grounds and as thy father's kin: [1]

(1) Inachos the father of Io (identified with the Argive river of the same name) was, like all rivers, a son of Okeanos, and therefore brother to the nymphs who had come to see Prometheus.

For to bewail and moan one's evil chance,
Here where one trusts to gain a pitying tear
From those who hear,—this is not labour lost.

   Io. I know not how to disobey your wish;
So ye shall learn the whole that ye desire
In speech full clear. And yet I blush to tell   660
The storm that came from God, and brought the loss
Of maiden face, what way it seized on me.
For nightly visions coming evermore
Into my virgin bower, sought to woo me
With glozing words. "O virgin greatly blest,
Why art thou still a virgin when thou might'st
Attain to highest wedlock? For with dart
Of passion for thee Zeus doth glow, and fain
Would make thee his. And thou, O child, spurn not
The bed of Zeus, but go to Lerna's field,   670
Where feed thy father's flocks and herds,
That so the eye of Zeus may find repose
From this his craving." With such visions **I**
Was haunted every evening, till I dared
To tell my father all these dreams of night,
And he to Pytho and Dodona sent
Full many to consult the Gods, that he
Might learn what deeds and words would please Heaven's
        lords.
And they came bringing speech of oracles
Shot with dark sayings, dim and hard to know.   680
At last a clear word came to Inachos
Charging him plainly, and commanding him
To thrust me from my country and my home,
To stray at large[1] to utmost bounds of earth;
And, should he gainsay, that the fiery bolt
Of Zeus should come and sweep away his race.
And he, by Loxias' oracles induced,

---

(1) **The words** used have an almost technical meaning as applied to
animals **that** were consecrated to the service of **a** God, and set free to
wander where they liked. The fate of Io, as at once devoted to Zeus and
animalised in form, was thus shadowed forth in the **very** language of the
Oracle.

Thrust me. against his will, against mine too,
And drove me from my home; but spite of all,
The curb of Zeus constrained him this to do.   690
And then forthwith my face and mind were changed;
And hornèd, as ye see me, stung to the quick
By biting gadfly, I with maddened leap
Rushed to Kerchneia's fair and limpid stream,
And fount of Lerna.[1] And a giant herdsman,
Argos, full rough of temper, followed me,
With many an eye beholding, on my track:
And him a sudden and unlooked-for doom
Deprived of life. And I, by gadfly stung,
By scourge from Heaven am driven from land to land.[700]
What has been done thou hearest. And if thou
Can'st tell what yet remains of woe, declare it;
Nor in thy pity soothe me with false words;
For hollow words, I deem, are worst of ills.
   Chor. Away, away, let be:
      Ne'er thought I that such tales
Would ever, ever come unto mine ears;
Nor that such terrors, woes, and outrages,
      Hard to look on, hard to bear,   710
Would chill my soul with sharp goad, double-edged.
      Ah fate! Ah fate!
I shudder, seeing Io's fortune strange.
   Prom. Thou art too quick in groaning, full of fear:
Wait thou a while until thou hear the rest.
   Chor. Speak thou and tell. Unto the sick 'tis sweet
Clearly to know what yet remains of pain.
   Prom. Your former wish ye gained full easily.
Your first desire was to learn of her   720
The tale she tells of her own sufferings;
Now therefore hear the woes that yet remain
For this poor maid to bear at Hera's hands.
And thou, O child of Inachos! take heed

---

(1) Lerna was a lake near the mouth of the Inachos, close to the sea.
Kerchneia may perhaps be identified with the Kenchreæ, the haven of
Korinth in later geographies.

To these my words, that thou may'st hear the goal
Of all thy wanderings. First then, turning hence
Towards the sunrise, tread the untilled plains,
And thou shalt reach the Skythian nomads, those[1]
Who on smooth-rolling waggons dwell aloft
In wicker houses, with far-darting bows
Duly equipped. Approach thou not to these,
But trending round the coasts on which the surf
Beats with loud murmurs,[2] traverse thou that clime.
On the left hand there dwell the Chalybes,[3]
Who work in iron. Of these do thou beware,
For fierce are they and most inhospitable ;
And thou wilt reach the river fierce and strong,
True to its name.[4] This seek not thou to cross,
For it is hard to ford, until thou come
To Caucasos itself, of all high hills
The highest, where a river pours its strength
From the high peaks themselves. And thou must cross
Those summits near the stars, must onward go
Towards the south, where thou shalt find the host
Of the Amâzons, hating men, whose home
Shall one day be around Thermôdon's bank,
By Themiskyra,[5] where the ravenous jaws
Of Salmydessos ope upon the sea,
Treacherous to sailors, stepdame stern to ships,[6]

(1) The wicker huts used by Skythian or Thrakian nomads (the Cal-mucks of modern geographers) are described by Herodotos (iv. 46) and are still in use.
(2) Sc., the N.E. boundary of the Euxine, where spurs of the Caucasos ridge approach the sea.
(3) The Chalybes are placed by geographers to the south of Colchis. The description of the text indicates a locality farther to the north.
(4) Probably the Araxes, which the Greeks would connect with a word conveying the idea of a torrent dashing on the rocks. The description seems to imply a river flowing into the Euxine from the Caucasos, and the condition is fulfilled by the Hypanis or Kouban.
(5) When the Amazons appear in contact with Greek history, they are found in Thrace. But they had come from the coast of Pontos, and near the mouth of the Thermôdon, (Thermeh.) The words of Prometheus point to yet earlier migrations from the East.
(6) Here, as in Soph. Antig. (970) the name Salmydessos represents the rockbound, havenless coast from the promontory of Thynias to the entrance of the Bosporos, which had given to the Black Sea its earlier name of Axenos, the "inhospitable."

And they with right good-will shall be thy guides;
And thou, hard by a broad pool's narrow gates,
Wilt pass to the Kimmerian isthmus. Leaving
This boldly, thou must cross Mæotic channel;[1]   750
And there shall be great fame 'mong mortal men
Of this thy journey, and the Bosporos[2]
Shall take its name from thee. And Europe's plain
Then quitting, thou shalt gain the Asian coast.
Doth not the all-ruling monarch of the Gods
Seem all ways cruel? For, although a God,
He, seeking to embrace this mortal maid,
Imposed these wanderings on her. Thou hast found,
O maiden! bitter suitor for thy hand;
For great as are the ills thou now hast heard,
Know that as yet not e'en the prelude's known.   760
  Io.   Ah woe! woe! woe!
  Prom. Again thou groan'st and criest. What wilt do
When thou shalt learn the evils yet to come?
  Chor. What! are there troubles still to come for her?
  Prom. Yea, stormy sea of woe most lamentable.
  Io. What gain is it to live? Why cast I not
Myself at once from this high precipice,
And, dashed to earth, be free from all my woes?
Far better were it once for all to die
Than all one's days to suffer pain and grief.   770
  Prom. My struggles then full hardly thou would'st
    bear,
For whom there is no destiny of death;
For that might bring a respite from my woes:
But now there is no limit to my pangs
Till Zeus be hurled out from his sovereignty.
  Io. What! shall Zeus e'er be hurled from his high
    state?

(1) The track is here in some confusion. From the Amazons south of
the Caucasos, Io is to find her way to the Tauric Chersonese (the Crimea)
and the Kimmerian Bosporos, which flows into the Sea of Azov, and so to
return to Asia.
(2) Here, as in a hundred other instances, a false etymology has become
the parent of a myth. The name Bosporos is probably Asiatic not Greek,
and has an entirely different signification.

Prom. Thou would'st rejoice, I trow, to see that fall.
Io. How should I not, when Zeus so foully wrongs me?
Prom. That this is so thou now may'st hear from me.
Io. Who then shall rob him of his sceptred sway?   780
Prom. Himself shall do it by his own rash plans.
Io. But how? Tell this, unless it bringeth harm.
Prom. He shall wed one for whom one day he'll grieve.
Io. Heaven-born or mortal? Tell, if tell thou may'st.
Prom. Why ask'st thou who? I may not tell thee that.
Io. Shall his bride hurl him from his throne of might?
Prom. Yea; she shall bear child mightier than his
        sire.
Io. Has he no way to turn aside that doom?
Prom. No, none; unless I from my bonds be loosed.[1]
Io. Who then shall loose thee 'gainst the will of
        Zeus?   790
Prom. It must be one of thy posterity.
Io. What, shall a child of mine free thee from ills?
Prom. Yea, the third generation after ten.[2]
Io. No more thine oracles are clear to me.
* *Prom.* Nay, seek not thou thine own drear fate to
        know.
Io. Do not, a boon presenting, then withdraw it.
Prom. Of two alternatives, I'll give thee choice.
Io. Tell me of what, then give me leave to choose.
Prom. I give it then.   Choose, or that I should tell
Thy woes to come, or who shall set me free.   800
Chor. Of these be willing one request to grant
To her, and one to me; nor scorn my words:
Tell her what yet of wanderings she must bear,
And me who shall release thee.   This I crave.
Prom. Since ye are eager, I will not refuse

---

(1) The lines refer to the story that Zeus loved Thetis the daughter of
Nereus, and followed her to Caucasos, but abstained from marriage with
her because Prometheus warned him that the child born of that union
should overthrow his father. Here the future is used of what was still
contingent only. In the lost play of the Trilogy the myth was possibly
brought to its conclusion and connected with the release of Prometheus.
(2) Heracles, whose genealogy was traced through Alcmena, Perseus,
Danaë, Danaos, and seven other names, to Epaphos and Io.

To utter fully all that ye desire.
Thee, Io, first I'll tell thy wanderings wild,
Thou, write it in the tablets of thy mind.
When thou shalt cross the straits, of continents
The boundary,[1] take thou the onward path
On to the fiery-hued and sun-tracked East.   810
[And first of all, to frozen Northern blasts
Thou'lt come, and there beware the rushing whirl,
Lest it should come upon thee suddenly,
And sweep thee onward with the cloud-rack wild;][2]
Crossing the sea-surf till thou come at last
Unto Kisthene's Gorgoneian plains,
Where dwell the grey-haired virgin Phorkides,[3]
Three, swan-shaped, with one eye between them all
And but one tooth; whom nor the sun beholds
With radiant beams, nor yet the moon by night:
And near them are their wingèd sisters three,
The Gorgons, serpent-tressed, and hating men,
Whom mortal wight may not behold and live.   820
* Such is one ill I bid thee guard against;
Now hear another monstrous sight: Beware
The sharp-beaked hounds of Zeus that never bark,[4]
The Gryphons, and the one-eyed, mounted host
Of Arimaspians, who around the stream
That flows o'er gold, the ford of Pluto, dwell:[5]

(1) Probably the Kimmerian Bosporos. The Tanais or Phasis has,
however, been conjectured.
(2) The history of the passage in brackets is curious enough to call for a
note. They are not in any extant, but they are found in a passage quoted
by Galen (v. p. 454,) as from the *Prometheus Bound*, and are inserted here
by Mr. Paley.
(3) Kisthene belongs to the geography of legend, lying somewhere on
the shore of the great ocean-river in Lybia or Ethiopia, at the end of the
world, a great mountain in the far West, beyond the Hesperides, the
dwelling-place, as here, of the Gorgons, the daughters of Phorkys.
Those first-named are the Graiæ.
(4) Here, like the "wingèd hound" of v. 1043, for the eagles that are
the messengers of Zeus.
(5) We are carried back again from the fabled West to the fabled East.
The Arimaspians, with one eye, and the Grypes or Gryphons, (the griffins
of mediæval heraldry,) quadrupeds with the wings and beaks of eagles,
were placed by most writers (Herod. iv. 13, 27) in the north of Europe,
in or beyond the *terra incognita* of Skythia. The mention of the "ford of
Pluto" and Æthiopia, however, may possibly imply (if we identify it, as

Draw not thou nigh to them.   But distant land
Thou shalt approach, the swarthy tribes who dwell
By the sun's fountain,[1] Æthiopia's stream :
By its banks wend thy way until thou come
To that great fall where from the Bybline hills
The Neilos pours its pure and holy flood ;
And it shall guide thee to Neilotic land,
Three-angled, where, O Io, 'tis decreed
For thee and for thy progeny to found
A far-off colony.   And if of this
Aught seem to thee as stammering speech obscure,
Ask yet again and learn it thoroughly :
Far more of leisure have I than I like.

    Chor. If thou hast aught to add, aught left untold
Of her sore-wasting wanderings, speak it out;   840
But if thou hast said all, then grant to us
The boon we asked.   Thou dost not, sure, forget it.

    Prom. The whole course of her journeying she hath
           heard,
And that she know she hath not heard in vain
I will tell out what troubles she hath borne
Before she came here, giving her sure proof
Of these my words.   The greater bulk of things
I will pass o'er, and to the very goal
Of all thy wanderings go.   For when thou cam'st
To the Molossian plains, and by the grove [2]
Of lofty-ridged Dodona, and the shrine
Oracular of Zeus Thesprotian,   850
And the strange portent of the talking oaks,

Mr. Paley does, with the Tartessos of Spain, or Bœtis—*Guadalquivir)*
that Æschylos followed another legend which placed them in the West.
There is possibly a *paronomasia* between Pluto, the God of Hades, and
Plutos, the ideal God of riches.

    (1) The name was applied by later writers (Quintus Curtius, iv 7, 22 ;
Lucretius, vi. 848) to the fountain in the temple of Jupiter Ammon in the
great Oasis. The "river Æthiops" may be purely imaginary, but it
may also suggest the possibility of some vague knowledge of the Niger,
or more probably of the Nile itself in the upper regions of its course.
The "Bybline hills" carry the name Byblos, which we only read of as
belonging to a town in the Delta, to the Second Cataract.

    (2) Comp, **Sophocles,** *Trachin,* v. 1168.

By which full clearly, not in riddle dark,
Thou wast addressed as noble spouse of Zeus,—
If aught of pleasure such things give to thee,—
Thence stung to frenzy, thou did'st rush along
The sea-coast's path to Rhea's mighty gulf,[1]
In backward way from whence thou now art vexed,
And for all time to come that reach of sea,
Know well, from thee Ionian shall be called,
To all men record of thy journeyings.   860
These then are tokens to thee that my mind
Sees somewhat more than that is manifest.
What follows (*to the Chorus*) I will speak to you and her
In common, on the track of former words
Returning once again. A city stands,
Canôbos, at its country's furthest bound,
Hard by the mouth and silt-bank of the Nile;
There Zeus shall give thee back thy mind again,[2]
With hand that works no terror touching thee,—
Touch only—and thou then shalt bear a child
Of Zeus begotten, Epaphos, "Touch-born,"   870
Swarthy of hue, whose lot shall be to reap
The whole plain watered by the broad-streamed Neilos:
And in the generation fifth from him
A household numbering fifty shall return
Against their will to Argos, in their flight
From wedlock with their cousins.[3] And they too,
(Kites but a little space behind the doves)
With eager hopes pursuing marriage rites
Beyond pursuit shall come; and God shall grudge
To give up their sweet bodies. And the land

(1) The Adriatic or Ionian Gulf.
(2) In the *Suppliants*, Zeus is said to have soothed her, and restored her
to her human consciousness by his "divine breathings." The thought
underlying the legend may be taken either as a distortion of some primitive tradition, or as one of the "unconscious prophecies" of heathenism.
The deliverer is not to be born after the common manner of men, and is
to have a divine as well as a human parentage.
(3) See the argument of the *Suppliants*, who, as the daughters of Danaos,
descended from Epaphos, are here referred to. The passage is noticeable
as showing that the theme of that tragedy was already present to the
poet's thoughts.

Pelasgian [1] shall receive them, when by stroke
Of woman's murderous hand these men shall lie
Smitten to death by daring deed of night :   880
For every bride shall take her husband's life,
And dip in blood the sharp two-edgèd sword
(So to my foes may Kypris show herself !) [2]
Yet one of that fair band shall love persuade
Her husband not to slaughter, and her will
Shall lose its edge; and she shall make her choice
Rather as weak than murderous to be known.
And she at Argos shall a royal seed
Bring forth (long speech 'twould take to tell this clear) 890
Famed for his arrows, who shall set me free [3]
From these my woes.   Such was the oracle
Mine ancient mother Themis, Titan-born,
Gave to me; but the manner and the means,—
That needs a lengthy tale to tell the whole,
And thou can'st nothing gain by learning it.

    Io. Eleleu ! Oh, Eleleu ! [4]
The throbbing pain inflames me, and the mood
       Of frenzy-smitten rage ;
       The gadfly's pointed sting,
       Not forged with fire, attacks,
And my heart beats against my breast with fear.   900
       Mine eyes whirl round and round :
       Out of my course I'm borne
By the wild spirit of fierce agony,
       And cannot curb my lips,
And turbid speech at random dashes on
Upon the waves of dread calamity.

---

(1) Argos. So in the *Suppliants,* **Pelasgos is the mythical king of the** Apian land who receives them.

(2) Hypermnæstra, who spared Lynceus, **and by him** became the mother of Abas and a line of Argive kings.

(3) Heracles, who came to Caucasos, and with his arrows slew the eagle that devoured Prometheus.

(4) The word is simply an interjection of pain, but one so characteristic that I have thought it better to reproduce it than to give any English equivalent.

STROPH. I.

Chor. Wise, very wise was he
Who first in thought conceived this maxim sage,
      And spread it with his speech,[1]—
That the best wedlock is with equals found,
And that a craftsman, born to work with hands,
      Should not desire to wed
Or with the soft luxurious heirs of wealth,
Or with the race that boast their lineage high.

ANTISTROPH. I.

Oh ne'er, oh ne'er, dread Fates,
May ye behold me as the bride of Zeus,
      The partner of his couch,
Nor may I wed with any heaven-born spouse!
For I shrink back, beholding Io's lot
      Of loveless maidenhood,
Consumed and smitten low exceedingly
By the wild wanderings from great Hera sent!

STROPH. II.

To me, when wedlock is on equal terms,
      It gives no cause to fear:
Ne'er may the love of any of the Gods,
      The strong Gods, look on me
      With glance I cannot 'scape!

ANTISTROPH. II.

That fate is war that none can war against,
      Source of resourceless ill;
Nor know I what might then become of me:
      I see not how to 'scape
      The counsel deep of Zeus.
Prom. Yea, of a truth shall Zeus, though stiff of will,
Be brought full low. Such bed of wedlock now
Is he preparing, one to cast him forth
In darkness from his sovereignty and throne.
And then the curse his father Cronos spake

(1) The maxim, "Marry with a woman thine equal," was ascribed to Pittacos.

Shall have its dread completion, even that
He uttered when he left his ancient throne;
And from these troubles no one of the Gods
But me can clearly show the way to 'scape.
I know the time and manner: therefore now
Let him sit fearless, in his peals on high
Putting his trust, and shaking in his hands
His darts fire-breathing.   Nought shall they avail
To hinder him from falling shamefully   930
A fall intolerable.   Such a combatant
He arms against himself, a marvel dread,
Who shall a fire discover mightier far
Than the red levin, and a sound more dread
Than roaring of the thunder, and shall shiver
That plague sea-born that causeth earth to quake,
The trident, weapon of Poseidon's strength:
And stumbling on this evil, he shall learn
How far apart a king's lot from a slave's.

> *Chor.* What thou dost wish thou mutterest against
> Zeus.
> *Prom.* Things that shall be, and things I wish, I
> speak.   950
> *Chor.* And must we look for one to master Zeus?
> *Prom.* Yea, troubles harder far than these are his.
> *Chor.* Art not afraid to vent such words as these?
> *Prom.* What can I fear whose fate is not to die?
> *Chor.* But He may send on thee worse pain than this.
> *Prom.* So let Him do: nought finds me unprepared.
> *Chor.* Wisdom is theirs who Adrasteia worship.[1]
> *Prom.* Worship then, praise and flatter him that
> rules;

My care for Zeus is nought, and less than nought:
Let Him act, let Him rule this little while,   960

---

(1) The Euhemerism of later scholiasts derived the name from a king
Adrastos, who was said to have been the first to build a temple to Nemesis,
and so the power thus worshipped was called after his name. A better
etymology leads us to see in it the idea of the "inevitable" law of retribution working unseen by men, and independently even of the arbitrary
will of the Gods, and bringing destruction upon the proud and haughty.

E'en as He will; for long He shall not rule
Over the Gods. But lo ! I see at hand
The courier of the Gods, the minister
Of our new sovereign. Doubtless he has come
To bring me tidings of some new device.

Enter HERMES.

Herm. **Thee do I** speak to,—thee, the teacher wise,
The bitterly o'er-bitter, who 'gainst Gods
Hast sinned in giving gifts to short-lived men—
I speak to thee, the filcher of bright fire.
The Father bids thee say what marriage thou
Dost vaunt, and who shall hurl Him from his might;
And this too not in dark mysterious speech,   970
But tell each point out clearly. **Give me not,**
Prometheus, task of double journey. **Zeus**
Thou seest, is not with such words appeased.

Prom. Stately of utterance, full of haughtiness
Thy speech, as fits a messenger of Gods.
Ye yet are young in your new rule, and think
To dwell in painless towers. Have **I** not
Seen **two** great rulers driven forth from **thence ?** [1]
And now the third, who reigneth, **I shall see**
In basest, quickest fall. Seem I to thee   980
To shrink and quail before these new-made Gods ?
Far, **very** far from that am **I.** But thou,
Track once again the path by which thou camest;
Thou shalt learn nought of what thou askest me.

Herm. It was by such self-will as this before
That thou did'st bring these sufferings on thyself.

Prom. I for my part, be sure, would never change
My evil state for that thy bondslave's lot.

Herm. To be the bondslave of this rock, **I trow,**
Is better than to be Zeus' trusty herald !   990

Prom. So it is meet the insulter to insult.

Herm. Thou waxest proud, 'twould seem, of this thy
        doom.

(1) Comp. *Agam.* 162-6.

Prom. Wax proud! God grant that I may see my foes
Thus waxing proud, and thee among the rest!
    Herm. Dost blame me then for thy calamities?
    Prom. In one short sentence—all the Gods I hate,
Who my good turns with evil turns repay.
    Herm. Thy words prove thee with no slight madness
        plagued.
    Prom. If to hate foes be madness, mad I am.
    Herm. Not one could bear thee wert thou pros-
        perous.   1000
    Prom. Ah me!
    Herm.   That word is all unknown to Zeus.
    Prom. Time waxing old can many a lesson teach.
    Herm. Yet thou at least hast not true wisdom learnt.
    Prom. I had not else addressed a slave like thee.
    Herm. Thou wilt say nought the Father asks, 'twould
        seem.
    Prom. Fine debt I owe him, favour to repay.
    Herm. Me as a boy thou scornest then, forsooth.
    Prom. And art thou not a boy, and sillier far,
If that thou thinkest to learn aught from me?
There is no torture nor device by which   1010
Zeus can impel me to disclose these things
Before these bonds that outrage me be loosed.
Let then the blazing levin-flash be hurled;
With white-winged snow-storm and with earth-born
    thunders
Let Him disturb and trouble all that is;
Nought of these things shall force me to declare
Whose hand shall drive him from his sovereignty.
    Herm. See if thou findest any help in this.
    Prom. Long since all this I've seen, and formed my
        plans.   1020
    Herm. O fool, take heart, take heart at last in time,
To form right thoughts for these thy present woes.
    Prom. Like one who soothes a wave, thy speech in vain
Vexes my soul. But deem not thou that I,
Fearing the will of Zeus, shall e'er become

As womanised in mind, or shall entreat
Him whom I greatly loathe, with upturned hand,
In woman's fashion, from these bonds of mine
To set me free. Far, far am I from that.

   Herm. It seems that I, saying much, shall speak in
       vain;
For thou in nought by prayers art pacified,
Or softened in thy heart, but like a colt   1030
Fresh harnessed, thou dost champ thy bit, and strive,
And fight against the reins. Yet thou art stiff
In weak device; for self-will, by itself,
In one who is not wise, is less than nought.
Look to it, if thou disobey my words,
How great a storm and triple wave of ills,[1]
Not to be 'scaped, shall come on thee; for first,
With thunder and the levin's blazing flash
The Father this ravine of rock shall crush,
And shall thy carcase hide, and stern embrace
Of stony arms shall keep thee in thy place.   1044
And having traversed space of time full long,
Thou shalt come back to light, and then his hound,
The wingèd hound of Zeus, the ravening eagle,
Shall greedily make banquet of thy flesh,
Coming all day an uninvited guest,
And glut himself upon thy liver dark.
And of that anguish look not for the end,
Before some God shall come to bear thy woes,
And will to pass to Hades' sunless realm,
And the dark cloudy depths of Tartaros.[2]   1050
Wherefore take heed. No feigned boast is this,

---

(1) **Either** a mere epithet of intensity, **as in** our "thrice blest," or
rising from the supposed fact that **every** third wave was larger and **more**
impetuous than the others, like the *fluctus decumanus* of the Latins, or
from the sequence of three great waves which some have noted **as a** common phenomenon in storms.

(2) Here again we have a strange shadowing forth of the mystery of
Atonement, and what we have learnt to call "vicarious" satisfaction.
In the later legend, Cheiron, suffering from the agony of his wounds, re-
signs his immortality, and submits to die in place of the ever-living death
to which Promethus was doomed.

K

But spoken all too truly; for the lips
Of Zeus know not to speak a lying speech,
But will perform each single word.   And thou,
Search well, be wise, nor think that self-willed pride
Shall ever better prove than counsel good.

   Chor. To us doth Hermes seem to utter words
Not out of season; for he bids thee quit
Thy self-willed pride and seek for counsel good.
Hearken thou to him.   To the wise of soul
It is foul shame to sin persistently.   1060

       Prom. To me who knew it all
      He hath this message borne;
      And that a foe from foes
      Should suffer is not strange.
      Therefore on me be hurled
      The sharp-edged wreath of fire;
      And let heaven's vault be stirred
      With thunder and the blasts
      Of fiercest winds; and Earth
      From its foundations strong,
      E'en to its deepest roots,
      Let storm-wind make to rock;
      And let the Ocean wave,
      With wild and foaming surge,
      Be heaped up to the paths   1070
      Where move the stars of heaven;
      And to dark Tartaros
      Let Him my carcase hurl,
      With mighty blasts of force:
      Yet me He shall not slay.

      Herm. Such words and thoughts from one
Brain-stricken one may hear.
What space divides his state
From frenzy?   What repose
Hath he from maddened rage?
But ye who pitying stand
And share his bitter griefs,   1080
Quickly from hence depart,

Lest the relentless roar
Of thunder stun your soul.
   Chor. With other words attempt
To counsel and persuade,
And I will hear: for now
Thou hast this word thrust in
That we may never bear.
How dost thou bid me train
My soul to baseness vile?
With him I will endure
Whatever is decreed.
Traitors I've learnt to hate,
Nor is there any plague   1090
That more than this I loathe.
   Herm. Nay then, remember ye
What now I say, nor blame
Your fortune: never say
That Zeus hath cast you down
To evil not foreseen.
Not so; ye cast yourselves:
For now with open eyes,
Not taken unawares,
In Atè's endless net
Ye shall entangled be
By folly of your own.   1100

   [*A pause, and then flashes of lightning and
     peals of thunder.*[1]

   Prom. Yea, now in very deed,
No more in word alone,
The earth shakes to and fro,
And the loud thunder's voice
Bellows hard by, and blaze

---

(1) It is noticeable that both Æschylos and Sophocles have left us tragedies which end in a thunderstorm as an element of effect. But the
contrast between the *Prometheus* and the *Œdipus at Colonos* as to the impression left in the one case of serene reconciliation, and in the other of
violent antagonism, is hardly less striking than the resemblance in the
outward phenomena, which are common to the two.

The flashing levin-fires;
And tempests whirl the dust,
And gusts of all wild winds
On one another leap,
In wild conflicting blasts,
And sky with sea is blent:
Such is the storm from Zeus   1110
That comes as **working fear,**
In terrors manifest.
O Mother venerable !
O Æther ! rolling round
The common light of all,
See'st thou what wrongs I **bear ?**

THE SUPPLIANTS

ARGUMENT.

When Io, after many wanderings, had found refuge in Egypt, and having been touched by Zeus, had given birth to Epaphos, it came to pass that he and his descendants ruled over the region of Canôpos, near one of the seven mouths of Neilos. And in the fifth generation there were two brothers, Danaos and Ægyptos, the sons of Belos, and the former had fifty daughters and the latter fifty sons, and Ægyptos sought the daughters of Danaos in marriage for his sons. And they, looking on the marriage as unholy, and hating those who wooed them, took flight and came to Argos, where Pelasgos then ruled as king, as to the land whence Io, from whom they sprang, had come. And thither the sons of Ægyptos followed them in hot pursuit.

Dramatis Personæ.

DANAOS.

PELASGOS, *king of* Argos.

Herald.

Chorus of the daughters of DANAOS.

THE SUPPLIANTS.

SCENE.—Argos, *the entrance of the gates. Statues of* ZEUS, ARTEMIS, *and other Gods, placed against the walls.*

[*Enter Chorus of the* Daughters of DANAOS,[1] *in the dress of Egyptian women, with the boughs of suppliants in their hands, and fillets of white wool twisted round them, chanting as they move in procession to take up their position round the thymele.*

> Zeus, the God of Suppliants, kindly
> Look on this our band of wanderers,
> That from banks at mouths of Neilos,
> Banks of finest sand, departed![2]
> Yea, we left the region sacred,
> Grassy plain on Syria's borders,[3]
> Not for guilt of blood to exile
> By our country's edict sentenced,
> But with free choice, loathing wedlock,
> Fleeing marriage-rites unholy
> With the children of Ægyptos.   10
> And our father Danaos, ruler,
> Chief of council, chief of squadrons,
> Playing moves on fortune's draught-board,[4]

(1) The daughters of Danaos are always represented as fifty in number. It seems probable, however, that the vocal chorus was limited to twelve, the others appearing as mutes.

(2) The alluvial deposit of the Delta.

(3) Syria is used obviously with a certain geographical vagueness, as including all that we know as Palestine, and the wilderness to the south of it, and so as conterminous with Egypt.

(4) Elsewhere in Æschylos (*Agam.* 33, *Fr.* 132) we trace allusion to games played with dice. Here we have a reference to one, the details of which

Chose what seemed the best of evils,
Through the salt sea-waves to hasten,
Steering to the land of Argos,
Whence our race has risen to greatness ;
Sprung, so boasts it, from the heifer
Whom the stinging gadfly harassed,
By the touch of Zeus love-breathing : [1]
And to what land more propitious
Could we come than this before us,
Holding in our hand the branches
Suppliant, wreathed with white wool fillets ?
O State ! O land ! O water gleaming !
Ye the high Gods, ye the awful,
In the dark the graves still guarding ;
Thou too with them, Zeus Preserver, [2]
Guardian of the just man's dwelling,
Welcome with the breath of pity,
Pity as from these shores wafted,
Us poor women who are suppliants.
And that swarm of men that follow,
Haughty offspring of Ægyptos,
Ere they set their foot among you
On this silt-strown shore, [3]—oh, send them
Seaward in their ship swift-rowing ;
There, with whirlwind tempest-driven,
There, with lightning and with thunder,
There, with blasts that bring the storm-rain,
May they in the fierce sea perish,
Ere they, cousin-brides possessing,
Rest on marriage-beds reluctant,
Which the voice of right denies them !

are not accurately known to us, but which seems to have been analogous
to draughts or chess.

(1) See the whole story, given as in prophecy, in the *Prometheus*, v. 865-880.

(2) The invocation is addressed —(1) to the Olympian Gods in the
brightness of heaven ; (2) to the Chthonian deities in the darkness below
the earth ; (3) to Zeus the Preserver, as the supreme Lord of both.

(3) An Athenian audience would probably recognise in this a description of the swampy meadows near the coast of Lerna. The descendants
of Io had come to the very spot where the tragic history of their ancestors
had had its origin.

Stroph. I.

And now I call on him, the Zeus-sprung steer,[1]   40
Our true protector, far beyond the sea,
Child of the heifer-foundress of our line,
    Who cropped the flowery mead,
Born of the breath, and named from touch of Zeus.
    *And lo! the destined time
    *Wrought fully with the name,
And she brought forth the "Touch-born," Epaphos.

Antistroph. I.

And now invoking him in grassy fields,   50
Where erst his mother strayed, to dwellers here
Telling the tale of all her woes of old,
    I surest pledge shall give;
And others, strange beyond all fancy's dream,
    Shall yet perchance be found;
    And in due course of time
Shall men know clearly all our history.

Stroph. II.

And if some augur of the land be near,
    Hearing our piteous cry,
    Sure he will deem he hears
    The voice of Tereus' bride,[2]
    Piteous and sad of soul,
The nightingale sore harassed by the kite.   60

Antistroph. II.

*For she, driven back from wonted haunts and streams,[3]
    Mourns with a strange new plaint
    The home that she has lost,
    And wails her son's sad doom,
    How he at her hand died,
Meeting with evil wrath unmotherly;

(1) The invocation passes on to Epaphos, as a guardian deity, able and willing to succour his afflicted children.
(2) Philomela. See the tale as given in the notes to *Agam.* 1113.
(3) "Streams," as flowing through the shady solitude of the groves which the nightingale frequented.

Stroph. III.

E'en so do I, to wailing all o'er-given,
In plaintive music of Ionian mood,[1]
*Vex the soft cheek on Neilos' banks that bloomed,
    And heart that bursts in tears,
And pluck the flowers of lamentations loud,
      Not without fear of friends,   70
        *Lest none should care to help
This flight of mine from that mist-shrouded shore.

Antistroph. III.

But, O ye Gods ancestral! hear my prayer,
Look well upon the justice of our cause,
Nor grant to youth to gain its full desire
    Against the laws of right,
But with prompt hate of lust, our marriage bless.
      *Even for those who come
      As fugitives in war
The altar serves as shield that Gods regard.

Stroph. IV.

    May God good issue give![2]   80
And yet the will of Zeus is hard to scan :
    Through all it brightly gleams,
E'en though in darkness and the gloom of chance
    For us poor mortals wrapt.

Antistroph. IV.

    Safe, by no fall tripped up,
The full-wrought deed decreed by brow of Zeus;
    For dark with shadows stretch
The pathways of the counsels of his heart,
    And difficult to see.

Stroph. V.

And from high-towering hopes He hurleth down   90
To utter doom the heir of mortal birth;

(1) "Ionian," as soft and elegiac, in contrast with the more military
character of Dorian music.
(2) In the Greek the *paronomasia* turns upon the supposed etymological
connexion between θεός and τίθημι. I have here, as elsewhere, attempted
an analogous rather than identical *jeu de mot*.

Yet sets He in array
No forces violent ;
All that Gods work is effortless and calm :
    Seated on holiest throne,
    Thence, though we know not how,
    He works His perfect will.

ANTISTROPH. V.

Ah, let him look on frail man's wanton pride,
With which the old stock burgeons out anew,
    By love for me constrained,
    In counsels ill and rash,   100
And in its frenzied, passionate resolve
    Finds goad it cannot shun ;
    But in deceivèd hopes,
    Shall know, too late, its woe.

STROPH. VI.

Such bitter griefs, lamenting, I recount,
    With cries shrill, tearful, deep,
      (Ah woe ! ah woe !)
That strike the ear with mourner's woe-fraught cry.
Though yet alive, I wail mine obsequies ;
    Thee, Apian sea-girt bluff,[1]
    I greet (our alien speech
    Thou knowest well, O land,)   110
And ofttimes fall, with rendings passionate,
On robe of linen and Sidonian veil.

ANTISTROPH. VI.

But to the Gods, for all things prospering well,
    When death is kept aloof,
    Gifts votive come of right.
    Ah woe ! Ah woe !
Oh, troubles dark, and hard to understand !

(1) The Greek word which I have translated "bluff" was one not
familiar to Attic ears, and was believed to be of Kyrenean origin.
Æschylos accordingly puts it into the lips of the daughters of Danaos, as
characteristic more or less of the "alien speech" of the land from which
they came.

Ah, whither will these waters carry me?
  Thee, Apian sea-girt bluff,   120
  I greet (our alien speech
  Thou knowest well, O land,)
And ofttimes fall, with rendings passionate,
On robe of linen and Sidonian veil.

Stroph. VII.

The oar indeed and dwelling, timber-wrought,
With sails of canvas, 'gainst the salt sea proof
    Brought me with favouring gales,
    By stormy wind unvexed;
Nor have I cause for murmur.   Issues good
May He, the all-seeing Father, grant, that, I,   130
    Great seed of Mother dread,
In time may 'scape, still maiden undefiled,
    My suitor's marriage-bed.

Antistroph. VII.

And with a will that meets my will may She,
The unstained child of Zeus, on me look down,
    *Our Artemis, who guards
    The consecrated walls;
And with all strength, though hunted down, uncaught,
May She, the Virgin, me a virgin free,   140
    Great seed of Mother dread,
That I may 'scape, still maiden undefiled,
    My suitor's marriage-bed.

Stroph. VIII.

    But if this may not be,
    We, of swarth sun-burnt race,
Will with our suppliant branches go to him,
    Zeus, sovereign of the dead,[1]
The Lord that welcomes all that come to him,
    Dying by twisted noose   150

(1) So in v. 235 Danaos speaks of the "second Zeus" who sit as Judge
in Hades. The feeling to which the Chorus gives utterance is that of—
    "Flectere si nequeo superos, Acheronta movebo."

If we the grace of Gods Olympian miss.
By thine ire, Zeus, 'gainst Io virulent,
 The Gods' wrath seeks us out,
 And I know well the woe
Comes from thy queen who reigns in heaven victorious;
 For after stormy wind
 The tempest needs must rage.

ANTISTROPH. VIII.

 And then shall Zeus to words
 Unseemly be exposed,
Having the heifer's offspring put to shame, 160
 Whom He himself begat,
And now his face averting from our prayers:
 Ah, may he hear on high,
Yea, pitying look and hear propitiously!
By thine ire, Zeus, 'gainst Io virulent,
 The Gods' wrath seeks us out,
 And I know well the woe
Comes from thy queen, who reigns in heaven victorious;
 For after stormy wind 170
 The tempest needs must rage,
 Danaos. My children, we need wisdom; lo! ye came
With me, your father wise and old and true,
As guardian of your voyage. Now ashore,
With forethought true I bid you keep my words,
As in a tablet-book recording them:
I see a dust, an army's voiceless herald,
Nor are the axles silent as they turn;
And I descry a host that bear the shield,
And those that hurl the javelin, marching on
With horses and with curvèd battle-cars.
Perchance they are the princes of this land, 180
Come on the watch, as having news of us;
But whether one in kindly mood, or hot
With anger fierce, leads on this great array,
It is, my children, best on all accounts
To take your stand hard by this hill of Gods

Who rule o'er conflicts.[1] Better far than towers
Are altars, yea, a shield impenetrable.
But with all speed approach the shrine of Zeus,
The God of mercy, in your left hand holding
The suppliants' boughs wool-wreathed, in solemn guise,[2]
And greet our hosts as it is meet for us,   190
Coming as strangers, with all duteous words
Kindly and holy, telling them your tale
Of this your flight, unstained by guilt of blood;
And with your speech, let mood not over-bold,
Nor vain nor wanton, shine from modest brow
And calm, clear eye. And be not prompt to speak,
Nor full of words; the race that dwelleth here
Of this is very jealous:[3] and be mindful
Much to concede; a fugitive thou art,
A stranger and in want, and 'tis not meet
That those in low estate high words should speak.

   Chor. My father, to the prudent prudently   200
Thou speakest, and my task shall be to keep
Thy goodly precepts. Zeus, our sire, look on us!
   Dan. Yea, may He look with favourable eye!
   Chor. I fain would take my seat not far from thee.
               [*Chorus moves to the altar not far from*
            DANAOS.
   Dan. Delay not then; success go with your plan.
   Chor. Zeus, pity us with sorrow all but crushed!
   Dan. If He be willing, all shall turn out well.
   Chor.   .   .   .
   Dan. Invoke ye now the mighty bird of Zeus.[4]

(1) Some mound dedicated to the Gods, with one or more altars and statues of the Gods on it, is on the stage, and the suppliants are told to take up their places there. The Gods of conflict who are named below, Zeus, Apollo, Poseidon, presided generally over the three great games of Greece. Hermes is added to the list.

(2) Comp. *Libation-Pourers*, 1024, *Eumen.* 44.

(3) The Argives are supposed to share the love of brevity which we commonly connect with their neighbours the Laconians.

(4) The "mighty bird of Zeus" seems here, from the answer of the Chorus, to mean not the "eagle" but the "sun," which roused men from their sleep as the cock did, so that "cock-crow" and "sunrise" were synonymous. It is, in any case, striking that Zeus, rather than Apollo, appears as the Sun-God.

Chor. We call the sun's bright rays to succour us.

Dan. Apollo too, the holy, in that He,   215

A God, has tasted exile from high heaven.[1]

Chor. Knowing that fate, He well may feel for men.

Dan. So may He feel, and look on us benignly !

Chor. Whom of the Gods shall I besides invoke ?

Dan. I see this trident here, a God's great symbol.[2]

Chor. Well hath He brought us, well may He receive !

Dan. Here too is Hermes,[3] as the Hellenes know him.

Chor. To us, as free, let Him good herald prove.

Dan. Yea, and the common shrine of all these Gods

Adore ye, and in holy precincts sit,

Like swarms of doves in fear of kites your kinsmen,   220

Foes of our blood, polluters of our race.

How can bird prey on bird and yet be pure ?

And how can he be pure who seeks in marriage

Unwilling bride from father too unwilling ?

Nay, not in Hades' self, shall he, vain fool,

Though dead, 'scape sentence, doing deeds like this ;

For there, as men relate, a second Zeus [4]

Judges men's evil deeds, and to the dead

Assigns their last great penalties. Look up,

And take your station here, that this your cause

May win its way to a victorious end.

Enter the KING *on his chariot, followed by* Attendants.

King. Whence comes this crowd, this non-Hellenic
       band,   230

In robes and raiment of barbaric fashion

So gorgeously attired, whom now we speak to ?

---

(1) The words refer to the myth of **Apollo's banishment from heaven** and servitude under Admetos.

(2) In the Acropolis at Athens the impress of a trident was seen on the rock, and was believed to commemorate the time when Poseidon had claimed it as his own by setting up his weapon there. Something of the same kind seems here to be supposed to exist at **Argos**, where a like legend prevailed.

(3) The Hellenic Hermes is distinguished from his Egyptian counterpart, Thoth, as being different in form and accessories.

(4) A possible reference to the Egyptian Osiris, as lord or judge of Hades. Comp. **v.** 145.

L

This woman's dress is not of Argive mode,
Nor from the climes of Hellas.   How ye dared,
Without a herald even or protector,
Yea, and devoid of guides too, to come hither
Thus boldly, is to me most wonderful.
And yet these boughs, as is the suppliant's wont,
Are set by you before the Gods of conflicts:
By this alone will Hellas guess aright.
Much more indeed we might have else conjectured,   240
Were there no voice to tell me on the spot.

   Chor. Not false this speech of thine about our garb:
But shall I greet thee as a citizen,
Or bearing Hermes' rod, or city ruling?[1]

   King. Nay, for that matter, answer thou and speak
Without alarm.   Palæchthon's son am I,
Earth-born, the king of this Pelasgic land;
And named from me, their king,[2] as well might be,
The race Pelasgic reaps our country's fruits;
*And all the land through which the Strymon pours   250
Its pure, clear waters to the West I rule;
And as the limits of my realm I mark
The land of the Perrhæbi, and the climes
Near the Pæonians, on the farther side
Of Pindos, and the Dodonæan heights;[3]
And the sea's waters form its bounds.   O'er all
Within these coasts I govern; and this plain,
The Apian land, itself has gained its name
Long since from one who as a healer lived;[4]
For Apis, coming from Naupactian land

(1) " Shall I," the Chorus asks, "speak to you as a private citizen, or
as a herald, or as a king?"
(2) It would appear from this that the king himself bore the name
Pelasgos.   In some versions of the story he is so designated.
(3) The lines contain a tradition of the wide extent of the old Pelasgic
rule, including Thessalia, or the Pelasgic Argos, between the mouths of
Peneus and Pindos, Perrhæbia, Dodona, and finally the Apian land or
Peloponnesos.
(4) The true meaning of the word "Apian," as applied to the Peloponnesos, seems to have been "distant."   Here the myth is followed
which represented it as connected with Apis the son of Telchin, (son of
Apollo, in the sense of being a physician-prophet,) who had freed the
land from monsters.

That lies beyond the straits, Apollo's son,
Prophet and healer, frees this land of ours   260
From man-destroying monsters, which the soil,
Polluted with the guilt of blood of old,
By anger of the Gods, brought forth,—fierce plagues,
The dragon-brood's dread, unblest company;
And Apis, having for this Argive land
Duly wrought out his saving surgery,
Gained his reward, remembered in our prayers;
And thou, this witness having at my hands,
May'st tell thy race at once, and further speak;
Yet lengthened speech our city loveth not.

   Chor. Full short and clear our tale. We boast that we
Are Argives in descent, the children true   270
Of the fair, fruitful heifer. And all this
Will I by what I speak show firm and true.

   King. Nay, strangers, what ye tell is past belief
For me to hear, that ye from Argos spring;
For ye to Libyan women are most like,[1]
And nowise to our native maidens here.
Such race might Neilos breed, and Kyprian mould,
Like yours, is stamped by skilled artificers
On women's features; and I hear that those   280
Of India travel upon camels borne,
Swift as the horse, yet trained as sumpter-mules,
E'en those who as the Æthiops' neighbours dwell.
And had ye borne the bow, I should have guessed,
Undoubting, ye were of th' Amâzon's tribe,
Man-hating, flesh-devouring. Taught by you,
I might the better know how this can be,
That your descent and birth from Argos come.

   Chor. They tell of one who bore the temple-keys
Of Hera, Io, in this Argive land.

   King. So was't indeed, and wide the fame prevails:
And was it said that **Zeus a mortal loved?**   290

(1) The description would seem to indicate—(1) that the daughter of
Danaos appeared on the stage as of swarthy complexion; and (2) that
Indians, Æthiopians, Kyprians, and Amazons, were all thought of as in
this respect alike.

Chor. And that embrace was not from Hera hid.
King. What end had then these strifes of sovereign Ones?
Chor. The Argive goddess made the maid a heifer.
King. Did Zeus that fair-horned heifer still approach?
Chor. So say they, fashioned like a wooing steer.
King. How acted then the mighty spouse of Zeus?
Chor. She o'er the heifer set a guard all-seeing.
King. What herdsman strange, all-seeing, speak'st
   thou of?
Chor. Argos, the earth-born, him whom Hermes
   slew.   300
King. What else then wrought she on the ill-starred
   heifer?
Chor. She sent a stinging gadfly to torment her.
 [Those who near Neilos dwell an *œstros* call it.]
King. Did she then drive her from her country far?
Chor. All that thou say'st agrees well with our tale.
King. And did she to Canôbos go, and Memphis?
Chor. Zeus with his touch, an offspring then begets.
King. What Zeus-born calf that heifer claims as
   mother?
Chor. *He from that touch which freed named Epa-
   phos.   310
King, [*What offspring then did Epaphos beget?*][1]
Chor. Libya, that gains her fame from greatest land
King. What other offspring, born of her, dost tell of?
Chor. Sire of my sire here, Belos, with two sons.
King. Tell me then now the name of yonder sage.
Chor. Danaos, whose brother boasts of fifty sons.
King. Tell me his name, too, with ungrudging speech.
Chor. Ægyptos: knowing now our ancient stock,
Take heed thou bid thine Argive suppliants rise.
 King. Ye seem, indeed, to make your ancient claim
To this our country good: but how came ye   320
To leave your father's house? What chance constrained
   you?

(1) The line is conjectural, but some question of this kind is implied in
the answer of the Chorus.

Chor. O king of the Pelasgi, manifold
Are ills of mortals, and thou could'st not find
The self-same form of evil anywhere.
Who would have said that this unlooked-for flight
Would bring to Argos race once native here,
Driving them forth in hate of wedlock's couch?
King. What seek'st thou then of these the Gods of
      conflicts,
Holding your wool-wreathed branches newly-plucked?
Chor. That I serve not Ægyptos' sons as slave.
King. Speak'st thou of some old feud, or breach of
      right?   330
Chor. Nay, who'd find fault with master that one
      loved?
King. Yet thus it is that mortals grow in strength.[1]
Chor. True; when men fail, 'tis easy to desert them.
King. How then to you may I act reverently?
Chor. Yield us not up unto Ægyptos' sons.
King. Hard boon thou ask'st, to wage so strange a war.
Chor. Nay, Justice champions those who fight with her.
King. Yes, if her hand was in it from the first.
Chor. Yet reverence thou the state-ship's stern thus
      wreathed,[2]
King. I tremble as I see these seats thus shadowed.   340

STROPH. I.

Chor. Dread is the wrath of Zeus, the God of sup-
      pliants:
      Son of Palæchthon, hear;
Hear, O Pelasgic king, with kindly heart.
Behold me suppliant, exile, wanderer,
      *Like heifer chased by wolves
      Upon the lofty crags,
      Where, trusting in her strength,

(1) By sacrificing personal likings to schemes of ambition, men and
women contract marriages which increase their power.
(2) The Gods of conflict are the pilots of the ship of the State. The
altar dedicated to them is as its stern; the garlands and wands of suppliants which adorn it are as the decorations of the vessels.

She lifteth up her voice
And to the shepherd tells her tale of grief.
    King. I see, o'ershadowed with the new - plucked
        boughs,
*Bent low, a band these Gods of conflict own ;
And may our dealings with these home-sprung stran-
    gers
Be without peril, nor let strife arise   350
To this our country for unlooked-for chance
And unprovided !   This our State wants not.

ANTISTROPH. I.

    Chor. Yea, may that Law that guards the suppliant's
        right
        Free this our flight from harm,
Law, sprung from Zeus, supreme Apportioner,
But thou, [*to the King,*] though old, from me, though
        younger, learn:
        If thou a suppliant pity
        Thou ne'er shalt penury know,
        So long as Gods receive
        Within their sacred shrines
Gifts at the hands of worshipper unstained.
    King. It is not at my hearth ye suppliant sit ;
But if the State be as a whole defiled,   360
Be it the people's task to work the cure.
I cannot pledge my promise to you first
Ere I have counselled with my citizens.[1]

STROPH. II.

    Chor. Thou art the State—yea, thou the common-
        wealth,
        Chief lord whom none may judge;
'Tis thine to rule the country's altar-hearth,

---

(1) Some editors have seen in this an attempt to enlist the constitutional sympathies of an Athenian audience in favour of the Argive king,
who will not act without consulting his assembly. There seems more
reason to think that the aim of the dramatist was in precisely the opposite direction, and that the words which follow set forth his admiration
for the king who can act, as compared with one who is tied and hampered
by restrictions.

With the sole vote of thy prevailing nod ;
     And thou on throne of state,
     Sole-sceptred in thy sway,
Bringest each matter to its destined end ;
     Shun thou the curse of guilt.
  King. Upon my foes rest that dread curse of guilt!   370
Yet without harm I cannot succour you,
Nor gives it pleasure to reject your prayers.
In a sore strait am I ; fear fills my soul
To take the chance, to do or not to do.

ANTISTROPH. II.

  Chor. Look thou on Him who looks on all from heaven,
     Guardian of suffering men
Who, worn with toil, unto their neighbours come
As suppliants, and receive not justice due :
     For these the wrath of Zeus,
     Zeus, the true suppliant's God,
Abides, by wail of sufferer unappeased.   380
  King. Yet if Ægyptos' sons have claim on thee
By their State's law, asserting that they come
As next of kin, who dare oppose their right ?
Thou must needs plead that by thy laws at home
They over thee have no authority.[1]

STROPH. III.

  Chor. Ah ! may I ne'er be captive to the might
     Of males ! Where'er the stars
Are seen in heaven, I track my way in flight,
As refuge from a marriage that I hate.
     But thou, make Right thy friend,
And honour what the Gods count pure and true,   390

---

(1) By an Attic law, analogous in principle to that of the Jews, (Num. xxxvi. 8; 1 Chron. xxiii. 22), heiresses were absolutely bound to marry their next of kin, if he claimed his right. The king at once asserts this as the law which was *prima facie* applicable to the case, and declares himself ready to surrender it if the petitioners can show that their own municipal law is on the other side. He will not thrust his country's customs upon foreigners, who can prove that they live under a different rule, but in the absence of evidence must act on the law which he is bound officially to recognise.

King. Hard is the judgment: choose not me as judge.
But, as I said before, I may not act
Without the people, sovereign though I be,
Lest the crowd say, should aught fall out amiss,
"In honouring strangers, thou the State did'st ruin."

ANTISTROPH. III.

Chor. Zeus, the great God of kindred, in these things
    Watches o'er both of us,
Holding an equal scale, and fitly giving
To the base evil, to the righteous blessing.
    Why, when these things are set
In even balance, fear'st thou to do right?   400
King. Deep thought we need that brings deliverance,
That, like a diver, mine eye too may plunge
Clear-seeing to the depths, not wine-bedrenched,
That these things may be harmless to the State,
And to ourselves may issue favourably:
That neither may the strife make you its prey,
Nor that we give you up, who thus are set
Near holy seat of Gods, and so bring in
To dwell with us the Avenger terrible,
God that destroyeth, who not e'en in Hades   510
Gives freedom to the dead.   Say, think ye not
That there is need of counsel strong to save?

STROPH. I.

Chor. Take heed to it, and be
Friend to the stranger wholly faithful found;
    Desert not thou the poor,
Driven from afar by godless violence.

ANTI TROPH. I.

    See me not dragged away,
O thou that rul'st the land! from seat of Gods:
    Know thou men's wanton pride,   420
And guard thyself against the wrath of Zeus.

STROPH. II.

Endure not thou to see thy suppliant,
    Despite of law, torn off,

As horses by their frontlets, from the forms
    Of sculptured deities,
Nor yet the outrage of their wanton hands,
    Seizing these broidered robes.

ANTISTROPH. II.

For know thou well, whichever course thou take,
    Thy sons and all thy house
*Must pay in war the debt that Justice claims,
    Proportionate in kind.   430
Lay well to heart these edicts, wise and true,
    Given by great Zeus himself.
   King. Well then have I thought o'er it. To this point
Our ship's course drives. Fierce war we needs must risk
Either with these (*pointing to the Gods*) or those. Set fast
    and firm
Is this as is the ship tight wedged in stocks;
And without trouble there's no issue out.
For wealth indeed, were our homes spoiled of that,
There might come other, thanks to Zeus the Giver,
More than the loss, and filling up the freight;   440
And if the tongue should aim its adverse darts,
Baleful and over-stimulant of wrath,
There might be words those words to heal and soothe.
But how to blot the guilt of kindred blood,
This needs a great atonement—many victims
Falling to many Gods—to heal the woe.
*I take my part, and turn aside from strife;
And I far rather would be ignorant
Than wise, forecasting evil. May the end,
Against my judgment, show itself as good!
   Chor. Hear, then, the last of all our pleas for pity.
   King. I hear; speak on. It shall not 'scape my
    heed.   450
   Chor. Girdles I have, and zones that bind my robes.
   King. Such things are fitting for a woman's state.
   Chor. With these then, know, as good and rare de-
    vice . . . .

King. Nay, speak. What word is this thou'lt utter
    now ?

Chor. Unless thou giv'st our band thy plighted
    word . . . .

King. What wilt thou do with this device of girdles ?

Chor. With tablets new these sculptures we'll adorn.

King. Thou speak'st a riddle. Make thy meaning plain.

Chor. Upon these Gods we'll hang ourselves at once.

King. I hear a word which pierces to the heart.   460

Chor. Thou see'st our meaning. Eyes full clear I've
    given.

King. Lo then! in many ways sore troubles come.
A host of evils rushes like a flood ;
A sea of woe none traverse, fathomless,
This have I entered ; haven there is none.
For if I fail to do this work for you,
Thou tellest of defilement unsurpassed ; [1]
And if for thee against Ægyptos' sons,
Thy kindred, I before my city's walls
In conflict stand, how can there fail to be
A bitter loss, to stain the earth with blood   470
Of man for woman's sake ? And yet I needs
Must fear the wrath of Zeus, the suppliant's God ;
That dread is mightiest with the sons of men.
Thou, then, O aged father of these maidens !
Taking forthwith these branches in thine arms,
Lay them on other altars of the Gods
Our country worships, that the citizens
May all behold this token of thy coming,
And about me let no rash speech be dropped ;
For 'tis a people prompt to blame their rulers.
And then perchance some one beholding them,   480
And pitying, may wax wrathful 'gainst the outrage
Of that male troop, and with more kindly will
The people look on you ; for evermore
Men all wish well unto the weaker side.

(1) *Sc.,* the pollution which the statues of the Gods would contract if
they carried into execution their threat of suicide.

Dan. This boon is counted by us of great price,
To find a patron proved so merciful.
And thou, send with us guides to lead us on,
And tell us how before their shrines to find
The altars of the Gods that guard the State,
*And holy places columned round about;
And safety for us, as the town we traverse.
Not of like fashion is our features' stamp; 490
For Neilos rears not race like Inachos.[1]
Take heed lest rashness lead to bloodshed here;
Ere now, unknowing, men have slain their friends.
 King (*to Attendants*). Go then, my men; full well the
   stranger speaks;
And lead him where the city's altars stand,
The seats of Gods; and see ye talk not not much
To passers-by as ye this traveller lead,
A suppliant at the altar-hearth of Gods.
     [*Exeunt* DANAOS *and Attendants.*
 Chor. Thou speak'st to him; and may he go as bidden!
But what shall I do? What hope giv'st thou me?
 King. Leave here those boughs, the token of your
   grief. 500
 Chor. Lo! here I leave them at thy beck and word.
 King. Now turn thy steps towards this open lawn.
 Chor. What shelter gives a lawn unconsecrate?[2]
 King. We will not yield thee up to birds of prey.
 Chor. Nay, but to foes far worse than fiercest dragons.
 King. Good words should come from those who good
   have heard.
 Chor. No wonder they wax hot whom fear enthrals.
 King. But dread is still for rulers all unmeet.
 Chor. Do thou then cheer our soul by words and deeds.
 King. Nay, no long time thy sire will leave thee
   lorn; 510

(1) Inachos, the river-God of Argos, and as such contrasted with
Neilos.
(2) *i.e.*, "Unconsecrate," marked out by no barriers, accessible to all,
and therefore seeming to offer but little prospect of a safe asylum. The
place described seems to have been an open piece of turf rather than a
grove of trees.

And I, all people of the land convening,
Will the great mass persuade to kindly words;
And I will teach thy father what to say.
Wherefore remain and ask our country's Gods,
With suppliant prayers, to grant thy soul's desire,
And I will go in furtherance of thy wish:
Sweet Suasion follow us, and Fortune good!   [*Exit.*

Stroph. I.

Chor. O King of kings! and blest
    Above all blessed ones,
And Power most mighty of the mightiest!
    O Zeus, of high estate!   520
    Hear thou and grant our prayer!
Drive thou far off the wantonness of men,
    The pride thou hatest sore,
And in the pool of darkling purple hue
Plunge thou the woe that comes in swarthy barque.

Antistroph. I.

    Look on the women's cause;
    Recall the ancient tale,
Of one whom Thou did'st love in time of old,
    The mother of our race:
    Remember it, O Thou
Who did'st on Io lay thy mystic touch.
    We boast that we are come
Of consecrated land the habitants,   530
And from this land by lineage high descended.

Stroph. II.

    Now to the ancient track,
    Our mother's, I have passed,
The flowery meadow-land where she was watched,—
    The pastures of the herd,
Whence Io, by the stinging gadfly driven,
    Flees, of her sense bereft,
Passing through many tribes of mortal men;
    And then by Fate's decree

> Crossing the billowy straits,
> On either side she leaves a continent.[1]

540

ANTISTROPH. II.

> Now through the Asian land
> She hastens o'er and o'er,
> Right through the Phrygian fields where feed the flocks;
> And passes Teuthras' fort,
> Owned by the Mysians,[2] and the Lydian plains;
> And o'er Kilikian hills,
> And those of far Pamphylia rushing on,
> By ever-flowing streams,
> On to the deep, rich lands,
> And Aphrodite's home in wheat o'erflowing.[3]

STROPH. III.

> And so she cometh, as that herdsman winged
> Pierces with sharpest sting,
> To holy plain all forms of life sustaining,
> Fields that are fed from snows,[4]
> Which Typhon's monstrous strength has traversèd,[5]
> And unto Neilos' streams,
> By sickly taint untouched,[6]
> Still maddened with her toil of ignominy,
> By torturing stings driven on, great Hera's frenzied slave.

550

ANTISTROPH. III.

> And those who then the lands inhabited,
> Quivered with pallid fear,

560

(1) Comp. the narrative as given in *Prometheus Bound*, vv. 660, *et seq.*
(2) Teuthras' fort, or Teuthrania, is described by Strabo (xii. p. 571) as lying between the Hellespont and Mount Sipylos, in Magnesia.
(3) Kypros, as dedicated to the worship of Aphrodite, and famous for its wine, and oil, and corn,
(4) The question, what caused the mysterious exceptional inundations of the Nile, occupied, as we see from Herodotos (ii. c. 19-27), the minds of the Greeks. Of the four theories which the historian discusses, Æschylos adopts that which referred it to the melting of the snows on the mountains of central Africa.
(5) Typhon, the mythical embodiment of the power of evil, was fabled to have wandered over Egypt, seeking the body of Osiris. Isis, to baffle him, placed coffins in all parts of Egypt, all empty but the one which contained the body.
(6) The fame of the Nile for the purity of its water, after the earthly matter held in solution had been deposited, seems to have been as great in the earliest periods of its history as it is now.

That filled their soul at that unwonted marvel,
 Seeing that monstrous shape,
 The human joined with brute,
Half heifer, and half form of woman fair : [1]
 And sore amazed were they.
 Who was it then that soothed
Poor Io, wandering in her sore affright,
Driven on, and ever on, by gadfly's maddening sting?

STROPH. IV.

 Zeus, Lord of endless time
 [Was seen All-working then;]
He, even He, for by his sovereign might
That works no ill, was she from evil freed;   570
 And by his breath divine
She findeth rest, and weeps in floods of tears
 Her sorrowing shame away;
 And with new burden big,
 Not falsely 'Zeus-born' named,
She bare a son that grew in faultless growth,

ANTISTROPH. IV.

 Prosperous through long, long years;
And so the whole land shouts with one accord,
" Lo, a race sprung from him, the Lord of life,
 In very deed, Zeus-born!   580
Who else had checked the plagues that Hera sent?"
 This is the work of Zeus:
 And speaking of our race
 That sprang from Epaphos
As such, thou would'st not fail to hit the mark.

STROPH. V.

Which of the Gods could I with right invoke
 As doing juster deeds?
He is our Father, author of our life,

---

(1) Io was represented as a woman with a heifer's head, and was probably a symbolic representation of the moon, with her crescent horns.
Sometimes the transformation is described (as in v. 294) in words which
imply a more thorough change.

The King whose right hand worketh all his will,
Our line's great author, in his counsels deep
    Recording things of old,
Directing all his plans, the great work-master, Zeus.

ANTISTROPH. V.

For not as subject hastening at the beck
    Of strength above his own,[1]
Reigns He subordinate to mightier powers;
Nor does He pay his homage from below,
While One sits throned in majesty above;[2]
    Act is for him as speech,
To hasten what his teeming mind resolves.

Re-enter DANAOS.

Dan. Be of good cheer, my children.   All goes well
With those who dwell here, and the people's voice
Hath passed decrees full, firm, irrevocable.
  Chor. Hail, aged sire, that tell'st me right good news!
But say with what intent the vote hath passed,
And on which side the people's hands prevail.
  Dan. The Argives have decreed without division,
So that my aged mind grew young again;
For in full congress, with their right hands raised
Rustled the air as they decreed their vote
That we should sojourn in their land as free,
Free from arrest, and with asylum rights;
And that no native here nor foreigner
Should lead us off; and, should he venture force,
That every citizen who gave not help
Dishonoured should be driven to exile forth.
Such counsel giving, the Pelasgian King
Gained their consent, proclaiming that great wrath

---

(1) Perhaps—
        " For not as subject sitting 'neath the sway
          Of strength above his own."
  (2) The passage takes its place among the noblest utterances of a faith
passing above the popular polytheism to the thought of one sovereign
Will ruling and guiding all things, as Will,—without effort, in the calmness of a power irresistible.

Of Zeus the God of suppliants ne'er would let
The city wax in fatness,—warning them
That double guilt[1] upon the State would come,
Touching at once both guests and citizens,
The food and sustenance of sore disease
That none could heal.   And then the Argive host,
Hearing these things, decreed by show of hands,
Not waiting for the herald's proclamation,
So it should be.   They heard, indeed, the crowd
Of those Pelasgi, all the winning speech,
The well-turned phrases cunning to persuade;
But it was Zeus that brought the end to pass.

  Chor. Come then, come, let us speak for Argives
    Prayers that are good for good deeds done; 620
    Zeus, who o'er all strangers watches,
    May He regard with his praise and favour
    The praise that comes from the lips of strangers,
    *And guide in all to a faultless issue.

STROPH. I.

Half-Chor. A. Now, now, at last, ye Gods of Zeus
    begotten,[2]
Hear, as I pour my prayers upon their race,
That ne'er may this Pelasgic city raise
From out its flames the joyless cry of War,
    War, that in other fields
    Reapeth his human crop:
    For they have mercy shown,
    And passed their kind decree, 630
Pitying this piteous flock, the suppliants of great Zeus.

ANTISTROPH. I.

They did not take their stand with men 'gainst women
Casting dishonour on their plea for help,

---

(1) Double, as involving a sin against the laws of hospitality, so far as
the suppliants were strangers—a sin against the laws of kindred, so far as
they might claim by descent the rights of citizenship.

(2) If, as has been conjectured, the tragedy was written with a view to
the alliance between Argos and Athens, made in B.C. 461, this choral ode
must have been the centre, if not of the dramatic, at all events of the
political interest of the play

*But looked to Him who sees and works from heaven,
*Full hard to war with.   Yea, what house could bear
      To see Him on its roof
      Casting pollution there? [1]
      Sore vexing there he sits.
      Yes, they their kin revere,
      Suppliants of holiest Zeus ;   640
Therefore with altars pure shall they the Gods delight.

STROPH. II.

Therefore from faces by our boughs o'ershadowed [2]
Let prayers ascend in emulous eagerness:
      Ne'er may dark pestilence
      This State of men bereave ;
      May no fierce party-strife
Pollute these plains with native carcases ;
      And may the bloom of youth
      Be with them still uncropt ;
And ne'er may Aphrodite's paramour,   650
      Ares the scourge of men,
      Mow down their blossoms fair !

ANTISTROPH. II.

And let the altars tended by the old
*Blaze with the gifts of men with hoary hairs ;
      So may the State live on
      In full prosperity !
      Let them great Zeus adore,
The strangers' God, the one Supreme on high,
      By venerable law
      Ordering the course of fate.
And next we pray that ever more and more
      Earth may her tribute bear,
And Artemis as Hecate preside [3]
      O'er woman's travail-pangs.   660

   (1) The image is that of a bird of evil omen, perched upon the roof, and
defiling the house, while it uttered its boding cries.
   (2) The suppliants' boughs, so held as to shade the face from view.
   (3) The name of Hecate connected Artemis as, on the one side, with
the unseen world of Hades, so, on the other, with child-birth, and the
purifications that followed on it.

STROPH. III.

Let no destroying strife come on, invading
    This city to lay waste,
    Setting in fierce array
    War, with its fruit of tears,
    Lyreless and danceless all,
    And cry of people's wrath;
    And may the swarm of plagues,
    Loathly and foul to see,
Abide far off from these our citizens,
And that Lykeian king, may He be found
    Benignant to our youth ![1]

ANTISTROPH. III.

And Zeus, may He, by his supreme decree,   670
    Make the earth yield her fruits
    Through all the seasons round,
    And grant a plenteous brood
    Of herds that roam the fields!
    May Heaven all good gifts pour,
    And may the voice of song
    Ascend o'er altar shrines,
    Unmarred by sounds of ill!
And let the voice that loves with lyre to blend
Go forth from lips of blameless holiness,
    In accents of great joy!

STROPH. IV.

*And may the rule in which the people share
Keep the State's functions as in perfect peace,
    E'en that which sways the crowd,
    *Which sways the commonwealth,   680
    By counsels wise and good;
And to the strangers and the sojourners
May they grant rights that rest on compacts sure,

(1) The name Lykeian, originally, perhaps, simply representing Apollo as the God of Light, came afterwards to be associated with the might of destruction (the Wolf-destroyer) and the darts of pestilence and sudden death. The prayer is therefore that he, the Destroyer, may hearken to the suppliants, and spare the people for whom they pray.

Ere War is roused to arms,
So that no trouble come !

ANTISTROPH. IV.

And the great Gods who o'er this country watch,
May they adore them in the land They guard,
    With rites of sacrifice,
    And troops with laurel boughs,
    As did our sires of old !
For thus to honour those who gave us life,
This stands as one of three great laws on high,[1]
    Written as fixed and firm,
    The laws of Right revered.

Dan. I praise these seemly prayers, dear children
    mine.   690
But fear ye not, if I your father speak
Words that are new, and all unlooked-for by you ;
For from this station to the suppliant given
I see the ship ; too clear to be mistaken
The swelling sails, the bulwark's coverings,
And prow with eyes that scan the onward way,[2]
But too obedient to the steerman's helm,
Being, as it is, unfriendly. And the men
Who sail in her with swarthy limbs are seen,
In raiment white conspicuous. And I see   700
Full clear the other ships that come to help ;
And this as leader, putting in to shore,
Furling its sails, is rowed with equal stroke.
'Tis yours, with mood of calm and steadfast soul,
To face the fact, and not to slight the Gods.
And I will come with friends and advocates ;
For herald, it may be, or embassy,
May come, and wish to seize and bear you off,
Grasping their prey. But nought of this shall be ;

(1) The "three great laws" were those ascribed to Triptolemos, "to
honour parents, to worship the Gods with the fruits of the earth, to hurt
neither man nor beast."
(2) The Egyptian ships, like those of many other Eastern countries,
had eyes (the eyes of Osiris, as they were called) painted on their bows.

Fear ye not them.   It were well done, however,
If we should linger in our help, this succour   716
In no wise to forget.   Take courage then ;
In their own time and at the appointed day,
Whoever slights the Gods shall pay for it.

Stroph. I.

Chor. I fear, my father, since the swift-winged ships
Are come, and very short the time that's left.
A shuddering anguish makes me sore afraid,
Lest small the profit of my wandering flight.
        I faint, my sire, for fear.
Dan. My children, since the Argives' vote is passed,
Take courage : they will fight for thee, I know.   726

Antistroph. I.

Chor. Hateful and wanton are Ægyptos' sons,
Insatiable of conflict, and I speak
To one who knows them.   They in timbered ships,
Dark-eyed, have sailed in wrath that hits its mark,
        With great and swarthy host.
Dan. Yet many they shall find whose arms are tanned
In the full scorching of the noontide heat.[1]

Stroph. II.

Chor. Leave me not here alone, I pray thee, father !
Alone, a woman is as nought, and war
Is not for her.   Of over-subtle mind,
And subtle counsel in their souls impure,   736
Like ravens, e'en for altars caring not,—
        Such, such in soul are they.
Dan. That would work well indeed for us, my children
Should they be foes to Gods as unto thee.

Antistroph. II.

Chor. No reverence for these tridents or the shrine
Of Gods, my father, will restrain their hands :

(1) A side-thrust, directed by the poet, who had fought at Marathon,
against the growing effeminacy of the Athenian youth, many of whom
were learning to shrink from all activity and exposure that might spoil
their complexions. Comp. Plato, *Phædros*, p. 239.

Full stout of heart, of godless mood unblest,
Fed to the full, and petulant as dogs,
And for the voice of high Gods caring not,—
    Such, such in soul are they.
  Dan. Nay, the tale runs that wolves prevail o'er dogs; 740
And byblos fruit excels not ear of corn.[1]
  Chor. But since their minds are as the minds of brutes,
Restless and vain, we must beware of force.
  Dan. Not rapid is the getting under weigh
Of naval squadron, nor their anchoring,
Nor the safe putting into shore with cables.
Nor have the shepherds of swift ships quick trust
In anchor-fastenings, most of all, as now,
When coming to a country havenless;
And when the sun has yielded to the night,
That night brings travail to a pilot wise,   750
[Though it be calm and all the waves sleep still;]
So neither can this army disembark
Before the ship is safe in anchorage.
And thou beware lest in thy panic fear
Thou slight the Gods whom thou hast called to help.
The city will not blame your messenger,
Old though he be, being young in clear voiced-thought.
                       Exit.

STROPH. I.

  Chor. Ah, me! thou land of jutting promontory
    Which justly all revere,
What lies before us? Where in Apian land
    Shall we a refuge find,
If still there be dark hiding anywhere?
    Ah! that I were as smoke

---

(1) The saying is somewhat dark, but the meaning seems to be that if
the "dogs" of Egypt are strong, the "wolves" of Argos are stronger;
that the wheat on which the Hellenes lived gave greater strength to limbs
and sinew than the "byblos fruit" on which the Egyptian soldiers and
sailors habitually lived. Some writers, however, have seen in the last
line, rendered—
       "The byblos fruit not always bears full ear,"
a proverb like the English,
        "There's many a slip
        'Twixt the cup and the lip."

That riseth full and black
Nigh to the clouds of Zeus,   760
Or soaring up on high invisible,
Like dust that vanishes,
Pass out of being with no help from wings !

ANTISTROPH. I.

*E'en so the ill admits not now of flight;
My heart in dark gloom throbs;
My father's work as watcher brings me low;
I faint for very fear,
And I would fain find noose that bringeth death,
In twisted cordage hung,
Before the man I loathe
Draws near this flesh of mine: 770
Sooner than that may Hades rule o'er me
Sleeping the sleep of death !

STROPH. II.

Ah, might I find a place in yon high vault,
Where the rain-clouds are passing into snow,
Or lonely precipice
Whose summit none can see,
Rock where the vulture haunts,
Witness for me of my abysmal fall,
Before the marriage that will pierce my heart
Becomes my dreaded doom !

ANTISTROPH. II.

I shrink not from the thought of being the prey   780
Of dogs and birds that haunt the country round;
For death shall make me free
From ills all lamentable:
Yea, let death rather come
Than the worse doom of hated marriage-bed !
What other refuge now remains for me
That marriage to avert ?

Stroph. III.

Yea, to the Gods raise thou
Cloud-piercing, wailing cry
Of songs and litanies,
Prevailing, working freedom out for me :
And thou, O Father, look,
Look down upon the strife,
With glance of wrath against our enemies
From eyes that see the right ;
With pity look on us thy suppliants,
O Lord of Earth, O Zeus omnipotent !

790

Antistroph. III.

For lo ! Ægyptos' house,
In pride intolerable,
O'er-masculine in mood,
Pursuing me in many a winding course,
Poor wandering fugitive,
With loud and wild desires,
Seek in their frenzied violence to seize :
But thine is evermore
The force that turns the balance of the scale :
What comes to mortal men apart from Thee ?

206

Ah ! ah ! ah ! ah !
*Here on the land behold the ravisher
Who comes on us by sea !
*Ah, may'st thou perish, ravisher, ere thou
Hast stopped or landed here !
*I utter cry of wailing loud and long,
*I see them work the prelude of their crimes,
Their crimes of violence.
Ah ! ah ! Ah me !
Haste in your flight for help !
The mighty ones are waxing fat and proud,
By sea and land alike intolerable.
Be thou, O King, our bulwark and defence !

810

Enter Herald *of the sons of* EYPTOS' *advancing to the*
daughters of DANAOS.

Her. Haste, haste with all your speed unto the barque.
Chor. Tearing of hair, yea, tearing now will come,
    And print of nails in flesh,
    And smiting off of heads,
    With murderous stream of blood.
Her. Haste, haste ye, to that barque that yonder lies,
    Ye wretches, curse on you.

STROPH. I.

Chor. Would thou had'st met thy death
Where the salt waves wildly surge,
Thou with thy lordly pride,
In nail-compacted ship :
*Lo ! they will smite thee, weltering in thy blood,   820
    *And drive thee to thy barque.
Her. I bid you cease perforce, the cravings wild
    Of mind to madness given.
    Ho there ! what ho ! I say;   830
Give up those seats, and hasten to the ship :
I reverence not what this State honoureth.

ANTISTROPH. I.

Chor. Ah, I may ne'er again
Behold the stream where graze the goodly kine,
    Nourished and fed by which [1]
The blood of cattle waxes strong and full !
    *As with a native's right,
    *And one of old descent,
I keep, old man, my seat, my seat, I say.
Her. Nay, in a ship, a ship thou shalt soon go,   840
    With or without thy will,
    By force, I say, by force :

(1) The words recall the vision of the "seven well-favoured kine and
fat-fleshed," which "came out of the river," as Pharaoh dreamed,
(Gen. xli. 1, 2,) and which were associated so closely with the fertility
which it ordinarily produced through the whole extent of the valley of
the Nile.

Come, come, provoke not evils terrible,
  Falling by these my hands.

STROPH. II.

Chor. **Ah me!** ah me!
Would thou may'st perish with no hand to help,
  Crossing the sea's **wide** plain,
  In wanderings far and wide,
Where Sarpedonian sand-bank [1] spreads its length,
  Driven by the sweeping blasts!
 Her. **Sob thou, and howl,** and call upon the Gods: 850
Thou shalt not 'scape that **barque** from Ægypt come,
Though thou **should'st pour a bitterer** strain of grief.

ANTISTROPH. II.

Chor. **Woe! woe!** Ah **woe! ah woe,**
For this **foul wrong!** **Thou utterest fearful things;**
*Thou art too bold and insolent of speech.
*May mighty Nile that reared thee turn away
  Thy wanton pride and lust
  That we behold it not!
 Her. I bid you go to yon ship **double-prowed,**[2]
With all your speed. Let no one lag **behind;**
But little shall my grasp your ringlets spare. 860
   [*Seizes on the leader of the Suppliants.*

STROPH. III.

Chor. Ah me! my father, ah!
The help of holiest statues turns to woe;
  He leads me to the sea,
  With motion spider-like,
Or like a dream, a dark **and dismal dream,**
  Ah **woe! ah woe! ah woe!**
O **mother Earth!** O Earth! O **mother mine!**
  . Avert that cry of fear,
O Zeus, thou king! O son of mother Earth!

(1) Two dangerous low headlands seem to have been known by this name, one on the coast of Kilikia, the other on that of the Thrakian Chersonese.
(2) No traces of ships of this structure are found in Egyptian art; but, if the reading be right, it implies the existence of boats of some kind, so built that they could be steered from either end.

Her. Nay, I fear not the Gods they worship here;
They did not rear nor lead me up to age.   574

ANTISTROPH. III.

Chor. Near me he rages now,

. . . .

That biped snake,
And like a viper bites me by the foot.
Oh, woe is me! woe! woe!
O mother Earth! O Earth! O mother mine!
Avert that cry of fear.
O Zeus, thou king! O son of mother Earth.
Her. If some one yield not, and to yon ship go,
The hand that tears her tunic will not pity.

STROPH. IV.

Chor. Ho! rulers of the State!   881
Ye princes! I am seized.
Her. It seems, since ye are slow to hear my words,
That I shall have to drag you by the hair.

ANTISTROPH. IV.

Chor. We are undone, undone!
We suffer, prince, unlooked-for outrages.
Her. Full many princes, heirs of great Ægyptos,
Ye soon shall see. Take courage; ye shall have
No cause to speak of anarchy as there.

Enter KING *followed by his* Bodyguard.

King. Ho there! What dost thou? and with what
intent
Dost thou so outrage this Pelasgic land?
Dost think thou comest to a town of women?   F.X
Too haughty thou, a stranger 'gainst Hellenes,
And, sinning much, hast nothing done aright.
Her. What sin against the right have I then done?
King. First, thou know'st not how stranger-guest
should act.

Her. How so ?   When I, but finding **what I lost . . .**
King. Whom among us dost thou then patrons call ?
Her. Hermes the Searcher, chiefest patron mine.[1]
King. Thou, Gods invoking, honourest not the Gods.
Her. The Gods of Neilos are the Gods I worship.
King. Ours then are nought, if I thy meaning catch. 900
Her. These girls I'll lead, if no one rescues **them.**
King. Lay hand **on them, and soon thou'lt pay the
          cost.**
Her. **I** hear a word in no wise hospitable.
King. **Who** rob the Gods I welcome not as guests.
Her. **I then** will tell Ægyptos' children this.
King, This threat is all unheeded in my mind.
Her. But that I, knowing all, may speak it plain,
(For it is **meet a herald should** declare
Each matter clearly,) what am I to say ?
By whom have I been robbed of that fair band
Of women whom I claim as kindred ? Nay,   910
But it is Ares that **shall try this cause,**
And not with witnesses, **nor money down,**
Settling the matter, but there **first must fall**
Full many a soldier, and of many **a life**
The rending in convulsive agony.
     King. Why **should I** tell my name ? In time thou'lt
                know it,
Thou **and thy** fellow-travellers.   But these maidens,
With their **consent** and free choice of their wills,
Thou may'st **lead** off, **if** godly speech persuade them :
But this decree our city's men have made
With one consent, that we **to force yield not**
This **company of women.   Here the** nail   *m.*
Is driven tight home to keep its place full firm ; [2]

(1) Hermes, **the** guardian deity of heralds, is here **described by the**
epithet which marked him out as being also the **patron of detectives.**
Every stranger arriving in a Greek port had to **place himself under a**
proxenos or patron of some kind.   The herald, **having no** *proxenos* **among**
the citizens, appeals to his patron deity.
     (2) The words refer to the custom of nailing decrees, proclamations,
treaties, and the like, engraved on metal or marble, upon the walls of
temples or public buildings.   Traces of the same idea may possibly be

These things are written not on **tablets** only,
[Nor signed and sealed in folds of byblos-rolls ;]
Thou hear'st them clearly from a tongue that speaks
With full, free speech.   Away, away, I say:
And with all speed from out my presence haste.

   Her. It is thy will then a rash war to wage :
May strength and victory on our males attend !

                                   [Exit.

   King. Nay, thou shalt find the dwellers of this land
Are also males, and drink not draughts of ale   930
From barley brewed.1   [*To the Suppliants.*]   But ye, and
     your attendants,
Take courage, go within the fencèd city,
Shut in behind its bulwark deep of towers ;
Yea, many houses **to the State** belong,
And I a palace own not meanly built,
If ye prefer to live with many others
In ease and plenty : **or if that suits better,**
Ye may inhabit separate abodes.
Of these two offers that which pleases best
Choose for yourselves, and I as your protector,   940
And all our townsmen, will defend the pledge
Which our decree has given you.   Why wait'st thou
For any better authorised than these ?

   Chor. **For** these thy good deeds done may'st **thou in**
     good,
All good, abound, great chief of the Pelasgi !
     But kindly send to us
Our father Danaos, brave and true of heart,
     To counsel and direct.
His **must the** first decision be where **we**
     Should dwell, **and where to find**
A kindly home; for ready is each **one**

---

found in the promise to Eliakim that he shall be "as a nail in a sure
place," (Isa. xxii. 23,) in the thanksgiving of Ezra that God had given
His people " a nail in his holy place," (Ezra ix. 8.)
  (1) As before, the bread of the Hellenes was praised to the disparage-
ment of the " byblos fruit " of Egypt, so here their wine to that of the
Egyptian beer, which was the ordinary drink of the lower classes.

To speak his word of blame 'gainst foreigners.   950
    But may all good be ours!
And so with fair repute and speech of men,
    Free from all taint of wrath,
So place yourselves, dear handmaids, in the land,
As Danaos hath for each of us assigned
    Dowry of handmaid slaves.

Enter DANAOS *followed by* Soldiers.

Dan. My children, to the Argives ye should pray,
And sacrifice, and full libations pour,
As to Olympian Gods, for they have proved,
With one consent, deliverers: and they heard
*All that I did towards those cousins there,   960
*Those lovers hot and bitter.   And they gave
To me as followers these that bear the spear,
That I might have my meed of honour due,
And might not die by an assassin's hand
A death unlooked-for, and thus leave the land
A weight of guilt perpetual: and 'tis fit
That one who meet such kindness should return,
*From his heart's depths, a nobler gratitude;
And add ye this to all already written,
Your father's many maxims of true wisdom,
That we, though strangers, may in time be known;   970
For as to aliens each man's tongue is apt
For evil, and spreads slander thoughtlessly;
But ye, I charge you, see ye shame me not,
With this your life's bloom drawing all men's eyes.
The goodly vintage is full hard to watch,
All men and beasts make fearful havoc of it,
Nay, birds that fly, and creeping things of earth;
And Kypris offers fruitage, dropping ripe,
*As prey to wandering lust, nor lets it stay; [1]
And on the goodly comeliness of maidens   980

(1) The words present a striking parallelism to the erotic imagery of
the *Song of Solomon:* "Take us the foxes, the little foxes that spoil our
vines, for our vines have tender grapes" (ii. 15).

Each passer-by, o'ercome with hot desire,
Darts forth the amorous arrows of the eye.
And therefore let us suffer nought of this,
Through which our ship has ploughed such width of sea,
Such width of trouble; neither let us work
Shame to ourselves, and pleasure to our foes.
This two-fold choice of home is open to you :
[Pelasgos offers his, the city theirs,]
To dwell rent-free.   Full easy terms are these :
Only, I charge you, keep your father's precepts,
Prizing as more than life your chastity.　　　　　900

   Chor. May the high Gods that on Olympos dwell
Bless us in all things ; but for this our vintage
Be of good cheer, my father; for unless
The counsels of the Gods work strange device,
I will not leave my spirit's former path.

STROPH. I.

  Semi-Chor. A. Go then and make ye glad the high
            Gods, blessed for ever,
Those who rule our towns, and those who watch over our
            city,
And they who dwell by the stream of Erasinos ancient.[1]
  Semi-Chor. B. And ye, companions true,
    Take up your strain of song.　　　　　1000
Let praise attend this city of Pelasgos ;
Let us no more no more adore the mouths of Neïlos
    With these our hymns of praise ;

ANTISTROPH. I.

  Semi-Chor. A. Nay, but the rivers here that pour calm
    streams through our country,[2]

---

(1) The Erasinos was supposed to rise in Arcadia, in Mount Stym-
phalos, to disappear below the earth, and to come to sight again in
Argolis.
   (2) In this final choral ode of the *Suppliants*, as in that of the *Seven
against Thebes*, we have the phenomenon of the division of the Chorus,
hitherto united, into two sections of divergent thought and purpose.
Semi-Chorus A. remains steadfast in its purpose of perpetual virginity
Semi-Chorus B. relents, and is ready to accept wedlock.

Parents of many a son, making glad the soil of our
        meadows,
With wide flood rolling on, in full and abounding rich-
        ness.
    Semi-Chor. B. And Artemis the chaste,
      May she behold our band   1010
With pity; ne'er be marriage rites enforcèd
On us by Kythereia : those who hate us,
    Let that ill prize be theirs.

STROPH. II.

    Semi-Chor. A. Not that our kindly strain does slight
        to Kypris immortal;
For she, together with Hera, as nearest to Zeus is mighty,
A goddess of subtle thoughts, she is honoured in mys-
        teries solemn.
    Semi-Chor. B. Yea, as associates too with that their
        mother belovèd,   1020
Are fair Desire and Suasion,[1] whose pleading no man can
      gainsay,
Yea, to sweet Concord too Aphrodite's power is entrusted,
    *And the whispering paths of the Loves.

ANTISTROPH. II.

    Simi-Chor. A. Yet am I sore afraid of the ship that
        chases us wanderers,
Of terrible sorrows, and wars that are bloody and hateful;
*Why else have they had fair gale for this their eager
      pursuing ?   1030
    Semi-Chor. B. Whate'er is decreed of us, I know that
        it needs must happen;
The mighty purpose of Zeus, unfailing, admits no trans-
      gression :

---

(1) The two names were closely connected in the local worship of
Athens, the temples of Aphrodite and Peitho (Suasion) standing at the
south-west angle of the Acropolis. If any special purpose is to be
traced in the invocation, we may see it in the poet's desire to bring out
the nobler, more ethical side of Aphrodite's attributes, in contrast
with the growing tendency to look on her as simply the patroness of
brutal lust.

*May this fate come to us, as to many women before us,
  *Fate of marriage and spouse!

Stroph. III.

Semi-Chor. A. Ah, may great Zeus avert
From me all marriage with Ægyptos' sons!
  Semi-Chor. B. Nay, all will work for gocd.
  Semi-Chor. A. Thou glozest that which will no glozing
      bear.   1040
  Semi-Chor. B. And thou know'st not what future
      comes to us.

Antistroph. III.

Semi-Chor. A. How can I read the mind
Of mightiest Zeus, to sight all fathomless?
  Semi-Chor. B. Well-tempered be thy speech!
  Semi-Chor. A. What mood of calmness wilt thou
      school me in?
  Semi-Chor. B. Be not o'er-rash in what concerns the
      Gods.

Stroph. IV.

Semi-Chor. A. Nay, may our great king Zeus avert
      that marriage
  With husbands whom we hate,
E'en He who, touching her with healing hand,
      Freed Io from her pain,
Putting an end from all her wanderings,
      Working with kindly force!   1050

Antistroph. V.

Semi-Chor. B. And may He give the victory to women!
      I choose the better part,
Though mixed with ill; and that the trial end
      Justly, as I have prayed,
By means of subtle counsels which God gives
      To liberate from ills.[1]

---

(1) The play, as acted, formed part of a trilogy, and the next play, the
Danaids, probably contained the sequel of the story, the acceptance by the
Suppliants of the sons of Ægyptos in marriage, the plot of Danaos for
the destruction of the bridegrooms on the wedding-night, and the execution of the deed of blood by all but Hypermnestra.

AGAMEMNON.

N

ARGUMENT.

Ten years had passed since Agamemnon, son of Atreus, king of
Mykenæ, had led the Hellenes to Troïa to take vengeance on
Alexandros (also known as Paris), son of Priam. For Paris
had basely wronged Menelaos, king of Sparta, Agamemnon's
brother, in that, being received by him as a guest, he enticed
his wife Helena to leave her lord and go with him to Troïa.
And now the tenth year had come, and Paris was slain, and
the city of the Troïans was taken and destroyed, and Agamemnon and the Hellenes were on their way homeward with
the spoil and prisoners they had taken. But meanwhile
Clytæmnestra too, Agamemnon's queen, had been unfaithful,
and had taken as her paramour Ægisthos, son of that Thyestes
whom Atreus, his brother, had made to eat, unknowing, of the
flesh of his own children. And now, partly led by her adulterer, and partly seeking to avenge the death of her daughter
Iphigeneia, whom Agamemnon had sacrificed to appease the
wrath of Artemis, and partly also jealous because he was
bringing back Cassandra, the daughter of Priam, as his concubine, she plotted with Ægisthos against her husband's life.
But this was done secretly, and she stationed a guard on the
roof of the royal palace to give notice when he saw the beacon-
fires, by which Agamemnon had promised that he would send
tidings that Troïa was taken.*

---

* The unfaithfulness of Clytæmnestra and the murder of Agamemnon had entered into the Homeric cycle of the legends of the house
of Atreus. In the *Odyssey*, however, Ægisthos is the chief agent in
this crime, (*Odyss.* iii. 264, iv. 91, 532, xi. 409); and the manner of it
differs from that which Æschylos has adopted. Clytæmnestra first
appears as slaying both her husband and Cassandra in Pindar (*Pyt.*
xi. 26.)

Dramatis Personæ.

Watchman.

Chorus of Argive Elders.

CLYTÆMNESTRA.

Herald, (TALTHYBIOS.)

AGAMEMNON.

CASSANDRA.

ÆGISTHOS.

AGAMEMNON.

SCENE.—Argos. *The Palace of* AGAMEMNON; *statues of the Gods in front. Watchman on the roof. Time, night.*

Watchman. I ask the Gods a respite from these toils,
This keeping **at my** post the whole year round,
Wherein, upon the Atreidæ's roof reclined,
Like dog, upon my elbow, I have learnt
To know night's goodly company of stars,
And those bright lords that deck the firmament,
And winter bring **to men, and harvest-tide ;**
[The rising and the **setting of the stars.**]
And now I watch **for sign of beacon-torch,**
The flash **of fire that bringeth news from** Troïa,
And tidings **of its capture.   So prevails**
*A woman's **manly-purposed, hoping** heart ;   10
And when I keep my bed of little ease,
Drenched **with the** dew, unvisited by dreams,
(For fear, instead of sleep, my comrade is,
So that in sound sleep ne'er I close mine eyes,)
And when I think to sing a **tune, or hum,**
(My medicine of song **to ward off sleep,**)
Then weep I, wailing for this house's **chance,**
No **more, as erst, right well administered.**
Well ! **may I now find blest release from toils,**   20
When fire **from out the dark brings tidings good.**

   ⌊*Pauses, then springs up suddenly, seeing a light
    in the distance.*

Hail ! thou torch-bearer of the night, that shedd'st
Light as of morn, and bringest full array

Of many choral bands in Argos met,
Because of this success.   Hurrah ! hurrah !
So clearly tell I Agamemnon's queen,
With all speed rising from her couch to raise
Shrill cry of triumph o'er this beacon-fire
Throughout the house, since Ilion's citadel
Is taken, as full well that bright blaze shows.   30
I, for my part, will dance my prelude now ;

[Leaps and dances.

For I shall score my lord's new turn of luck,
This beacon-blaze my throw of triple six.[1]
Well, would that I with this mine hand may touch
The dear hand of our king when he comes home !
As to all else, the word is " Hush !"   An ox [2]
Rests on my tongue ; had the house a voice
'Twould tell too clear a tale.   I'm fain to speak
To those who know, forget with those who know not.

[Exit.

*Enter Chorus of twelve Argive elders, chanting as they
march to take up their position in the centre of the stage.
A procession of women bearing torches is seen in the
distance.*

Lo ! the tenth year now is passing   40
Since, of Priam great avengers,
Menelaos, Agamemnon,

(1) The form of gambling from which the phrase is taken, had clearly become common in Attica among the class to which the watchman was supposed to belong, and had given rise to proverbial phrases like that in the text. The Greeks themselves supposed it to have been invented by the Lydians, (Herod. i. 94), or Palamedes, one of the heroes of the tale of Troïa, but it enters also into Egyptian legends (Herod. ii. 122,) and its prevalence from remote antiquity in the farther East, as in the Indian story of Nala and Damayanti, makes it probable that it originated there. The game was commonly played, as the phrase shows, with three dice, the highest throw being that which gave three sixes. Æschylos, it may be noted, appears in a lost drama, which bore the title of *Palamedes,* to have brought the game itself into his plot. It is referred to, as invented by that hero, in a fragment of Sophocles, (*Fr.* 380,) and again in the proverb,—
"The dice of Zeus have ever lucky throws."—(*Fr.* 763.)

(2) Here, also, the watchman takes up another common proverbial phrase, belonging to the same group as that of " kicking against the pricks " in v. 1624. He has his reasons for silence, weighty as would be the tread of an ox to close his lips.

Double-throned and double-sceptred,
Power from sovran Zeus deriving—
Mighty pair of the Atreidæ—
Raised a fleet of thousand **vessels**
Of the Argives from our country,
Potent helpers in their warfare,
Shouting cry of Ares fiercely;
E'en **as** vultures shriek who hover,
Wheeling, whirling o'er **their eyrie**,   50
In wild sorrow for their nestlings,
With their oars of stout wings rowing,
Having lost the toil that bound them
To their callow fledglings' couches.
But on high One,—or Apollo,
Zeus, or Pan,—the shrill cry hearing,
Cry of birds that are his clients,[1]
Sendeth forth on men transgressing,
Erinnys, slow but sure avenger;
So against young Alexandros[2]
Atreus' sons the great King sendeth,
Zeus, of host and guest protector: 60
He, for bride with many a lover,
Will to Danai give and Troïans
Many conflicts, **men's** limbs straining,
When the knee in dust is crouching,
And the spear-shaft in the onset
Of the battle snaps asunder.
But **as** things are now, so are **they**,
So, **as** destined, shall the end **be**.
Nor by tears, nor yet libations
Shall he soothe the wrath unbending
Caused by sacred rites left fireless.[3]   70

(1) The vultures stand, *i.e.*, **to** the rulers of Heaven, in the same relation as the foreign sojourners **in** Athens, the *Metoecs*, did **to** the citizens
under whose protection they placed themselves.
(2) Alexandros, the other name of Paris, the seducer of Helen.
(3) The words, perhaps, refer to the grief of Menelaos, as leading him
to neglect the wonted sacrifices to Zeus, but it seems better to see in
them a reference to the sin of Paris. He, at least, who had carried off
his host's wife, had not offered acceptable sacrifices, had neglected all

We, with old frame little honoured,
Left behind that host are staying,
Resting strength that equals childhood's
On our staff: for in the bosom
*Of the boy, life's young sap rushing,
Is of old age but the equal;
Ares not as yet is found there:
And the man in age exceeding,
When the leaf is sere and withered,
Goes with three feet on his journey; [1]   80
Not more Ares-like than boyhood,
Like a day-seen dream he wanders.

[*Enter* CLYTÆMNESTRA, *followed by the procession
    of torch-bearers.*

Thou, of Tyndareus the daughter,
Queen of Argos, Clytæmnestra,
What has happened? what news cometh?
What perceiving, on what tidings
Leaning, dost thou put in motion
All this solemn, great procession?
Of the Gods who guard the city,
Those above and those beneath us,
Of the heaven, and of the market,   90
Lo! with thy gifts blaze the altars;
And through all the expanse of Heaven,
Here and there, the torch-fire rises,
With the flowing, pure persuasion
Of the holy unguent nourished,
*And the chrism rich and kingly
From the treasure-store's recesses.
Telling what of this thou canst tell,
What is right for thee to utter,
    Be a healer of my trouble,

sacrifices to Zeus Xenios, the God of host and guest. The allusion to the
sacrifice of Iphigenia, which some (Donaldson and Paley) have found
here, and the wrath of Clytæmnestra, which Agamemnon will fail to
soothe, seems more far-fetched.
    (1) An allusion, such as the audience would catch and delight in, to the
well-known enigma of the Sphinx. See Sophocles, (*Trans.*,) p. 1.

Trouble now my soul disturbing, 100
*While anon fond hope displaying
Sacrificial **signs** propitious,
Wards **off care** that no rest knoweth,
Sorrow **mind** and heart corroding.
[*The Chorus, taking their places round the central
thymele, begin their song.*[1]

STROPHE.

Able am I to utter, setting forth
The might from **omens** sprung
*What met the heroes as they journeyed on,
(For still, by God's great gift,
My age, **yet linked with** strength,
*Breathes **suasive** power of song,)
How the Achæans' twin-throned majesty,
Accordant rulers of the youth of Hellas, 110
With spear and vengeful hand,
Were sent by fierce, strong bird 'gainst Teucrian **shore,**
Kings of the birds to kings of ships appearing,
One black, with white tail one,
Near to the palace, on the spear-hand side,
On station **seen of** all,
A pregnant hare devouring with her young,
Robbed of all runs to come:

(1) The Chorus, though **too to** take part in **the** expedition, are yet
able to tell both of what passed as the expedition started, and of the
terrible fulfilment of the omens which they had seen. The two eagles are,
of course, in the symbolism of prophecy, the two chieftains, Menelaos
and Agamemnon. The "white feathers" of the one may point to the
less heroic character of Menelaos: so, in v. 123, they are of "diverse
mood." The hare whom they devour is, in the first instance, Troia, and
so far the omen is good, portending the success of the expedition; but,
as Artemis hates the fierceness of the eagles, so there is, in the eyes of
the seer, a dark token of danger from her wrath against the Atreidæ.
Either their victory will be sullied by cruelty which will bring down vengeance, or else there is some secret sin in the past which must be atoned
for by a terrible sacrifice. In the legend followed by Sophocles, (*Electr.*
566,) Agamemnon had offended Artemis by slaying a doe sacred to her, as
he was hunting. In the manifold meanings of such omens there is,
probably, a latent suggestion of the sacrifice of Iphigeneia by the two
chieftains, though this was at the time hidden from the seer. The fact
that they are seen on the right, not on the left hand, was itself ominous
of good.

Wail as for Linos, wail, wail bitterly,
    And yet may good prevail ! [1]   [120]

ANTISTROPHE.

And the wise prophet of the army seeing
    The brave Atreidæ twain
Of diverse mood, knew those that tore the hare,
    And those that led the host;
    And thus divining spake:
    "One day this armament
Shall Priam's city sack, and all the herds
Owned by the people, countless, by the towers,
    Fate shall with force lay low.
Only take heed lest any wrath of Gods   [130]
Blunt the great curb of Troïa yet encamped,
    Struck down before its time;
For Artemis the chaste that house doth hate,
    Her father's wingèd hounds,
Who slay the mother with her unborn young,
    And loathes the eagles' feast.
Wail as for Linos, wail, wail bitterly;
    And yet may good prevail !

EPODE.

" *For she, the fair One, though so kind of heart
*To fresh-dropt dew from mighty lion's womb,[2]
    And young that suck the teats

---

(1) The song of Linos, originally the dirge with which men mourned for the death of Linos, the minstrel-son of Apollo and Urania, brother of Orpheus, who was slain by Heracles,—a type, like Thammuz and Adonis, of life prematurely closed and bright hopes never to be fulfilled,—had come to be the representative of all songs of mourning. So Hesiod (in Eustath. on Hom. Il., vii. 569) speaks of the name, as applied to all funeral dirges over poets and minstrels. So Herodotos (ii. 79) compares it, as the type of this kind of music among the Greeks, with what he found in Egypt connected with the name of Maneros, the only son of the first king of Egypt, who died in the bloom of youth. The name had, therefore, as definite a connotation for a Greek audience as the words *Miserere* or *Jubilate* would have for us, and ought not, I believe, to disappear from the translation.

(2) The comparison of a lion's whelps to dew-drops, bold as the figure is, has something in it analogous to that with which we are more familiar, describing the children, or the army of a king, as the "dew" from "the womb of the morning" (Ps. cx. 3).

Of all that roam the fields,
   *Yet prays Him bring to pass
   The portents of those birds,
The omens good yet also full of dread.
   And Pæan I invoke
As Healer, lest she on the Danai send
   Delays that keep the ships
   Long time with hostile blasts.
So urging on a new, strange sacrifice,
   Unblest, unfestivalled,[1]
By natural growth artificer of strife,
Bearing far other fruit than wife's true fear,
   For there abideth yet,
   Fearful, recurring still,
Ruling the house, full subtle, unforgetting,
   Vengeance for children slain." [2]
Such things, with great good mingled, Calchas spake,
   In voice that pierced the air,
As destined by the birds that crossed our path
   To this our kingly house:
   And in accord with them,
Wail as for Linos, wail, wail bitterly;
   And yet may good prevail.

STROPH. I.

   O Zeus—whate'er He be,[3]
   If that Name please Him well,
   By that on Him I call:

(1) The sacrifice, i.e., was to be such as could not, according to the customary ritual, form a feast for the worshippers.

(2) The dark words look at once before and after, back to the murder of the sons of Thyestes, forward, though of this the seer knew not, to the sacrifice of Iphigeneia. Clytemnestra is the embodiment of the Vengeance of which the Chorus speaks.

(3) As a part of the drama the whole passage that follows is an assertion by the Chorus that in this their trouble they will turn to no other God, invoke no other name, but that of the Supreme Zeus. But it can hardly be doubted that they have a meaning beyond this, and are the utterance by the poet of his own theology. In the second part of the Promethean trilogy (all that we now know of it) he had represented Zeus as ruling in the might of despotic sovereignty, the representative of a Power which men could not resist, but also could not love, inflicting needless sufferings on the sons of men. Now he has grown wiser. The

Weighing all other names I fail to guess
Aught else but Zeus, if I would cast aside,
  Clearly, in very deed,
From off my soul this idle weight of care.   160

Antistroph. I.

Nor He who erst was great,[1]
Full of the might to war,
 *Avails now; He is gone;
And He who next came hath departed too,
His victor meeting; but if one to Zeus,
  High triumph-praise should sing,
His shall be all the wisdom of the wise;

Stroph. II.

Yea, Zeus, who leadeth men in wisdom's way, 170
  And fixeth fast the law,
  That pain is gain;
And slowly dropping on the heart in sleep
  Comes woe-recording care,
And makes the unwilling yield to wiser thoughts:
And doubtless this too comes from grace of Gods,
*Seated in might upon their awful thrones.

Antistroph. II.

And then of those Achæan ships the chief,[2]
  The elder, blaming not
  Or seer or priest;

sovereignty of Zeus is accepted as part of the present order of the world; trust in Him brings peace; the pain which He permits is the one only way to wisdom. The stress laid upon the name of Zeus implies a wish to cleave to the religion inherited from the older Hellenes, as contrasted with those with which their intercourse with the East had made the Athenians familiar. Like the voice which came to Epimenides, as he was building a sanctuary to the Muses, bidding him dedicate it not to them but to Zeus, (Diog. Laert. i. 10,) it represents a faint approximation to a truer, more monotheistic creed than that of the popular mythology.

(1) The two mighty ones who have passed away are Uranos and Cronos, the representatives in Greek mythology of the earlier stages of the world's history, (1) mere material creation, (2) an ideal period of harmony, a golden, Saturnian age, preceding the present order of divine government with its mingled good and evil. Comp. Hesiod, *Theogon*, 459.

(2) The Chorus returns, after its deeper speculative thoughts, to its interrupted narrative.

But tempered to the fate that on him smote. . . .   180
      When that Achæan host
Were vexed with adverse winds and failing stores,
Still kept where Chalkis in the distance lies,
And the vexed waves in Aulis ebb and flow;

Stroph. III.

And breezes from the Strymon sweeping down,
Breeding delays and hunger, driving forth
      Our men in wandering course,
      On seas without a port.
Sparing nor ships, nor rope, nor sailing gear,
With doubled months wore down the Argive host;   190
      And when, for that wild storm,
Of one more charm far harder for our chiefs
The prophet told, and spake of Artemis,[1]
      In tone so piercing shrill,
The Atreidæ smote their staves upon the ground,
      And could not stay their tears.

Antistroph. III.

And then the old king lifted up his voice,
And spake, " Great woe it is to disobey;
      Great too to slay my child,   200
      The pride and joy of home, ·
Polluting with the streams of maiden's blood
Her father's hands upon the altar steps.
      What course is free from ill?
How lose my ships and fail of mine allies?
'Tis meet that they with strong desire should seek
      A rite the winds to soothe,
E'en though it be with blood of maiden pure;
      May all end well at last!"   210

Stroph. III.

      So when he himself had harnessed
      To the yoke of Fate unbending,

---

(1) The seer saw his augury fulfilled. When he uttered the name of
Artemis it was pregnant with all the woe which he had foreboded at the
outset.

With a blast of strange, new feeling,
Sweeping o'er his heart and spirit,
Aweless, godless, and unholy,
He his thoughts and purpose altered
To full measure of all daring,
(Still base counsel's fatal frenzy,
Wretched primal source of evils,
Gives to mortal hearts strange boldness,)
And at last his heart he hardened
His own child to slay as victim,
Help in war that they were waging,
To avenge a woman's frailty,
Victim for the good ships' safety.

Antistroph. III.

All her prayers and eager callings   220
On the tender name of Father,
All her young and maiden freshness,
They but set at nought, those rulers,
In their passion for the battle.
And her father gave commandment
To the servants of the Goddess,
When the prayer was o'er, to lift her,
Like a kid, above the altar,
In her garments wrapt, face downwards,—[1]
Yea, to seize with all their courage,
And that o'er her lips of beauty
Should be set a watch to hinder
Words of curse against the houses,
With the gag's strength silence-working.[2]

Stroph. IV.

And she upon the ground
Pouring rich folds of veil in saffron dyed,   230
Cast at each one of those who sacrificed
A piteous glance that pierced,

(1) So that the blood may fall upon the altar, as the knife was drawn
across the throat.
(2) The whole passage should be compared with the magnificent description in Lucretius i. 84-101.

Fair as a pictured form; [1]
And wishing,—all in vain,—
To speak; for oftentimes
In those her father's hospitable halls
She sang, a maiden pure with chastest song,
 *And her dear father's life
That poured its threefold cup of praise to God, [2]
 Crowned with all choicest good,
 She with a daughter's love
 Was wont to celebrate.

ANTISTROPH. IV.

What then ensued mine eyes
Saw not, nor may I tell, but Calchas' arts
Were found not fruitless.   Justice turns the scale
 For those to whom through pain
 At last comes wisdom's gain.
 *But for our future fate,
 *Since help for it is none,
*Good-bye to it before it comes, and this
Has the same end as wailing premature;
 For with to-morrow's dawn
It will come clear; may good luck crown our fate!
 So prays the one true guard,
 Nearest and dearest found,
 Of this our Apian land. [3]

240

[*The Chief of the Chorus turns to* CLYTÆMNESTRA, *and
her train of handmaids, who are seen approaching.*

Chor. I come, O Clytæmnestra, honouring

---

(1) Beautiful as a picture, and as motionless and silent also. The art,
young as it was, had already reached the stage when it supplied to the
poet an ideal standard of perfection. Other allusions to it are found in
vv. 774, 1300.

(2) The words point to the ritual of Greek feasts, which assigned the
first libation to Zeus and the Olympian Gods, the second to the Heroes,
the third to Zeus in his special character as Saviour and Preserver; the
last was commonly accompanied by a pæan, hymn of praise. The life of
Agamemnon is described as one which had good cause to offer many
such libations. Iphigeneia had sung many such pæans.

(3) The mythical explanation of this title for the Argive territory is
found in the *Suppl.* v. 256, and its real meaning will be discussed in a note
on that passage.

Thy majesty: 'tis meet to pay respect
To a chief's wife, the man's throne empty left: **2t.**
But whether thou hast heard good news, or else
In hopes of tidings glad dost sacrifice,
I fain would hear, yet will not silence blame.

   Clytæm. May Morning, as the proverb runs, appear
Bearing glad tidings from his mother Night![1]
Joy thou shalt learn beyond thy hope to hear;
For Argives now have taken Priam's city.

   Chor. What? Thy words sound so strange they flit by
     me.

   Clytæm. The Achœans hold Troïa. Speak I clear
     enough?   **200**

   Chor. Joy creeps upon me, drawing forth my tears.

   Clytæm. Of loyal heart thine eyes give token true.

   Chor. What witness sure hast thou of these events?

   Clytæm. Full clear (how else?) unless the God deceive.[2]

   Chor. Reliest thou on dreams or visions seen?

   Clytæm. I place no trust in mind weighed down with
     sleep.[3]

   Chor. Hath then some wingless omen charmed thy
     soul?[4]

   Clytæm. My mind thou scorn'st, as though 'twere but
     a girl's.

   Chor. What time has passed since they the city sacked?

---

(1) To speak of Morning as the child of Night was, we may well
believe, among the earliest parables of nature. In its mythical form it
appears in Hesiod., (*Theogon.* 123,) but its traces are found wherever, as
among Hebrews, Athenians, Germans, men reckoned by nights rather
than by days, and spoke of "the evening and the morning" rather than
of "day and night."

(2) The God thought of is, as in v. 272, Hephæstos, as being Lord of
the Fire, that had brought the tidings.

(3) It is not without significance that Clytæmnestra scorns the channel
of divine instruction of which the Chorus had spoken with such reverence. The dramatist puts into her mouth the language of those who
scoffed at the notion that truth might come to the soul in "visions of the
night," when "deep sleep falleth upon men." So Sophocles puts like
thoughts into the mouth of Jocasta, (*Œd. King*, vv. 709, 858.)

(4) Omens came from the flight of birds. An omen which was not
trustworthy, or belonged to some lower form of divination, might therefore be spoken of as "wingless." But the word may possibly be inten-
sive, not negative, "swift-winged," and then refer generically to that
form of divination.

Clytæm. This very night, the mother of this morn. 270
Chor. What herald could arrive with speed like this?
Clytæm. Hephæstos flashing forth bright flames from
        Ida:
Beacon to beacon from that courier-fire
Sent on its tidings; Ida to the rock [1]
Hermæan named, in Lemnos: from the isle
The height of Athos, dear to Zeus, received
A third great torch of flame, and lifted up,
So as on high to skim the broad sea's back,
The stalwart fire rejoicing went its way;
The pine-wood, like a sun, sent forth its light
Of golden radiance to Makistos' watch;   280
And he, with no delay, nor unawares
Conquered by sleep, performed his courier's part:
Far off the torch-light, to Euripos' straits
Advancing, tells it to Messapion's guards:
They, in their turn, lit up and passed it on,
Kindling a pile of dry and aged heath.
Still strong and fresh the torch, not yet grown dim,
Leaping across Asôpos' plain in guise
Like a bright moon, towards Kithæron's rock,
Roused the next station of the courier flame.   290
And that far-travelled light the sentries there
Refused not, burning more than all yet named:
And then the light swooped o'er Gorgôpis' lake,
And passing on to Ægiplanctos' mount,
Bade the bright fire's due order tarry not;

(1) The description that follows, over and above its general interest, had, probably, for an Athenian audience, that of representing the actual succession of beacon-stations, by which they, in the course of the wars under Pericles, had actually received intelligence from the coasts of Asia. A glance at the map will show the fitness of the places named—Ida, Lemnos, Athos, Makistos, (a mountain in Euboea,) Messapion, (on the coast of Boeotia,) over the plains of the Asôpos to Kithæron, in the south of the same province, then over Gorgopis, a bay of the Corinthian Gulf, to Ægiplanctos in Megaris, then across to a headland overlooking the Saronic Gulf, to the Arachnæan hill in Argolis. The word "*courier*-fire" connects itself also with the system of posts or messengers, which the Persian kings seem to have been the first to organise, and which impressed the minds both of Hebrews (Esth. viii. 14) and Greeks (Herod. viii. 98) by their regular transmission of the king's edicts, or of special news.

O

And they, enkindling boundless store, send on
A mighty beard of flame, and then it passed
The headland e'en that looks on Saron's gulf,
Still blazing.   On it swept, until it came
To Arachnæan heights, the watch-tower near;   300
Then here on the Atreidæ's roof it swoops,
This light, of Ida's fire no doubtful heir.
Such is the order of my torch-race games;
One from another taking up the course,[1]
But here the winner is both first and last;
And this sure proof and token now I tell thee,
Seeing that my lord hath sent it me from Troïa.

 Chor. I to the Gods, O Queen, will pray hereafter,
But fain would I hear all thy tale again,
E'en as thou tell'st, aud satiate my wonder.   310

 Clytæm. This very day the Achæans Troïa hold.
I trow full diverse cry pervades the town:
Pour in the same vase vinegar and oil,
*And you would call them enemies, not friends;
And so from conquerors and from captives now

---

(1) Our ignorance of the details of the *Lampadephoria*, or "torch-race
games," in honour of the fire-God, Prometheus, makes the allusion to
them somewhat obscure. As described by Pausanias, (I. xxx. 2,) the
runners started with lighted torches from the altar of Prometheus in the
Academeia and ran towards the city.   The first who reached the goal with
his torch still burning became the winner. If all the torches were extin-
guished, then all were losers.   As so described, however, there is no
succession, no taking the torch from one and passing it on to another,
like that described here and in the well-known line of Lucretius, (ii. 78,)

  " Et quasi cursores vitaï lampada tradunt."
  (And they, as runners, pass the torch of life.)

On the other hand, there are descriptions which show that such a transfer
was the chief element of the game.   This is, indeed, implied both in this
passage and in the comparison between the game and the Persian courier-
system in Herod. viii. 98.   The two views may be reconciled by supposing
(1) that there were sets of runners, vying with each other as such, rather
than individually, or (2) that a runner whose speed failed him though
his torch kept burning, was allowed to hand it on to another who was
more likely to win the race, but whose torch was out.   The next line
seems meant to indicate where the comparison failed.   In the torch-race
which Clytæmnestra describes there had been no contest.   One and the
self-same fire (the idea of succession passing into that of continuity) had
started and had reached the goal, and so had won the prize.   An alternative rendering would be,—

  " He wins who is first in, though starting last."

The cries of varied fortune one may hear.
For these, low-fallen on the carcases
Of husbands and of brothers, children too
By aged fathers, mourn their dear ones' death,
And that with throats that are no longer free.   320
And those the hungry toil of sleepless guard,
After the battle, at their breakfast sets;
Not billeted in order fixed and clear,
But just as each his own chance fortune grasps,
They in the captive houses of the Troïans
Dwell, freed at last from all the night's chill frosts,
And dews of heaven, for now, poor wretches, they
Will sleep all night without the sentry's watch;
And if they reverence well the guardian Gods
Of that new-conquered country, and their shrines,   330
Then they, the captors, will not captured be.
Ah! let no evil lust attack the host
Conquered by greed, to plunder what they ought not:
For yet they need return in safety home,
Doubling the goal to run their backward race.[1]
*But should the host come sinning 'gainst the Gods,
Then would the curse of those that perishèd
Be watchful, e'en though no quick ill might fall.
Such thoughts are mine, mere woman though I be.
May good prevail beyond all doubtful chance!   340
For I have got the blessing of great joy.
   Chor. Thou, lady, kindly, like a sage, dost speak,
And I, on hearing thy sure evidence,
Prepare myself to give the Gods due thanks;
For they have wrought full meed for all our toil.
                [*Exit* CLYTÆM. *with her train.*
    O Zeus our King! O Night beloved,
    Mighty winner of great glories,
    Who upon the towers of Troïa
    Casted'st snare of closest meshes,

---

(1) The complete foot-race was always to the column which marked the
end of the course, round it, and back again. In getting to Troïa, therefore, but half the race was done.

So that none full-grown or youthful   350
Could o'erleap the net of bondage,
Woe of universal capture ;—
Zeus, of host and guest protector,
Who hath brought these things, I worship ;
He long since on Alexandros
Stretched his bow that so his arrow
Might not sweep at random, missing,
Or beyond the stars shoot idly.

STROPH. L.

Yes, one may say, 'tis Zeus whose blow they feel ;
   This one may clearly trace :
   They fared as He decreed :
   Yea, one there was who said,   360
" The Gods deign not to care for mortal men [1]
By whom the grace of things inviolable
   Is trampled under foot."
   No fear of God had he :
*Now is it to the children manifest [2]
   Of those who, overbold,
Breathed rebel War beyond the bounds of Right,
Their houses overfilled with precious store
   *Above the golden mean.
*Ah ! let our life be free from all that hurts,   370
   So that for one who gains
   Wisdom in heart and soul,
   That lot may be enough.

---

(1) Dramatically the words refer to the practical impiety of evildoers
like Paris, with, perhaps, a half-latent allusion to that of Clytæmnestra.
But it can hardly be doubted that for the Athenian audience it would
have a more special significance, as a protest against the growing scepticism, what in a later age would have been called the Epicureanism, of
the age of Pericles. It is the assertion of the belief of Æschylos in the
moral government of the world. The very vagueness of the singular,
" One there was," would lead the hearers to think of some teacher like
Anaxagoras, whom they suspected of Atheism.

(2) The Chorus sees in the overthrow of Troïa, an instance of this
righteous retribution. The audience were, perhaps, intended to think
also of the punishment which had fallen on the Persians for the sacrilegious acts of their fathers. The "things inviolable" are the sanctities
of the ties of marriage and hospitality, both of which Paris had set at
nought.

Since still there is no bulwark strong in wealth
    Against destruction's doom,
For one who in the pride of wantonness
Spurns the great altar of the Right and Just.

ANTISTROPH. I.

Him woeful, subtle Impulse urges on,
    Resistless in her might,
    Atè's far-scheming child:
    All remedy is vain.
It is not hidden, but is manifest,
That mischief with its horrid gleaming light;
    And, like to worthless bronze,[1]
    By friction tried and tests,
It turns to tarnished blackness in its hue:
    Since, boy-like, he pursues
A bird upon its flight, and so doth bring
Upon his city shame intolerable:
    And no God hears his prayer,
    But bringeth low the unjust,
    Who deals with deeds like this.
    Thus Paris came to the Atridæ's home,
    And stole its queen away,
And so left brand of shame indelible
Upon the board where host and guest had sat.

STROPH. II.

She, leaving to her countrymen at home
Wild din of spear and shield and ships of war,
    And bringing, as her dower,
    To Ilion doom of death,
Passed very swiftly through the palace gates,
    Daring what none should dare;

---

(1) Here, and again in v. 612, we have a similitude drawn from the
metallurgy of Greek artists. Good bronze, made of copper and tin, takes
the green rust which collectors prize, but when rubbed, the brightness
reappears. If zinc be substituted for tin, as in our brass, or mixed
largely with it, the surface loses its polish, oxidizes and becomes black.
It is, however, doubtful whether this combination of metals was at the
time in use, and the words may simply refer to different degrees of excellence in bronze properly so called.

And many a wailing cry
They raised, the minstrel prophets of the house,
    " Woe for that kingly home!
Woe for that kingly home and for its chiefs!   405
Woe for the marriage-bed and traces left
    Of wife who loved her lord!"
* There stands he silent; foully wronged and yet
        *Uttering no word of scorn,[1]
*In deepest woe perceiving she is gone;
        And in his yearning love
        For one beyond the sea,
A ghost shall seem to queen it o'er the house;
        The grace of sculptured forms[2]
        Is loathèd by her lord,
And in the penury of life's bright eyes
        All Aphroditè's charm
        To utter wreck has gone.

                ANTISTROPH. II.

And phantom shades that hover round in dreams   410
Come full of sorrow, bringing vain delight;
        For vain it is, when one
        Sees seeming shows of good,
And gliding through his hands the dream is gone,
        After a moment's space,
        On wings that follow still
Upon the path where sleep goes to and fro.
        Such are the woes at home
Upon the altar hearth, and worse than these.

(1) In a corrupt passage like this, the text of which has been so va-
riously restored and rendered, it may be well to give at least one alternative version:
        " There stands she silent, with no honour met,
                Nor yet with words of scorn,
                Sweetest to see of all that he has lost."

The words, as so taken, refer to the vision of Helen, described in the
lines that follow. Another, for the line "In deepest woe," &c., . . .
would give,
        " Believing not he sees the lost one there."

(2) The art of Pheidias had already made it natural at Athens to speak
of kings as decorating their palaces with the life-size busts or statues of
those they loved.

But on a wider scale for those who went
    From Hellas' ancient shore,
A sore distress that causeth pain of heart   426
    Is seen in every house.
Yea, many things there are that touch the quick:
    For those whom each did send
    He knoweth; but, instead
Of living men, there come to each man's home
    Funereal urns alone,
    And ashes of the dead.

STROPH. III.

For Ares, trafficking for golden coin
    The lifeless shapes of men,
And in the rush of battle holding scales,
    Sends now from Ilion
    Dust from the funeral pyre,
A burden sore to loving friends at home,
    And bitterly bewailed,
    Filling the brazen urn
With well-smoothed ashes in the place of men;   430
    And with high praise they mourn
This hero skilled and valiant in the fight,
And that who in the battle nobly fell,
    All for another's wife:
And other words some murmur secretly;
    And jealous discontent
Against the Atreidæ, champions in the suit,
    Creeps on all stealthily;
    And some around the wall,
In full and goodly form have sepulture
    There upon Ilion's soil,   440
And their foes' land inters its conquerors.

ANTISTROPH. III.

And so the murmurs of their subjects rise
    With sullen discontent,
And do the dread work of a people's curse;
    And now my boding fear

Awaits some news of ill,
As yet enwrapt in blackness of the night.
Not heedless are the Gods
Of shedders of much blood,
And the dark-robed Erinnyes in due time,
By adverse chance of life,
Place him who prospers in unrighteousness
In gloom obscure; and once among the unseen,
There is no help for him:
Fame in excess is but a perilous thing;
For on men's quivering eyes
Is hurled by Zeus the blinding thunder-bolt.
I praise the good success
That rouses not God's wrath;
Ne'er be it mine a city to lay waste,[1]
Nor, as a prisoner, see
My life wear on beneath another's power!

Epode.

And now at bidding of the courier flame,
The herald of good news,
A rumour swift spreads through the city streets,
But who knows clearly whether it be true,
Or whether God has mingled lies with it?
Who is so childish or so reft of sense,
As with his heart a-glow
At that fresh uttered message of the flame,
Then to wax sad at changing rumour's sound?
It suits the mood that sways a woman's mind
To pour thanksgiving ere the truth is seen:
Quickly, with rapid steps, too credulous,
The limit which a woman sets to trust
Advances evermore;[2]
And with swift doom of death
A rumour spread by woman perishes.

(1) Here again one may note a protest against the aggressive policy of
Pericles, an assertion of the principle that a nation should be content
with independence, without aiming at supremacy.
(2) Perhaps passively, "Soon suffers trespassers."

[*As the Chorus ends, a Herald is seen approaching, his head wreathed with olive.*[1]

Soon we shall know the sequence of the torches
Light-giving, and of all the beacon-fires,
If they be true ; **or if**, as 'twere a dream,
This sweet light coming hath beguiled our minds.
I see a herald coming from the shore,
With olive boughs o'ershadowed, and the **dust,**[2]
Dry sister-twin of mire,[3] announces this,
That neither without voice, nor kindling blaze
Of wood upon the mountains, he will signal   480
With smoke from fire, but either he will come,
With clear speech bidding us rejoice, or else . . . [*pauses.*
The word opposed to this I much mislike.
Nay, may good issue good beginnings crown !
Who for our city utters other prayers,
May he himself his soul's great error reap !
   Herald. Hail, soil of this my Argive fatherland.
Now in the light of the tenth year I reach thee,
Though many hopes are shattered, gaining one.
For never did I think in Argive land
To die, and share the tomb that most I craved.   490
Now hail ! thou land ; and hail ! thou light of day :
Zeus our great ruler, and thou Pythian king,
No longer darting arrows from thy bow.[4]
Full hostile wast thou by Scamandros' banks ,
Now be thou Saviour, yea, and Healer found,
O king Apollo ! and the Gods of war,

(1) As the play opens on the morning of the day on which Troïa was
taken, and now we have the arrivals, first, of the herald, and then of
Agamemnon, after the capture has been completed, and the spoil divided,
and the fleet escaped a storm, an interval of some days must be supposed
between the two parts of the play, the imaginary law of the unities not-
withstanding.

(2) The customary adornment of heralds **who** brought good news.
Comp. Sophocles, *Œd. K.* v. 83. The custom prevailed for many cen-
turies. and is recognised by Dante, *Purg.* ii. 70, as usual in his time in
Italy.

(3) **So in** the *Seven against Thebes*, (v. 494,) smoke is called "the sister of
fire."

(4) A probable reference, not only to the story, but to the actual words
of Homer, *Il.* i. 45-52.

These I invoke; my patron Hermes too,
Dear herald, whom all heralds reverence,—
Those heroes, too, that sent us,[1]—graciously
To welcome back the host that war has spared.   500
Hail, O ye royal dwellings, home beloved!
Ye solemn thrones, and Gods who face the sun![2]
If e'er of old, with cheerful glances now
After long time receive our king's array.
For he is come, in darkness bringing light
To you and all, our monarch, Agamemnon.
Salute him with all grace; for so 'tis meet,
Since he hath dug up Troïa with the spade
Of Zeus the Avenger, and the plain laid waste;
Fallen their altars and the shrines of Gods;   510
The seed of all the land is rooted out,
This yoke of bondage casting over Troïa,
Our chief, the elder of the Atreidæ, comes,
A man full blest, and worthiest of high honour
Of all that are.   For neither Paris' self,
Nor his accomplice city now can boast
Their deed exceeds its punishment.   For he,
Found guilty on the charge of rape and theft,[3]
Hath lost his prize and brought his father's house,
With lands and all, to waste and utter wreck;
And Priam's sons have double forfeit paid.[4]   520

(1) Specially the Dioscuri, Castor and Polydeukes.
(2) Such a position (especially in the case of Zeus or Apollo) was common in the temples both of Greece and Rome, and had a very obvious signification. As the play was performed, the actual hour of the day probably coincided with that required by the dramatic sequence of events, and the statues of the Gods were so placed on the stage as to catch the rays of the morning sun when the herald entered. Hence the allusion to the bright "cheerful glances" would have a visible as well as ethical fitness.
(3) It formed part of the guilt of Paris, that, besides his seduction of Helena, he had carried off part of the treasures of Menelaos.
(4) The idea of a payment twofold the amount of the wrong done, as a complete satisfaction to the sufferer, was common in the early jurisprudence both of Greeks and Hebrews, (Exod. xxii, 4-7.) In some cases it was even more, as in the four or fivefold restitution of Exod. xxii. 1. In the grand opening of Isaiah's message of glad tidings the fact that Jerusalem has received "double for all her sins" is made the ground on which she may now hope for pardon. Comp. also Isa. lxi. 7; Zech. ix. 12.

Chor. Joy, joy, thou herald of the Achæan host !
Her. All joy is mine : I shrink from death no more.
Chor. Did love for this thy fatherland so try thee ?
Her. So that mine eyes weep tears for very joy.
Chor. Disease full sweet then this ye suffered from . . .
Her. How so ?   When taught, I shall thy meaning
     master.
Chor. Ye longed for us who yearned for you in turn.
Her. Say'st thou this land its yearning host yearned
     o'er ?
Chor. Yea, so that oft I groaned in gloom of heart.
Her. Whence came these bodings that an army hates ? [530]
Chor. Silence I've held long since a charm for ill.
Her. How, when your lords were absent, feared ye any ?
Chor. To use thy words, death now would welcome be.
Her. Good is the issue ; but in so long time
Some things, one well might say, have prospered well,
And some give cause for murmurs.   Save the Gods,
Who free from sorrow lives out all his life ?
For should I tell of toils, and how we lodged
Full hardly, seldom putting in to shore,[1]
And then with couch full hard. . . . What gave us not
Good cause for mourning ?   What ill had we not   [540]
As daily portion ?   And what passed on land,
That brought yet greater hardship : for our beds
Were under our foes' walls, and meadow mists
From heaven and earth still left us wringing wet,
A constant mischief to our garments, making
Our hair as shaggy as the beasts'.[2]   And if
One spoke of winter frosts that killed the birds,
By Ida's snow-storms made intolerable,[3]
Or heat, when Ocean in its noontide couch

(1) Perhaps—
     "Full hardly, and the close and crowded decks."
(2) So stress is laid upon this form of hardship, as rising from the
climate of Troïa, by Sophocles, *Aias*, 1206.
(3) One may conjecture that here also, as with the passage describing
the succession of beacon fires, (vv. 281-314,) the description would have
for an Athenian audience the interest of recalling personal reminiscences
of some recent campaign in Thrakè, or on the coasts of Asia.

Windless reclined and slept without a wave. . . .
But why lament o'er this?   Our toil is past;   650
Past too is theirs who in the warfare fell,
So that no care have they to rise again.
Why should I count the number of the dead,
Or he that lives mourn o'er a past mischance?
To change and chance I bid a long Farewell:
With us, the remnant of the Argive host,
Good fortune wins, no ills as counterpoise.
So it is meet to this bright sun we boast,
Who travel homeward over land and sea;
"The Argive host who now have captured Troïa,   560
These spoils of battle[1] to the Gods of Hellas
Hang on their pegs, enduring prize and joy."[2]
Hearing these things we ought to bless our country
And our commanders; and the grace of Zeus
That wrought this shall be honoured.   My tale's told.
    Chor. Thy words o'ercome me, and I say not nay;
To learn good keeps youth's freshness with the old.
'Tis meet these things should be a special care
To Clytæmnestra and the house, and yet
That they should make me sharer in their joy.

                    Enter CLYTÆMNESTRA.

    Clytæm. I long ago for gladness raised my cry,   570
When the first fiery courier came by night,
Telling of Troïa taken and laid waste:
And then one girding at me spake, "Dost think,
Trusting in beacons, Troïa is laid waste?
This heart elate is just a woman's way."
In words like these they made me out distraught;
Yet still I sacrificed, and with a strain

(1) We may, perhaps, think of the herald, as he speaks, placing some
representative trophy upon the pegs on the pedestals of the statues of
the great Gods of Hellas, whom he had invoked on his entrance.
    (2) Or,
            "So that to this bright morn our sons may boast,
            As they o'er land and ocean take their flight,
            'The Argive host of old, who captured Troïa,
            These spoils of battle to the Gods of Hellas,
            Hung on their pegs, a trophy of old days.'"

Shrill as a woman's, **they, now** here, now there,
Throughout the city hymns of blessing raised
In shrines of Gods, and lulled to gentle sleep
The **fragrant flame** that on the incense fed.   580
And now why need'st thou lengthen out thy words?
I from the king himself the tale shall learn;
And that I show all zeal to welcome back
My honoured lord on his return (for what
Is brighter joy for wife to see than this,
When God has brought her husband back from war,
To open wide her gates?) tell my lord this,
"**To come** with all his speed, the city's idol;"
And "**may he find** a faithful wife at home,
Such **as** he left her, noble watch-dog still   590
For him, and hostile to his enemies;
And like in all things else, who has not broken
One seal of his in all this length of time."[1]
No pleasure have I known, nor scandal ill
With any other more than . . . stains on bronze.[2]   *dyeing*
Such is my vaunt, and being full of truth,
Not shameful for a noble wife to speak.[3]   [*Exit.*

(1) **The husband,** on his departure, sealed up his special treasures. It was the **glory of the** faithful wife or the trusty steward to keep these seals unbroken.

(2) There is an ambiguity, possibly an intentional one, in the comparison which Clytæmnestra uses. If there was no such art as that of "staining bronze" (or copper) known at the time, the words would be a natural phrase enough to describe what was represented as an impossibility. Later on in the history of art, however, as in the time of Plutarch, a process so described (perhaps analogous to enamelling) is described (*De Pyth. Orac.* § 2) as common. If we suppose the art to have been a mystery known to the few, but not to the many, in the time of Æschylos, then the words would have for the hearers the **point** of a *double entendre.* She seems to the **mass** to disclaim what yet, to those in the secret she acknowledges.

Another rendering refers "bronze" to the "sword," **and** makes the stains those of blood; as though **she** said, "I am as guiltless of adultery as of murder," while yet she knew that she had committed the one, and meant to commit the other. The possibility of such a meaning is certainly **in** the words, and with a sharp-witted audience catching at ænigmas **and dark** sayings may have added to their suggestiveness. The ambiguous comment of the Chorus shows that they read, as between the lines, the shameful secret which they knew, but of which the Herald was **ignorant.**

(3) **The** last two lines are by some editors assigned to the Herald.

Chor. [*to Herald.*] She hath thus spoken in thy hear-
        ing now
A goodly word for good interpreters.
But tell me, herald, tell of Menelaos,   600
If, coming home again in safety he
Is with you, the dear strength of this our land.
  Her. I cannot make report of false good news,
So that my friends should long rejoice in it.
  Chor. Ah! could'st thou good news speak, and also
        true!
These things asunder are not well concealed.
  Her. The chief has vanished from the Achæan host,
He and his ship.   I speak no falsehood here.
  Chor. In sight of all when he from Ilion sailed?
Or did a storm's wide evil part him from you?   610
  Her. Like skilful archer thou hast hit the mark,
And in few words hast told of evil long.———
  Chor. And was it of him as alive or dead
The whisper of the other sailors ran?
  Her. None to that question answer clear can give,
Save the Sun-God who feeds the life of earth.
  Chor. How say'st thou? Did a storm come on our fleet,
And do its work through anger of the Gods?
  Her. It is not meet a day of tidings good
To mar with evil news.   Apart for each   620
Is special worship.   But when courier brings
With louring face the ills men pray against,
And tells a city that its host has fallen,
That for the State there is a general wound,
That many a man from many a home is driven,
As banned by double scourge that Ares loves,
Woe doubly-barbed, Death's two-horsed chariot this . . .
When with such griefs as freight a herald comes,
'Tis meet to chant the Erinnyes' dolorous song;
But for glad messenger of good deeds wrought
That bring deliverance, coming to a town   630
Rejoicing in its triumph, . . . how shall I
Blend good with evil, telling of a storm

That smote the Achæans, not without God's wrath?
For they a compact swore who erst were foes,
Ocean and Fire, and their pledges gave,
Wrecking the ill-starred army of the Argives;
And in the night rose ill of raging storm:
For Thrakian tempests shattered all the ships,
Each on the other.   Some thus crashed and bruised,
By the storm stricken and the surging foam
Of wind-tost waves, soon vanished out of sight,   640
Whirled by an evil pilot.   And when rose
The sun's bright orb, behold, the Ægæan sea
Blossomed with wrecks of ships and dead Achæans.
And as for us and our uninjured ship,
Surely 'twas some one stole or begged us off,
Some God, not man, presiding at the helm;
And on our ship with good will Fortune sat,
Giver of safety, so that nor in haven
Felt we the breakers, nor on rough rock-beach
Ran we aground.   But when we had escaped   650
The hell of waters, then in clear, bright day,
Not trusting in our fortune, we in thought
O'er new ills brooded of our host destroyed,
And eke most roughly handled.   And if still
Breathe any of them they report of us
As having perished.   How else should they speak?
And we in our turn deem that they are so.
God send good ending!   Look you, first and chief,
For Menelaos' coming; and indeed,
If any sunbeam know of him alive
And well, by help of Zeus who has not willed   660
As yet to blot out all the regal race,
Some hope there is that he'll come back again.
Know, hearing this, that thou the truth hast heard.

                                         [Exit Herald.

STROPH. I.

   Chor. Who was it named her with such wondrous truth?
      (Could it be One unseen,

In strange prevision of her destined work,
      Guiding the tongue through chance?)
Who gave that war-wed, strife-upstirring one
The name of Helen, ominous of ill?[1]
      For all too plainly she
      Hath been to men, and ships,
      And towers, as doom of Hell.
From bower of gorgeous curtains forth she sailed
With breeze of Zephyr Titan-born and strong;[2]
      And hosts of many men,
      Hunters that bore the shield,
Went on the track of those who steered their boat
Unseen to leafy banks of Simois,
      On her account who came,
Dire cause of strife with bloodshed in her train.

ANTISTROPH. I.

And so the wrath which works its vengeance out
      Dear bride to Ilion brought,
(Ah, all too truly named!) exacting still[3]
      After long lapse of time
The penalty of foul dishonour done
To friendship's board and Zeus, of host and guest
      The God, from those who paid
      Their loud-voiced honour then
      Unto that bridal strain,
That hymeneal chorus which to chant

(1) It need hardly be said that it is as difficult to render a *paronomasia* of this kind as it is to reproduce those, more or less analogous, which we find in the prophets of the Old Testament, (comp. especially Micah i.;) but it seems better to substitute something which approaches, however imperfectly, to an equivalent than to obscure the reference to the *nomen et omen* by abandoning the attempt to translate it. "Hell of men, and hell of ships, and hell of towers," has been the rendering adopted by many previous translators. The Greek fondness for this play on names is seen in Sophocles, *Aias*, v. 401.

(2) Zephyros, Boreas, and the other great winds were represented in the *Theogony* of Hesiod (v. 134) as the offspring of Astræos and Eôs, and Astræos was a Titan. The west wind was, of course, favourable to Paris as he went with Helen from Greece to Troïa.

(3) Here again the translator has to meet the difficulty of a pun. As an alternative we might take—

      "To Ilion brought, well-named,
      A marriage marring all."

Fell to the lot of all the bridegroom's kin.[1]
    But learning other song,
    Priam's ancient city now   640
Bewaileth sore, and calls on Paris' name,
Wedded in fatal wedlock; all the time
    * Enduring tear-fraught life
* For all the blood its citizens had lost.

STROPH. II.

    So once a lion's cub,
    A mischief in his house,
    As foster child one reared,[2]
    While still it loved the teats;
    In life's preluding dawn
    Tame, by the children loved,   700
    And fondled by the old,[3]
    Oft in his arms 'twas held,
    Like infant newly born,
With eyes that brightened to the hand that stroked,
And fawning at the hest of hunger keen.

ANTISTROPH. II.

    But when full-grown, it showed
    The nature of its sires;
    For it unbidden made
    A feast in recompense
    Of all their fostering care,
    * By banquet of slain sheep;   720
    With blood the house was stained,

(1) The sons of Priam are thought of as taking part in the celebration of Helen's marriage with Paris, and as, therefore, involving themselves in the guilt and the penalty of his crime.

(2) Here, too, it may be well to give an alternative rendering—

    "A mischief in his house,
    A man reared, not on milk."

Home-reared lions seem to have been common as pets, both among Greeks and Latins, (Arist., *Hist. Anim.* ix. 31; Plutarch, *de Cohib. irâ*, § 14, p. 822,) sometimes, as in Martial's Epigram, ii. 25, with fatal consequences. The text shows the practice to have been common enough in the time of Pericles to supply a similitude.

(3) There may, possibly, be a half allusion here to the passage in the *Iliad*, (vv. 154-160,) which describes the fascination which the beauty of Helen exercised on the Trojan elders.

P

A curse no slaves could check,
   Great mischief murderous :
By God's decree a priest of Atè thus
Was reared, and grew within the man's own house.

Stroph. III.

So I would tell that thus to Ilion came
Mood as of calm when all the air is still,
The gentle pride and joy of kingly state,
   A tender glance of eye,
The full-blown blossom of a passionate love,
   Thrilling the very soul ;
   And yet she turned aside,
And wrought a bitter end of marriage feast,
   Coming to Priam's race,
   Ill sojourner, ill friend,
Sent by great Zeus, the God of host and guest—
Erinnys, for whom wives weep many tears.

Antistroph. III.

There lives an old saw, framed in ancient days,[1]
In memories of men, that high estate
Full-grown brings forth its young, nor childless dies,
   But that from good success
Springs to the race a woe insatiable.
   But I, apart from all,
   Hold this my creed alone :
For impious act it is that offspring breeds,
   Like to their parent stock :
   For still in every house
That loves the right their fate for evermore
Rejoiceth in an issue fair and good.

(1) The poet becomes a prophet, and asserts what it has been given him to know of the righteous government of God. The dominant creed of Greece at the time was, that the Gods were envious of man's prosperity, that this alone, apart from moral evil, was enough to draw down their wrath, and bring a curse upon the prosperous house. So, *e.g.*, Amasis tells Polycrates (Herod. iii. 40) that the unseen Divinity that rules the world is envious, that power and glory are inevitably the precursors of destruction. Comp. also the speech of Artabanus, (Herod. vii. 10, 46.) Against this, in the tone of one who speaks single-handed for the truth, Æschylos, through the Chorus, enters his protest.

But Recklessness of old
Is wont to breed another Recklessness,
    Sporting its youth in human miseries,
Or now, or then, whene'er the fixed hour comes :   143
    That in its youth, in turn,
    Doth full-flushed Lust beget,
And that dread demon-power unconquerable,
    Daring that fears not God,—
Two curses black within the homes of men,
.   Like those that gendered them.

But Justice shineth bright
In dwellings that are dark and dim with smoke,
    And honours life law-ruled,
While gold-decked homes conjoined with hands defiled   750
    She with averted eyes
    Hath left, and draweth near   .
To holier things, nor worships might of wealth,
    If counterfeit its praise ;
But still directeth all the course of things
    Towards its destined goal.
        [AGAMEMNON *is seen approaching in his chariot,*
        followed by *another chariot, in which* CAS-
        SANDRA *is standing, carrying her prophet's
        wand in her hand, and wearing fillets round
        her temples, and by a great train of soldiers
        bearing* **trophies.** *As they come on the stage
        the Chorus sings its welcome.*
Come then, king, thou son of Atreus,
Waster of the towers of Troïa,
What of greeting and of homage
Shall I give, nor overshooting,
Nor due need of honour missing ?
Men there are who, right transgressing,
Honour semblance more than being.   760
    O'er the sufferer all are ready

Wail of bitter grief to utter,
Though the biting pang of sorrow
Never to their heart approaches;
So with counterfeit rejoicing
Men strain faces that are smileless;
But when one his own sheep knoweth,
Then men's eyes cannot deceive him,
When they deem with kindly purpose,   770
And with fondness weak to flatter.
Thou, when thou did'st lead thine army
For Helen's sake—(I will not hide it)—
Wast to me as one whose features
Have been limned by unskilled artist,
Guiding ill the helm of reason,
Giving men to death's doom sentenced
* Courage which their will rejected.[1]
Now nor from the spirit's surface,
Nor with touch of thought unfriendly,
All the toil, I say, is welcome,
If men bring it to good issue.
And thou soon shalt know, enquiring,   780
Him who rightly, him who wrongly
Of thy citizens fulfilleth
Task of office for the city.[2]

Agam. First Argos, and the Gods who guard the land,
'Tis right to greet; to them in part I owe
This my return, and vengeance that I took
On Priam's city. Not on hearsay proof
Judging the cause, with one consent the Gods
Cast in their votes into the urn of blood
For Ilion's ruin and her people's death;
* I' the other urn Hope touched the rim alone,   790

(1) *Sc.*, Agamemnon, by the sacrifice of Iphigenia, had induced his
troops to persevere in an expedition from which, in their inmost hearts,
they shrank back with strong dislike   A conjectural reading gives,
    "By the sacrifice he offered
    Giving death-doomed men false boldness."

(2) The tone of ambiguous irony mingles, it will be seen, even here,
with the praises of the Chorus.

Still far from being filled full.[1]   And even yet
The captured city by its smoke is seen,
* The incense clouds of Atè live on still;
And, in the act of dying with its prey,
From richest store the dust sends savours sweet.
For these things it is meet to give the Gods
Thank-offerings long-enduring; for our nets
Of vengeance we set close, and for a woman
Our Argive monster laid the city low,[2]
Foaled by the mare, a people bearing shield,
Taking its leap when set the Pleiades;[3]
And, bounding o'er the tower, that ravenous lion   800
Lapped up its fill of blood of kingly race.
This prelude to the Gods I lengthen out;
And as concerns thy feeling (this I well
Remember hearing) I with thee agree,
And thou in me may'st find an advocate.
With but few men is it their natural bent
To honour without grudging prosperous friend:
For ill-souled envy that the heart besets,
Doubles his woe who suffers that disease:
He by his own griefs first is overwhelmed,
And groans at sight of others' happier lot.   810
* And I with good cause say, (for well I know,)
They are but friendship's mirror, phantom shade,
Who seemed to be my most devoted friends.
Odysseus only, who against his will[4]
Sailed with us, still was found true trace-fellow:
And this I say of him or dead or living.

(1) Possibly an allusion to Pandora's box. Here, too, Hope alone was
left, but it only came up to where the curve of the rim began, not to its
top. The imagery is drawn from the older method of voting, in which
(as in *Eumenides*, v. 678) the votes for condemnation and acquittal were
cast into separate urns.
(2) The lion, as the symbol of the house of **Atreus**, still seen **in the**
sculptures of Mykenæ; the horse, in allusion to the stratagem by **which**
Troïa had been taken.
(3) At the end of autumn, and therefore at a season when a storm like
that described by the herald would be a probable incident enough.
(4) So in Sophocles, Philoctetes (v. 1025) taunts Odysseus :—

    " And yet thou sailedst with them by constraint,
    By tricks fast bound."

But as for all that touches on the State,
Or on the Gods, in full assembly we,
Calling our council, will deliberate :
For what goes well we should with care provide
How longest it may last ; and where there needs
A healing charm, there we with all good-will,
By surgery or cautery will try
To turn away the mischief of disease.
And now will I to home and household hearth
Move on, and first give thanks unto the Gods
Who led me forth, and brought me back again.
Since Victory follows, long may she remain !

Enter CLYTÆMNESTRA, *followed by female attendants
carrying purple tapestry.*

Clytæm. Ye citizens, ye Argive senators,
I will not shrink from telling you the tale
Of wife's true love. As time wears on one drops   630
All over-shyness.   Not learning it from others,
I will narrate my own unhappy life,
The whole long time my lord at Ilion stayed.
For first, that wife should sit at home alone
Without her husband is a monstrous grief,
Hearing full many an ill report of him,
Now one and now another coming still,
Bringing news home, worse trouble upon bad.
Yea, if my lord had met as many wounds
As rumour told of, floating to our house,   640
He had been riddled more than any net ;
And had he died, as tidings still poured in,
Then he, a second Geryon[1] with three lives,
Had boasted of a threefold coverlet
Of earth above, (I will not say below him,)[2]

(1) Geryon appears in the myth of Hercules as a monster with three
heads and three bodies, ruling over the island Erytheia, in the far West,
beyond Hesperia. To destroy him and seize his cattle was one of the
"twelve labours," with which Hesiod (*Theogon*, vv. 287-294) had already
made men familiar.
(2) When a man is buried, there is earth above and earth below him.
Clytæmnestra having used the words "coverlet," pauses to make her

Dying one death for each of those his forms;
And so, because of all these ill reports,
Full many a noose around my neck have others
Loosed by main force, when I had hung myself.
And for this cause no son is with me now,   850
Holding in trust the pledges of our love,
As he should be, Orestes. Wonder not;
For now a kind ally doth nurture him,
Strophios the Phokian, telling me of woes
Of twofold aspect, danger on thy side
At Ilion, and lest loud-voiced anarchy
Should overthrow thy council, since 'tis still
The wont of men to kick at those who fall.
No trace of guile bears this excuse of mine;
As for myself, the fountains of my tears
Have flowed till they are dry, no drop remains,   860
And mine eyes suffer from o'er-late repose,
Watching with tears the beacons set for thee,[1]
Left still unheeded. And in dreams full oft
I from my sleep was startled by the gnat
With thin wings buzzing, seeing in the night
Ills that stretched far beyond the time of sleep.[2]
Now, having borne all this, with mind at ease,
I hail my lord as watch-dog of the fold,
The stay that saves the ship, of lofty roof   870
Main column-prop, a father's only child,
Land that beyond all hope the sailor sees,
Morn of great brightness following after storm,

language accurate to the very letter. She is speaking only of the earth
which would have been laid over her husband's corpse, had he died as
often as he was reported to have done. She will not utter anything so
ominous as an allusion to the depths below him stretching down to
Hades.

(1) Or—

"Weeping because the torches in thy house
No more were lighted as they were of yore."

(2) The words touch upon the psychological fact that in dreams, as in
other abnormal states of the mind, the usual measures of time disappear,
and we seem to pass through the experiences of many years in the slumber of a few minutes.

Clear-flowing fount to thirsty traveller.[1]
Yes, it is pleasant to escape all straits :
With words of welcome such as these I greet thee ;
May jealous Heaven forgive them ! for we bore
Full many an evil in the past ; and now,
Dear husband, leave thy car, nor on the ground,
O King, set thou the foot that Ilion trampled.   840
Why linger ye, [*turning to her attendants,*] ye maids,
    whose task it was
To strew the pathway with your tapestries ?
Let the whole road be straightway purple-strown,
That Justice lead to home he looked not for.
All else my care, by slumber not subdued,
Will with God's help work out what fate decrees.[2]

(*The handmaids advance, and are about to lay the purple
    carpets on the ground.*)

Agam. O child of Leda, guardian of my home,
Thy speech hath with my absence well agreed—
For long indeed thou mad'st it—but fit praise
Is boon that I must seek at other hands.   850
I pray thee, do not in thy woman's fashion
Pamper my pride, nor in barbaric guise
Prostrate on earth raise full-mouthed cries to me ;
Make not my path offensive to the Gods
By spreading it with carpets.[3]   They alone

---

(1) The rhetoric of the passage, with all its multiplied similitudes, fine
as it is in itself, receives its dramatic significance by being put into the
lips of Clytæmnestra. She "doth protest too much." A true wife would
have been content with fewer words.
(2) The last three lines of the speech are of course intentionally ambiguous, carrying one meaning to the ear of Agamemnon, and another to
that of the audience.
(3) There is obviously a side-thrust, such as an Athenian audience
would catch at, at the token of homage which the Persian kings required
of their subjects, the prostration at their feet, the earth spread over with
costly robes. Of the latter custom we have examples in the history of
Jehu, (2 Kings ix. 13,) in our Lord's entry into Jerusalem, (Mark xi. 8,)
in the usages of modern Persian kings, (Malcolm's *Persia*, i. 580 ;)
perhaps also in the true rendering of Ps. xlv. 14, "She shall be brought
unto the king *on* raiment of needle-work." In the march of Xerxes
across the Hellespont myrtle-boughs strown on the bridge of boats took
the place of robes, (Herod. vii. 54.) To the Greek character, with its
strong love of independence, such customs were hateful. The case of

May claim that honour ; but for mortal men
To walk on fair embroidery, to me
Seems nowise without peril. So I 'bid you
To honour me as man, and not as God.
Apart from all foot-mats and tapestry
My fame speaks loudly ; and God's greatest gift   900
Is not to err from wisdom. We must bless
Him only who ends life in fair estate.[1]
Should I thus act throughout, good hope were mine.

> *Clytæm.* Nay, say not this my purposes to thwart.
> *Agam.* Know I change not for the worse my pur-
>   pose.
> *Clytam.* In fear, perchance, thou vowèd'st thus to act.
> *Agam.* If any, I, with good ground spoke my will.[2]
> *Clytæm.* What think'st thou Priam, had he wrought
>   such deeds . . . ?
> *Agam.* Full gladly he, I trow, had trod on carpets.
> *Clytæm.* Then shrink not thou through fear of men's
>   dispraise.   910
> *Agam.* And yet a people's whisper hath great might.[3]
> *Clytæm.* Who is not envied is not enviable.
> *Agam.* 'Tis not a woman's part to crave for strife.
> *Clytam.* True, yet the prosperous e'en should some-
>   times yield.
> *Agam.* Dost thou then prize that victory in the strife ?
> *Clytæm.* Nay, list ; with all good-will yield me this
>   boon.

Agam. Well, then, if thou wilt have it so, with speed
Let some one loose my buskins,[4] (servants they

Pausanias, who offended the national feeling by assuming the outward
state of the Persian kings, must have been recalled to the minds of the
Athenians, intentionally or otherwise, by such a passage as this.
    (1) The "old saying, famed of many men," which we find in the
Trachiniæ of Sophocles, (v. 1,) and in the counsel of Solon to Crœsus,
(Herod i. 32.)
    (2) He who had suffered so much from the wrath of Artemis at Aulis
knew what it was to rouse the wrath and jealousy of the Gods.
    (3) An echo of a line in Hesiod, (*Works and Days*, 763)—
> "No whispered rumours which the many spread
> Can ever wholly perish."
    (4) Here, too, we may trace a reference to the Oriental custom of
recognising the sanctity of a consecrated place by taking the shoes from

Doing the foot's true work,) and as I tread
Upon these robes sea-purpled, may no wrath
From glance of Gods smite on me from afar !   420
Great shame I feel to trample with my foot
This wealth of carpets, costliest work of looms ;
So far for this.   This stranger [*pointing to* CASSANDRA]
      lead thou in
With kindliness.   On him who gently wields
His power God's eye looks kindly from afar.
None of their own will choose a bondslave's life ;
And she, the chosen flower of many spoils,
Has followed with me as the army's gift.
But since I turn, obeying thee in this,
I'll to my palace go, on purple treading.   430
      Clytæm. There is a sea,—and who shall drain it dry ?
Producing still new store of purple juice,
Precious as silver, staining many a robe.
And in our house, with God's help, O my king,
'Tis ours to boast our palace knows no stint.
Trampling of many robes would I have vowed,
Had that been ordered me in oracles,
When for my lord's return I then did plan
My votive gifts.   For while the root lives on,
The foliage stretches even to the house,
And spreads its shade against the dog-star's rage ;   440
So when thou comest to thy hearth and home,
Thou show'st that warmth hath come in winter time;
And when from unripe clusters Zeus matures
The wine,[1] then is there coolness in the house,
If the true master dwelleth in his home.
Ah, Zeus ! the All-worker, Zeus, work out for me

off the feet, as in Exod. iii. 5, in the services of the Tabernacle and
Temple, through all their history, (Juven., *Sat.* vi. 159,) in all mosques to
the present day.   Agamemnon, yielding to the temptress, seeks to make
a compromise with his conscience. He will walk upon the tapestry, but
will treat it as if it, of right, belonged to the Gods, and were a consecrated thing.   It is probably in connexion with this incident that
Æschylos was said to have been the first to bring actors on the stage in
these boots or buskins, (Suidas. s. v. ἀρβύλη.)
   (1) The words of Isaiah, (xviii. 5,) "when the sour grape is ripening in
the flower," present an almost verbal parallel.

All that I pray for; let it be thy care
To look to what Thou purposest to work.[1]

> [*Exeunt* AGAMEMNON, *walking on the* tapestry,
> CLYTÆMNESTRA, *and her attendants.*

STROPH. I.

Chor. Why thus continually
Do haunting phantoms hover at the gate ?
  Of my foreboding heart ?   950
Why floats prophetic song, unbought, unbidden ?
  Why doth no steadfast trust
  Sit on my mind's dear throne,
To fling it from me as a vision dim ?
Long time hath passed since stern-ropes of our ships
Were fastened on the sand, when our great host
  Of those that sailed in ships
  Had come to Ilion's towers :[2]

ANTISTROPH. I.

. And now from these mine eyes   960
I learn, myself reporting to myself,
  Their safe return; and yet
My mind within itself, taught by itself,
  Chanteth Erinnys' dirge,
  The lyreless melody,
And hath no strength of wonted confidence.
Not vain these inner pulses, as my heart
Whirls eddying in breast oracular.
  I, against hope, will pray
  It prove false oracle.   970

STROPH. II.

  Of high, o'erflowing health
There is no bound that stays the wish for more,
For evermore disease, as neighbour close
  Whom but a wall divides,

---

(1) The ever-recurring ambiguity of Clytæmnestra's language is again
traceable, as is also her fondness for rhetorical similitudes.
(2) The Chorus speaks in perplexity. It cannot get rid of its forebodings, and yet it would seem as if the time for the fulfilment of the dark
words of Calchas must have passed long since. It actually sees the safe
return of the leader of the host, yet still its fears haunt it.

Upon it presses ; and man's prosperous state
      *Moves on its course, and strikes
         Upon an unseen rock ;
But if his fear for safety of his freight,
A part, from well-poised sling, shall sacrifice,
      Then the whole house sinks not,
      O'erfilled with wretchedness,
      Nor does he swamp his boat :
      So, too, abundant gift
From Zeus in bounteous fulness, and the fruit
      Of globe at harvest tide
Have caused to cease sore hunger's pestilence ;

ANTISTROPH. II.

      But blood that once hath flowed
In purple stains of death upon the ground
At a man's feet, who then can bid it back
      By any charm of song ?
Else him who knew to call the dead to life[1]
      * Zeus had not sternly checked,
      * As warning unto all ;
But unless Fate, firm-fixed, had barred our fate
From any chance of succour from the Gods,
      Then had my heart poured forth
      Its thoughts, outstripping speech.[2]
      But now in gloom it wails
      Sore vexed, with little hope
At any time hereafter fitting end
      To find, unravelling,
My soul within me burning with hot thoughts.

Re-enter CLYTÆMNESTRA.

Clytæm. [to CASSANDRA, who has remained in the chariot
                during the choral ode.]
Thou too—I mean Cassandra—go within ;.

----

(1) Asclepios, whom Zeus smote with his thunderbolt for having restored
Hippolytos to life.
(2) The Chorus, in spite of their suspicions and forebodings, have
given the king no warning. They excuse themselves by the plea of
necessity, the sovereign decree of Zeus overruling all man's attempts to
withstand it.

Since Zeus hath made it thine, and not in wrath,
To share the lustral waters in our house,
Standing with many a slave the altar nigh
Of Zeus, who guards our goods.[1]   Now get thee down
From out this car, nor look so over proud.
They say that e'en Alcmena's son endured[2]
Being sold a slave, constrained to bear the yoke:
And if the doom of this ill chance should come,
Great boon it is to meet with lords who own
Ancestral wealth.   But whoso reap full crops   1010
They never dared to hope for, these in all,
And beyond measure, to their slaves are harsh:[3]
From us thou hast what usage doth prescribe.

   Chor. So ends she, speaking words full clear to thee:
And seeing thou art in the toils of fate,
If thou obey, thou wilt obey; and yet,
Perchance, obey thou wilt not.

   Clytæm. Nay, but unless she, like a swallow, speaks
A barbarous tongue unknown, I, speaking now
Within her apprehension, bid obey.   1020

   Chor. [*to* CASSANDRA, *still standing motionless*] Go with
         her.   What she bids is now the best;
Obey her: leave thy seat upon this car.

   Clytæm. I have no leisure here to stay without:
For as regards our central altar, there
The sheep stand by as victims for the fire;
For never had we hoped such thanks to give:
If thou wilt do this, make no more delay;

---

(1) Cassandra is summoned to an act of worship. The household is
gathered, the altar to Zeus Ktesios, (the God of the family property,
slaves included,) standing in the servants' hall, is ready. The new slave
must come in and take her place with the others.

(2) As in the story which forms the groundwork of the *Trachiniæ* of
Sophocles, vv. 250-280, that Heracles had been sold to Omphale as a slave,
in penalty for the murder of Iphitos.

(3) Political as well as dramatic. The Eupatrid poet appeals to public
opinion against the *nouveaux riches*, the tanners and lamp-makers, who
were already beginning to push themselves forward towards prominence
and power. The way was thus prepared in the first play of the Trilogy
for what is known to have been the main object of the last. Comp. Arist.,
Rhet. ii. 32.

But if thou understandest not my words,
Then wave thy foreign hand in lieu of speech.

> [CASSANDRA *shudders as in horror, but*
> *makes no sign.*

Chor. The stranger seems a clear interpreter
To need.   Her look is like a captured deer's.   1030
Clytæm. Nay, she is mad, and follows evil thoughts,
Since, leaving now her city, newly-captured,
She comes, and knows not how to take the curb,
Ere she foam out her passion in her blood.
I will not bear the shame of uttering more.   [*Exit.*
Chor. And I—I pity her, and will not rage:
Come, thou poor sufferer, empty leave thy car;
Yield to thy doom, and handsel now the yoke.

> [CASSANDRA *leaves the chariot, and bursts*
> *into a cry of wailing.*

STROPH. I.

Cass.   Woe! woe, and well-a-day!
                Apollo! O Apollo!   1040
Chor. Why criest thou so loud on Loxias?
The wailing cry of mourner suits not him.

ANTISTROPH. I.

Cass.   Woe! woe, and well-a-day!
                Apollo! O Apollo!
Chor. Again with boding words she calls the God,
Though all unmeet as helper to men's groans.

STROPH. II.

Cass.   Apollo! O Apollo!
God of all paths, Apollo true to me;
For still thou dost appal me and destroy.[1]
Chor. She seems her own ills like to prophecy: 1050
The God's great gift is in the slave's mind yet.

---

(1) Here again the translator has the task of finding an English *paro-*
nomasia which approximates to that of the Greek, between Apollo and
ἀπόλλων *the destroyer.*   To Apollo, as the God of paths, (*Aguieus,*) an
altar stood, column-fashion, before the street-door of every house, and to
such an altar, placed by the door of Agamemnon's palace, Cassandra turns,
with the twofold play upon the name.

ANTISTROPH. II.

Cass.　　　Apollo! O Apollo!
God of all paths, Apollo true to me;
What path hast led me? To what roof hast brought?
　Chor. To that of the Atreidæ. This I tell,
If thou know'st not. Thou wilt not find it false.

STROPH. III.

Cass.　　　Ah! Ah! Ah me!
Say rather to a house God hates—that knows
　　Murder, self-slaughter, ropes,[1]
* A human shamble, staining earth with blood.　　1060
　Chor. Keen scented seems this stranger, like a hound,
And sniffs to see whose murder she may find.

ANTISTROPH. III.

Cass.　　　Ah! Ah! Ah me!
Lo! [*looking wildly, and pointing to the house,*] there the
　　witnesses whose word I trust,—
　　Those babes who wail their death,
The roasted flesh that made a father's meal.
　Chor. We of a truth had heard thy seeress fame,
But prophets now are not the race we seek.[2]

STROPH. IV.

Cass. Ah me! O horror! What ill schemes she now?
　　What is this new great woe?　　　1070
Great evil plots she in this very house,
Hard for its friends to bear, immedicable;
　　And help stands far aloof.
　Chor. These oracles of thine surpass my ken;
Those I know well. The whole town rings with them.[3]

(1) This refers, probably, to the death of Hippodamcia, the wife of
Pelops, who killed herself, in remorse for the death of Chrysippos, or
fear of her husband's anger. The horrors of the royal house of Argos
pass, one by one, before the vision of the prophetess, and this leads
the procession, followed by the spectres of the murdered children of
Thyestes.
(2) The Chorus, as in their last ode, had made up their minds, though
foreboding ill, to let destiny take its course. They do not wish that
policy of non-interference to be changed by any too clear vision of the
future.
(3) The Chorus understands the vision of the *clairvoyante* as regards the

ANTISTROPH. IV.

Cass. Ah me! O daring one! what work'st thou here,
    Who having in his bath
Tended thy spouse, thy lord, then . . . How tell the rest?
For quick it comes, and hand is following hand,
    Stretched out to strike the blow.   1060
Chor. Still I discern not; after words so dark
I am perplexed with thy dim oracles.

STROPH. V.

Cass. Ah, horror, horror! What is this I see?
    Is it a snare of Hell?
Nay, the true net is she who shares his bed,
    Who shares in working death. *who shares the crime*
Ha! let the Band insatiable in hate[1]
Howl for the race its wild exulting cry
    O'er sacrifice that calls
    For death by storm of stones.

STROPH. VI.

Chor. What dire Erinnys bidd'st thou o'er our house
To raise shrill cry? Thy speech but little cheers;
    And to my heart there rush
    Blood-drops of saffron hue,[2]   1070
    * Which, when from deadly wound
They fall, together with life's setting rays
End, as it fails, their own appointed course:
    And mischief comes apace.

ANTISTROPH. V.

Cass. See, see, I say, from that fell heifer there.
    Keep thou the bull:[3] in robes

past tragedy of the house of Atreus, but not that which seems to portend another actually imminent.

(1) Fresh visions come before the eyes of the seeress. She beholds the company of Erinnyes hovering over the accursed house, and calls on them to continue their work till the new crime has met with its due punishment. The murder which she sees as if already wrought, demands death by stoning.

(2) The "yellow" look of fear is thought of as being caused by an actual change in the colour of the blood as it flows through the veins to the heart.

(3) Here there is prevision as well as clairvoyance. The deed is not yet

Entangling him, she with her weapon gores
  Him with the swarthy horns;[1]
Lo! in that bath with water filled he falls,
Smitten to death, and I to thee set forth
  Crime of a bath of blood,
  By murderous guile devised.

ANTISTROPH. VI.

Chor. I may not boast that I keen insight have
In words oracular; yet bode I ill.   1100
  What tidings good are brought
  By any oracles
  To mortal men? These arts,
  In days of evils sore, with many words,
Do still but bring a vague, portentous fear
  For men to learn and know.

STROPH. VII.

Cass. Woe, woe! for all sore ills that fall on me!
It is my grief thou speak'st of, blending it
  With his.[2] [*Pausing, and then crying out.*] Ah!
    wherefore then
  Hast thou[3] thus brought me here,
  Only to die with thee?
  What other doom is mine?

STROPH. VIII.

Chor. Frenzied art thou, and by some God's might
    swayed,   1110
  And utterest for thyself
A melody which is no melody,
  Like to that tawny one,

---

done. The sacrifice and the feast are still going on, yet she sees the crime in all its circumstances.

(1) As before (v. 115) the black eagle had been the symbol of the warrior-chief, so here the black-horned bull, that being one of the notes of the best breed of cattle. A various reading gives "with *her* swarthy horn."

(2) What the Chorus had just said as to the fruitlessness of prophetic insight tallied all too well with her own bitter experience.

(3) The ecstasy of horror interrupts the tenor of her speech, and the second "thou" is addressed not to the Chorus, but to Agamemnon, whose death Cassandra has just witnessed in her vision.

Q

Insatiate in her wail,
The nightingale, who still with sorrowing soul,
       And "Itys, Itys," cry,[1]
Bemoans a life o'erflourishing in ills.

ANTISTROPH. VII.

Cass. Ah, for the doom of clear-voiced nightingale!
The Gods gave her a body bearing wings,
       And life of pleasant days
       With no fresh cause to weep:
       But for me waiteth still
       Stroke from the two-edged sword.

ANTISTROPH. VIII.

Chor. From what source hast thou these dread agonies
       Sent on thee by thy God,
Yet vague and little meaning; and thy cries   1120
       Dire with ill-omened shrieks
       Dost utter as a chant,
And blendest with them strains of shrillest grief?
       Whence treadest thou this track
Of evil-boding path of prophecy?

STROPH. IX.

Cass. Woe for the marriage-ties, the marriage-ties
Of Paris that brought ruin on his friends!
       Woe for my native stream,
       Scamandros, that I loved!
Once on thy banks my maiden youth was reared,
       (Ah, miserable me!)
Now by Cokytos and by Acheron's shores   1130
I seem too likely soon to utter song
       Of wild, prophetic speech.

---

(1) The song of the nightingale, represented by these sounds, was connected with a long legend, specially Attic in its origin. Philomela,
daughter of Pandion, king of Attica, suffered outrage at the hands of
Tereus, who was married to her sister Procne, and was then changed into
a nightingale, destined ever to lament the fate of Itys, her sister's son.
The earliest form of the story appears in the Odyssey, (xix. 518). Comp.
Sophocles, *Electr.* v. 148.

Stroph. X.

Chor. What hast thou spoken now
With utterance all too clear?
*Even a boy its gist might understand;
I to the quick am pierced
With throe of deadly pain,
Whilst thou thy moaning cries art uttering
Over thy sore mischance,
Wondrous for me to hear.

Antistroph. IX.

Cass. Woe for the toil and trouble, toil and trouble
Of city that is utterly destroyed!
Woe for the victims slain
Of herds that roamed the fields,   1140
My father's sacrifice to save his towers!
No healing charm they brought
To save the city from its present doom:
And I with hot thoughts wild myself shall cast
Full soon upon the ground.

Antistroph. X.

Chor. This that thou utterest now
With all before agrees.
Some Power above dooms thee with purpose ill,
Down-swooping heavily,
To utter with thy voice
Sorrows of deepest woe, and bringing death.
And what the end shall be
Perplexes in the extreme.
Cass. Nay, now no more from out of maiden veils
My oracle shall glance, like bride fresh wed;[1]   1150
But seems as though 'twould rush with speedy gales
In full, clear brightness to the morning dawn;
So that a greater woe than this shall surge

---

(1) In the marriage-rites of the Greeks of the time of Æschylos, the bride for three days after the wedding wore her veil; then, as now no longer shrinking from her matron life, she laid it aside and looked on her husband with unveiled face.

Like wave against the sunlight.[1]   Now I'll teach
No more in parables.   Bear witness ye,
As running with me, that I scent the track
Of evil deeds that long ago were wrought:
For never are they absent from this house,
That choral band which chants in full accord,
Yet no good music; good is not their theme.
And now, as having drunk men's blood,[2] and so
Grown wilder, bolder, see, the revelling band,   1160
Erinnyes of the race, still haunt the halls,
Not easy to dismiss.   And so they sing,
Close cleaving to the house, its primal woe,[3]
And vent their loathing in alternate strains
On marriage-bed of brother ruthless found
To that defiler.   *Miss I now, or hit,
Like archer skilled? or am I seeress false,
A babbler vain that knocks at every door?
Yea, swear beforehand, ere I die, I know
(And not by rumour only) all the sins
Of ancient days that haunt and vex this house.

    Chor. How could an oath, how firm soe'er confirmed,
Bring aught of healing?   Lo, I marvel at thee,   1170
That thou, though born far off beyond the sea,
Should'st tell an alien city's tale as clear
As though thyself had stood by all the while.

    Cass. The seer Apollo set me to this task.
    Chor. Was he, a God, so smitten with desire?
    Cass. There was a time when shame restrained my
        speech.
    Chor. True; they who prosper still are shy and coy.
    Cass. He wrestled hard, breathing hot love on me.
    Chor. And were ye one in act whence children spring?

---

(1) The picture might be drawn by any artist of power, but we may,
perhaps, trace a reproduction of one of the grandest passages in the *Iliad*,
(iv. 422-426.)
(2) So in the *Eumenides*, (v. 293,) the Erinnyes appear as vampires,
drinking the blood of their victims.
(3) The death of Myrtilos as the first crime in the long history of the
house of Pelops.   Comp. Soph. *Electr.* v. 470.   The "defiler" is Thyestes,
who seduced Aerope, the wife of Atreus.

Cass. I promised Loxias, then I broke my vow.

Chor. Wast thou e'en then possessed with arts
  divine?   1180

Cass. E'en then my country's woes I prophesied.

Chor. How wast thou then unscathed by Loxias' wrath?

Cass. I for that fault with no man gained belief.

Chor. To us, at least, thou seem'st to speak the truth.

-*Cass.* [*Again speaking wildly, as in an ecstasy*] Ah, woe
  is me! Woe's me! Oh, ills on ills!

Again the dread pang of true prophet's gift
With preludes of great evil dizzies me.
See ye those children sitting on the house
In fashion like to phantom forms of dreams?   1190
Infants who perished at their own kin's hands,
Their palms filled full with meat of their own flesh,
Loom on my sight, the heart and entrails bearing,
(A sorry burden that!) on which of old
Their father fed.[1] And in revenge for this,
I say a lion, dwelling in his lair,
With not a spark of courage, stay-at-home,
Plots 'gainst my master, now he's home returned,
(Yes mine—for still I must the slave's yoke bear;)
And the ship's ruler, Ilion's conqueror,
Knows not what things the tongue of that lewd bitch
Has spoken and spun out in welcome smooth,   1200
And, like a secret Atè, will work out
With dire success: thus 'tis she plans: the man
Is murdered by the woman. By what name
Shall I that loathèd monster rightly call?
An Amphisbæna? or a Skylla dwelling[2]
Among the rocks, the sailors' enemy?

(1) The horror of the Thyestes banquet again haunts her as the source
of all the evils that followed, of the deaths both of Iphigeneia and Agamemnon. The "stay-at-home" is Ægisthos.

(2) Both words point to the Sindbad-like stories of distant marvels
brought back by Greek sailors. The Amphisbæna, (double-goer), wrig-
gling itself backward and forward, believed to have a head at each
extremity, was looked upon as at once the most subtle and the most
venomous of serpents. Skylla, already famous in its mythical form from
the story in the Odyssey, (xii. 85-100,) was probably a "development" of
the monstrous cuttle-fish of the straits of Messina.

Hades' fierce raging mother, breathing out
Against her friends a curse implacable?
Ah, how she raised her cry, (oh, daring one!)
As for the rout of battle, and she feigns
To hail with joy her husband's safe return!
And if thou dost not credit this, what then?
What will be will.   Soon, present, pitying me   1210
Thou'lt own I am too true a prophetess.

   Chor. Thyestes' banquet on his children's flesh
I know and shudder at, and fear o'ercomes me,
Hearing not counterfeits of fact, but truths;
Yet in the rest I hear and miss my path.

    Cass. I say thou'lt witness Agamemnon's death.

    Chor. Hush, wretched woman, close those lips of
        thine!

    Cass. For this my speech no healing God's at hand.

    Chor. True, if it must be; but may God avert it!   1220

    Cass. Thou utterest prayers, but others murder plot.

    Chor. And by what man is this dire evil wrought?

    Cass. Sure, thou hast seen my bodings all amiss.

    Chor. I see not his device who works the deed.

    Cass. And yet I speak the Hellenic tongue right well.

    Chor. So does the Pythian, yet her words are hard.

    Cass. [*In another access of frenzy.*] Ah me, this fire!
        It comes upon me now!

Ah me, Apollo, wolf-slayer! woe is me!
This biped lioness who takes to bed
A wolf in absence of the noble lion,   1230
Will slay me, wretched me.   And, as one
Mixing a poisoned draught, she boasts that she
Will put my price into her cup of wrath,
Sharpening her sword to smite her spouse with death,
So paying him for bringing me.   Oh, why
Do I still wear what all men flout and scorn,
My wand and seeress wreaths around my neck?[1]

---

(1) As in Homer (*Il.* i. 14) so here, the servant of Apollo bears the
wand of augury, and fillets or wreaths round head and arms.   The
divining garments, in like manner, were of white linen.

Thee, ere myself I die I will destroy: [*breaks her wand.*]
Perish ye thus: [*casting off her wreaths,*] I soon shall
    follow you:
Make rich another Atè[1] in my place;
Behold Apollo's self is stripping me   1240
Of my divining garments, and that too,
When he has seen me even in this garb
Scorned without cause among my friends and kin,
*By foes, with no diversity of mood.
Reviled as vagrant, wandering prophetess,
Poor, wretched, famished, I endured to live:
And now the Seer who me a seeress made
Hath brought me to this lot of deadly doom.
Now for my father's altar there awaits me
A butcher's block, where I am smitten down
By slaughtering stroke, and with hot gush of blood.
But the Gods will not slight us when we're dead;   1250
Another yet shall come as champion for us,
A son who slays his mother, to avenge
His father; and the exiled wanderer
Far from his home, shall one day come again,
Upon these woes to set the coping-stone:
For the high Gods have sworn a mighty oath,
His father's fall, laid low, shall bring him back.
Why then do I thus groan in this new home,[2]
When, to begin with, Ilion's town I saw
Faring as it did fare, and they who held
That town are gone by judgment of the Gods?   1260
I too will fare as they, and venture death:
So I these gates of Hades now address,
And pray for blow that bringeth death at once,
That so with no fierce spasm, while the blood
Flows in calm death, I then may close mine eyes.
           [*Goes towards the door of the palace.*

(1) If we adopt this reading, we must think of Cassandra as identifying
herself with the woe (Atè) which makes up her life, just as afterwards
Clytæmnestra speaks of herself as one with the avenging Demon (Alastor)
of the house of Atreus, (1473.) The alternative reading gives,—
        "Make rich in woe another in my place."
(2) Perhaps, "in home not mine."

Chor. O thou most wretched, yet again most wise:
Long hast thou spoken, lady, but if well
Thou know'st thy doom, why to the altar go'st thou,
Like heifer driven of God, so confidently ? [1]   1270

Cass. For me, my friends, there is no time to 'scape. [2]
Chor. Yea; but he gains in time who comes the last.
Cass. The day is come : small gain for me in flight.
Chor. Know then thou sufferest with a heart full
    brave.
Cass. Such words as these the happy never hear.
Chor. Yet mortal man may welcome noble death.
Cass. [*Shrinking back from opening the door.*] Woe's
    me for thee and thy brave sons, my father ! [3]
Chor. What cometh now ? What fear oppresseth thee ?
Cass. [*Again going to the door and then shuddering in
    another burst of frenzy.*] Fie on't, fie !
Chor. Whence comes this " Fie ? " unless from mind
    that loathes ?   ..   [1280
Cass. The house is tainted with the scent of death.
Chor. How so ? This smells of victims on the hearth.
Cass. Nay, it is like the blast from out a grave.
Chor. No Syrian ritual tell'st thou for our house. [4]
Cass. Well then I go, and e'en within will wail
My fate and Agamemnon's. And for me,
Enough of life. Ah, friends ! Ah ! not for nought
I shrink in fear, as bird shrinks from the brake. [5]
When I am dead do ye this witness bear,
When in revenge for me, a woman, Death
A woman smites, and man shall fall for man   1290

(1) When the victim, instead of shrinking and struggling, went, as with
good courage, to the altar, it was noted as a sign of divine impulse. Such
a strange, new courage the Chorus notices in Cassandra.
(2) Possibly,
    " My one escape, **my friends, is** but delay."
(3) The implied thoughts of **the** words is that Priam and **his sons,**
though they had died nobly, were yet miserable, and not happy.
(4) The Syrian ritual had, it would seem, become proverbial for **its**
lavish use of frankincense and other spices.
(5) The close parallel of Shakspeare's *Henry VI.*, **Act. v.** sc. 6, is worth
quoting—
   " The bird that hath been limed in a bush,
    With trembling **eyes** misdoubteth every bush."

In evil wedlock wed.   This friendly office,
As one about to die, I pray you do me.
   Chor. Thy doom foretold, poor sufferer, moves my pity.
   Cass. I fain would speak once more, yet not to wail
Mine own death-song; but to the Sun I pray,
To his last rays, that my avengers wreak
Upon my hated murderers judgment due
For me, who die a slave's death, easy prey.
Ah, life of man! when most it prospereth,
* It is but limned in outline;[1] and when brought
To low estate, then doth the sponge, full soaked,   1300
Wipe out the picture with its frequent touch :
And this I count more piteous e'en than that.[2]
                [*Passes through the door into the palace.*
   Chor. 'Tis true of all men that they never set
A limit to good fortune; none doth say,
      As bidding it depart,
* And warding it from palaces of pride,
     " Enter thou here no more."
To this our lord the Blest Ones gave to take
     Priam's city; and he comes
Safe to his home and honoured by the Gods;
     But if he he now shall pay
The forfeit of blood-guiltiness of old,
And, dying, so work out for those who died,
By his own death another penalty,   1310
     Who then of mortal men,
     Hearing such things as this,
     Can boast that he was born
     With fate from evil free ?
   Agam. [*from within.*] Ah, me! I am struck down
       with deadly stroke.
   Chor. Hush! Who cries out with deadly stroke sore
      smitten ?
   Agam. Ah me, again! struck down a second time! [*Dies.*

(1) The older reading gives—
          " A shadow might o'erturn it."
  (2) Her own doom, hard as it was, touches her less than the common
lot of human suffering and mutability.

Chor. By the king's groans I judge the deed is done;
B .t let us now confer for counsels safe.[1]

Chor. a. I give you my advice to summon here,
Here to the palace, all the citizens.   1320

Chor. b. I think it best to rush at once on them,
And take them in the act with sword yet wet.

Chor. c. And I too give like counsel, and I vote
For deed of some kind.   'Tis no time to pause.

Chor. d. Who will see, may.—They but the prelude
        work
Of tyranny usurped o'er all the State.

Chor. e. Yes, we are slow, but they who trample down
The thought of hesitation slumber not.

Chor. f. I know not what advice to find or speak:
He who can act knows how to counsel too.   1330

Chor. g. I too think with thee; for I have no hope
With words to raise the dead again to life.

Chor. h. What! Shall we drag our life on and submit
To these usurpers that defile the house?

Chor. i. Nay, that we cannot bear: To die were better;
For death is gentler far than tyranny.

Chor. k. Shall we upon this evidence of groans
Guess, as divining that our lord is dead?

Chor. l. When we know clearly, then should we
        discuss:
To guess is one thing, and to know another.   1340

Chor.[2] So vote I too, and on the winning side,
Taking the votes all round that we should learn
How he, the son of Atreus, fareth now.

    Enter CLYTÆMNESTRA *from the palace, in robes with
    stains of blood, followed by soldiers and attendants.
    The open doors show the corpses of* AGAMEMNON
    and CASSANDRA, *the former lying in a silvered
    bath.*

Clytæm. Though many words before to suit the time

---

(1) So far the dialogue has been sustained by the Coryphæos, or leader
of the Chorus. Now each member of it speaks and gives his counsel.
(2) The Coryphæos again takes up his part, sums up, and pronounces
his decision.

Were spoken, now I shall not be ashamed
The contrary to utter: How could one
By open show of enmity to foes
Who seemed as friends, fence in the snares of death
Too high to be o'erleapt? But as for me,
Not without forethought for this long time past,
This conflict comes to me from triumph old [1]
Of his, though slowly wrought.   I stand where I   1350
Did smite him down, with all my task well done.
So did I it, (the deed deny I not,)
That he could nor avert his doom nor flee:
I cast around him drag-net as for fish,
With not one outlet, evil wealth of robe:
And twice I smote him, and with two deep groans
He dropped his limbs: And when he thus fell down
I gave him yet a third, thank-offering true [2]
To Hades of the dark, who guards the dead.
So fallen, he gasps out his struggling soul,
And breathing forth a sharp, quick gush of blood,
He showers dark drops of gory rain on me,   1360
Who no less joy felt in them than the corn,
When the blade bears, in glad shower given of God.
Since this is so, ye Argive elders here,
Ye, as ye will, may hail the deed, but I
Boast of it.   And were't fitting now to pour
Libation o'er the dead,[3] 'twere justly done,
Yea more than justly; such a goblet full
Of ills hath he filled up with curses dire
At home, and now has come to drain it off.

   Chor. We marvel at the boldness of thy tongue,   1370
Who o'er thy husband's corpse speak'st vaunt like this.

(1) *i.e.* He had had his triumph over her when, forgetful of her
mother's feelings, he had sacrificed Iphigeneia. She has now repaid him
to the full.

(2) The third libation at all feasts was to Zeus, as the Preserver or
Guardian Deity. Clytæmnestra boasts that her third blow was as an
offering to a God of other kind, to Him who had in his keeping not the
living, but the dead.

(3) So in the *Choëphori*, (vv. 351, 476,) the custom of pouring libations
on the burial-place of the dead is recognised as an element of their blessedness or shame in Hades, and Agamemnon is represented as lacking the
honour which comes from them till he receives it at the hand of Orestes.

Clytæm. Ye test me as a woman weak of mind;
But I with dauntless heart to you that know
Say this, and whether thou dost praise or blame,
Is all alike :—here Agamemnon lies,
My husband, now a corpse, of this right hand,
As artist just, the handiwork : so stands it.

STROPHE.

Chor. What evil thing, O Queen, or reared on earth,
   Or draught from salt sea-wave   1380
   Hast thou fed on, to bring
   Such incense on thyself,[1]
   A people's loud-voiced curse ?
   'Twas thou did'st sentence him,
   'Twas thou did'st strike him down ;
   But thou shalt exiled be,
Hated with strong hate of the citizens.
Clytæm. Ha! now on me thou lay'st the exile's doom,
My subjects' hate, and people's loud-voiced curse,
Though ne'er did'st thou oppose my husband there,
Who, with no more regard than had been due
To a brute's death, although he called his own
Full many a fleecy sheep in pastures bred,
Yet sacrificed his child, the dear-loved fruit   1390
Of all my travail-pangs, to be a charm
Against the winds of Thrakia.   Should'st thou not
Have banished him from out this land of ours,
As meed for all his crimes ?   Yet hearing now
My deeds, thou art a judge full stern.   But I
Tell thee to speak thy threats, as knowing well
I am prepared that thou on equal terms
Should'st rule, if thou dost conquer.   But if God
Should otherwise decree, then thou shalt learn,
Late though it be, the lesson to be wise.

---

(1) Incense was placed on the head of the victim. The Chorus tells
Clytæmnestra that she has brought upon her own head the incense, not of
praise and admiration, but of hatred and wrath, as though some poison
had driven her mad.

Chor. Yea, thou art stout of heart, and speak'st big 1400
        words;
    And maddened is thy soul
    As by a murderous hate;
    And still upon thy brow
    Is seen, not yet avenged,
    The stain of blood-spot foul;
    And yet it needs must be,
    One day thou, reft of friends,
  Shalt pay the penalty of blow for blow.

Clytæm. Now hear thou too my oaths of solemn dread:
By my accomplished vengeance for my child,
By Atè and Erinnys, unto whom
I slew him as a victim, I lock not
That fear should come beneath this roof of mine,
So long as on my hearth Ægisthos kindles 1410
The flaming fire, as well disposed to me
As he hath been aforetime. He to us
Is no slight shield of stoutest confidence.
There lies he, [*pointing to the corpse of* AGAMEMNON,] one
    who foully wronged his wife,
The darling of the Chryseïds at Troïa;
And there [*pointing to* CASSANDRA] this captive slave, this
    auguress,
His concubine, this seeress trustworthy,
* Who shared his bed, and yet was as well known
To the sailors as their benches! . . . They have fared
Not otherwise than they deserved: for he
Lies as you see. And she who, like a swan,[1]
Has chanted out her last and dying song, 1420

(1) The species of swan referred to is said to be in the *Cygnus Musicus*. Aristotle (*Hist. Anim.* ix. 12) describes swans of some kind as having been heard by sailors near the coast of Libya, "singing with a lamentable cry." Mrs. Somerville (*Phys. Geog.*, c. xxxiii. 3) describes their note as "like that of a violin." The same fact is reported of the swans of Iceland and other regions of the far North. The strange, tender beauty of the passage in the *Phædo* of Plato, (p. 85, a,) which speaks of them as singing when at the point of death, has done more than anything else to make the illustration one of the commonplaces of rhetoric and poetry.

Lies close to him she loved, and so has brought
The zest of a new pleasure to my bed.

Stroph. I.[1]

Chor. Ah me, would death might come
Quickly, with no sharp throe of agony,
  Nor long bed-ridden pain,
  Bringing the endless sleep;
Since he, the watchman most benign of all,
  Hath now been smitten low,
And by a woman's means hath much endured,
And at a woman's hand hath lost his life!

Stroph. II.

Alas! alas! O Helen, evil-souled,   1430
  Who, though but one, hast slain
Many, yea, very many lives at Troïa.[2]
  *   *   *   *   *

Stroph. III.

* But now for blood that may not be washed out
  * Thou hast to full bloom brought
*A deed of guilt for ever memorable,
  For strife was in the house,
  Wrought out in fullest strength,
  Woe for a husband's life.

Stroph. IV.

Clytæm. Nay, pray not thou for destiny of death,
  Oppressed with what thou see'st;
Nor turn thou against Helena thy wrath,   1448
  As though she murderess were,
And, though but one, had many Danaï's souls
Brought low in death, and wrought o'erwhelming woe.

Antistroph. I.

Chor.   O Power that dost attack

---

(1) The structure of the lyrical dialogue that follows is rather compli-
cated, and different editors have adopted different arrangements. I have
followed Paley's.
(2) Several lines seem to have dropped out by some accident of tran-
scription.

Our palace and the two **Tantalidæ**,[1]
　　*And dost through women wield
　　*A might that grieves my heart ![2]
And o'er the body, **like a raven foul**,
　　Against all laws **of** right,
*Standing, she **boasteth in** her pride of heart [3]
That she can chant **her pœan** hymn of praise.　　　　1450

ANTISTROPH. IV.

Clytæm. Now thou dost guide aright **thy** speech and
　　　　thought,
　　Invoking **that dread Power**,
*The thrice-gorged evil genius of **this house**;
　　For he it is **who feeds**
In the heart's depth the raging lust of blood:
Ere the old wound is healed, new bloodshed comes.

STROPH. V.

Chor.　　Yes, of **a Power thou tell'st**
*Mighty and very **wrathful to this house**;
Ah me! ah me! **an evil tale enough**　　　　1460
　　Of baleful **chance of doom**,
　　Insatiable **of ill**:
　　Yet, ah! it is **through Zeus**,
The all-appointing **and all-working One**;
　　For what with mortal men
　　Is wrought apart from Zeus?
What of all this is not **by God decreed?**[4]

STROPH. VI.

　　Ah me! ah me!
My **king, my king**, how shall I weep for thee?

(1) Agamemnon and **Menelaos**, as descended from Tantalos, the **father** of Pelops.

(2) In each case women, Helen and Clytæmnestra, **had been the** unconscious instruments of the Divine Nemesis, to which the **Chorus traces** the ruin of the house of Atreus.

(3) Or, with another reading,—

　　"**He** (*sc.* the avenging Demon) boasteth in his pride of heart."

(4) It is characteristic of the teaching of Æschylos that the Chorus passes from the thought of the agency of any lower Power to the supreme will of Zeus.

What shall I speak from heart that truly loves?
And now thou lie'st there, breathing out thy life,   1470
     In impious deed of death,
     In this fell spider's web,—

Stroph. VII.

(Yes, woe is me! woe, woe!
Woe for this couch of thine dishonourable!)—
     Slain by a subtle death,[1]
With sword two-edged which her right hand did wield.

Stroph. VIII.

Clytæm. Thou speak'st big words, as if the deed were
        mine;
     Yet think thou not of me,
     As Agamemnon's spouse;
But in the semblance of this dead man's wife,
The old and keen Avenger of the house
Of Atreus, that cruel banqueter of old,
     Hath wrought out vengeance full
     On him who lieth here,   1480
     And full-grown victim slain
     Over the younger victims of the past.[2]

Antistroph. V.

Chor. That thou art guiltless found
Of this foul murder who will witness bear?
How can it be so, how? And yet, perchance,
     As helper to the deed,
     Might come the avenging Fiend
     Of that ancestral time;
And in this rush of murders of near kin
     Dark Ares presses on,
     Where he will vengeance work
For clotted gore of children slain as food.   1490

---

(1) Or,   "Dying, as dies a slave."
(2) Clytæmnestra still harps (though in ambiguous words, which may
refer also to the murder of the children of Thyestes) upon the death of
Iphigeneia as the crime which it had been her work to avenge.

ANTISTROPH. VI.

Ah me ! ah me !
My king, my king, how shall I weep for thee ?
What shall I speak from heart that truly loves ?
And now thou lie'st there, breathing out thy life,
 In impious deed of death,
 In this fell spider's web,—

ANTISTROPH. VII.

(Yes, woe is me ! woe, woe !
Woe for this couch of thine dishonourable !)—
 Slain by a subtle death,
With sword two-edged which her right hand did wield.

ANTISTROPH. VIII.

Clytæm. Nay, not dishonourable
 His death doth seem to me :
 Did he not work a doom,
 In this our house with guile ? [1]   1500
Mine own dear child, begotten of this man,
Iphigeneia, wept with many a tear,
He slew ; now slain himself in recompense,
 Let him not boast in Hell,
 Since he the forfeit pays,
 Pierced by the sword in death,
For all the evil that his hand began.

STROPH. IX.

Chor. I stand perplexed in soul, deprived of power
 Of quick and ready thought,
 Where now to turn, since thus   1510
 Our home is falling low.
I shrink in fear from the fierce pelting storm
Of blood that shakes the basement of the house;
 No more it rains in drops :
And for another deed of mischief dire,
 Fate whets the righteous doom
 On other whetstones still.

(1) Perhaps,   "And that, too, not a slave's."
н

Antistroph. II.

O Earth ! O Earth ! Oh, would thou had'st received me,
　　　Ere I saw him on couch
Of bath with silvered walls thus stretched in death !
Who now will bury him, who wail ?　Wilt thou,
When thou hast slain thy husband, have the heart　　　1520
To mourn his death, and for thy monstrous deeds
Do graceless grace ?　And who will chant the dirge
　　　　With tears in truth of heart,
　　　　Over our godlike chief ?

Stroph. X.

Clytæm. It is not thine to speak ;
　　　'Twas at our hands he fell,
　　　Yea, he fell low in death,
　　　And we will bury him,　　　　　　1830
Not with the bitter tears of those who weep
　　　As inmates of the house ;
But she, his child, Iphigeneia, there
Shall meet her father, and with greeting kind,
E'en as is fit, by that swift-flowing ford,
　　　　Dark stream of bitter woes,
　　　　Shall clasp him in her arms,
　　　　And give a daughter's kiss.

Antistroph. IX.

Chor. Lo ! still reproach upon reproach doth come ;
　　　Hard are these things to judge :
　　　The spoiler still is spoiled,
　　　The slayer pays his debt ;
Yea, while Zeus liveth through the ages, this　　　1540
Lives also, that the doer dree his weird ;
　　　For this is law fast fixed.
Who now can drive from out the kingly house
　　　The brood of curses dark ?
　　　The race to Atè cleaves.

Antistroph. X.

Clytæm. Yes, thou hast touched with truth
　　　That word oracular ;

But I for my part wish,
(Binding with strongest oath
The evil dæmon of the Pleisthenids,)[1]
Though hard it be to bear,
To rest content with this our present lot;
And, for the future, that he go to vex
Another race with homicidal deaths.   1550
Lo! 'tis enough for me,
Though small my share of wealth,
At last to have freed my house
From madness that sets each man's hand 'gainst each.

Enter ÆGISTHOS.

Ægis. Hail, kindly light of day that vengeance brings!
Now I can say the Gods on high look down,
Avenging men, upon the woes of earth,
Since lying in the robes the Erinnyes wove
I see this man, right welcome sight to me,
Paying for deeds his father's hand had wrought.   1560
Atreus, our country's ruler, this man's father,
Drove out my sire Thyestes, his own brother,
(To tell the whole truth,) quarrelling for rule,
An exile from his country and his home.
And coming back a suppliant on the hearth,
The poor Thyestes found a lot secure,
Nor did he, dying, stain the soil with blood,
There in his home.   But this man's godless sire,[2]
Atreus, more prompt than kindly in his deeds,
On plea of keeping festal day with cheer,
To my sire banquet gave of children's flesh,   1570
His own.   The feet and finger-tips of hands
* He, sitting at the top, apart concealed;
And straight the other, in his blindness taking
The parts that could not be discerned, did eat

(1) Here the genealogy is carried one step further to Pleisthenes, the
father of Tantalos.
(2) Ægisthos, in his version of the story, suppresses the adultery
of Thyestes with the wife of Atreus, which led the latter to his horrible
revenge.

A meal which, as thou see'st, perdition works
For all his kin.   And learning afterwards
The deed of dread, he groaned and backward fell,
Vomits the feast of blood, and imprecates
On Pelops' sons a doom intolerable,
And makes the o'erturning of the festive board,
With fullest justice, as a general curse,
That so might fall the race of Pleisthenes.   158x
And now thou see'st how here accordingly
This man lies fallen; I, of fullest right,
The weaver of the plot of murderous doom.
For me, a babe in swaddling-clothes, he banished
With my poor father, me, his thirteenth child;
And Vengeance brought me back, of full age grown:
And e'en far off I wrought against this man,
And planned the whole scheme of this dark device.
And so e'en death were now right good for me,
Seeing him into the nets of Vengeance fallen.

   Chor. I honour not this arrogance in guilt,   159a
Ægisthos.   Thou confessest thou hast slain
Of thy free will our chieftain here,—that thou
Alone did'st plot this murder lamentable;
Be sure, I say, thy head shall not escape
The righteous curse a people hurls with stones.

   Ægisth. Dost thou say this, though seated on the bench
Of lowest oarsmen, while the upper row
Commands the ship?[1]   But thou shalt find, though old,
How hard it is at such an age to learn,
When the word is, 'keep temper.'   But a prison
And fasting pains are admirably apt,   1600
As prophet-healers even for old age.
Dost see, and not see this?   Against the pricks
Kick not,[2] lest thou perchance should'st smart for it.

---

(1) The image is taken from the trireme with its three benches full of
rowers.   The Chorus is compared to the men on the lowest, Ægisthos and
Clytæmnestra to those on the uppermost bench.
  (2) The earliest occurrence of the proverb with which we are familiar
through the history of St. Paul's conversion, Acts ix. 5, xxvi. 14.

Chor. Thou, thou, O Queen, when thy lord came from
>war,
While keeping house, thy husband's bed defiling,
Did'st scheme this death for this our hero-chief.

Ægisth. These words of thine shall parents prove of
>tears:
But this thy tongue is Orpheus' opposite;
He with his voice led all things on for joy,
But thou, provoking with thy childish cries,
Shalt now be led; and then, being kept in check,
Thou shalt appear in somewhat gentler mood.   1610

Chor. As though thou should'st o'er Argives ruler be,
Who even when thou plotted'st this man's death
Did'st lack good heart to do the deed thyself?

Ægisth. E'en so; to work this fraud was clearly part
Fit for a woman. I was foe, of old
Suspected. But now will I with his wealth
See whether I his subjects may command,
And him who will not hearken I will yoke
In heavy harness as a full-fed colt,
Nowise as trace-horse;[1] but sharp hunger joined
With darksome dungeon shall behold him tamed.   1620

Chor. Why did'st not thou then, coward as thou art,
Thyself destroy him? but a woman with thee,
Pollution to our land and our land's Gods,
She slew him. Does Orestes see the light,
Perchance, that he, brought back by Fortune's grace,
May for both these prove slayer strong to smite?

Ægisth. Well, since thou think'st to act, not merely talk,
Thou shalt know clearly . . . .
>[*Calling his Guards from the palace.*
On then, my troops, the time for deeds is come.

Chor. On then, let each man grasp his sword in hand.

Ægisth. With sword in hand, I too shrink not from
>death.   1630

Chor. Thou talkest of thy death; we hail the word;
And make our own the fortune it implies.

(1) The trace-horse, as not under the pressure of the collar, was taken
as the type of free, those that wore the yoke, of enforced submission.

Clytæm. Nay, let us not do other evil deeds,
Thou dearest of all friends.   An ill-starred harvest
It is to have reaped so many.   Enough of woe:
Let no more blood be shed: Go thou—[*to the Chorus*]—
     go ye,
Ye aged sires, to your allotted homes,
Ere ye do aught amiss and dree your weird:
* This that we have done ought to have sufficed;
But should it prove we've had enough of ills,
We will accept it gladly, stricken low
In evil doom by heavy hand of God.
This is a woman's counsel, if there be
That deigns to hear it.
     Ægisth.   But that these should fling
The blossoms of their idle speech at me,   1640
And utter words like these, so tempting Fate,
And fail of counsel wise, and flout their master . . . . !
     Chor. It suits not Argives on the vile to fawn.
     Ægisth. Be sure, hereafter I will hunt thee down.
     Chor. Not so, if God should guide Orestes back.
     Ægisth. Right well I know how exiles feed on hopes.
     Chor. Prosper, wax fat, do foul wrong—'tis thy day.
     Ægisth. Know thou shalt pay full price for this thy
          folly.
     Chor. Be bold, and boast, like cock beside his mate.
     Clytæm. Nay, care not thou for these vain howl-
          ings; I   1650
And thou together, ruling o'er the house,
Will settle all things rightly.   [*Exeunt.*

CHOËPHORI,

OR

THE LIBATION-POURERS.

ARGUMENT.

It came to pass, after Agamemnon had been slain, that Clytæmnestra and Ægisthos ruled in Argos, and all things seemed
to go well with them. Orestes, who was heir to Agamemnon,
they had sent away to the care of Strophios of Phokis, and
there he abode. Electra his sister, mourned in secret over
her father's death, and prayed for vengeance, but no avenger
came. And when Orestes grew up to man's estate, he went
to ask counsel of the God at Delphi, and the God straitly
charged him to take vengeance on his father's murderers;
and so he started on his journey with his trusty friend
Pylades, and arrived at Argos. And it chanced that a
little while before he came, the Gods sent Clytæmnestra a
fearful dream, that troubled her soul greatly; and in her
terror she bade Electra go with her handmaids to pour libations on the tomb of Agamemnon, that so she might appease
his soul, and propitiate the Powers that rule over the dark
world of the dead.

Dramatis Personæ.

ORESTES.

ELECTRA.

CLYTÆMNESTRA.

ÆGISTHOS.

PYLADES.

Nurse.

Servant.

Chorus of Captive Women.

THE LIBATION-POURERS.

SCENE.—Argos, *in front of the palace of the Atreidæ.*
The tomb of AGAMEMNON (*a raised mound of* earth)
is seen in the background.

Enter ORESTES *and* PYLADES *from the left;* ORESTES
advances to the mound, and, as he speaks, *lays on it a*
lock of his hair.

Orest. O Hermes of the darkness 'neath the earth,
Who hast the charge of all thy Father's [1] sway,
To me who pray deliverer, helper be ;
For I to this land come, from exile come,
And on the raised mound of this monument
I bid my father hear and list.   One tress,
Thank-offering for the gifts that fed my youth,
To Inachos I consecrate, and this
The second as the token of my grief ; [2]

---

(1) Hermes is invoked, (1.) as the watcher over the souls of the dead in
Hades, and therefore the natural patron of the murdered Agamemnon ;
(2.) as exercising an authority delegated by Zeus, and therefore capable of
being, like Zeus himself, the deliverer and helper of suppliants. So
Electra, further on, invokes Hermes in the same character. The line
may, however, be rendered,

"Who stand'st as guardian of my father's house."

The three opening lines are noticeable, as having been chosen by Aristophanes as the special object for his satirical criticism (*Frogs*, 1126-1176,)
abounding in a good score of ambiguities and tautologies.

(2) The words point to the two symbolic aspects of one and the same
practice. In both there are some points of analogy with the earlier and
later forms of the Nazarite vow among the Jews. (1.) As being part of
the body, and yet separable from it without mutilation, it became the
representative of the whole man, and as such was the sign of a votive
dedication. As early as Homer, it was the custom for youths to keep one
long, flowing lock as consecrated, and when they reached manhood, they
cut it off, and offered it to the river-god of their country, throwing it
into the stream, as that to which, directly and indirectly, they owed

For mine it was not, father, being by,
Over thy death to groan, nor yet to stretch
My hand forth for the burial of thy corpse.

> [*As he speaks,* ELECTRA, *followed by a train of
> captive women in black garments bearing liba-
> tions, wailing and tearing their clothes, comes
> forth from the palace.*

What see I now? What company of women
Is this that comes in mourning garb attired?
What chance shall I conjecture as its cause?   10
Does a new sorrow fall upon this house?
Or am I right in guessing that they bring
Libations to my father, soothing gifts
To those beneath?   It cannot but be so.
I think Electra, mine own sister, comes,
By wailing grief conspicuous.   Thou, O Zeus,
Grant me full vengeance for my father's death,
And of thine own good will my helper be !
Come, Pylades, and let us stand aside,
That I may clearly learn what means this train
Of women offering prayers.   20

STROPH. I.

Chor. Sent from the house I come,
With quick, sharp beatings of the hands in grief,
   To pour libations here;
* And see, my cheeks with bloody marks are tracked,[1]

their nurture. Here the offering is made to Inachos, as the hero-founder
of Argos, identified with the river that bore his name. (2.) They shaved
their head, wholly or in part, as a token of grief, and then, because true
grief for the dead was an acceptable and propitiatory offering, this
became the natural offering for suppliants who offered their prayers at
the tombs of the departed. So in the *Aias* of Sophocles (v. 1174) Teucros
calls on Eurysakes to approach the corpse of his father, holding in his
hands locks of his own hair, his mother's, and that of Teucros. In the
offe·ing which Achilles makes over the grave of Patroclos of the hair
which he had cherished for the river-god of his fatherland, Spercheios,
we have the union of the two customs. Homer, *Il.* xxiii. 141-151.

(1) After the widespread fashion of the East, the handmaids of Clytæmnestra (originally Trojan captives) had to rend their clothes, beat their
breasts, and lacerate their faces till the blood came. The higher civilisation of Solon's laws had forbidden these wild, barbarous forms of grief at
Athens. Plutarch, *Solon*, p. 164.

The new-cut furrows which my nails have made,
And evermore my heart is fed with groans;
  And folds of mantles tied
  Across the breast are rent
  To shreds and rags in grief,
* Marring the grace of linen vestments fair,
* Since we by woes that shut out smiles are smitten. ³⁰

ANTISTROPH. I.

  * Full clear a spectre came
That made each single hair to stand on end,
  Dream-prophet of this house,
That e'en in sleep breathes out avenging wrath;
And from the secret chamber cried in fear
A cry that broke the silence of the night,
  There, where the women dwell,
  Falling with heaviest weight;
  And those who judge such dreams
Told, calling God to witness, that the souls
Below were wroth and vexed with those that slew
  them. ⁴⁰

STROPH. II.

On such a graceless deed of grace, as charm
To ward off ill, (O Earth! O mother kind!)
  A godless woman now
  Sends me with eager heart;
And yet I dread to utter that same prayer;
  What ransom has been found
  For blood on earth once poured?
  Oh! hearth all miserable!
Oh! utter overthrow of house and home!
Yea, mists of darkness, sunless, loathed of men, ⁵⁰
  Cover both home and house
  With its lords' bloody deaths.

ANTISTROPH. II.

Yea, all the majesty that awed of old,
Unchecked, unconquered, irresistible,

Thrilling the people's heart
As well as ears, is gone ;
There are, may be, that fear ;[1] but now Success
Is man's sole God and more ;
Yet stroke of Vengeance swift
Smites some in life's clear day,
For some who tarry long their sorrows wait
In twilight dim, on darkness' borderland,
     * And some an endless night
Of nothingness holds fast.

STROPH. III.

Because of blood that mother earth has drunk,
The guilt of slaughter that will vengeance work
     Is fixed indelibly ;
     And Atè, working grief,
Permits awhile the guilty one to wait,
That so he may be full and overflow
     * With all-devouring ill.

60

ANTISTROPH. III.

For him whose foul touch stains the marriage bed[2]
No remedy avails ; and water-streams,
     Though all as from one source
     Should pour to cleanse the guilt
* Of murder that the sin-stained hand defiles,
     * Would yet flow all in vain
     * That guilt to purify.

EPODE.

But now to me, since the high Gods have sent
A doom of bondage round my city's walls,
     (For from my father's home

---

(1) Purposely, perhaps, **obscure. They seem to** say that the **old**
reverence for Agamemnon has passed **away, and** instead of it there **is**
only a slavish fear for Ægisthos. For **the** more acute, however, they
imply that those who have cause to fear **are** Ægisthos and Clytæmnestra
themselves.

(2) The words, **in** their generalising sententiousness, refer specially to
the twofold crime **of** Ægisthos as an adulterer and murderer. Then, in
the Epode, the Chorus justify themselves for their seeming inconsistency
in thus abhorring the guilt, and yet acting as instruments of the guilty in
their attempts to escape punishment.

They have brought on me fate of slavery,)
    Deeds right and wrong alike
Have been as things 'twas meet I should accept,   70
    Since this slave-life began,
Where deeds are done by violence and force,—
    And I must needs suppress
* The bitter loathing of my inmost heart,
* And now beneath my cloak I weep and wail
* For all the frustrate fortunes of my lords.[1]
    Chilled through with secret grief.
    Elect. Ye handmaids, ye who deftly tend this house,
Since ye are here companions in my task
As suppliants, give me your advice in this,
What shall I say as these funereal gifts
I pour? How shall I speak acceptably?   80
How to my father pray? What? Shall I say
" I bring from loving wife to husband loved
Gifts "—from my mother? No, I am not bold
Enough for that, nor know I what to speak,
Pouring this chrism on my father's tomb,[2]
Or shall I say this prayer, as men are wont,
" Good recompense make thou to those who bring
These garlands," yea, a gift full well deserved
By deeds of ill? Or dumb, with ignominy
Like that with which he perished, shall I pour
Libations on the earth, and like a man
That flings away the lustral filth, shall I
Throw down the urn and walk with eyes not turned ?[3]   90

(1) The mourners speak, of course, of Agamemnon and Orestes, not of Ægisthos and Clytæmnestra.

(2) A mixture of meal, honey, and oil formed the half-liquid substance commonly used for these funereal libations. The " garlands" may be wreaths of flowers or fillets, or the word may be used figuratively for the libation itself, as crowning the mound in which Agamemnon lay.

(3) The words point to a strange Athenian custom. When a house was cleansed of that which defiled it, morally or physically, the filth was carried in an earthen vessel to a place where three ways met, and the worshipper flung the vessel behind him, and walked away without turning to look at it. To Electra's mind, the libation which her mother sends is equally unclean, and should be treated in the same way. So in Hom. *Il.* i. 314, the Argives purify themselves, and then cast the lustral water they have used into the sea. Lev vi. 11, gives us an analogous usage. Comp. also Theocritos, *Idyll* xxiv., vv. 22-97.

Be sharers in my counsels, O my friends;
A common hate we cherish in the house;
Hide nothing in your heart through fear of man.
Fate's doom firm-fixed awaits alike the free,
And those in bondage to another's hand.
Speak, if thou can'st a better counsel give.   100

    Chor. [*laying their hands on Agamemnon's tomb.*] Thy
        father's tomb as altar honouring,
I, as thou bidd'st, will speak my heart-thoughts out!

    Elect. Speak, then, as thou my father's tomb dost
        honour.

    Chor. Say, as thou pour'st, good words for those that
        love.

    Elect. Which of my friends shall I address as such ?

    Chor. First then thyself, and whoso hates Ægisthos.

    Elect. Shall I for thee, as for myself, pray thus ?

    Chor. Now that thou'rt learning, judge of that thyself.

    Elect. Whom shall I add then to this company ?

    Chor. Far though Orestes be, forget him not.

    Elect. Right well is this: thou teachest admirably.

    Chor. Then, for the blood-stained ones remembering
        say. . . . .

    Elect. What then ?   Explain, and teach my igno-
        rance.[1]   110

    Chor. That there may come to them some God or
        man . . . .

    Elect. Shall I " as judge " or as " avenger " say ?

    Chor. Say it out plain! " to give them death for
        death." . . . .

    Elect. May prayers like these consist with piety ?

    Chor. Why not,—a foe with evils to requite ?

    Elect. [*moving to the tomb, and pouring libations as she*
    speaks.] * O mightiest herald of the Gods on high
And those below, O Hermes of the dark,
Call thou the Powers beneath, and bid them hear

---

(1) Partly it is the youth of Electra that seeks counsel from those who
had more experience ; partly she shrinks from the responsibility of being
the first to utter the formula of execration.

The prayers that look towards my father's house ;
And Earth herself, who all things bringeth forth,   120
And rears them and again receives their fruit.
And I to human souls libations pouring,
Say, calling on my father, " Pity me ;
How shall we bring our dear Orestes home ? "
For now as sold to ill by her who bore us,
We poor ones wander. She as husband gained
Ægisthos, who was partner in thy death ;
And I am as a slave, and from his wealth
Orestes now is banished, and they wax
Full haughty in the wealth thy toil had gained.   130
And that Orestes hither with good luck
May come, I pray. Hear thou that prayer, my father !
And to myself grant thou that I may be
Than that my mother wiser far of heart,
Holier in act. For us this prayer I pour ;
And for our foes, my father, this I pray,
That Justice may as thine avenger come,
And that thy murderers perish. Thus I place
Midway in prayer for good that now I speak,
My prayer 'gainst them for evil. Be thou then
The escort[1] of these good things that I ask,   140
With help of Gods, and Earth, and conquering Justice.
With prayers like these my votive gifts I pour ;
And as for you [*turning to the Chorus*] 'tis meet with cries
    to crown
The pæan ye utter, wailing for the dead.

STROPH.

  Chor. * Pour ye the pattering tear,
     * Falling for fallen lord,
* Here by the tomb that shuts out good and ill,—
Here, where the full libations have been poured
That turn aside the curse men deprecate,

---

(1) The word "escort" has a special reference to the function of
Hermes in the unseen world. As he was wont to act as guide to the
souls of the dead in their downward journey, so now Electra prays that
he may lead the blessings she asks for upward from the dark depths of
Earth.

S

Hear me, O Thou my Dread,   156
Hear thou, O Sire, the words my dark mind speaks !

ANTISTROPHE.

Oh, woe is me, woe, woe !
Woe, woe, and woe is me !
* What warrior strong of spear
Shall come the house to free,
Or Ares with his Skythian bow[1] in hand,
Shaking its pliant strength in deeds of war,
* Or guiding in encounter closer yet
The weapons made with hilts ?

[*During the choral ode* ELECTRA, *after going to the
mound, and pouring the libations on it, returns
holding in her hands the lock of hair which*
ORESTES *had left there.*

Elect. The gifts the earth hath drunk, my father hath
them :
Now this new wonder come and share with me.
Chor. Speak on, my heart goes pit-a-pat with fear,
Elect. There on the tomb I see this lock cut off.   160
Chor. What man or maid low-girdled can it claim ?
Elect. Full easy this for any one to guess.
Chor. Old as I am, may I from younger learn ?
Elect. None but myself could cut off lock like this.
Chor. Yea, foes are they that should with grief-locks
mourn.
Elect. Yes, surely, 'tis indeed the self same hair . . .
Chor. But as what tresses ? This I seek to know.
Elect. And of a truth 'tis very like to ours. . . . .
Chor. Did then Orestes send this secret gift ?[2]

(1) The Skythian bow, long and elastic, bending either way, like those
of the Arabians, (Herod. **vii.** 69.) The connexion of Ares with the wild,
fierce tribes of Thrakia **and** Skythia meets us again and again **in** the
literature of Greece. He was the only God to whom they built temples,
(Ibid., **iv.** 59.) They sacrificed human victims to an iron sword as his
more appropriate symbol, (iv. 62.) The use of iron for weapons of war
came to the Greeks from them, (*Seven ag. Th.* 729 ; *Prom.* 714.)
(2) It may be worth while to compare the methods adopted by the
three dramatists of Greece in bringing the recognition of the
brother by the sister. (1.) Here the lock of hair in its peculiar colour and
texture, resembling her own, followed by the likeness of his footsteps to

Elect. It is most like those flowing locks of his.   170

Chor. Yet how had he adventured to come hither?

Elect. He to his father sent the lock as gift.

Chor. Not less regretful than before, thy words,
If on this soil his foot shall never tread.

Elect. Yea, on me too there rushed heart-surge of gall
And I was smitten as with dart that pierced;
And from mine eyes there fell the thirsty drops
That pour unchecked, of this full bitter flood,
As I this lock beheld.   How can I think
That any other townsman owns this hair?   180
Nay, she who slew . . . . she did not cut it off,
My mother . . . . who towards her children shows
A godless mood that little suits the name;
And yet that I should this assert outright,
The precious gift is his whom most of men
I love, Orestes. . . . . Nay, hope flatters me.
Alas! alas!
Would, herald-like, it had a kindly voice!
So should I not turn to and fro in doubt;
But either it had told me with all clearness
To loathe this tress, if cut from hated head;   190
Or, being of kin, had sought to share my grief,
To deck the tomb and do my father honour.

Chor. Well, on the Gods we call, on those who know
In what storms we, like sailors, now are tossed:
But if deliverance may indeed be curs,

From a small seed a mighty trunk may grow.[1]

   Elect. Here too are foot-prints as a second proof,
Just like . . . . yea, close resembling those of mine.
For here are outlines of two separate feet,
His own and those of fellow-traveller,
And all the heels and impress of the feet,
When measured, fit well with my footsteps here . . . .
Pangs come on me, and sore bewilderment.

        [*As she ceases speaking* ORESTES *comes forward from*
         his concealment.

   Orest. Pray, uttering to the Gods no fruitless prayer,
For good success in what is yet to come.

   Elect. What profits now to me the Gods' good will?

   Orest. Thou see'st those here whom most thou did'st
       desire.

   Elect. Whom called I on, that thou hast knowledge of?

   Orest. Right well I know how thou dost prize Orestes.

   Elect. In what then find I now my prayers fulfilled? 210

   Orest. Behold me! Seek no dearer friend than I!

   Elect. Nay, stranger, dost thou weave a snare for me?

   Orest. Then do I plot my schemes against myself.

   Elect. Thou seekest to make merry with my grief.

   Orest. With mine then also, if at all with thine.

   Elect. Art thou indeed Orestes that I speak to?

   Orest. Though thou see'st him, thou'rt slow to learn
       'tis I;

Yet when thou saw'st this lock of mourner's hair,
And did'st the foot-prints track my feet had made,
Agreeing with thine own, as brother's true,
Then did'st thou deem in hope thou looked'st on me.   220
Fit then this lock where it was cut, and see;
See too this woven robe, thine own hands' work,

---

(1) The saying is probably one of the wide-spread proverbs which
imply parables. The idea is obviously that with which we are familiar
in the Gospel "grain of mustard seed." Here, as in the "kicking
against the pricks" of Acts ix. 5, xxvi. 14, and *Agam.* v. 1604, we are
carried back to a period which lies beyond the range of history as that in
which men took note of the analogies and embodied them in forms like
this.

The shuttle's stroke, and forms of beasts[1] of chase.

[ELECTRA *starts, as if about to cry aloud for joy.*

Restrain thyself, nor lose thy head for joy:
Our nearest kin, I know, are foes to us.

Elect. [*embracing* ORESTES] Thou whom thy father's
house most loves, most prays for,
Our one sole hope, bewept with many a tear,
Of issue that shall work deliverance!
Thine own might trusting, thou thy father's house
Shalt soon win back.   O pleasant fourfold name!   230
I needs must speak to thee as father dear;[2]
The love I owe my mother turns to thee,
(She with full right to me is hateful now,)
My sister's too, who ruthlessly was slain;
And thou wast ever faithful brother found,
And one whom I revered.   May Might and Right,
And sovran Zeus as third, my helpers be!

Orest. Zeus! Zeus! be Thou a witness of our troubles,
See the lorn brood that calls an eagle sire,
Eagle that perished in the coils and folds   240
Of a fell viper.   Now on them bereaved
Presses gaunt famine.   Not as yet full-grown
Are they to bring their father's booty home.
Thus it is thine to see in me and her,
(I mean Electra) children fatherless,
Both suffering the same exile from our home.

Elect. And should'st Thou havoc make of brood of sire
Who at thine altar greatly honoured Thee,
Whence wilt Thou get a festive offering
From hand as free? Nor, should'st Thou bring to nought
The eagle's nestlings, would'st thou have at hand   250
A messenger to bear thy will to man
In signs persuasive; nor when withered up
This royal stock shall be, will it again
Wait on thine altars at high festivals:

(1) So in the *Odyssey*, (xix. 228,) Odysseus appears as wearing a
woollen cloak, on which are embroidered the figures of a fawn and
a dog.
(2) An obvious reproduction of the words of Andromache, (*Il.* vi. 429.)

Oh, bring it back, and then Thou too wilt raise
From low estate a lofty house, which now
Seems to have fallen, fallen utterly.

   Chor. Ah, children! saviours of your father's house,
Hush, hush, lest some one hear you, children dear,
And for mere talking's sake report all this
To those that rule.   Ah, would I might behold them
Lie dead 'midst oozing fir-pyre blazing high![1]   2/4

   Orest. Nay, nay, I tell you, Loxias' oracle,
In strength excelling, will not fail us now,
That bade me on this enterprise to start,
And with clear voice spake often, warning me
Of chilling pain-throes at the fevered heart,
Unless my father's murderers I should chase,
Bidding me kill them in the self-same fashion,
Stirred by the wrongs that pauperise my life,
And said that I with many a mischief ill
Should pay for that fault with mine own dear life.
For making known to men the charms earth-born   270
* That soothe the wrathful powers,[2] he spake for us
Of ills as follows, leprous sores that creep
All o'er the flesh, and as with cruel jaws
Eat out its ancient nature, and white hairs[3]
On that foul ill to supervene: and still
He spake of other onsets of the Erinnyes,
As brought to issue from a father's blood;

(1) The words seem to imply that burning alive was known among the Greeks as a punishment for the more atrocious crimes. The "oozing pitch," if we adopt that rendering, apparently describes something like the "*tunica molesta*" of Juvenal. (*Sat.* viii. 235.) Hesychios (s. v. Κωνῆσαι) mentions the practice as alluded to in a lost play of Æschylos.

(2) The words are both doubtful and obscure. Taking the reading which I have adopted, they seem to mean that while men in general had means of propitiating the Erinnyes and other Powers for the guilt of unavenged bloodshed, Orestes and Electra had no such way of escape open to them. If they, the next of kin, failed to do their work, they would be exposed to the full storm of wrath. But a conjectural emendation of one word gives us,
        "For making known to men the earth-born ills
          That come from wrathful Powers."

(3) Either that old age would come prematurely, or that the hair itself would share the leprous whiteness of the flesh.

For the dark weapon of the Gods below
Winged by our kindred that lie low in death,
And beg for vengeance, yea, and madness too,
And vague, dim fears at night disturb and haunt me,
*Seeing full clearly, though I move my brow [1]   280
In the thick darkness . . . . and that then my frame,
Thus tortured, should be driven from the city
With brass-knobbed scourge : and that for such as I
It was not given to share the wine-cup's taste,
Nor votive stream in pure libation poured ;
And that my father's wrath invisible
Would drive me from all altars, and that none
Should take me in, or lodge with me ; at last,
That, loathed of all and friendless, I should die,
A wretched mummy, all my strength consumed.
Must I not trust such oracles as these ?
Yea, though I trust not, must the deed be done ;   290
For many motives now in one converge,—
The God's command, great sorrow for my father ;
My lack of fortune, this, too, urges me
Never to leave our noble citizens,
With noblest courage Troïa's conquerors,
To be the subjects to two women thus ;
Yea, his soul is as woman's : [2] an' it be not,
He soon shall know the issue.
   Chor. Grant ye from Zeus, O mighty Destinies !
      That so our work may end
As Justice wills, who takes our side at last ;   300
Now for the tongue of bitter hate let tongue

---

(1) The words, as taken in the text, refer to Orestes seeing even in sleep the spectral forms of the Erinnyes. By some editors the verse is placed after v 276, and the lines then read thus :—

  "And that he calls fresh onsets of the Erinnyes
  As brought to issue from a father's blood,
  Seeing clearly, though he move his brow in darkness."

So taken, the last line refers to Agamemnon, who, though in the darkness of Hades, sees the penalties which will fall upon his son should he neglect to take vengeance on his father's murderers.
(2) Stress is laid here, as in *Agam.* 1224, on the effeminacy of the adulterer.

Of bitter hate be given.   Loud and long
The voice of Vengeance claiming now her debt;
    And for the murderous blow
Let him who slew with murderous blow repay.
"That the wrong-doer bear the wrong he did,"
Thrice-ancient saying of a far-off time,[1]
    This speaketh as we speak.

Stroph. I.

Orest. O father, sire ill-starred,
    What deed or word could I
    Waft from afar to thee,
    Where thy couch holds thee now,   310
*To be a light with dark commensurate?
    Alike, in either case,
The wail that tells their praise is welcome gift
To those Atreidæ, guardians of our house.

Stroph. II.

Chor. My child, my child, the mighty jaws of fire[2]
Bind not the mood and spirit of the dead!
But e'en when that is past he shows his wrath.
    When he that dies is wailed,
    The murderer stands revealed: 320
The righteous cry for parents that begat,
    To fullest utterance roused,
    Searches the whole truth out.

Antistroph. I.

Elect. Hear then, O father, now
    Our tearful griefs in turn;
    From us thy children twain
    The funeral wail ascends;

---

(1) The great law of retribution is repeated from *Agam.* 1564. As one
of the earliest utterances of man's moral sense, it was referred popularly
among the Greeks to Rhadamanthos, who with Minos judged the souls of
the dead in Hades. Comp. Aristot, *Ethic. Nicom.*, v. 8.

(2) The funeral pyre, which consumes the body, leaves the life and
power of the man untouched. The spirit survives, and calls on the Gods
that dwell in darkness to avenge him. The very cry of wailing tends, as
a prayer to them, to the exposure of the murderer.

And we, as suppliants and as exiles too,
    Find shelter at thy tomb.
What of all this is good, what void of ills?   339
Is not this now a woe invincible?
  Chor. Yet, even yet, from evils such as these,
God, if He will, may bring more pleasant strains:
And for the dirge we utter by the tomb,
A pæan in the royal house may raise
    Welcome to new-found friend.

STROPH. III.

  Orest. Had'st thou beneath the walls
    Of Ilion, O my sire,
    Been slain by Lykian foe,[1]
    Pierced through and through with spear,
    Leaving high fame at home,   340
    And laying strong and sure
    *Thy children's paths in life,
    Then had'st thou had as thine
    Far off across the sea
    A mound of earth heaped high,
To all thy kith and kin endurable.

ANTISTROPH. II.

  Chor. Yea, and as friend with friends
    That nobly died, he then
    Had dwelt in high estate
    A sovereign ruler, held
    Of all in reverence,
    High in their train who ru'e
    Supreme in that dark world;   350
    For he, too, while he lived,
    As monarch ruled o'er those
    Whose hands the sceptre held
    That mortal men obey.[2]

(1) The Lykians, of whom Glaucos and Sarpedon are the representative heroes in the *Iliad*, are named as the chief allies of the Troïans.

(2) The words embody the widespread feeling that the absence of funereal honours affected the spirit of the dead, and that the souls with whom he dwelt held him in high or low esteem according as they had been given or withheld.

ANTISTROPH. III.

Elect. Not even 'neath the walls
　　Of Troïa, O my Sire,
　　With those the spear hath slain,
　　Would I have had thee lie
　　By fair Scamandros' stream:
　　No, this my prayer shall be
　　That those who slew thee fall,
　　*By their own kin struck down,　　　　　360
　　That one might hear far off,
　　Untried by woes like this,
The fate that brings inevitable death.
　　Chor. Of blessings more than golden, O my child,
Greater than greatest fortune, or the bliss
Of those beyond the North [1] thou speakest now;
　　　For this is in thy grasp;
But hold; e'en now this thud of double scourge [2]
　　Finds its way on to him;
Already these find helpers 'neath the earth,
But of those rulers whom we loathe and hate
　　　Unholy are the hands:　　　　　　　　　370
　　　And children gain the day.

STROPH. IV.

Elect. Ah! this, like arrow, pierces through the ear!
O Zeus! O Zeus! who sendest from below
　　　A woe of tardy doom
Upon the bold and subtle hands of men . . . . .
　　　Nay, though they parents be,
　　　Yet all shall be fulfilled.

---

(1) Pindar, (*Pyth.* x. 47,) the contemporary of Æschylos, had made the
name of these Hyperborei well known to all Greeks. The vague dreams
of men, before the earth had been searched out, pictured a happy land
as lying beyond their reach. There were Islands of the Blest in the far
West; Æthiopians, peaceful and long-lived, in the South; and far
away, beyond the cold North, a people exempt from the common evils
of humanity. The latter have been connected with the old Aryan
belief in the paradise of Mount Meru. Comp. also Herod. iv. 421;
Prom. 812.
(2) *Sc.,* the beating of both **hands upon the breast, as the Chorus**
uttered their lamentations.

Strophe. V.

Chor. May it be mine to chant o'er funeral pyre
*Cry well accordant with the pine-fed blaze,[1]
    When first the man is slain,
    And his wife perisheth!   380
Why should I hide what flutters round my heart?
On my heart's prow a blast blows mightily,
    Keen wrath and loathing fierce.

Antistroph. IV.

Orest. And when shall Zeus, the orphan's guardian true,
Lay to his hand and smite the guilty heads?
    So may our land learn faith!
Vengeance I claim from those who did the wrong.   390
    Hear me O Earth, and ye,
    *Powers held in awe below!
Chor. Yea, the law saith that gory drops once shed
Upon the ground for yet more blood should crave;
*For lo! fell slaughter on Erinnys calls,
To come from those that perished long ago,
And on one sorrow other sorrow bring.

Stroph. VI.

Elect. *Ah, ah, O Earth, and Lords of those below!
Behold, ye mighty Curses of the slain,
Behold the remnant of the Atreidæ's house
    Brought to extremest strait,   400
    Bereaved of house and home!
Whither, O Zeus, can any turn for help?

Antistroph. V.

Chor. Ah, my fond heart is quivering in dismay,
*Hearing this loud lament most lamentable:
    Now have I little cheer,
    And blackened is my heart,
*Hearing that speech; but then again when hope

---

(1) Perhaps, simply "the sharp and bitter cry." But the rendering in
the text seems justified as repeating the wish already expressed, (v. 260,)
that the murderers may die by this form of death.

*On strength uplifts me, far it drives my grief,
      *Propitious seen at last.

Antistroph. VI.

Orest. What could we speak more fitly than the woes   410
We suffer, yea, and from a parent's hands?
Well, she may fawn; our mood remains unsoothed;
      For like a wolf untamed,
      We from our mother take
A wrathful soul that to no fawning yields.

Stroph. VII.

Chor. *I strike an Arian stroke, and in the strain
      Of Kissian mourner skilled,[1]
Ye might have seen the stretching forth of hands,
With rendings of the hair, and random blows,
      In quick succession given,
Dealt from above with arm at fullest length,
And with the beating still my head is stunned,   420
      Battered and full of woe.
Elect. O mother, hostile found, and daring all!
      With burial as of foe
Thou had'st the heart a ruler to inter,
      His citizens not there,
A spouse unwept, with no lamentings loud.

Stroph. VIII.

Orest. Ah! thou hast told the whole full tale of shame;
Shall she not pay then for that outrage dire
            Unto my father done,
            So far as Gods prevail,
            So far as my hands work?
May it be mine to smite her and then die!   430

(1) **The Chorus** at this point renew their words and cries of lamentation, smiting on their breasts. By some critics this speech and Antistroph. VII. are assigned to Electra, Antistroph. VIII. to the Chorus, with
a corresponding change in the pronouns "my" and "thy." The Chorus,
as consisting of Trojan captives, is represented as adopting the more
vehement Asiatic forms of wailing. Among these the Arians, Kissians,
and Mariandynians (*Pers.*, 920) seem to have been most conspicuous for
their skill in lamentation, and, as such, were in request where hired
mourners were wanted. Compare the opening chorus, **v. 22.**

ANTISTROPH. VII.

Chor. Yea, he was maimed ![1] (that thou the tale may'st
    know)
And as she slaughtered, so she buried him,
    Seeking to work a doom
For thy young life all unendurable.
    Now thou dost hear the woes
Thy father suffered, stained with foulest shame.

ANTISTROPH. VIII.

Elect. Thou tellest of my father's death, but I
    Stood afar off, contemned,
Counted as nought, and like a cursèd hound
Shut up within, I poured the tide of tears
    (More ready they than smiles)
Uttering in secret wail of weeping full.   440
Hear thou these things, and write them in my mind.
  Chor. Let the tale pierce thine ears,
While thy soul onward moves with tranquil step:
    So much, thou know'st, stands thus;
Seek thou with all desire to know the rest;
    'Tis meet to enter now
Within the lists with mind inflexible.

STROPH. IX.

Orest. I bid thee, O my father, help thy friends.
Elect. Bitterly weeping, these my tears I add.
Chor. With full accord so cries our company.
    Come then to light, and hear;   450
    Be with us 'gainst our foes.

ANTISTROPH. IX.

Orest. My Might their Might, my Right their Right
    must meet.
Elect. *Ye Gods, give righteous issue in our cause.

---

(1) The practice of mutilating the corpse of a murdered man by cutting
off his hands and feet and fastening them round his waist, seems to have
been looked on as rendering him powerless to seek for vengeance. Comp.
Soph. *Elect.*, v. 437. This kind of mutilation, and not mere wanton
outrage, is what the Chorus refer to.

Chor. **Fear creeps** upon me as I hear **your prayers.**
            Long tarries destiny,
            But comes to those who pray.

STROPH. X.

Semi-Chor. A. **Oh, woe** that haunts the race,
And harsh, shrill stroke of Atè's bloody scourge !
            Woes **sad and hard** to bear,   460
            Calling for wailing loud,
Ah, woe is me, a grief immedicable.

ANTISTROPH. X.

Semi-Chor. B. **Yea, but as cure for this,**
And healing salve, 'tis yours with your own hands,
            With no help from without,
            *To press your suit of blood;**
So runs our hymn **to those** great **Gods below.**
    Chor. **Yea,** hearing now, ye blest **Ones 'neath** the earth,
This prayer, send ye your children **timely help**
            That worketh victory.
    Orest. **O sire, who** in no kingly fashion died'st,   470
Hear thou my prayer; grant victory o'er this house.
    Elect. **I,** father, ask this prayer, that I may work
*Ægisthos' **death, and** then acquittal **gain.**
    Orest. **Yea,** thus the banquets that men give the **dead**
Would for thee too be held, but otherwise
*Dishonoured wilt thou lie 'mid those that **feast,**[1]
Robbed of thy country's rich burnt-offerings.
    Elect. **I too from out** my father's house will **bring**
Libations from mine own inheritance,
As marriage **offerings.   Chief and first of all,**
Will I do honour **to this sepulchre.**   [480
    Orest. **Set** free my **sire, O Earth, to watch the** battle.

(1) **As in v.** 351 the loss of honour among the dead was represented as
one consequence of the absence of funereal rites from those who loved the
dead, so here the restoration of the children to their rights appears as the
condition without which that dishonour must continue. If they succeed,
then, and then only, can they offer funereal banquets, year by year, as
was the custom. There may be a special reference to an Argive custom
mentioned by Plutarch (*Quæst. Græc.*, c. 24) of sacrificing immediately after
the death of a relative to Apollo, and thirty days later to Hermes.

Elect. O Persephassa, goodly victory grant!

Orest. Remember, sire, the bath in **which they slew
thee!**

Elect. *Remember** thou the net they handselled so!

Orest. In fetters not of brass wast thou snared, father.

Elect. Yea, basely with that mantle they devised.

Orest. Art thou not roused by these reproaches, father?

Elect. Dost thou not lift thine head for those thou lov'st?

Orest. **Or send thou Vengeance** to assist thy friends;
Or let them get like grasp of those thy foes,
If thou, o'ercome, dost wish to conquer them.   490

Elect. **And hear thou this last prayer of mine, my
father,**
Seeing us thy nestlings sitting at thy tomb,
Have mercy on thy boy and on thy girl;
Nor blot thou out the seed of Pelopids:
So thou, though thou hast died, art yet not dead;
For children are the voices that preserve
Man's memory when **he dies: so bear the net**
The corks that float the flax-mesh from the deep.
Hear thou: **This is our wailing cry for thee,**
And thou, our prayer regarding, sav'st thyself.   500

Chor. Unblamed have **ye your utterance lengthened
out,**
Amends for that his tomb's unwept-for lot.
But as to what remains, since thou'rt resolved
To act, **act now; make trial** of thy Fate.

Orest. So shall it be.   Yet 'tis not out of course
To ask why she libations sent, why thus
Too late she cares for ill she cannot cure?
Yea, to a dead man heeding not 'twas sent,
A sorry offering.   Why, I fail **to guess:**
The gifts are far **too** little for the fault;   510
For should a man pour **all he** has to pay
For one small drop **of blood,** the toil were vain:
So runs the saying.   But if **thou dost know,**
Tell this to me as wishing **much** to learn.

Chor. I know, my child, **for I** was by.   Stirred on

By dreams and wandering terrors of the night,
That godless woman these libations sent.

   Orest. And have ye learnt the dream, to tell it right?
   Chor. As she doth say, she thought she bare a snake.
   Orest. How ends the tale, and what its outcome then?
   Chor. She nursed it, like a child, in swaddling
      clothes.   520
   Orest. What food did that young monster crave for
      then?
   Chor. She in her dream her bosom gave to it.
   Orest. How 'scaped her breast by that dread beast
      unhurt?
   Chor. Nay, with the milk it sucked out clots of blood.
   Orest. Ah, not in vain comes this dream from her lord.
   Chor. She, roused from sleep, cries out all terrified,
And many torches that were quenched in gloom
Blazed for our mistress' sake within the house.
Then these libations for the dead she sends,
Hoping they'll prove good medicine of ills.   530
   Orest. Now to Earth here and my sire's tomb I pray,
They leave not this strange vision unfulfilled.
So I expound it that it all coheres;
For if, the self-same spot that I left leaving,
*The snake was then wrapt in my swaddling clothes,
And sucked the very breast that nourished me,
And mixed the sweet milk with a clot of blood,
And she in terror wailed the strange event,
So must she, as that monster dread she nourished,
Die cruel death: and I, thus serpentised,   540
Am here to slay her, as this dream portends;
I take thee as my dream-interpreter.
   Chor. So be it; but in all else guide thy friends;
*Bid some do this, some that, some nought at all.
   Orest. Simple my orders, that she [*pointing to* ELECTRA]
      go within;
And you, I charge you, hide these plans of mine,
That they who slew a noble soul by guile,
By guile may die and in the self-same snare

Be caught, as Loxias gave his oracle,
The king Apollo, seer that never lied: 550
For like a stranger in full harness clad
Will I draw near with this man, Pylades,
To the great gates, a stranger I, and he,
Ally in arms. And then we both will speak
Parnassian speech, and imitate the tone
Of Phokian tongue. And should no porter there
Give us good welcome, on the ground that now
The house with ills is haunted, there we'll stay,
So that a man who passeth by the house
Will guess, and thus will speak, " Why drives Ægisthos
The suppliant from his gate, if he's at home   [560
And knows it ?" But if I should pass the threshold
Of the great gate, and find him seated there
Upon my father's throne, or if he comes
And meets me, face to face, and lifts his eyes,
And drops them, then be sure, before he says,
" Whence is this stranger ?"—I will lay him dead,
With my swift-footed brazen weapon pierced;
And then Erinnys, stinted not in slaughter,
Shall drink her third draught of unmingled blood.[1]
Thou, then, [to ELECTRA] watch well what passes in the
    house,   570
So that these things may dovetail close and well :
And you [to the Chorus] I bid to keep a tongue discreet,
Silent, if need be, or the right word speaking,
And Him[2] [pointing to the statue of Apollo] I call to look
    upon me here,
Since he has set me on this strife of swords.
        [Exeunt ORESTES, PYLADES, and ELECTRA.]
             STROPH. I.

   Chor. Many dread forms of evils terrible
        Earth bears, and Ocean's bays
        With monsters wild and fierce

---

(1) Another reference to the third cup of undiluted wine which men
drank to the honour of Zeus the Preserver. Comp. *Agam.* v. 245.
(2) Possibly the pronoun refers to Pylades.

T

*O'erflow, and through mid-air the meteor lights   590
  Sweep by; and wingèd birds
And creeping things can tell the vehement rage
  Of whirling storms of winds.

    ANTISTROPH. I.

But who man's temper overbold may tell,
  Or daring passionate loves
  Of women bold in heart,
Passions close bound with men's calamities?
  Love that true love disowns,
That sways the weaker sex in brutes and men,   598
  Usurps o'er wedlock's ties.

    STROPH. II.

Whoso is not bird-witted, let him think
  What scheme she learnt to plan,
Of subtle craft that wrought its will by fire,
That wretched child of Thestios, who to slay
  Her son did set a-blaze
  The brand that glowed blood-red,
Which had its birth when first from out the womb
  He came with infant's wail,
And spanned the measure of its life with his,   609
  On to the destined day.[1]

    ANTISTROPH. II.

Another, too, must we with loathing name,
  Skylla, with blood defiled.[2]
Who for the sake of foes a dear one slew,

(1) The story of **Althæa** has recently been **made** familiar to English readers by Mr. Swinburne's *Atalanta in Calydon*. More briefly told, the legend ran that she, being the wife of Œneus, **bare a** son, who was believed to be the child of Ares—that the Fates came to her when the boy, who was named Meleagros, was seven days old, and told her that his life should last until the firebrand then burning on the earth should be consumed. She took the firebrand, and quenched it, and laid it by in a chest; but when Meleagros grew up, he joined in the chase of the great boar of Calydon, and when he had slain it, gave the skin as a trophy to Atalanta, and when his mother's brothers, the sons of Thestios, claimed it as their right, he waxed wroth with them and slew them. And then Althæa, in her grief, caring more for her brothers than her son, took the brand from the chest, and threw it into the fire, and so Meleagros died. Phrynichos is said to have made the myth the subject of a drama. In Homer, (*Il.* x. 566,) Althæa brings about her son's death by her curses.

(2) Skylla (**not to be confounded with** the sea-monster of Messina) **was**

Won by the gold-chased bracelets brought from Crete,
    The gifts that Minos gave,
    And knowing not the end,
Robbed Nisos of his lock of deathless life,
    She with her dog-like heart   610
Surprising him deep-breathing in his sleep;
    But Hermes comes on her.[1]

STROPH. III.

And since I tell the tale of ruthless woes. . . . [2]
    Yet now 'tis not the time
* To tell of evil marriage which this house
    Doth loathe and execrate,
And of a woman's schemes and stratagems
    Against a warrior chief,
* Chief whom his people honoured as was meet,
I give my praise to hearth from hot broils free,
    And praise that woman's mood
    That dares no deed of ill.

ANTISTROPH. III.

But of all crimes the Lemnian foremost stands;[3]   620
    * And the Earth mourns that woe
As worthy of all loathing. Yes, this guilt
    One might have well compared
With Lemnian ills; and now that race is gone,
    To lowest shame brought down
By the foul guilt the Gods abominate:

the daughter of Nisos, king of Megaris, who had on his head a lock of purple hair, which was a charm that preserved his life from all danger. And the Cretans under Minos attacked Nisos, and besieged him in his city; and Minos won the love of Skylla, and tempted her with gifts, and she cut off her father's lock of hair, and so he perished. But Minos, scorning her for her deed, bound her by the feet to the stern of his ship and drowned her.

(1) Hermes, i.e. in his office as the escort of the souls of the dead to Hades.

(2) The Chorus apparently is represented as on the point of completing its catalogue of crimes committed by women with the story of Clytæmnestra's guilt. Something leads them to check themselves, and they are contented with a dark and vague allusion.

(3) The story of the Lemnian women is told by Herodotos, (vi. 138.) They rose up against their husbands and put them all to death; and the deed passed into a proverb, so that all great crimes were spoken of as Lemnian. This guilt is that alluded to in Stroph. III.

For no man honours what the Gods condemn,
        Which instance of all these
        Do I not rightly urge ? [1]

STROPH. IV.

And now the sword already at the heart,
Sharp-pointed, strikes a blow that pierces through,
        While Vengeance guides the hand ;   630
        For lo ! the lawlessness
Of one who doth transgress all lawlessly
The might and majesty of Zeus, lies not
        As trampled under foot. [2]

ANTISTROPH. IV.

The anvil-block of Vengeance firm is set,
And Fate, the sword-smith, hammers on the bronze
        Beforehand ; and the child
        Is brought unto his home,
And in due time the debt of guilt is paid
By the dark-souled Erinnys, famed of old,
        For blood of former days.

ORESTES and PYLADES enter, *disguised as Phokian travel-*
lers, go to the door of the palace, and knock loudly.

Orest. What ho, boy! hear us knocking at the gate.   640
Who is within, boy ? who, boy ?—hear, again ;
A third time now I give my summons here,
If good Ægisthos' house be hospitable.

[*A Slave opens the door.*

Slave. Hold, hold; I hear. What stranger comes, and
        whence ?

Orest. Tell thou thy lords who over this house rule,
To whom I come and tidings new report ;
And make good speed, for now the dusky car
Of night comes on apace, and it is time
For travellers in hospitable homes

---

(1) In every case of which the Chorus had spoken guilt had been followed by retribution. So, it is implied, it will be in that which is present
to their thoughts.

(2) Sc., is not forgotten or overlooked, but will assuredly meet with its
due punishment.

To cast their anchor; and let some one come
From out the house who hath authority;
The lady, if so be one ruleth here,
But, seemlier far, her lord; for then no shame
In converse makes our words obscure and dim;
But man with man gains courage to speak out,
And makes his mission manifest as day.

Enter CLYTÆMNESTRA.

Clytæm. If ye need aught, O strangers, speak; for here
Is all that's fitting for a house like ours;
Warm baths,[1] and bed that giveth rest from toil,
And presence of right honest faces too;
If there be aught that needeth counsel more,
That is men's business, and to them we'll tell it.

Orest. A Daulian traveller, from Phokis come,
Am I, and as I went on business bound,
My baggage with me, unto Argos, I
(Just as I set forth,) met a man I knew not,
Who knew not me, and he then, having asked
My way and told me his, the Phokian Strophios
(For so I learnt in talking) said to me,
"Since thou dost go, my friend, for Argos bound,
In any case, tell those who gave him birth,
Remembering it right well, Orestes' death;
See thou forget it not, and whether plans
Prevail to fetch him home, or bury him
There where he is, a stranger evermore,
Bear back the message as thy freight for us;
For now the ribbed sides of an urn of bronze
The ashes hide of one whom men have wept."
So much I heard and now have told; and if
I speak to kin that have a right in him
I know not, but his father sure should know it.

Clytæm. Ah, thou hast told how utterly our ruin
Is now complete! O Curse of this our house,
Full hard to wrestle with! How many things,

---

(1) So in Homer, (*Il.* xxii. 444,) the warm bath is prepared by Andromache for Hector on his return from the battle in which he fell.

Though lying out of reach, thou aimest at,
And with well-darted arrows from afar
Dost bring them low !   And now thou strippest me,
Most wretched one, of all that most I loved.
A lucky throw Orestes now was making,
Getting his feet from out destruction's slough ;
But now the hope of high, exulting joy,
*Which this house had as healer, he scores down
As present in this fashion that we see.

  Orest. I could have wished to come to prosperous hosts,
As known and welcomed for my tidings good ;
For who to hosts is friendlier than a guest ?   690
But 'twould have been as impious in my thoughts
Not to complete this matter for my friends,
By promise bound and pledged as guest to host.

  Clytæm. Thou shalt not meet with less than thou
    deserv'st ;
Nor wilt thou be to this house less a friend;
Another would have brought news all the same :
But since 'tis time that strangers who have made
A long day's journey find the things they need,
Lead him [*to her Slave, pointing to* ORESTES] to these our
  hospitable halls,
And these his fellow-travellers and servants :   700
There let them meet with what befits our house.
I bid thee act as one who gives account;
And we unto the masters of our house
Will tell this news, and with no lack of friends
Deliberate of this calamity.[1]

   [*Exeunt* CLYTÆMNESTRA, ORESTES, PYLADES,
    and Attendants.

  Chor. Come then, handmaids of the palace,
   When shall we with full-pitched voices
   Shew our feeling for Orestes ?

(1) As in her speeches in the *Agamemnon*, (vv. 595, 884,) Clytæmnestra's words here also are full of significant ambiguity. The "things
that befit the house," the proposed conference with Ægisthos, her
separation of Orestes from his companions, are all indications of suspicion already half-aroused. The last three lines were probably spoken as
an "aside."

O earth revered! thou **height revered, too,**
Of the mound piled o'er the **body**
Of our navy's kingly captain, 710
Oh, hear us now; oh, come and **help us;**
For 'tis time for subtle Suasion[1]
To go with them to the conflict,
And that Hermes act as escort,
He who dwells in earth's deep darkness,
In the strife where swords work mischief.

Enter KILISSA.

Chor. **The stranger seems about to work some ill;**
And here I see Orestes' nurse in tears.
Where then, Kilissa, art thou bound, that thus
Thou tread'st the palace-gates, and with thee comes
Grief as a fellow-traveller unbidden? 720
Kilis. Our mistress bids me with all **speed to call**
Ægisthos to the strangers, that he come
And hear more clearly, as a man from man,
This **newly-brought report. Before her slaves,**
Under set eyes of melancholy cast,
She hid her inner **chuckle at the events**
That have been brought to **pass—too well for her,**
But for this house and hearth most miserably,—
As in the tale the strangers **clearly told.**
He, **when he** hears **and** learns the story's gist,
Will joy, I trow, in heart. Ah, wretched me! 730
How those old troubles, **of** all sorts made up,
Most hard to bear, in Atreus' palace-halls
Have made my heart full heavy in **my breast!**
But never have **I known** a woe like **this.**
For other ills I bore full patiently,
But as **for dear** Orestes, my sweet **charge,**
Whom **from his mother I received and nursed . . . .**
And then the shrill cries rousing me o' nights.
And many and unprofitable **toils**
For me who bore them. For one needs must **rear**

(1) Suasion is personified, and invoked to come and win Clytæmnestra
to trust herself in the power of the two avengers.

The heedless infant like an animal,   748
(How can it else be?) as his humour serves.
For while a child is yet in swaddling clothes,
* It speaketh not, if either hunger comes,
Or passing thirst, or lower calls of need;
And children's stomach works its own content.
And I, though I foresaw this, call to mind
How I was cheated, washing swaddling clothes,
And nurse and laundress did the self-same work.
I then with these my double handicrafts,
Brought up Orestes for his father dear;
And now, woe's me! I learn that he is dead,   750
And go to fetch the man that mars this house:
And gladly will he hear these words of mine.
 Chor. And how equipped then doth she bid him come?
 Nurse. 'How?' Speak again that I may better learn.
 Chor. By spearmen followed, or himself alone?
 Nurse. She bids him bring his guards with lances armed.
 Chor. Nay, say not that to him thy lord doth hate,[1]
But bid him 'come alone,' (that so he hear
 Without alarm,) 'full speed, with joyous mind,'
Since 'secret speech with messengers goes best.'   760
 Nurse. And art thou of good cheer at this my tale?
 Chor. But what if Zeus will turn the tide of ill?
 Nurse. How so? Orestes, our one hope is gone.
 Chor. Not yet; a sorry seer might know thus much.
 Nurse. What say'st thou? Know'st thou aught be-
  sides my tale?
 Chor. Go tell thy message; do thine errand well:
The Gods for what they care for, care enough.
 Nurse. I then will go, complying with thy words:
May all, by God's gift, end most happily!

STROPH. I.

 Chor. Now to my prayer, O Father of the Gods   770
  Of high Olympos, Zeus,

(1) An alternative rendering is,
  "Nay, say not that to him with show of hate."

Grant that their fortune may be blest indeed
* Who long to look on goodness prospering well,
    Yea, with full right and truth
I speak the word—O Zeus, preserve thou him !

Stroph. II.

Yea, Zeus, set him whom now the palace holds,
    Set him above his foes ;
      For if thou raise him high,
Then shalt thou have, to thy heart's full content,
Payment of two-fold, three-fold recompense.

Antistroph. I

Know that the son of one who loved thee well   790
    *Like colt of sire bereaved,
*Is to the chariot of great evils yoked,
*And set thy limit to his weary path.
    *Ah, would that one might see
*His panting footsteps, as he treads his course,
*Keeping due measure through this plain of ours !

Stroph. III.

    And ye within the gate,
    Ye Gods, in purpose one,
    Who dwell in shrines enriched
    With all good things, come ye,
    And now with vengeance fresh
    Atone for murder foul
    Of those that fell long since :   700
    *And let that blood of old,
    *When these are justly slain,
    Breed no more in our house.

Mesode.

O Thou [1] that dwellest in the cavern vast,
    Adorned with goodly gifts,
Grant our lord's house to look up yet once more,
    And that it now may glance,
    In free and glorious guise

    (1) Apollo in the shrine at Delphi.

With loving kindly eyes,
From out its veil of gloom.
Let Maia's son [1] too give
His righteous help, and waft
Good end with prosperous gale.

Antistroph. III.

*And things that now are hid,   800
He, if he will, will bring
As to the daylight clear;
But when it pleases him
Dark, hidden words to speak,
As in thick night he bears
Black gloom before his face; [2]
Nor is he in the day
One whit more manifest.

Stroph. IV.

*And then our treasured store, [3]
*The price as ransom paid
To free the house from ill,
A woman's gift on breath
Of favouring breeze onborne,
We then with clamorous cry,
To sound of cithern sweet,
Will in the city pour;
And if this prospers well,
*My gains, yea, mine, 'twill swell, and Atè then
From those I love stands far.   810

Antistroph. II.

But thou, take courage, when the time is come
For action, and cry out,
Shouting thy father's name,

(1) Hermes invoked once more, as at once the patron of craft and the
escort of the dead.
(2) Or "before our eyes."
(3) The "treasured store" is explained by the words that follow to
mean the cry of exultation which the Chorus will raise when the deed of
vengeance is accomplished; or, possibly (as Mr. Paley suggests), the
funereal wail over the bodies of Ægisthos and Clytæmnestra, which the
Chorus would raise to avert the guilt of the murder from Orestes.

When she shall cry aloud the name of " son,"
And work thou out a woe that none will blame.

ANTISTROPH. IV.

And have thou in thy breast
The heart that Perseus had,[1]
And for thy friends beneath,
And those on earth who dwell,
Go thou and work the deed
Acceptable to them,
Of bitter, wrathful mood,
And consummate within
*The loathly work of blood;
[And bidding Vengeance come as thine ally,]
Destroy the murderer.

Enter ÆGISTHOS.

Ægis. Not without summons came I, but by word
Of courier fetched, and learn that travellers bring
Their tale of tidings new, in no wise welcome.
As for Orestes' death, with it to charge
The house would be a burden dropping fear
To one by that old bloodshed sorely stung.[2]
How shall I count these things ?   As clear and true ?
Or are they vague reports of woman's fears,
That leap up high and die away to nought ?
What can'st thou say that will my mind inform ?

Chor. We heard, 'tis true; but go thou in and ask
Of these same strangers.   Nought is found in words
Of messengers like asking, man from man.

Ægis. I wish to see and probe the messenger,
If he himself were present at the death,
Or tells it hearing of a vague report :
They shall not cheat a mind with eyes wide open. [*Exit.*

(1) As Perseus could only overcome the **Gorgon**, Medusa, by turning
away his eyes, lest looking on her he should **turn to** stone, so Orestes was
to avoid meeting his mother's glance, lest **that** should unman him and
blunt his purpose.

(2) Ægisthos had suffered enough, he says, for his share in Agamemnon's death. He has no wish that fresh odium should fall on him, as being
implicated also in the death of Orestes, of which he has just heard.

Chor. Zeus! Zeus! what words shall I   840
    Now speak, whence start in prayer,
    *Invoking help of Gods?
    How with all wish for good
    Shall I speak fitting words?
    For now the sharp sword-points,
    Red with the blood of man,
    Will either work for aye
    The utter overthrow
    Of Agamemnon's house,
    Or, kindling fire and torch
    For freedom thus achieved,
    Will he the sceptre wield
    Of duly-ordered sway,
    His father's pride and state: 850
    Such is the contest he,
    Orestes, godlike one,
    Now wages all alone,
    The one sole combatant,[1]
    In place of him who fell,
Against those twain.   May victory be his!
Ægisth. [*groaning within*]. Ah! ah! Woe's me!
  Chor.   Hark! hark! How goes it now?
What issue has been wrought within the house?
Let us hold back while they the deed are doing,
That we may seem as guiltless of these ills:
For surely now the fight has reached its end.

Enter Servant *from the chief door.*

  Serv. Alas! alas! my master perishes!   860
Alas! alas! a third time yet I call.
Ægisthos is no more; but open now
With all your speed, and loosen ye the bolts
That bar the women's gates. A man's full strength
Is needed; not indeed that that would help

---

(1) The word (*ephedros*) was applied technically to one who sat by
during a conflict between two athletes, prepared to challenge the victor to
a fresh encounter. Orestes is such a combatant, taking the place of
Agamemnon.

A man already slain.
> [*Rushes to the gate of the women's half of the
> palace.*
Ho there! I say:
I speak to the deaf; to those that sleep I utter
In vain my useless cries.   And where is she?
Where's Clytæmnestra?   What doth she do now?
Her neck upon the razor's edge doth seem,
To fall, down-stricken by a vengeance just.   670

Enter CLYTÆMNESTRA *from the side door.*

Clytæm. What means all this?   What cry is this thou
> mak'st?
Serv. I say the dead are killing one who lives.
Clytæm. Ah, me!   I see the drift of thy dark speech;
By guile we perish, as of old we slew:
Let some one hand at once axe strong to slay;
Let's see if we are conquered or can conquer,
For to that point of evil am I come.

Enter ORESTES *and* PYLADES *from the other door.*

Orest. 'Tis thee I seek: he there has had enough.
Clytæm. Ah me! my loved Ægisthos! Art thou dead?
Orest. Lov'st thou the man?   Then in the self-same
> tomb   680
Shalt thou now lie, nor in his death desert him.
Clytæm. [*baring her bosom*] Hold, boy!   Respect this
> breast of mine, my son,[1]
Whence thou full oft, asleep, with toothless gums,
Hast sucked the milk that sweetly fed thy life.
Orest. What shall I do, my Pylades?   Shall I
Through this respect forbear to slay my mother?
Pyl.[2] Where, then, are Loxias' other oracles,

_____

(1) So, in Homer, (*Il.* xxii. 79,) Hecuba, when the entreaties of Priam
had been in vain, makes this the last appeal—
> "Then to the front his mother rushed, in tears,
> Her bosom bare, with either hand her breast
> Sustaining, and with tears addressed him thus,
> 'Hector, my son, thy mother's breast revere.'"
(2) The reader will note this as the only speech put into the lips of

The Pythian counsels, and the fast-sworn vows?
Have all men hostile rather than the Gods.

   Orest. My judgment goes with thine; thou speakest
       well:

[*To* CLYTÆMNESTRA] Follow: I mean to slay thee
       where he lies,   890
For while he lived thou held'st him far above
My father.   Sleep thou with him in thy death,
Since thou lov'st him, and whom thou should'st love
       hatest.

   Clytæm. I reared thee, and would fain grow old with
       thee.   .

   Orest. What!   Thou live with me, who did'st slay my
       father?

   Clytæm. Fate, O my son, must share the blame of that.

   Orest. This fatal doom, then, it is Fate that sends.

   Clytæm. Dost thou not fear a parent's curse, my son?

   Orest. Thou, though my mother, did'st to ill chance
       cast me.

   Clytæm. No outcast thou, so sent to house allied.   900

   Orest. I was sold doubly, though of free sire born.

   Clytæm. Where is the price, then, that I got for thee?

   Orest. I shrink for shame from pressing that charge
       home.

   Clytæm. Nay, tell thy father's wantonness as well.

   Orest. Blame not the man that toils when thou'rt at
       ease.[1]

   Clytæm. 'Tis hard, my son, for wives to miss their
       husband.

   Orest. The husband's toil keeps her that sits at home.[1]

   Clytæm. Thou seem'st, my son, about to slay thy
       mother.

   Orest. It is not I that slay thee, but thyself.

Pylades, though he is present as accompanying Orestes throughout great
part of the drama.

  (1) The different ethical standard applied to the guilt of the husband
and the wife was, we may well believe, that which prevailed among the
Athenians generally.   It has only too close a parallel in the ballads and
romances of our own early literature.

Clytæm. Take heed, beware a mother's vengeful hounds.[1]   910

Orest. How, slighting this, shall I escape my father's?

Clytæm. I seem in life to wail as to a tomb.[2]

Orest. My father's fate ordains this doom for thee.

Clytæm. Ah me! the snake is here I bare and nursed.[3]

Orest. An o'er-true prophet was that dread dream-born;

Thou slewest one thou never should'st have slain,
Now suffer fate should never have been thine.

> [*Exit* ORESTES, *leading* CLYTÆMNESTRA *into the palace, and followed by* PYLADES.

Chor. E'en of these two I wail the twin mischance;
But since long line of murder culminates
In poor Orestes, this we yet accept,
That he, our one light, fall not utterly.   920

STROPH. I.

Late came due vengeance on the sons of Priam,
          Just forfeit of sore woe;—
Late came there too to Agamemnon's house,
          Twin lions, two-fold Death.[4]
The exile who obeyed the Pythian hest
          Hath gained his full desire,
Sped on his way by counsel from the Gods.

STROPH. II.

Shout ye, loud shout for the escape from ills
          Our master's house has seen,
And from the wasting of his ancient wealth
          By that defiled pair,   930
          Ill fate intolerable.

---

(1) The line is memorable as prophetic of the whole plot of the *Eumenides*.
(2) The phrase "wail as to a tomb" seems to have been a bye-word for fruitless entreaty and lamentation.
(3) Clytæmnestra sees now the import of the dream referred to in vv. 518-522.
(4) The words must be left in their obscurity. Commentators have conjectured Orestes and Pylades, or the deaths of Agamemnon and Iphigeneia, or those of Ægisthos and Clytæmnestra, as the "two lions" spoken of. The first seems most in harmony with the context.

Antistroph. I.

And so on one who loves the war of guile
    Revenge came subtle-souled;
And in the strife of hands the child of Zeus
      · In very deed gave help,
(We mortals call her Vengeance, hitting well
    The meetest name for her,)
Breathing destroying wrath against her foes.

Stroph. III.

She, she it is whom Loxias summons now,   *940*
Who dwelleth in Parna'ssia's cavern vast,
    *Calling on her who still
    *Is guileful without guile,
*Halting of foot and tarrying over-long:
The will of Gods is strangely overruled;
    It may not help the vile;[1]
'Tis meet to adore the Power that rules in Heaven:
    At last we see the light.

Antistroph. II.

*Now is the bit that curbed the slaves ta'en off:[2]
    Arise, arise, O house:
Too long, too long, all prostrate on the ground   *950*
    Ye have been used to lie.

    ·   ·   ·   ·

Antistroph. III.

Quickly all-working Time will bring a change
Across the threshold of the palace old,
    When from the altar-hearth
    It shall drive all the guilt,
With cleansing rites that chase away our woes;

---

(1) **The Eternal** Justice which orders all things is mightier than any
arbitrary will, such as men attribute to the Gods. That will, even if we
dare to think of it as changeable or evil, is held in restraint. It cannot,
even if it would, protect the evil-doers.
(2) The Chorus feel that they have been too long silent; now, at last,
they can speak. As slaves dreading punishment they had been gagged
before; now the gag is removed.

And Fortune's throws shall fall with gladsome cast,
      *Once more benign to see,[1]
For new-come strangers settled in the house:
      At last we see the light.

Enter ORESTES, PYLADES, *and followers from the* **palace.**
  His attendants bear the robe in which AGAMEMNON
  had been murdered.

  Orest. See ye this country's tyrant rulers twain,   960
My father's murderers, wasters of his house;
Stately were they, seen sitting on their thrones,
Friends too e'en now, to argue from their fate,
Whose oaths are kept to every pledge they gave.
Firmly they swore that they would slay my father,
And die together. Well those oaths are kept:
And ye who hear these ills, behold ye now
Their foul device, as bonds for my poor father,
Handcuffs, and fetters both his feet to bind.
Come, stretch it out, and standing all around,   970
Show ye the snare that wrapt him o'er, that He
May see, our Father,—not of mine I speak,
But the great Sun that looks on all we do,—
My mother's deeds, defilèd and impure,
That He may be a witness in my cause,
That I did justly bring this doom to pass
Upon my mother. . . . . Of Ægisthos' fate
No word I speak. He bears the penalty,
As runs the law, of an adulterer's guilt;
But she who planned this crime against a man
By whom she knew the weight of children borne
Beneath her girdle, once a burden loved,
But now, as it is proved, a grievous ill,   980
What seems she to you? Had she viper been,
Or fell myræna,[2] she with touch alone,
*Rather than bite, had made a festering sore

---

(1) Or, "Once more for those who wail."
(2) It is not clear with what form of animal life the *myræna* is to be
identified. The idea implied is that of some sea-monster whose ouch
was poisonous, but this does not hold good of the "lamprey."

U

With that bold daring of unrighteous mood.
What shall I call it, using mildest speech?
A wild beast's trap?—a pall that wraps a bier,
And hides a dead man's feet?—A net, I trow,
A snare, a robe entangling, one might call it.
Such might be owned by one to plunder trained,
Practised in duping travellers, and the life
That robs men of their money; with this trap   992
Destroying many, many deeds of ill
His fevered brain might hatch.   May such as she
Ne'er share my dwelling!   May the hand of God
Far rather smite me that I childless die!

    Chor. [*looking on* AGAMEMNON's *robe.*] Ah me! ah me!
       these deeds most miserable!
By hateful murder thou wast done to death.
       Woe, woe is me!
And evil buds and blooms for him that's left.

    Orest. Was the deed hers or no?   Lo! this same robe
Bears witness how she dyed Ægisthos' sword,
And the blood-stain helps Time's destroying work,   1000
Marring full many a tint of pattern fair:
*Now name I it, now as eye-witness wail;[1]
And calling on this robe that slew my father,
Moan for all done and suffered, wail my race,
Bearing the foul stains of this victory.

    Chor. No mortal man shall live a life unharmed,
*Stout-hearted and rejoicing evermore.
       Woe, woe is me!
One trouble vexes now, another comes.

    Orest. (*wildly, as one distraught.*) Nay, know ye—for I
       know not how 'twill end;   1010
Like chariot-driver with his steeds I'm dragged
Out of my course; for passion's moods uncurbed
Bear me their victim headlong.   At my heart

---

(1) As the text stands, Orestes says that at last he can speak of the
murder over which he had long brooded in silence.   Another reading
makes him speak of the oscillations in his own mind—

    " Now do I praise myself, now wail and blame."

Stands terror ready or to sing or dance
In burst of frenzy.   While my reason stays,
I tell my friends here that I slew my mother,
Not without right, my father's murderess,
Accursed, and hated of the Gods.   And I
As chiefest spell that made me dare this deed
Count Loxias, Pythian prophet, warning me
That doing this I should be free from blame,   1020
But slighting . . . . I pass o'er the penalty [1] . . . .
For none, aim as he will, such woes will hit.
And now ye see me, in what guise equipped,

> [*Putting on the suppliant's wreaths of wool, and
> taking an olive branch in his hand.*

With this my bough and chaplet I will gain
Earth's central shrine, the home where Loxias dwells,
And the bright fire that is as deathless known,[2]
Seeking to 'scape this guilt of kindred blood ;
And on no other hearth, so Loxias bade,
May I seek shelter.   And I charge you **all,**
Ye Argives, bear ye witness in due time   1030
How these dark deeds of wretched ill were wrought :
But I, a wanderer, exiled from my land,
Shall live, and leaving these my prayers in death, . . .

   Chor. Nay, thou hast prospered : burden not thy lips
With evil speech, nor speak ill-boding words,
When thou hast freed the Argive commonwealth,
By **good chance** lopping **those** two serpents' heads.

> [*The Erinnyes are seen in the background, visible
> to Orestes only, in black robes, and with snakes
> in their hair.*

   Orest. Ah ! ah ! ye handmaids : see, like **Gorgons** these,
Dark-robed, and all their tresses hang entwined
With many serpents.   I can bear no more.

---

(1) Comp. vv. 270-288.
(2) Delphi was to the Greek (as Jerusalem was to mediæval Christendom) the centre at once of his religious life and of the material earth.
It's rock was the *omphalos* of the world.   Consecrated widows watched
over the sacred and perpetual fire.   Once only up to the time of Æschylos,
when the Temple itself was desecrated by the Persians, had it ceased to
burn.

Chor. What phantoms vex thee, best beloved of
      sons   1040
By thy dear sire ? Hold, fear not, victory's thine.
    Orest. These are no phantom terrors that I see :
Full clear they are my mother's vengeful hounds.
    Chor. The blood fresh-shed is yet upon thy hands,
And thence it is these troubles haunt thy soul.
    Orest. O King Apollo ! See, they swarm, they swarm,
And from their eyes is dropping loathsome blood.
    Chor. One way of cleansing is there ; Loxias' form
Clasp thou, and he will free thee from these ills.
    Orest. These forms ye see not, but I see them there :
They drive me on, and I can bear no more.   [*Exit.*
    Chor. Well, may'st thou prosper ; may the gracious
      God   1050
Watch o' and guard thee with a chance well timed !

Here, then, upon this palace of our kings
    A third storm blows again ;
The blast that haunts the race has run its course.
First came the wretched meal of children's flesh ;
    Next what befell our king :
Slain in the bath was he who ruled our host,
    Of all the Achæans lord ;
And now a third has come, we know not whence,[1]
    To save . . . or shall I say,
    To work a doom of death ?
Where will it end ? Where will it cease at last,
    The mighty Atè dread,
    Lulled into slumber deep ?

(1) Once again we have the thought of the third cup offered as a
libation to Zeus as saviour and deliverer. The Chorus asks whether this
third deed of blood will be true to that idea and work out deliverance.

EUMENIDES.

ARGUMENT.

The Erinnyes who appeared to Orestes after the murder of Clytæmnestra made his life miserable, and drove him without
rest from land to land. And he, seeking to escape them,
had recourse to the Oracle of Apollo at Delphi, believing that
he who had sent him to do the work of vengeance would also
help to free him from this wretchedness. But the Erinnyes
followed him there also, and took their places even within the
holy shrine of the Oracle, and while Orestes knelt on the
central hearth as a suppliant, they sat upon the seats there,
and for very weariness fell asleep.

Dramatis Personæ.

PYTHIAN PRIESTESS.

APOLLO.

ATHENA.

Ghost of Clytæmnestra.

ORESTES.

HERMES.

Chorus of the Erinnyes.

Athenian Citizens, Women, and Girls.

EUMENIDES.

SCENE.—*The Outer Court of the Oracle at* Delphi. *Inner shrine in the background, with doors leading into it.*

Enter the PYTHIAN PRIESTESS.

Pyth. First, with this prayer, of all the Gods I honour
The primal seeress Earth, and Themis next,[1]
Who in due order filled her mother's place,
(So runs the tale,) and in the third lot named,
With her goodwill and doing wrong to none,
Another of the Titans' offspring sat,
Earth's daughter Phœbe, and as birthday gift
She gives it up to Phœbos,[2] and he takes
His name from Phœbe. And he, leaving then
The pool[3] and rocks of Delos, having steered
To the ship-traversed shores that Pallas owns,   10
Came to this land and to Parnassos' seat:
And with great reverence they escort him on,
Hephæstos' sons, road-makers,[4] turning thus

(1) The succession is, in part, accordant with that in the *Theogonia* of Hesiod, (vv. 116-136,) but the special characteristic of the Æschylean form of the legend is that each change is a step in a due, rightful succession, as by free gift, not accomplished (as in other narratives of the same transition) by vi·lence and wrong.

(2) Phœbe, in the *Theogonia*, marries Coios, and becomes the mother of Leto, or Latona, and so the grandmother of Apollo. The "birthday gift" was commonly presented on the eighth day after birth, when the child was named. The oracle is spoken of as such a gift to Apollo, as bearing the name of Phœbos.

(3) The sacred circular pool of Delos is the crater of an extinct volcano. There Apollo was born, and thence he passed through Attica to Parnassos, to take possession of the oracle, according to one form of the myth, depriving Themis of it and slaying the dragon Python that kept guard over it.

(4) The people of Attica are thus named, either as being mythically

The wilderness to land no longer wild;
And when he comes the people honour him,
And Delphos too,[1] chief pilot of this land.
And him Zeus sets, his mind with skill inspired,
As the fourth seer upon these sacred seats;
And Loxias is his father Zeus's prophet.
These Gods in prologue of my prayer I worship;   20
Pallas Pronaia[2] too claims highest praise;
The Nymphs adore I too where stands the rock
Korykian,[3] hollow, loved of birds and haunt
Of Gods. [And Bromios[4] also claims this place,
Nor can I now forget it, since the time
When he, a God, with help of Bacchants warred,
And planned a death for Pentheus, like a hare's.[5]]
Invoking Pleistos'[6] founts, Poseidon's might,
And Zeus most High, supreme Accomplisher,
I in due order sit upon this seat
As seeress, and I pray them that they grant
To find than all my former divinations   30
One better still. If Hellas pilgrims sends,
Let them approach by lot, as is our law;

descended from Erichthonios the son of Hephæstos, or as artificers, who
own him as their father. The words refer to the supposed origin of the
Sacred Road from Athens to Delphi, passing through Bœotia and Phokis.
When the Athenians sent envoys to consult the oracle they were preceded by men bearing axes, in remembrance of the original pioneering
work which had been done for Apollo. The first work of active civilisation was thus connected with the worship of the giver of Light and
Wisdom.
(1) Delphos, the hero *Eponymos* (name-giving) of Delphi, was honoured
as the son of Poseidon. Hence the Priestess invokes the latter as one of
the guardian deities of the shrine.
(2) Pronaia, as having her shrine or statue in front of the temple of
Apollo.
(3) The Korykian rock in Parnassos, as in Soph., *Antig.*, v. 1128; known
also as the "Nymphs' cavern."
(4) Bromios, a name of Dionysos, embodying the special attributes of
loud, half-frenzied revelry.
(5) In the legend which Euripides follows, Kithæron, not Parnassos, is
the scene of the death of Pentheus. He, it was said, opposed the wild or
frantic worship of the Pelasgic Bacchos, concealed himself that he might
behold the mysteries of the Mænads, and was torn in pieces by his mother
and two others, on whose eyes the God had cast such glamour that they
took him for a wild beast. English readers may be referred to Dean Mil-
man's translation of the *Bacchanals* of Euripides.
(6) Pleistos, topographically, a river flowing through the vale of Delphi
mythically the father of the nymphs of Korykos.

For as the God guides I give oracles.[1]

> *[She passes through the door to the adytum, and*
> *after a pause returns trembling and crouch-*
> *ing with fear, supporting herself with her*
> *hands against the walls and columns. The*
> *door remains open, and Orestes and the*
> *Erinnyes are seen in the inner sanctuary.*

Dread things to tell, and dread for eyes to see,
Have sent me back again from Loxias' shrine,
*So that strength fails, nor can I nimbly move,
But run with help of hands, not speed of foot;
A woman old and terrified is nought,
A very child. Lo! into yon recess
With garlands hung I go, and there I see
Upon the central stone [2] a God-loathed man,
Sitting as suppliant, and with hands that dripped
Blood-drops, and holding sword but newly drawn,
And branch of olive from the topmost growth,
With amplest tufts of white wool meetly wreathed;
For this I will say clearly.[3] And a troop
Of women strange to look at sleepeth there,
Before this wanderer, seated on their stools;
Not women they, but Gorgons[4] I must call them;

(1) At one time the Oracle had been open to questioners once in the
year only, afterwards once a month. The pilgrims, after they had made
their offerings, cast lots, and the doors were opened to him to whom the
lot had fallen. Plutarch, *Qu. Grac.*, p. 292.

(2) The altar of the adytum, on the very centre, as men deemed, of the
whole earth. Zeus, it was said, had sent forth two eagles at the same
moment; one from the East and the other from the West, and here it
was that they had met. The stone was of white marble, and the two
eagles were sculptured on it. Strabo, ix. 3.

(3) The priestess dwells upon the outward tokens, which showed that
the suppliant came as one whose need was specially urgent. On the ritual
of supplication generally comp. *Suppl.*, **vv.** 22, 348, 641, Soph., *Œd. King*, **v.**
3; *Œd. Col.*, vv. 469-489.

(4) Æschylos apparently follows the *Theogonia* of Hesiod, (l 278,) who
describes the Gorgons as three in number, daughters of Phorkys and
Keto, and bearing the names of Stheno, Euryale, and Medusa. The last
enters into the Perseus cycle of myths, as one of the monsters whom he
conquered, with a face once beautiful, but with her hair turned to serpents
by the wrath of Athena, and so dreadful to look upon that those who
gazed on her were turned to stone. When Perseus had slain her,
Athena placed her head in her ægis, and thus became the terror of all
who were foes to herself or her people. A wild legendary account of

Nor yet can I to Gorgon forms compare them ·
I have seen painted shapes that bear away
The feast of Phineus.[1]   Wingless, though, are these,
And swarth, and every way abominable.
*They snort with breath that none may dare approach,
And from their eyes a loathsome humour pours,
And such their garb as neither to the shrine
Of Gods is meet to bring, nor mortal roof.
Ne'er have I seen a race that owns this tribe,
Nor is there land can boast it rears such brood,
Unhurt and free from sorrow for its pains.
Henceforth be it the lot of Loxias,
Our mighty lord, himself to deal with them :
True prophet-healer he, and portent-seer,
And for all others cleanser of their homes.

>   *Enter* APOLLO *from the inner adytum, attended by*
>   HERMES.

Apol. [*To* ORESTES.] Nay, I'll not fail thee, but as
        close at hand
Will guard thee to the end, or though far off,
Will not prove yielding to thine adversaries ;
And now thou see'st these fierce ones captive ta'en,
These loathly maidens fallen fast in sleep.
Hoary and ancient virgins they, with whom
Nor God, nor man, nor beast, holds intercourse.
They owe their birth to evils ; for they dwell
In evil darkness, yea in Tartaros
Beneath the earth, and are the hate and dread
Of all mankind, and of Olympian Gods.
Yet fly thou, fly, and be not faint of heart ;

---

them meets us in the *Prom. Bound*, v. 812. As works of **art**, the Gorgon
images are traceable to the earliest or Kyclopian period.
   (1) Here also we have a reference to a familiar subject of early Greek
art, probably to some painting familiar to an Athenian audience. The
name of Phineus indicates that the monstrous forms spoken of are those
of the Harpies, birds with women's faces, or women with birds' wings,
who were sent to vex the blind seer for his cruelty to the children of his
first marriage. Comp. Soph. *Antig.*, v. 973. In the *Æneid* they appear
(III. 225) as dwelling in the Strophades, and harassing Æneas and his
companions.

For they will chase thee over mainland wide,
As thou dost tread the soil by wanderers tracked,
And o'er the ocean, and by sea-girt towns;
And fail thou not before the time, as brooding
O'er this great toil.   But go to Pallas' city,
And sit, and clasp her ancient image [1] there;   80
And there with judges of these things, and words
Strong to appease, will we a means devise
To free thee from these ills for evermore;
For I urged thee to take thy mother's life.

   Orest. Thou know'st, O king Apollo, not to wrong:
And since thou know'st, learn also not to slight:
Thy strength gives full security for act.

   Apol. Remember, let no fear o'ercome thy soul;
And [*To* HERMES,] thou, my brother, of one father born,
My Hermes, guard him; true to that thy name,
Be thou his Guide, true shepherd of this man,
Who comes to me as suppliant: Zeus himself   90
*Reveres this reverence e'en to outcasts due,
When it to mortals comes with guidance good.[2]

        [*Exit* ORESTES *led by* HERMES.   APOLLO *retires*
          within the adytum.   The Ghost of CLYTÆM-
          NESTRA *rises from the ground.*

   Clytœm. What ho! Sleep on!   What need of sleepers
      now?
And I am put by you to foul disgrace
Among the other dead, nor fails reproach
Among the shades that I a murderess am;
And so in shame I wander, and I tell you
That at their hands I bear worst form of blame.
And much as I have borne from nearest kin,   100
Yet not one God is stirred to wrath for me,

<hr>

(1) The old image of Pallas, carved in olive-wood, as distinguished from
later sculpture.
(2) The early code of hospitality bound the host, who as such had once
received a guest under the shelter of his roof, not to desert him, even
though he might discover afterwards that he had been guilty of great
crimes, but to escort him safely to the boundary of his territory. Thus
Apollo, as the host with whom Orestes had taken refuge, sends Hermes,
the escort God, to guide and defend him on his way to Athens.

Though done to death by matricidal hands.
See ye these heart-wounds, whence and how they came ?
Yea, when it sleeps, the mind is bright with eyes; [1]
But in the day it is man's lot to lack
All true discernment.   Many a gift of mine
Have ye lapped up, libations pure from wine, [2]
And soothing rites that shut out drunken mirth ;
And I dread banquets of the night would offer
On altar-hearth, at hour no God might share.
And lo ! all this is trampled under foot.   110
He is escaped, and flees, like fawn, away ;
And even from the midst of all your toils
Has nimbly slipped, and draws wide mouth at you.
Hear ye; for I have spoken for my life :
Give heed, ye dark, earth-dwelling Goddesses,
I, Clytæmnestra's phantom, call on you.
                    [*The Erinnyes moan in their sleep.*
Moan on, the man is gone, and flees far off :
My kindred find protectors; I find none.
                              [*Moan as before.*
Too sleep-oppressed art thou, nor pitiest me :
Orestes, murderer of his mother, 'scapes.   120
                              [*Noises repeated.*
Dost snort ? Dost drowse ? Will thou not rise and speed ?
What have ye ever done but work out ill ?
                              [*Noises as before.*
Yea, sleep and toil, supreme conspirators,
Have withered up the dreaded dragon's strength.
    Chor. [*starting up suddenly with a yell.*] Seize him,
        seize, seize, yea, seize : look well to it.

---

(1) The thought that the highest wisdom came to men rather in
" visions of the night, when deep sleep falleth on men," than through the
waking senses, which we have already met with in *Agam.*, v. 173, is traceable to the mysticism of Pythagoras, more distinctly perhaps to that of
Epimenides.
    (2) Wine, as in Soph. *Œd. Col.*, vv. 100, 481, was rigidly excluded from
the *cultus* of the Eumenides, and to them only as daughters of Night were
midnight sacrifices offered. We must not lose sight of the thought thus
implied, that Clytæmnestra had herself lived, after her deed of guilt, in
perpetual terror of the Erinnyes, seeking to soothe them by her
sacrifices.

Clytæm. Thou, phantom-like,[1] dost hunt thy prey, and
    criest,
Like hound that never rests from care of toil.
What dost thou ? (*to one Erinnys.*) Rise and let not toil
    o'ercome thee,
Nor, lulled to sleep, lose all thy sense of loss.
Let thy soul (*to another*) feel the pain of just reproach : [130]
The wise of heart find that their goad and spur.
And thou (*to a third*), breathe on him with thy blood-
    flecked breath,
And with thy vapour, thy maw's fire, consume him ;
Chase him, and wither with a fresh pursuit.
    Leader of the Chor. Wake, wake, I say ; wake her, as
      I wake thee.
Dost slumber ? Rise, I say, and shake off sleep.
Let's see if this our prelude be in vain.

STROPH. I.

Pah! pah! Oh me! we suffered, O my friends. . . . .
Yea, many mine own sufferings undeserved. . . . .
We suffered a great sorrow, full of woe,   140
    An evil hard to bear.
Out of the nets he's slipped, our prey is gone :
O'ercome by sleep I have my quarry lost.

ANTISTROPH. I.

Ah, son of Zeus, a very robber thou,
Though young, thou didst old Goddesses ride down,[2]
Honouring thy suppliant, godless though he be,
    One whom his parents loathe :
Thou, though a God, a matricide hast freed :
Of which of these acts can one speak as just ?

(1) **The common** rendering "in a dream" gives a sufficient meaning,
and is, of course, tenable enough. But there is a force in the repetition of the same word, as in v. 116, which is thus lost, and which I
have endeavoured to preserve. The Erinnyes, thus impotent in their
rage, are as much mere dream-like spectres as is the ghost of Clytæmnestra.

(2) Here, as throughout Æschylos, the Olympian divinities are thought
of as new comers, thrusting from their thrones the whole Chthonian and
Titanic dynasty, Gods of the conquering Hellenes superseding those of
the Pelasgi.

Yea, this reproach that came to me in dreams   138
          Smote me, as charioteer
Smites with a goad he in the middle grasps,
          Beneath my breast, my heart;
'Tis ours to feel the keen, the o'er keen smart,
As by the public scourger fiercely lashed.

Such are the doings of these younger Gods,
          Beyond all bounds of right
Stretching their power. . . . . A clot of blood besmeared
          Upon the base, the head, ...
Earth's central shrine itself we now may see   160
Take to itself pollution terrible.

And thou, a seer, with guilt that stains thy hearth
Hast fouled thy shrine, self-prompted, self-impelled,
Against God's laws a mortal honouring,
          And bringing low the Fates
          Born in the hoary past.

Me he may vex, but shall not rescue him;
Though 'neath the earth he flee, he is not freed;
For he, blood-stained, shall find upon his head
          Another after me,
          Destroyer foul and dread.
          [APOLLO *advances from the Adytum and confronts*
               them.
     Apol. Out, out, I bid you, quickly from this temple;
Go forth, and leave this shrine oracular,   170
Lest, smitten with a serpent winged and bright,
Forth darted from my bow-string golden-wrought,
Thou in sore pain bring up dark foam, and vomit
The clots of blood thou suck'dst from human veins.
This is no house where ye may meetly come,

But there where heads upon the scaffold lie,[1]
And eyes are gouged, and throats of men are cut,
*And mutilation mars the bloom of youth,
Where men are maimed and stoned to death, and groan
With bitter wailing, 'neath the spine impaled;   180
Hear ye what feast ye love, and so become
Loathed of the Gods?   Yes, all your figure's fashion
Points clearly to it.   Such as ye should dwell
In cave of lion battening upon blood,
Nor tarry in these sacred precincts here,
Working defilement.   Go, and roam afield
Without a shepherd, for to flock like this
Not one of all the Gods is friendly found.

   Chor. O king Apollo, hear us in our turn:
No more accomplice art thou of these things,   190
But guilty art in full as principal.
   Apol. How then?   Prolong thy speech to tell me this.
   Chor. Thou bad'st this stranger be a matricide.
   Apol. I bade him to avenge his sire.   Why not?
   Chor. Then thou did'st welcome here the blood just
     shed.
   Apol. I bade him seek this shrine as suppliant.
   Chor. Yet us who were his escort thou revilest.
   Apol. It is not meet that ye come nigh this house.
   Chor. Yet is this self-same task appointed us.
   Apol. What function's this?   Boast thou of nobler
     task?   200
   Chor. We drive from home the murderers of their
     mothers.
   Apol. What?   Those who kill a wife that slays her
     spouse?
   Chor. That deed brings not the guilt of blood of kin.[2]

(1) The accumulation of horrid forms of cruelty had, probably, a special significance for the Athenians. These punishments belonged to their enemies, the Persians, not to the Hellenic race, and the poet's purpose was to rekindle patriotic feeling by dwelling on their barbarity, as in *Agam.*, v. 894, he points in like manner to their haughtiness and luxury.

(2) The argument of the Erinnyes is, to some extent, like that of the Antigone of Sophocles, (*Antig.*, 909-913,) and the wife of Intaphernes, (Herod. III., 119.) The tie which binds the husband to the wife is less sacred than that between the mother and the son. This, therefore, brings

X

Apol. *Truly thou mak'st dishonoured, and as nought,
The marriage-vows of Zeus and Hera great ;
And by this reasoning Kypris too is shamed,
From whom men gain the ties of closest love.
For still to man and woman marriage bed,
Assigned by Fate and guided by the Right,
Is more than any oath.   If thou then deal   210
So gently, when the one the other slays,
And dost not even look on them with wrath,
I say thou dost not justly chase Orestes ;
For thou, in the one case, I know, dost rage ;
I' the other, clearly tak'st it easily :
The Goddess Pallas shall our quarrel judge.
   Chor. That man I ne'er will leave for evermore.
   Apol. Chase him then, chase, and gain yet more of toil.
   Chor. Curtail thou not my functions by thy speech.
   Apol. Ne'er by my choice would I thy functions own.
   Chor. True ; great thy name among the thrones of
           Zeus :   220
But I, his mother's blood constraining me,
Will this man chase, and track him like a hound.
   Apol. And I will help him and my suppliant free ;
For dreadful among Gods and mortals too
. The suppliant's curse, should I abandon him.

                                              [*Exeunt.*

Scene changes to Athens, *in front of the Temple of Athena
         Polias, on the Acropolis.*[1]
                Enter ORESTES.
   Orest. [*clasping the statue of the Goddess.*] O Queen
           Athena, I at Loxias' hest

on the slayer the guilt of blood of kin, while murder in the other case is
reduced to simple homicide. Orestes therefore was not justified in per-
petrating the greater crime as a retribution for the less. Apollo, in
meeting this plea, asserts the sacredness of the marriage bond as standing
on the same level as that of consanguinity.
   (1) The ideal interval of time between the two parts of the drama is
left undefined, but it would seem from vv. 230, 274-6, and 429, to have
been long enough to have allowed of many wanderings to sacred places,
Orestes does not go straight from Delphi to Athens. He appears now,
not as before dripping and besmeared with blood, but with hands and
garments purified.

Am come: do thou receive me graciously,
Sin-stained though I have been: no guilt of blood
Is on my soul, nor is my hand unclean,
But now with stain toned down and worn away,
In other homes and journeyings among men,[1] 230
O'er land and water travelling alike,
Keeping great Loxias' charge oracular,
I come, O Goddess, to thy shrine and statue:
Here will I stay and wait the trial's issue.

Enter the Erinnyes in pursuit.

Chor. Lo! here are clearest traces of the man:
Follow thou up that dumb informer's[2] hints;
For as the hound pursues a wounded fawn,
So by red blood and oozing gore track we.
My lungs are panting with full many a toil,
Wearing man's strength down. Every spot of earth 240
Have I now searched, and o'er the sea in flight
Wingless I came pursuing, swift as ship;
And now full sure he's crouching somewhere here:
The smell of human blood wafts joy to me.
See, see again, look round ye every way,
Lest he, the murderer, slip away unscathed.
Ho, it is true, in full security,
Clasping the statue of the deathless goddess,
Would fain now take his trial at our hands. 250
This may not be; a mother's blood out-poured
(Pah! pah!) can never be raised up again,
The life-blood shed is poured out and gone,
But thou must give to us to suck the blood
Red from thy living members; yea, from thee,
May I gain meal of drink undrinkable!

(1) The story of Adrastos and Crœsos in Herod. **I. 35**, illustrates the
gradual purification of which Orestes speaks. The penitent who has the
stain of blood-guiltiness upon him comes to the king, and the king, as
his host, performs the lustral rites for him. Here Orestes urges that he
has been received at many homes, and gone through many such lustrations. He has been cleansed from the pollution of sin: what he now
seeks, to use the terminology of a later system, is a forensic justifi-
cation.

(2) *Sc.*, the scent of blood, which though no longer visible to the eyes of
men, still lingers round him and is perceptible to his pursuers.

And, having dried thee up, I'll drag thee down
Alive to bear the doom of matricide.
There thou shalt see if any other man
Has sinned in not revering God or guest,
Or parents dear, that each receiveth there					260
The recompense of sin that Vengeance claims.
For Hades is a mighty arbiter
Of those that dwell below, and with a mind
That writes true record all man's deeds surveys.

   Orest. I, taught by troubles, know full many a form
Of cleansing rites,—to speak, when that is meet,
And when 'tis not, keep silence, and in this
I by wise teacher was enjoined to speak;
For the blood fails and fades from off my hands;
The guilt of matricide is washed away.					270
For when 'twas fresh, it then was all dispelled,
At Phœbos' shrine, by spells of slaughtered swine.
Long would the story be, if told complete,
Of all I joined in harmless fellowship.
Time waxing old, too, cleanses all alike :
And now with pure lips, I in words devout,
Call Athenæa, whom this land owns queen,
To come and help me : So without a war
Shall she gain me, my land, my Argive people,					280
Full faithful friends, allies for evermore;[1]
But whether in the climes of Libyan land,
Hard by her birth-stream's foam, Tritonian named,[2]
She stands upright, or sits with feet enwrapt,
Helping her friends, or o'er Phlegræan plains,
Like a bold chieftain, she keeps watchful guard,[3]

(1) Here, too, we trace the political bearing of the play. In the year when it was produced (B.C. 458) an alliance with Argos was the favourite measure of the more conservative party at Athens.

(2) The names Triton and Tritonis, wherever found in classical geography, (Libya, Crete, Thessaly, Bœotia,) are always connected with the legend that Athena was born there. Probably both name and legend were carried from Greece to Libya, and then amalgamated with the indigenous local worship of a warlike goddess. Hesiod (iv. 180, 188) connects the Libyan lake with the legend of Jason and Argonauts.

(3) In the war with the giants fought in the Phlegræan plains (the volcanic district of Campania) Athena had helped her father Zeus by her

Oh, may she come ! (far off a God can hear,)
And work for me redemption from these ills !
　　Chor. Nay, nor Apollo, nor Athena's might
Can save thee from the doom of perishing,　　　　　．　290
Outcast, not knowing where to look for joy,
The bloodless food of demons, a mere shade.
Wilt thou not answer ?　Scornest thou my words,
A victim reared and consecrate to me ?
Alive thou'lt feed me, not at altar slain ;
And thou shalt hear our hymn as spell to bind thee.

The Erinnyes, as they sing the ode that follows, move round
　　and round in solemn and weird measure.

　　Come, then, let us form our chorus ;
　　Since 'tis now our will to utter
　　Melody of song most hateful,
　　Telling how our band assigneth
　　All the lots that fall to mortals ;　　　　　300
　　And we boast that we are righteous :
　　Not on one who pure hands lifteth
　　Falleth from us any anger,
　　But his life he passeth scatheless ;
　　But to him who sins like this man,
　　And his blood-stained hands concealeth,
　　Witnesses of those who perish,
　　Coming to exact blood-forfeit,
　　We appear to work completeness.　　　　　310

Stroph. I.

O mother who did'st bear me, mother Night,
A terror of the living and the dead,
　　Hear me, oh hear !
The son of Leto puts me to disgrace
　　And robs me of my spoil,

wise counsel, and was honoured there as keeping in check the destructive
Titanic forces which had been so subdued, burying Enkelados, *e.g.*, in
Sicily. The "friends" are her Libyan worshippers. The passage is
interesting, as showing the extent of Æschylos's acquaintance with the
African and Italian coasts of the Mediterranean.

This crouching victim for a mother's blood:
   And over him as slain,
We raise this chant of madness, frenzy-working,[1]
   The hymn the Erinnyes love,
A spell upon the soul, a lyreless strain
   That withers up men's strength.

Antistroph. I.

This lot the all-pervading Destiny   320
Hath spun to hold its ground for evermore,
   That we should still attend
On him on whom there rests the guilt of blood
   Of kin shed causelessly,
Till earth lie o'er him; nor shall death set free.
   And over him as slain,
We raise this chant of madness, frenzy-working,
   The hymn the Erinnyes love,
A spell upon the soul, a lyreless strain
   That withers up men's strength.

Stroph. II.

Such lot was then assigned us at our birth:
From us the Undying Ones must hold aloof: 330
   Nor is there one who shares
   The banquet-meal with us;
In garments white I have nor part nor lot;[2]
My choice was made for overthrow of homes,
Where home-bred slaughter works a loved one's death:
   Ha! hunting after him,
   Strong though he be, 'tis ours
To wear the newness of his young blood down.[3]

---

(1) The Choral ode here is brought in as an incantation. This weapon
is to succeed where others have failed, and this too, the frenzy which
seizes the soul in the remembrance of its past transgression, is soothed
and banished by Athena.

(2) White, as the special colour of festal joy, was not used in the worship
of the Erinnyes.

(3) Another rendering gives—
  "To dim the bright hue of the fresh-shed blood."

ANTISTROPH. II.

*Since 'tis our work another's task to take,[1]   840
*The Gods indeed may bar the force of prayers
      Men offer unto me,
      But may not clash in strife;
For Zeus doth cast us from his fellowship,
" Blood-dropping, worthy of his utmost hate." . . .
For leaping down as from the topmost height,
      I on my victim bring
      The crushing force of feet,
Limbs that o'erthrow e'en those that swiftly run,
      An Atè hard to bear.   350

STROPH. III.

And fame of men, though very lofty now
      Beneath the clear, bright sky,
Below the earth grows dim and fades away
Before the attack of us, the black-robed ones,
      And these our dancings wild,
      Which all men loathe and hate.

ANTISTROPH. III.

Falling in frenzied guilt, he knows it not;
      So thick the blinding cloud
*That o'er him floats; and Rumour widely spread
With many a sigh reports the dreary doom,
      A mist that o'er the house
      In gathering darkness broods.

STROPH. IV.

Fixed is the law, no lack of means find we;   360
      We work out all our will,

---

(1) The thought which underlies the obscurity of a corrupt passage
seems to be that, as they relieve the Gods from the task of being avengers
of blood, all that the Gods on their side can legitimately do against them
is to render powerless the prayers for vengeance offered by the kindred
of the slain. Their very isolation, as Chthonian deities, from the Gods of
Olympos should protect them from open conflict. But an alternative
rendering of the second line gives, perhaps, a better meaning—
      "And by the prayers men offer unto me
        Work freedom for the Gods;"
i.e., by being the appointed receivers of such prayers for vengeance, they
leave the Gods free for a higher and serener life.

We, the dread Powers, the registrars of crime,
    Whom mortals fail to soothe,
Fulfilling tasks dishonoured, unrevered,
    Apart from all the Gods,
    *In foul and sunless gloom,[1]
Driving o'er rough steep road both those that see,
    And those whose eyes are dark.

ANTISTROPHE. IV.

What mortal man then doth not bow in awe
    And fear before all this,
Hearing from me the destined ordinance·
    Assigned me by the Gods?   370
This task of mine is one of ancient days;
    Nor meet I here with scorn,
    Though 'neath the earth I dwell,
And live there in the darkness thick and dense,
    Where never sunbeam falls.

Enter ATHENA, *appearing in her chariot, and then alights.*

Athena. I heard far off the cry of thine entreaty
E'en from Scamandros,[2] claiming there mine own,
The land which all Achaia's foremost leaders,
As portion chief from out the spoils of war,
Gave to me, trees and all, for evermore,
A special gift for Theseus' progeny.   300
Thence came I plying foot that never tires,
Flapping my ægis-folds, no need of wings,
My chariot drawn by young and vigorous steeds:
And seeing this new presence in the land,
I have no fear, though wonder fills mine eyes;
Who, pray, are ye? To all of you I speak,

---

(1) Perhaps,   "With torch of sunless gloom."
(2) The words contain an allusion to the dispute between Athens and Mitylene in the time of Peisistratos, as to the possession of Sigeion. Athena asserts that it had been given to her by the whole body of Achæans at the time when they had taken Troïa. Comp. Herod. vv. 94, 95. It probably entered into the political purposes of the play to excite the Athenians to a war in this direction, so as to draw them off from the constitutional changes proposed by Pericles and Ephialtes.

And to this stranger at my statue suppliant.
And as for you, like none of Nature's births,
Nor seen by Gods among the Goddess-forms,
Nor yet in likeness of a mortal shape 390
But to speak ill of neighbours blameless found
Is far from just, and Right holds back from it.

Chor. Daughter of Zeus, thou shalt learn all in brief;
Children are we of everlasting Night;
[At home, beneath the earth, they call us Curses.]

   Athena. Your race I know, and whence ye take your
       name.

Chor. Thou shalt soon know then what mine office is.

   Athena. Then could I know, if ye clear speech would
       speak.

Chor. We from their home drive forth all murderers.

   Athena. Where doth the slayer find the goal of
       flight? 400

Chor. Where to find joy in nought is still his wont.

   Athena. And whirrest thou such flight on this man
       here?

Chor. Yea, for he thought it meet to slay his mother.

   Athena. Was there no other power whose wrath he
       feared?

Chor. What impulse, then, should prick to matricide?

   Athena. Two sides are here, and I but half have heard.

Chor. But he nor takes nor tenders us an oath.[1]

---

(1) Here, and throughout the trial, we have to bear in mind the technicalities of Athenian judicial procedure. The prosecutor, in the first instance, tendered to the accused an oath that he was not guilty. This he might accept or refuse. In the latter case, the course of the trial was at least stopped, and judgment might be recorded against him. If he could bring himself to accept it, he was acquitted of the special charge of which he was accused, but was liable to a prosecution afterwards for that perjury. If, on the other hand, he tendered an oath affirming his guilt to the prosecutor, he placed himself in his hands. Orestes, not being able to deny the fact, will not declare on oath that he is "not guilty," but neither will he place himself in the power of his accusers. The peculiarities of this use of oaths were: (1.) That they were taken by the parties to the suit, not by witnesses. (2.) That if both parties agreed to that mode of decision, the oath was either way decisive. An allusion to the latter practice is found in Heb. vi. 16, and traces of it are found, as the Yelverton *cause célèbre* has recently reminded us, in the law-proceedings of Scotland. If either party refused, the cause had to be tried in the usual way, and witnesses were called.

Athena. Thou lov'st the show of Justice more than act.
Chor. How so?　Inform me.　Skill thou dost not
　　　　lack!
Athena. 'Tis not by oaths a cause unjust shall win.[1] ⁴¹⁰
Chor. Search out the cause, then, and right judgment
　　　　judge.
Athena. And would ye trust to me to end the cause?[2]
Chor. How else?　Thy worth, and worthy stock we
　　　　honour.
Athena. What dost thou wish, O stranger, to reply?
Tell thou thy land, thy race, thy life's strange chance,
And then ward off this censure aimed at thee,
Since thou sitt'st trusting in thy right, and hold'st
This mine own image, near mine altar hearth,
A suppliant, like Ixion,[3] honourable.
Answer all this in speech intelligible.　　　　　⁴²⁰

Orest. O Queen Athena, from thy last words starting,
I first will free thee from a weighty care:
I am not now defiled: no curse abides
Upon the hand that on thy statue rests;
And I will give thee proof full strong of this.
The law is fixed the murderer shall be dumb,
Till at the hand of one who frees from blood,
The purple stream from yeanling swine run o'er him;[4]
Long since at other houses these dread rites[5]

(1) Æschylos seems here to attach himself to the principles of those
who were seeking to reform the practice described in the previous note
as being at once cumbrous and unjust, throwing its weight into the scale
of the least scrupulous conscience, and to urge a simpler, more straight-
forward trial.　The same objection is noticed by Aristotle in his discussion of the subject. (*Rhet.* i. 15.)

(2) Athena offers herself, not as arbitrator or sovereign judge, but as
presiding over the court of jurors whom she proceeds to appoint.

(3) Ixion appeared in the mythical history of Greece as the prototype of
all suppliants for purification.　When he had murdered Deioneus,
Zeus had had compassion to him, received him as a guest, cleansed
him from his guilt.　His ingratitude for this service was the special
guilt of his attempted outrage upon Hera.　The case is mentioned again
in v. 687.

(4) In heathen, as in Jewish sacrifices, the blood was the very instru-
ment of purification,　It was sprinkled or poured upon men, and they
became clean.　But this could not be done by the criminal himself, nor
by any chance person.　The service had to be rendered by a friend, who
of very love gave himself to this mediatorial work.

(5) In the legend related by Pausanias (*Corinth.* c. 3), Trœzen was the

We have gone through, slain victims, flowing streams:
This care, then, I can speak of now as gone.   430
And how my lineage stands thou soon shalt know:
An Argive I, my sire well known to thee,
Chief ruler of the seamen, Agamemnon,
With whom thou madest Troïa, Ilion's city,
To be no city.   He, when he came home,
Died without honour; and my dark-souled mother
Enwrapt and slew him with her broidered toils,
Which bore their witness of the murder wrought
There in the bath; and I, on my return,   440
(Till then an exile,) did my mother kill,
(That deed I'll not deny,) in forfeit due
Of blood for blood of father best beloved;
And Loxias, too, is found accomplice here,
Foretelling woes that pricked my heart to act,
If I did nought to those accomplices
In that same crime.   But thou, judge thou my cause,
If what I did were right or wrong, and I,
Whate'er the issue, will be well content.
   Athena. Too great this matter, if a mortal man
Think to decide it.   Nor is't meet for me
To judge a cause of murder stirred by wrath;   450
*And all the more since thou with contrite soul
Hast come to this my house a suppliant,
Harmless and pure.   I now, in spite of all,
Take thee as one my city need not blame; [1]
But these hold office that forbids dismissal,
And should they fail of victory in this cause,
Hereafter from their passionate mood will poison [2]

first place where Orestes was thus received, and in his time the descendants of those who had thus helped held periodical feasts in commemora-
tion of it.
   (1) The course which Athena takes is: (1.) to receive Orestes as a
settler with the rights which attached to such persons on Athenian
soil, not a criminal fugitive to be simply surrendered; (2.) to offer to
the Erinnyes, as being too important to be put out of court, a fair and open
trial; (3.) to acknowledge that he and they are equally "blameless," as
far as she is concerned.   She has no complaint to make of them.
   (2) The red blight of vines and wheat was looked on as caused by drops
of blood which the Erinnyes had let fall.

Fall on the land, disease intolerable,
And lasting for all time. E'en thus it stands;
And both alike, their staying or dismissal,
Are unto me perplexing and disastrous.
But since the matter thus hath come on me,
I will appoint as judges of this murder
Men bound by oath, a law for evermore;[1]
And ye, call ye your proofs and witnesses,
Sworn pledges given to help the cause of right.
And I, selecting of my citizens
Those who are best, will come again that they
May judge this matter truly, taking oaths
To utter nought against the law of right.   [Exit.

Stroph. I.

Chor. Now will there be an outbreak of new laws:
          If victory shall rest
Upon the wrong right of this matricide,
          This deed will prompt forthwith
All mortal men to callous recklessness.
          And many deaths, I trow,
At children's hands their parents now await
          Through all the time to come.

Antistroph. I.

For since no wrath on evil deeds will creep
          Henceforth from those who watch
With wild, fierce souls the evil deeds of men,
          I will let loose all crime;
*And each from each shall seek in eager quest,
          *Speaking of neighbours' ills,
*For pause and lull of woes;[2] yet wretched man,
          He speaks of cures that fail.

(1) Stress is laid on the fact that the judges of the Areopagos, in contrast with those of the inferior tribunes of Athens, discharged their duty
under the sanction of an oath.
(2) Perhaps
          "And each from each shall learn, as he predicts
              His neighbour's ills, that he
          Shares in the same and harbours them, and speaks,
              Poor wretch, of cures that fail."

STROPH. II.

Henceforth let none call us,
When smitten by mischance,
Uttering this cry of prayer,
"O Justice, and O ye, Erinnyes' thrones!"
Such wail, perchance, a father then shall utter,
Or mother newly slain,
Since, fallen low, the shrine of Justice now
Lies prostrate in the dust.

400

ANTISTROPH. II.

There are with whom 'tis well
That awe should still abide,
As watchman o'er their souls.
Calm wisdom gained by sorrow profits much :
For who that in the gladness of his heart,
Or man or commonwealth,
Has nought of this, would bow before the Right
Humbly as heretofore ? [1]

STROPH. III.

Praise not the lawless life,   500
Nor that which owns a despot's sovereignty ;
To the true mean in all God gives success,[2]
And with far other mood,
On other course looks on ;
And I will say, with this in harmony,
That Pride is truly child of Godlessness ;
While from the soul's true health
Comes the fair fortune, loved of all mankind,
And aim of many a prayer.

ANTISTROPH. III.

And now, I say in sum,   510

(1) At a more advanced period of human thought, Cicero (*Orat. pro Roscio*, c. 24) could point to the "thoughts that accuse each other," the horror and remorse of the criminal, as the true Erinnyes, the "assiduæ domesticæque Furiæ." Æschylos clings to the mythical symbolism as indispensable for the preservation of the truth which it shadowed forth.

(2) Once again we have the poet of constitutional conversatism keeping the *via media* between Peisistratos and Pericles.

Revere the altar reared to Justice high,
Nor, thine eye set on gain, with godless foot
    Treat it contemptuously:
    For wrath shall surely come;
The appointed end abideth still for all.
Therefore let each be found full honour giving
    To parents, and to those,
The honoured guests that gather in his house,
    Let him due reverence show.

STROPH. IV.

And one who of his own free will is just,
    Not by enforced constraint,
    He shall not be unblest,
Nor can he e'er be utterly o'erthrown;
But he that dareth, and transgresseth all,
    In wild, confusèd deeds,
    Where Justice is not seen,
I say that he perforce, as time wears on,
    Will have to take in sail,
When trouble make him hers, and each yard-arm
    Is shivered by the blast.

ANTISTROPH. IV.

And then he calls on those who hear him not,
    And struggles all in vain,
    In the fierce waves' mid-whirl;
And God still mocks the man of fevered mood,
When he sees him who bragged it ne'er would come,
    With woes inextricable
    Worn out, and failing still
To weather round the perilous promontory;
    And for all time to come,
Wrecking on reefs of Vengeance bliss once high,
    He dies unwept, unseen.

The scene changes to the Areopagos. Enter ATHENA,
  followed by Herald and twelve Athenian citizens.

  Athena. Cry out, O herald; the great host hold back;

Then let Tyrrhenian trumpet,[1] piercing heaven,
Filled with man's breath, to all that host send forth
The full-toned notes, for while this council-hall   ₆₄₀
Is filling, it is meet men hold their peace.

                    [Herald blows his trumpet.

And let the city for all time to come
Learn these my laws, and this accused one too,
That so the trial may be rightly judged.[2]

                   [As ATHENA *speaks,* APOLLO *enters.*

  Chor. O King Apollo, rule thou o'er thine own;
But what hast thou to do with this our cause?

  Apol. I am come both as witness,—for this man
Is here as suppliant, that on my hearth sat,
And I his cleanser am from guilt of blood,—
And to plead for him as his advocate:
I bear the blame of that his mother's death.
But thou, whoe'er dost act as president,
Open the suit in way well known to thee.[3]   ₆₅₀

  Athena, [*to the Erinnyes.*] 'Tis yours to speak; I thus
        the pleadings open,
For so the accuser, speaking first, shall have,
Of right, the task to state the case to us.

  Chor. Many are we, but briefly will we speak;
And answer thou [*to* ORESTES], in thy turn, word for
        word;
First tell us this, did'st thou thy mother slay?

  Orest. I slew her: of that fact is no denial.

  Chor. Here, then, is one of our three bouts[4] decided.

---

(1) The Tyrrhenian trumpet, with its bent and twisted tube, retained its proverbial pre-eminence from the days of Æschylos and Sophocles, (*Aias*, 17) to those of Virgil, (*Æn.,* viii. 526.)

(2) The fondness of the Athenians for litigation, and the large share which every citizen took in the administration of justice, would probably make the scene which follows, with all its technicalities, the part of the play into which they would most enter.

(3) It was necessary that some one, sitting as President of the Court, should formally open the pleadings, by calling on this side or that to begin. Here Athena takes that office on herself, and calls on the Erinnyes.

(4) The technicalities of the Areopagos are still kept up. The three points on which the Erinnyes, as prosecutors, lay stress are: (1.) the fact of the murder; (2.) the mode; (3.) the motive. "Three bouts," as referring to the rule of the arena, that three struggles for the mastery should be decisive.

Orest. Thou boastest this o'er one not yet thrown
    down.   660

Chor. This thou at least must tell, how thou did'st slay
    her.

Orest. E'en so; her throat I cut with hand sword-armed.

Chor. By whom persuaded, and with whose advice?

Orest. [*Pointing to* APOLLO.] By His divine command:
    He bears me witness.

Chor. The prophet-God prompt thee to matricide!

Orest. Yea, and till now I do not blame my lot.

Chor. Nay, when found guilty, soon thou'lt change thy
    tone.

Orest. I trust my sire will send help from the tomb.

Chor. Trust in the dead, thou murderer of thy
    mother!

Orest. Yes; for in her two great pollutions met.   670

Chor. How so, I pray? Inform the court of this.

Orest. She both her husband and my father slew.

Chor. Nay then, thou liv'st, and she gets quit by
    death.

Orest. Why, while she lived, did'st thou to chase her
    fail?

Chor. The man she slew was not of one blood with her.[1]

Orest. And does my mother's blood then flow in me?

Chor. E'en so; how else, O murderer, reared she thee
Within her womb? Disown'st thou mother's blood?

Orest. [*Turning to* APOLLO.] Now bear thou witness, and
    declare to me,   680

Apollo, if I slew her righteously;
For I the deed, as fact, will not deny.
But whether right or wrong this deed of blood
Seem in thine eyes, judge thou that these may hear.

(1) The pleas put in by the Erinnyes as prosecutors are: (1.) That
Clytæmnestra had been adequately punished by her death, while Orestes
was still alive; and (2.) when asked why they had not intervened to
bring about that punishment, that the relationship between husband
and wife was less close than that between mother and son. They drew,
in other words, a distinction between consanguinity and affinity, and
upon this the rest of the discussion turns. Orestes, and Apollo as his
counsel, on the other hand, meet this with the rejoinder, that there is no
blood-relationship between the mother and her offspring.

Apol. I will to you, Athena's solemn council,
Speak truly, and as prophet will not lie.
Ne'er have I spoken on prophetic throne,
Of man, or woman, or of commonwealth,
But as great Zeus, Olympian Father, bade;
And that ye learn how much this plea avails,
I bid you [*Turning to the court of jurymen*] follow out my
    Father's will;   590
No oath can be of greater might than Zeus.[1]
  Chor. Zeus, then, thou say'st, did prompt the oracle
That this Orestes here, his father's blood
Avenging, should his mother's rights o'erthrow?
  Apol. 'Tis a quite other thing for hero-chief,
Bearing the honour of Zeus-given sceptre,
To die, and at a woman's hands, not e'en
By swift, strong dart, from Amazonian bow,[2]
But as thou, Pallas, now shalt hear, and those
Who sit to give their judgment in this cause;   600
For when he came successful from the trade
Of war with largest gains, receiving him
With kindly words of praise, she spread a robe
Over the bath, yes, even o'er its edge,
As he was bathing, and entangling him
In endless folds of cloak of cunning work,
She strikes her lord down. Thus the tale is told
Of her lord's murder, chief whom all did honour,
The ships' great captain. So I tell it out,
E'en as it was, to thrill the people's hearts,
Who now are set to give their verdict here.
  Chor. Zeus then a father's death, as thou dost say, 610
Of highest moment holds, yet He himself
Bound fast in chains his aged father, Cronos;[3]

(1) *Sc.*, Their oath to give a verdict according to the evidence must
yield to the higher obligation of following the Divine will rather than the
letter of the law.

(2) To have died in health by the arrows of a woman-warrior might
have been borne. To be slain by a wife treacherously in his bath was to
endure a far worse outrage.

(3) In this new argument, and the answer to it, we may trace, as in the
Prometheus and the *Agamemnon*, the struggles of the questioning intellect

Y

Are not thy words at variance with the facts?
I call on you [*To the Court*] to witness what he says.

   Apol. O hateful creatures, loathèd of the Gods,
Those chains may be undone, that wrong be cured,
And many a means of rescue may be found :
But when the dust has drunk the blood of men,
No resurrection comes for one that's dead :
No charm for these things hath my sire devised ;
But all things else he turneth up or down,   620
And orders without toil or weariness.[1]

   Chor. Take heed how thou help this man to escape ;
Shall he who stained earth with his mother's blood
Then dwell in Argos in his father's house ?
What public altars can he visit now?
What lustral rite of clan or tribe admit him ?[2]

   Apol. This too I'll say ; judge thou if I speak right :
The mother is not parent of the child
That is called hers, but nurse of embryo sown
He that begets is parent :[3] she, as stranger,   630
For stranger rears the scion, if God mar not ;
And of this fact I'll give thee proof full sure.
A father there may be without a mother :
Here nigh at hand, as witness, is the child
Of high Olympian Zeus, for she not e'en
Was nurtured in the darkness of the womb,[4]

against the more startling elements of the popular religious belief. Zeus
is worshipped as the supreme Lord, yet His dominion seems founded on
might as opposed to goodness, on the unrighteous expulsion of another.
Here, in Apollo's answer, there is the glimmer of a possible reconciliation. The old and the new, the sovereignty of Cronos and that of Zeus
may be reconciled, and one supreme God be "all in all."

   (1) Comp. the thought and language of the *Suppliants*, v. 93.

   (2) The last argument is, that the acquittal can be, at the best, partial
only, not complete ; formal, not real. There would remain for ever the
pollution which would exclude Orestes from the *Phratria*, the clan-bro-
therhood, by which, as by a sacramental bond, all the members were held
together.

   (3) The question seems to have been one of those which occupied men's
minds in their first gropings towards the mysteries of man's physical life,
and both popular metaphors and primary impressions were in favour of
the hypothesis here maintained. Euripides (*Orest.*, v. 534) puts the same
argument into the mouth of Orestes.

   (4) The story of Athena's birth, full-grown, from the head of Zeus, is
next referred to as the leading case bearing on the point at issue.

Yet such a scion may no God beget.
I, both in all else, Pallas, as I know,
Will make thy city and thy people great,
And now this man have sent as suppliant
Upon thy hearth, that he may faithful prove   (4)
Now and for ever, and that thou, O Goddess,
May'st gain him as ally, and all his race,
And that it last as law for evermore,
That these men's progeny our treaties own.

   Athena. [*To jurors.*] I bid you give, according to your
        conscience,
A verdict just; enough has now been said.

   Chor. We have shot forth our every weapon now:
I wait to hear what way the strife is judged.

   Athena. [*To Chorus.*] How shall I order this, unblamed
      by you?

   Chor. [*To jurors.*] Ye heard what things ye heard,
      and in your hearts
Reverence your oaths, and give your votes, O friends.   650

   Athena. Hear ye my order, O ye Attic people,
In act to judge your first great murder-cause.
And henceforth shall the host of Ægeus' race [1]   *
For ever own this council-hall of judges:
And for this Ares' hill, the Amazons' seat
And camp when they, enraged with Theseus, came [2]
In hostile march, and built as counterwork
This citadel high-reared, a city new,

(1) Here, of course, the political interest of the whole drama reached its
highest point.   What seems comparatively flat to us must, to the
thousands who sat as spectators, have been fraught with the most intense
excitement, showing itself in shouts of applause, or audible tokens of
clamorous dissent.   The rivalry of Whigs and Tories over Addison's
Cato, the sensation produced in times of Papal aggression by the king's
answer to Pandulph in *King John*, present analogies which are worth
remembering.

(2) The story ran that the tribe of women-warriors from the Caucasos,
or the Thermodon, known by this name, had invaded Attica under
Oreithyia, when Theseus was king, to revenge the wrongs he had done
them, and to recover her sister Hippolyta.   Ares, the God of Thrakians,
Skythians, and nearly all the wilder barbaric tribes, was their special
deity; and when they occupied the hill which rose over against the Acropolis, they sacrificed to him, and so it gained the name of the *Areopagos*,
or " hill of Ares."

And sacrificed to Ares, whence 'tis named
As Ares' hill and fortress: in this, I say,   660
The reverent awe its citizens shall own,
And fear, awe's kindred, shall restrain from wrong
By day, nor less by night, so long as they,
The burghers, alter not themselves their laws :
But if with drain of filth and tainted soil
Clear river thou pollute, no drink thou'lt find.[1]
I give my counsel to you, citizens,
To reverence and guard well that form of state
Which is nor lawless, nor tyrannical,
And not to cast all fear from out the city ;[2]
For what man lives devoid of fear and just ?
But rightly shrinking, owning awe like this,   670
Ye then would have a bulwark of your land,
A safeguard for your city, such as none
Boast or in Skythia's[3] or in Pelops' clime.
This council I establish pure from bribe,
Reverend, and keen to act, for those that sleep[4]
An ever-watchful sentry of the land.
This charge of mine I thus have lengthened out
For you, my people, for all time to come.
And now 'tis meet ye rise, and take your ballots,[5]

(1) As in the *Agamemnon*, (v. 1010,) so here we find the aristocratic
conservative poet showing his colours protesting against the admission to
the Archonship, and therefore to the Areopagos, of men of low birth or
in undignified employments.

(2) The words, like all political clap-trap, are somewhat vague; but, as
understood at the time, the "lawless" policy alluded to was that of
Pericles and Ephialtes, who sought to deface and to diminish the jurisdiction of the Areopagos, and the "tyrannical," that which had crushed
the independence of Athens under Peisistratos. Between the two was
the conservative party, of which Kimon had been the leader.

(3) The Skythians may be named simply as representing all barbarous,
non-Hellenic races ; but they appear, about this time, wild and nomadic
as their life was, to have impressed the minds of the Greeks somewhat in
the same way as the Germans did the minds of the Romans in the time of
Tacitus. Tales floated from travellers' lips of their wisdom and their
happiness—of sages like Zamolxis and Aristarchos, who rivalled those of
Hellas—of the Hyperborei, in the far north, who enjoyed a perpetual and
unequalled blessedness.—Comp. *Libation-Pourers*, v. 366.

(4) Two topics of praise are briefly touched on : (1.) the lower, popular
courts of justice at Athens might be open to the suspicion of corruption,
but no breath of slander had ever tainted the fame of the Areopagos ; (2.)
it met by night, keeping its watch, that the citizens might sleep in peace.

(5) The first of the twelve jurymen rises and drops his voting-ballot

And so decide the cause, maintaining still
Your reverence for your oath. My speech is said.   680

   Chor. And I advise you not to treat with scorn
A troop that can sit heavy on your land.
   Apol. And I do bid you dread my oracles,
And those of Zeus, nor rob them of their fruit.
   Chor. Uncalled thou com'st to take a murderer's part;
No longer pure the oracles thou'lt speak.
   Apol. And did my father then in purpose err,
Then the first murderer he received, Ixion ?[1]
   Chor. Thou talk'st, but should I fail in this my cause,
I will again dwell here and vex this land.
   Apol. Alike among the new Gods and the old   690
Art thou dishonoured : I shall win the day.
   Chor. This did'st thou also in the house of Pheres,[2]
Winning the Fates to make a man immortal.
   Apol. Was it not just a worshipper to bless
In any case,—then most, when he's in want ?
   Chor. Thou did'st o'erthrow, yea, thou, laws hoar
        with age,
And drug with wine the ancient Goddesses.[3]
   Apol. Nay, thou, non-suited in this cause of thine,
Shalt venom spit that nothing hurts thy foes.   700
   Chor. Since thou, though young, dost ride me down,
        though old,
I wait to hear the issue of the cause,
Still wavering in my wrath against this city.

into one of the urns, and is followed by another at the end of each of the
short two-line speeches in the dialogue that follows. The two urns of
acquittal and condemnation stand in front of them. The plan of voting
with different coloured balls (black and white) in the same urn, was a
later usage.

(1) Campare note on v. 419.

(2) In the legend of Admetos son of Pheres, and king of Pheræ in
Thessalia, Apollo is represented as having first given wine to the
Destinies, and then persuaded them to allow Admetos, whenever the hour
of death should come, to be redeemed from Hades, if father, or mother,
or wife were willing to die for him. The self-surrender of his wife,
Alkestis, for this purpose, forms the subject of the noblest of the tragedies
of Euripides.

(3) Partly as setting at nought the power of Erinnyes and the Destinies, partly as giving wine to those whose libations were wineless.-
Comp. Sophocles, *Œd. Col.* v. 100.

Athena. 'Tis now my task to close proceedings here;
And this my vote I to Orestes add;
For I no mother own that brought me forth,
And saving that I wed not, I prefer
The male with all my heart, and make mine own
The father's cause, nor will above it place
A woman's death, who slew her own true lord,
The guardian of her house.   Orestes wins,   710
E'en though the votes be equal.   Cast ye forth
With all your speed the lots from out the urns,
Ye jurors unto whom that office falls.

   Orest. Phœbos Apollo! what will be the judgment?
   Chor. Dark Night, my mother! dost thou look on this?
   Orest. My goal is now the noose, or full, clear day.
   Chor. Ours too to come to nought, or work on still.

       [*A pause.   The jurors take out the voting tablets
         from the two urns (one of bronze, the other of
         wood) for acquittal or condemnation.*

   Apol. Now count ye up the votes thrown out, O friends,
And be ye honest, as ye reckon them;
One sentence lacking, sorrow great may come,   720
And one vote given hath ofttimes saved a house.

       [*A pause, during which the urns are emptied and
         the votes are counted.*

   Athena. The accused is found "not guilty" of the
         murder:
For lo! the numbers of the votes are equal.[1]

   Orest. O Pallas, thou who hast redeemed my house,
Thou, thou hast brought me back when I had been
Bereaved of fatherland, and Hellenes now
Will say, "The man's an Argive once again,
And dwells upon his father's heritage,
Because of Pallas and of Loxias,
And Zeus, the true third Saviour, all o'erruling,
Who, touched with pity for my father's fate,   730

---

(1) The practice of the Areopagos is accurately reproduced.   When the
votes of the judges were equal a casting vote was given in favour of the
accused, and was known as that of Athena.

Saves me, beholding these my mother's pleaders."
And I will now wend homeward, giving pledge
To this thy country and its valiant host,
To stand as firm for henceforth and for ever,
That no man henceforth, chief of Argive land,
Shall bring against it spearmen well equipped:
For we ourselves, though in our sepulchres,
On those who shall transgress these oaths of ours,
Will with inextricable evils work,
Making their paths disheartening, and their ways   740
Ill-omened, that they may their toil repent.
But if these oaths be kept, to those who honour
This city of great Pallas, our ally,
Then we to them are more propitious yet.
Farewell then, Thou, and these who guard thy city.
Mayst thou so wrestle that thy foes escape not,
And so win victory and deliverance!

STROPHE.

Chor. Ah! ah! ye younger God!
Ye have ridden down the laws of ancient days,
  And robbed me of my prey.
But I, dishonoured, wretched, full of wrath,   750
  Upon this land, ha! ha!
Will venom, venom from my heart let fall,
  In vengeance for my grief,
  A dropping which shall smite
  The earth with barrenness!
And thence shall come, (O Vengeance!) on the plain
Down swooping, blight of leaves and murrain dire
That o'er the land flings taint of pestilence.   760
  Shall I then wail and groan?
  Or what else shall I do?
Shall I become a woe intolerable
Unto these men for wrongs I have endured?
  Great, very great are they,
Ye virgin daughters of dim Night, ill-doomed,
  Born both to shame and woe!

Athena. Nay, list to me, and be not over-grieved;
Ye have not been defeated, but the cause
Came fairly to a tie, no shame to thee.
But the clear evidence of Zeus was given,
And he who spake it bare his witness too
That, doing this, Orestes should not suffer.
Hurl ye not then fierce rage on this my land;
Nor be ye wroth, nor work ye barrenness,
*By letting fall the drops of evil Powers,[1]
The baleful influence that consumes all seed.
For lo! I promise, promise faithfully,
That, seated on your hearths with shining thrones,
Ye shall find cavern homes in righteous land,
Honoured and worshipped by these citizens.

ANTISTROPHE.

Chor. Ah! ah! ye younger Gods!
Ye have ridden down the laws of ancient days,
   And robbed me of my prey.
And I, dishonoured, wretched, full of wrath,
   Upon this land, ha! ha!
Will venom, venom from my heart let fall,
   In vengeance for my grief,
   A dropping which shall smite
   The earth with barrenness!
And thence shall come, (O Vengeance!) on the plain
Down-swooping, blight of leaves and murrain dire
That o'er the land flings taint of pestilence.
   Shall I then wail and groan?
   Or what else shall I do?
Shall I become a woe intolerable
Unto these men for wrongs I have endured?
   Great, very great are they,
Ye virgin daughters of dim Night, ill-doomed,
   Born both to shame and woe!
  Athena. Ye are not left unhonoured; be not hot
In wrath, ye Goddesses, to mar man's land,

770

784

(1) Another reading gives—
  "By spurting from your throats those **venom drops.**"

I too, yes I, trust Zeus.   Need I say more ?   790
I only of the high Gods know the keys
Of chambers where the sealed-up thunder lies ;
But that I have no need of.   List to me,
Nor cast upon the earth thy rash tongue's fruit,
That brings to all things failure and distress ;
Lull thou the bitter storm of that dark surge,
As dwelling with me, honoured and revered ;
And thou with first-fruits of this wide champaign,
Offerings for children's birth and wedlock-rites,
Shalt praise these words of mine for evermore.   800
   Chor. That I should suffer this, fie on it ! fie !
That I, with thoughts of hoar antiquity,[1]
      Should now in this land dwell,
      Dishonoured, deemed a plague !
I breathe out rage, and every form of wrath.
      Oh, Earth ! fie on it ! fie !
What pang is this that thrills through all my breast ?
      Hear thou, O mother Night,
      Hear thou my vehement wrath !
For lo ! deceits that none can wrestle with
Have thrust me out from honours old of Gods,
      And made a thing of nought.
   Athena. Thy wrath I'll bear, for thou the elder art,   810
[And wiser too in that respect than I ;]
Yet to me too Zeus gave no wisdom poor ;
And ye, if ye an alien country seek,
Shall yearn in love for this land.   This I tell you ;
For to this people Time, as it runs on,
Shall come with fuller honours, and if thou
Hast honoured seat hard by Erechtheus' home,
Thou shalt from men and women reap such gifts
As thou would'st never gain from other mortals ;
But in these fields of mine be slow to cast   820
Whetstones of murder's knife, to young hearts bale,

---

(1) The conservative poet enters his protest through the Erinnyes
against the innovating spirit that looked with contempt upon the principles of a past age.

Frenzied with maddened passion, not of wine;
Nor, as transplanting hearts of fighting-cocks,[1]
Make Ares inmate with my citizens,
In evil discord, and intestine broils;
Let them have war without, not scantily,
For him who feels the passionate thirst of fame:
Battle of home-bred birds . . I name it not;
This it is thine to choose as gift from me;
Well-doing, well-entreated, and well-honoured,   836
To share the land best loved of all the Gods.

   Chor. That I should suffer this, fie on it! fie!
That I, with thoughts of hoar antiquity,
       Should now in this land dwell,
       Dishonoured, deemed a plague,
I breathe out rage, and every form of wrath;
       Ah, Earth! fie on it! fie!
What pang is this that thrills through all my breast?
       Hear thou, O mother Night,
       Hear thou my vehement wrath!
For lo! deceits that none can wrestle with
Have thrust me out from honours old of Gods,
       And made a thing of nought.   840

   Athena. I will not weary, telling thee of good,
That thou may'st never say that thou, being old,
Wert at the hands of me, a younger Goddess,
And those of men who in my city dwell,
Driven in dishonour, exiled from this plain.
But if the might of Suasion thou count holy,
And my tongue's blandishments have power to soothe,
Then thou wilt stay; but if thou wilt not stay,
Not justly would'st thou bring upon this city,
Or wrath, or grudge, or mischief for its host.
It rests with thee, as dweller in this spot,[2]   850
To meet with all due honour evermore.

---

(1) Cock fighting took its place among the recognised sports of the
Athenians. Once a year there was a public performance in the
theatre.
(2) The Temple of the Eumenides or Semnœ ("venerable ones") stood
near the Areopagos.

Chor. Athena, Queen, what seat assign'st thou me?
Athena. One void of touch of evil; take thou it.
Chor. Say I accept. What honour then is mine?
Athena. That no one house apart from thee shall
    prosper.
Chor. And wilt thou work that I such might may have?
Athena. His lot who worships thee we'll guide aright.
Chor. And wilt thou give thy warrant for all time?
Athena. What I work not I might refrain from speaking.
Chor. It seems thou sooth'st me: I relax my wrath. ⁸⁶⁰
Athena. In this land dwelling thou new friends shalt
    gain.
Chor. What hymn then for this land dost bid me raise?
Athena. Such as is meet for no ill-victory.[1]

And pray that blessings upon men be sent,
And that, too, both from earth, and ocean's spray,
And out of heaven; and that the breezy winds,
In sunshine blowing, sweep upon the land,
And that o'erflowing fruit of field and flock
May never fail my citizens to bless,
Nor safe deliverance for the seed of men.
But for the godless, rather root them out: 870
For I, like gardener shepherding his plants,
This race of just men freed from sorrow love.
So much for thee: and I will never fail
To give this city honour among men,
Victorious in the noble games of war.

Strophe. I.

Chor. I will accept this offered home with Pallas,
    Nor will the city scorn,
    Which e'en All-ruling Zeus
And Ares give as fortress of the Gods,
The altar-guarding pride of Gods of Hellas;   880
    And I upon her call,
    With kindly auguries,

(1) Some two or three lines have probably been lost here.

That so the glorious splendour of the sun
May cause life's fairest portion in thick growth
>*To burgeon from the earth.
>>*Athena.* Yea, I work with kindliest feeling
>>For these my townsmen, having settled
>>Powers great, and hard to soothe among them:
>>Unto them the lot is given,
>>All things human still to order;   890
>>He who hath not felt their pressure
>>Knows not whence life's scourges smite him:
>>For the sin of generations
>>Past and gone;—a dumb destroyer,—
>>Leads him on into their presence,
>>And with mood of foe low bringeth
>>Him whose lips are speaking proudly.

ANTISTROPH. I.

>*Chor.* Let no tree-blighting canker breathe on them,
>>(I tell of boon I give,)
>>>Nor blaze of scorching heat,
That mars the budding eyes of nursling plants,   900
And checks their spreading o'er their narrow bounds;
>>And may no dark, drear plague
>>Smite it with barrenness.
But may Earth feed fair flock in season due,
Blest with twin births, and earth's rich produce pay
>>To the high heavenly Powers,
>>Its gift for treasure found.[1]
>*Athena.* Hear ye then, ye city's guardians,
>>What she offers? Dread and mighty   910
>>With the Undying is Erinnys;
>>And with Those beneath the earth too,
>>And full clearly and completely
>>Work they all things out for mortals,
>>Giving these the songs of gladness,
>>Those a life bedimmed with weeping.

(1) Probably an allusion to the silver-mine at Laureion, which about the time formed a large element of the revenues of Athens, and of which a tithe was consecrated to Athena.

STROPH. II.

Chor. **Avaunt, all evil chance**
That brings men low in death before their time!
And for the maidens lovely and beloved,
Give, ye whose work it is,
Life with a husband true,
And ye, O Powers of self-same mother born,   920
Ye Fates who rule aright,
Partners in every house,
Awe-striking through all time,
With presence full of righteousness and truth,
Through all the universe
Most honoured of the Gods!
Athena. Much I joy that thus ye promise
These boons to my land in kindness;
And I love the glance of Suasion,
That she guides my speech and accent
Unto these who gainsaid stoutly.   930
But the victory is won by
Zeus, the agora's protector;
And our rivalry in blessings
Is the conqueror evermore.

ANTISTROPH. II.

Chor. For this too I will pray,
That Discord, never satiate with ill,
May never ravine in this commonwealth,
Nor dust that drinks dark blood
From veins of citizens,
Through eager thirst for vengeance, from the State
Snatch woes as penalty
For deeds of murderous guilt.
But may they give instead
With friendly purpose acts of kind intent,   940
And if need be, may hate
With minds of one accord;
For this is healing found to mortal men
Of many a grievous woo.

Athena. Are they not then waxing wiser,
    And at last the path discerning
    Of a speech more good and gentle ?
    Now from these strange forms and fearful,
    See I to my townsmen coming,
    E'en to these, great meed of profit;
    For if ye, with kindly welcome,
    Honour these as kind protectors,
    Then shall ye be famed as keeping,
    Just and upright in all dealings,
    Land and city evermore.

STROPHE. III.

Chor. Rejoice, rejoice ye in abounding wealth,
    Rejoice, ye citizens,
    Dwelling near Zeus himself,[1]   850
Loved of the virgin Goddess whom ye loved,
    In due time wise of heart,
You, 'neath the wings of Pallas ever staying,[2]
    The Father honoureth.
Athena. Rejoice ye also, but before you
    I must march to show your chambers,
    By your escorts' torches holy ;
    Go, and with these dread oblations   860
    Passing to the crypt cavernous,
    Keep all harm from this our country,
    Send all gain upon our city,
    Cause it o'er its foes to triumph.
    Lead ye on, ye sons of Cranaos,[3]
    Lead, ye dwellers in the city,
    Those who come to sojourn with you,
    And may good gifts work good purpose
    In my townsmen evermore !

(1) Reference is made to another local sanctuary, the temple on the Areopagos dedicated to the Olympian Zeus.
(2) The figure of Athena, as identical with Victory, and so the tutelary Goddess of Athens, was sculptured with outspread wings.
(3) Cranaos, the son of Kecrops, the mythical founder of Athens.

Antistrophe. III.

Chor. Rejoice, rejoice once more, ye habitants! 970
   I say it yet again,
   Ye Gods, and mortals too,
Who dwell in Pallas' city. Should ye treat
   With reverence us who dwell
As sojourners among you, ye shall find
   No cause to blame your lot.
 Athena. I praise these words of yours, the prayers ye
  offer,
And with the light of torches flashing fire,
Will I escort you to your dark abode,[1]
Low down beneath the earth, with my attendants,
Who with due honour guard my statue here,
For now shall issue forth the goodly eye
Of all the land of Theseus; fair-famed troop 980
Of girls and women, band of matrons too,
In upper vestments purple-dyed arrayed:
*Now then advance ye; and the blaze of fire,
Let it go forth, that so this company
Stand forth propitious, henceforth and for aye,
In rearing race of noblest citizens,

*Enter an array of women, young and old, in procession,
 leading the Erinnyes—now, as propitiated, the Eumenides or Gentle Ones—to their shrines.*

Chorus of *Athenian* women.

Stroph. I.

Go to your home, ye great and jealous Ones,
Children of Night, and yet no children ye;[2]
   With escort of good-will,
   Shout, shout, ye townsmen, shout.

Antistroph. I.

There in the dark and gloomy caves of earth,
With worthy gifts and many a sacrifice 990

---

(1) The sanctuaries of the Eumenides were crypt-like chapels, where
they were worshipped by the light of lamps or torches.
(2) Perhaps, "Children of Night, yourselves all childless left."

Consumèd in the fire—
Shout, shout ye, one and all.

Stroph. II.

Come, come, with thought benign,
Propitious to our land,
Ye dreaded Ones, yea, come,
While on your progress onward ye rejoice,
In the bright light of fire-devourèd torch;
Shout, shout ye to our songs.

Antistroph. II.

Let the drink-offerings come,
In order meet behind,
While torches fling their light;
*Zeus the All-seeing thus hath joined in league
*With Destiny for Pallas' citizens;
Shout, shout ye to our songs.

[*The procession winds its way,* ATHENA *at its head, then
the Eumenides, then the women, round the Areopagos
towards the ravine in which the dread Goddesses were to
find their sanctuary.*]

FRAGMENTS.

z

FRAGMENTS.

38.

APHRODITE loquitur.

The pure, bright heaven still yearns to blend with earth,
And earth is filled with love for marriage-rites,
And from the kindly sky the rain-shower falls
And fertilises earth, and earth for men
Yields grass for sheep, and corn, Demêter's gift;
And from its wedlock with the South the fruit
Is ripened in its season; and of this,
All this, I am the cause accessory.

123.

So, in the Libyan fables, it is told
That once an eagle, stricken with a dart,
Said, when he saw the fashion of the shaft,
"With our own feathers, not by others' hands,
Are we now smitten."

147.

Of all the Gods, Death only craves not gifts:
Nor sacrifice, nor yet drink-offering poured
Avails; no altars hath he, nor is soothed
By hymns of praise. From him alone of all
The powers of Heaven Persuasion holds aloof.

151.

When 'tis God's will to bring an utter doom
Upon a house, He first in mortal men
Implants what works it out.

162.

The words of Truth are ever simplest found.

163.

What good is found in life that still brings pain?

174.

To many mortals silence great gain brings.

229.

O Death the Healer, scorn thou not, I pray,
To come to me: of cureless ills thou art
The one physician. Pain lays not its touch
Upon a corpse.

230.

                      When the wind
Nor suffers us to leave the port, nor stay.

243.

And if thou wish to benefit the dead,
'Tis all as one as if thou injured'st them,
And they nor sorrow nor delight can feel:
Yet higher than we are is Nemesis,
And Justice taketh vengeance for the dead.

266.

Thetis on the death of Achilles.

Life free from sickness, and of many years,
And in a word a fortune like to theirs
Whom the Gods love, all this He spake to me
As pæan-hymn, and made my heart full glad:
And I full fondly trusted Phœbos' lips
As holy and from falsehood free, of art
Oracular an ever-flowing spring,
And He who sang this, He who at the feast
Being present, spake these things,—yea, He it is
That slew my son.

267.

The man who does ill, ill must suffer too.

268.

Evil on mortals comes full swift of foot,
And guilt on him who doth the right transgress.

269.

Thou see'st a vengeance voiceless and unseen
For one who sleeps or walks or sits at ease :
It takes its course obliquely, here to-day,
And there to morrow.   Nor does night conceal
Men's deeds of ill, but whatsoe'er thou dost,
Think that some God beholds it.

270.

" All have their chance :" good proverb for the rich.

271.

Wise is the man who knows what profiteth,
Not he who knoweth much.

272.

Full grievous burden is a prosperous fool.

272A.

From a just fraud God turneth not away.

273.

There is a time when God doth falsehood prize.

274.

The polished brass is mirror of the form,
Wine of the soul.

275.

Words are the parents of a causeless wrath.

276,

Men credit gain for oaths, not oaths for them.

277.

God ever works with those that work with will.

278.

Wisdom to learn is e'en for old men good.

281.

The base who prosper are intolerable.

282.

The seed of mortals broods o'er passing things,
And hath nought surer than the smoke-cloud's shadow.

283.

Old age hath stronger sense of right than youth.

286,

Yet though a man gets many wounds in breast,
He dieth not, unless the appointed time,
The limit of his life's span, coincide;
Nor does the man who by the hearth at home
Sits still, escape the doom that Fate decrees.

287.

How far from just the hate men bear to death,
Which comes as safeguard against many ills.

288.

TO FORTUNE.

Thou did'st beget me; thou too, as it seems,
Wilt now destroy me.

289.

The fire-moth's silly death is that I fear.

290.

I by experience know the race full well
That dwells in Æthiop land, where seven-mouthed Nile
Rolls o'er the land with winds that bring the rain,
What time the fiery sun upon the earth
Pours its hot rays, and melts the snow till then
Hard as the rocks; and all the fertile soil
Of Egypt, filled with that pure-flowing stream,
Brings forth Demêter's ears that feed our life.

291.

This hoopoo, witness of its own dire ills,
He hath in varied garb set forth, and shows
In full array that bold bird of the rocks
Which, when the spring first comes, unfurls a wing
Like that of white-plumed kite; for on one breast
It shows two forms, its own and eke its child's,
And when the corn grows gold, in autumn's prime,
A dappled plumage all its form will clothe;
And ever in its hate of these 't will go
Far off to lonely thickets or bare rocks.

292.

Still to the sufferer comes, as due from God,
A glory that to suffering owes its birth.

293.

The air is Zeus, Zeus earth, and Zeus the heaven,
Zeus all that is, and what transcends them all.

297.

Take courage; pain's extremity soon ends.

298.

When Strength and Justice are true yoke-fellows,
Where can be found a mightier pair than they?

APPENDIX OF RHYMED CHORUSES

AGAMEMNON.

NINE weary years are gone and spent
Since Menelaos' armament
Sped forth, on work of vengeance bent,
 For Priam's guilty land;
And with him Agamemnon there
Throne, sceptre, army all did share;
And so from Zeus the Atreidæ bear,
 Their two-fold high command.
They a fleet of thousand sail,
Strong in battle to prevail,
Led from out our Argive coast,
Shouting war-cries to the host;
E'en as vultures do that utter
Shrillest screams as round they flutter,
Grieving for their nestlings lost,
Plying still their oary wings
In many lonely wanderings,
Robbed of all the sweet unrest
That bound them to their young ones' nest.
And One on high of solemn state,
Apollo, Pan, or Zeus the great,
When he hears that shrill wild cry
Of his clients in the sky,
On them, the godless who offend,
Erinnys slow and sure doth send.
So 'gainst Alexandros then
The sons of Atreus, chiefs of men,
Zeus sent to work his high behest,
True guardian of the host and guest.

He, for bride of many a groom,
On Danai, Troïans sendeth doom,
Many wrestlings, sinew-trying
Of the knee in dust down-lying,
Many a spear-shaft snapt asunder
In the prelude of war's thunder.
What shall be, shall, and still we see
Fulfilled is destiny's decree.
Nor by tears in secret shed,
Nor by offerings o'er the dead,
Will he soothe God's vengeful ire
For altar hearths despoiled of fire.

And we with age outworn and spent
Are left behind that armament,
With head upon our staff low bent.
Weak our strength like that of boy;
Youth's life-blood, in its bounding joy,
For deeds of might is like to age,
And knows not yet war's heritage:
And the man whom many a year
Hath bowed in withered age and sere,
As with three feet creepeth on,
Like phantom form of day-dream gone,
Not stronger than his infant son.

And now, O Queen, who tak'st thy name
From Tyndareus of ancient fame,
Our Clytæmnestra whom we own
As rightly sharing Argos' throne!
What tidings joyous hast thou heard,
Token true or flattering word,
That thou send'st to every shrine
Solemn pomp in stately line,—
Shrines of Gods who reign in light,
Or those who dwell in central night,
Who in Heaven for aye abide,
Or o'er the Agora preside.

Lo, thy gifts on altars blaze,
And here and there through heaven's wide ways
The torches fling their fiery rays,
Fed by soft and suasive spell
Of the clear oil, flowing well
From the royal treasure-cell.
Telling what of this thou may,
All that's meet to us to say,
Do thou our haunting cares allay,
Cares which now bring sore distress,
While now bright hope, with power to bless,
From out the sacrifice appears,
And wardeth off our restless fears,
The boding sense of coming fate,
That makes the spirit desolate.

Strophe. I.

Yes, it is mine to tell
What omens to our leaders then befell,
Giving new strength for war,
(For still though travelled far
In life, by God's great gift to us belong
The suasive powers of song,)
To tell how those who bear
O'er all Achæans sway in equal share,
Ruling in one accord
The youth of Hellas that own each as lord,
Were sent with mighty host
By mighty birds against the Troïan coast,
Kings of the air to kings of men appearing
Near to the palace, on the right hand veering;
On spot seen far and near,
They with their talons tear
A pregnant hare with all her unborn young,
All her life's course in death's deep darkness flung.
Oh raise the bitter cry, the bitter wail;
Yet pray that good prevail!

ANTISTROPH. I.

And then the host's wise seer
Stood gazing on the Atreidæ standing near,
　Of diverse mood, and knew
　Those who the poor hare slew,
And those who led the host with shield and spear,
　And spake his omens clear:
　" One day this host shall go,
And Priam's city in the dust lay low,
　And all the kine and sheep
Countless, which they before their high towers keep,
　Fate shall with might destroy:
Only take heed that no curse mar your joy,
Nor blunt the edge of curb that Troïa waiteth,
Smitten too soon, for Artemis still hateth
　The wingèd hounds that own
　Her father on his throne,
Who slay the mother with the young unborn,
And looks upon the eagle's feast with scorn,
Ah! raise the bitter cry, the bitter wail;
　Yet pray that good prevail.

EPODE.

For she, the Fair One, though her mercy shields
　The lion's whelps, like dew-drops newly shed,
And yeanling young of beasts that roam the fields,
　Yet prays her sire fulfil these omens dread,
　The good, the evil too.
And now I call on him, our Healer true,
Lest she upon the Danai send delays
That keep our ships through many weary days,
　Urging a new strange rite,
Unblest alike by man and God's high law,
Evil close clinging, working sore despite,
　Marring a wife's true awe.
　For still there lies in wait,
　Fearful and ever new,
Watching the hour its eager thirst to sate,

Vengeance on those who helpless infants slew."
Such things, ill mixed with good, great Calchas spake,
As destined by the birds' strange auguries;
And we too now our echoing answer make
     In loud and woeful cries:
Oh raise the bitter cry, the bitter wail;
     Yet pray that good prevail.

STROPH. II.

    O Zeus, whoe'er Thou be,
    If that name please Thee well,
    By that I call on Thee;
For weighing all things else I fail to tell
    Of any name but Zeus;
    If once for all I seek
Of all my haunting, troubled thoughts a truce,
    That name I still must speak.

ANTISTROPH. II.

    For He who once was great,
    Full of the might to war,
    Hath lost his high estate;
And He who followed now is driven afar,
    Meeting his Master too:
    But if one humbly pay
With 'bated breath to Zeus his honour due,
    He walks in wisdom's way,—

STROPH. III.

To Zeus, who men in wisdom's path doth train,
    Who to our mortal race
Hath given the fixèd law that pain is gain;
    For still through his high grace
True counsel falleth on the heart like dew,
    In deep sleep of the night,
The boding thoughts that out of ill deeds grew;
This too They work who sit enthronèd in their might.

ANTISTROPH. III.

And then the elder leader of great fame
    Who ruled the Achæans' ships,

Not bold enough a holy seer to blame
  With words from reckless lips,
But tempered to the fate that on him fell;—
  And when the host was vexed
With tarryings long, scant stores, and surging swell,
Chalkis still far off seen, and baffled hopes perplexed;

STROPH. IV.

And stormy blasts that down from Strymon sweep,
And breed sore famine with the long delay,
Hurl forth our men upon the homeless deep
  On many a wandering way,
Sparing nor ships, nor ropes, nor sailing gear,
Doubling the weary months, and vexing still
  The Argive host with fear.
Then when as mightier charm for that dread ill,
  Hard for our ships to bear,
From the seer's lips did "Artemis" resound,
The Atreidæ smote their staves upon the ground,
And with no power to check, shed many a bitter tear.

ANTISTROPH. IV.

And then the elder of the chiefs thus cried:
" Great woe it is the Gods to disobey;
Great woe if I my child, my home's fond pride,
  With my own hands must slay,
Polluting with the streams of maiden's blood
A father's hands, the holy altar near.
  Which course hath least of good?
How can I loss of ships and comrades bear?
  Right well may men desire,
With craving strong, the blood of maiden pure
As charm to lull the winds and calm ensure;
Ah, may there come the good to which our hopes aspire!"

STROPH. V.

  Then, when he his spirit proud
  To the yoke of doom had bowed,
  While the blasts of altered mood
  O'er his soul swept like a flood,

Reckless, godless and unblest ;
Thence new thoughts upon him pressed,
Thoughts of evil, frenzied daring,
(Still doth passion, base guile sharing,
Mother of all evil, hold
The power to make men bad and bold,)
And he brought himself to slay
His daughter, as on solemn day,
Victim slain the ships to save,
When for false wife fought the brave.

Antistroph. V.

All her cries and loud acclaim,
Calling on her father's name,—
All her beauty fresh and fair,
They heeded not in their despair,
Their eager lust for conflict there.
And her sire the attendants bade
To lift her, when the prayer was said,
Above the altar like a kid,
Her face and form in thick veil hid;
Yea, with ruthless heart and bold,
O'er her gracious lips to hold
Their watch, and with the gag's dumb pain
From evil-boding words restrain.

Stroph. VI.

And then upon the ground
Pouring the golden streams of saffron veil,
She cast a glance around
That told its piteous tale,
At each of those who stood prepared to slay,
Fair as the form by skilful artist drawn,
And wishing, all in vain, her thoughts to say;
For oft of old in maiden youth's first dawn,
Within her father's hall,
Her voice to song did call,
To chant the praises of her sire's high state.
His fame, thrice blest of Heaven, to celebrate.

A A

What then ensued mine eyes
Saw not, nor may I tell, but not in vain
    The arts of Calchas wise;
    For justice sends again,
The lesson "pain is gain" for them to learn:
  But for our piteous fate since help is none,
With voice that bids "Good-bye," we from it turn
  Ere yet it come, and this is all as one
    With weeping ere the hour,
    For soon will come in power
To-morrow's dawn, and good luck with it come!
So speaks the guardian of this Apian home.

Verses 346—471.

O great and sovran Zeus, O Night,
Great in glory, great in might,
Who round Troïa's towers hast set,
Enclosing all, thy close-meshed net,
So that neither small nor great
Can o'erleap the bond-slave's fate,
Or woe that maketh desolate;
Zeus, the God of host and guest,
Worker of all this confessed,
He by me shall still be blest.
Long since, 'gainst Alexandros He
Took aim with bow that none may flee,
·That so his arrows onward driven,
Nor miss their mark, nor pierce the heaven.

Stroph. I.

Yes, they lie smitten low,
If so one dare to speak, by stroke of Zeus;
    Well one may trace the blow;
The doom that He decreed their soul subdues.
    And though there be that say
The Gods for mortal men care not at all,
Though they with reckless feet tread holiest way,
    These none will godly call.

Now is it to the **children's children clear**
    Of those who, overbold,
More than was meet, breathed Discord's spirit drear ;
While yet their houses all rich store did hold
    Beyond the perfect mean.
Ah ! may my lot be free from all that harms,
    My soul may nothing wean
From calm contentment with her tranquil charms ;
    For nought is there in **wealth**
That serves as bulwark 'gainst the subtle stealth
    Of Destiny and Doom,
For one **who,** in the pride of wanton mood,
Spurns **the great altar of the Right and Good.**

ANTISTROPH. I.

    Yea, a strange impulse **wild**
Urges him on, resistless in its **might,**
    Atè's far-scheming **child.**
It knows no healing, **is not hid in night,**
    That mischief **lurid, dark ;**
Like bronze that will **not stand the test of wear,**
A tarnished blackness in its hue **we mark ;**
And like a boy who doth a bird pursue
    Swift-floating **on the** wing,
He to **his country** hopeless woe doth bring ;
    And no God hears their prayer,
But sendeth down the unrighteous to despair,
    Whose hands are stained with sin.
    So was it Paris came
His entrance **to the** Atreidæ's home **to win,**
    And brought its queen to shame,
To shame **that** brand indelible hath set
Upon the **board** where host and guest were met.

STROPH. II.

And leaving to **her countrymen to** bear
Wild whirl of ships **of war and** shield and spear.
    And bringing as her dower,
    Death's doom to Ilion's tower,

She hath passed quickly through the palace gate,
    Daring what none should dare;
And lo! the minstrel seers bewail the fate
    That home must henceforth share;
" Woe for the kingly house and for its lord;
Woe for the marriage-bed and paths which still
    A vanished love doth fill!
There stands he, wronged, yet speaking not a word
    Of scorn from wrathful will,
Seeing with utter woe that he is left,
    Of her fair form bereft;
    And in his yearning love
For her who now is far beyond the sea,
A phantom queen through all the house shall rove;
    And all the joy doth flee
The sculptured forms of beauty once did give;
And in the penury of eyes that live,
    All Aphroditè's grace
    Is lost in empty space.

Antistroph. II.

And spectral forms in visions of the night
Come, bringing sorrow with their vain delight:
    For vain it is when one
    Thinks that great joy is near,
And, passing through his hands, the dream is gone
    On gliding wings, that bear
The vision far away on paths of sleep."
    Such woes were felt at home
Upon the sacred altar of the hearth,
And worse than these remain for those who roam
    From Hellas' parent earth:
In every house, in number measureless,
    Is seen a sore distress:
    Yea, sorrows pierce the heart:
For those who from his home he saw depart
    Each knoweth all too well;
And now, instead of warrior's living frame,

There cometh to the home where each did dwell
The scanty ashes, relics of the flame,
    The urns of bronze that keep
    The dust of those that sleep.

STROPH. III.

For Ares, who from bodies of the slain
    Reapeth a golden gain,
And holdeth, like a trafficker, his scales,
E'en where the torrent rush of war prevails,
    From Ilion homeward sends
But little dust, yet burden sore for friends,
O'er which, smooth-lying in the brazen urn,
    They sadly weep and mourn,
Now for this man as foremost in the strife,
And now for that who in the battle fell,
    Slain for another's wife.
And muttered curses some in secret tell,
    And jealous discontent
Against the Atreidæ who as champions led
    The mighty armament;
And some around the wall, the goodly dead,
Have there in alien land their monument,
    And in the soil of foes
Take in the sleep of death their last repose.

ANTISTROPH. III.

And lo! the murmurs which our country fill
    Are as a solemn curse,
And boding anxious fear expecteth still
    To hear of evil worse.
Not blind the Gods, but giving fullest heed
To those who cause a nation's wounds to bleed;
And the dark-robed Erinnyes in due time
    By adverse chance and change
Plunge him who prospers though defiled by crime
In deepest gloom, and through its formless range
    No gleams of help appear.
O'er-vaunted glory is a perilous thing;

For on it Zeus, whose glance fills all with fear,
    His thunderbolts doth fling.
    That fortune fair I praise
That rouseth not the Gods to jealousy.
May I ne'er tread the devastator's ways,
    Nor as a prisoner see
My life wear out in drear captivity!

EPODE.

And now at bidding of the courier-flame,
    Herald of great good news,
A murmur swift through all the city came;
But whether it with truth its course pursues,
Who knows? or whether God who dwells on high,
    With it hath sent a lie?
Who is so childish, or of sense bereft,
    As first to feel the glow
That message of the herald fire has left,
    And then to sink down low,
Because the rumour changes in its sound?
    It is a woman's mood
To accept a boon before the truth is found:
Too quickly she believes in tidings good,
    And so the line exact
    That marks the truth of fact
Is over-passed, and with quick doom of death
A rumour spread by woman perisheth.

VERSES 665—782.

STROPH. I.

Who was it named her with such foresight clear?
    Could it be One of might,
In strange prevision of her work of fear,
    Guiding the tongue aright?
Who gave that war-wed, strife-upstirring one
    The name of Helen, ominous of ill?
For 'twas through her that Hellas was undone.
    That woes from Hell men, ships, and cities fill.
Out from the curtains, gorgeous in their fold,

Wafted by **breeze of** Zephyr, earth's **strong child,**
　　She her swift way doth hold;
And hosts of mighty men, as hunters bold
　　That bear the spear and shield,
Wait on the track of those who steered their way
Unseen where Simois flows by leafy field,
Urged by a strife that came with power to slay.

ANTISTROPH. I.

And so the wrath which doth its work **fulfil**
　　To Ilion brought, well-named,
A marriage marring all, avenging still
　　For friendship wronged and shamed,
And outrage foul on Zeus, of host and guest
　　The guardian God, from those who then did raise
The bridal hymn of marriage-feast unblest
　　Which called the bridegroom's kin to shouts of praise
　　　But now by woe oppressed
Priam's ancient city waileth very **sore,**
And **calls** on Paris unto dark doom wed,
　　Suffering yet more and more
For all the blood **of heroes vainly shed,**
And bearing through **the long protracted years**
A life **of** wailing grief and **bitter tears.**

STROPH. II.

　One was there who did rear
A lion's whelp within his home to dwell,
　A monster waking fear,
Weaned from the mother's **milk it loved so well:**
　Then in life's dawning light,
Loved by **the children,** petted by the old,
　Oft **in** his arms clasped tight,
As **one an** infant newly-born **would** hold,
With eye that gleamed beneath **the** fondling hand,
And fawning as at hunger's strong command.

ANTISTROPH. II.

　But soon of age full grown,
It showed **the** inbred nature of its sire,

And wrought unasked, alone,
A feast to be that fostering nurture's hire;
    Gorged full with slaughtered sheep,
The house was stained with blood as with a curse
    No slaves away could keep,
A murderous mischief waxing worse and worse,
Sent as from God a priest from Atè fell,
And reared within the man's own house to dwell.

Stroph. III.

So I would say to Ilion then there came
    Mood as of calm when every wind is still,
The gentle pride and joy of noble fame,
The eye's soft glance that all the soul doth thrill;
        Love's full-blown flower that brings
        The thorn that wounds and stings;
        And yet she turned aside,
And of the marriage feast wrought bitter end,
Coming to dwell where Priam's sons abide,
        Ill sojourner, ill friend,
Sent by great Zeus the God of host and guest,
A true Erinnys, by all wives unblest.

Antistroph. III.

There lives a saying framed of ancient days,
    And in men's minds imprinted firm and fast,
That great good fortune never childless stays,
    But brings forth issue,—that on fame at last
        There rushes on apace
        Great woe for all the race;
        But I, apart, alone,
Hold a far other and a worthier creed:
The impious act is by ill issue known,
        Most like the parent deed;
While still for all who love the Truth and Right,
Good fortune prospers, fairer and more bright.

Stroph. IV.

But wanton Outrage done in days of old
    Another wanton Outrage still doth bear,

And mocks at human woes with scorn o'erbold,
　Or soon or late as they their fortune share.
　　That other in its turn
　　Begets Satiety,
And lawless Might that doth all hindrance spurn,
　　And sacred right defy,
Two Atès fell within their dwelling-place,
　　Like to their parent race.

ANTISTROPH. IV.

Yet Justice still shines bright in dwellings murk
　And dim with smoke, and honours calm content;
But gold-bespangled homes, where guilt doth lurk,
　She leaves with glance in horror backward bent,
　　And draws with reverent fear
　　To places holier far,
And little recks the praise the prosperous hear,
　　Whose glories tarnished are;
But still towards its destined goal she brings
　　The whole wide course of things.

　　Say then, son of Atreus, thou
　　Who com'st as Troïa's conqueror now,
　　What form of welcome right and meet,
　　What homage thy approach to greet,
　　Shall I now use in measure true,
　　Nor more nor less than that is due ?
　　Many men there are, I wis,
　　Who in seeming place their bliss,
　　Caring less for that which is.
　　If one suffers, then their wail
　　Loudly doth the ear assail;
　　Yet have they nor lot nor part
　　In the grief that stirs the heart;
　　So too the joyous men will greet
　　With smileless faces counterfeit :
　　But shepherd who his own sheep knows
　　Will scan the lips that fawn and gloze,

Ready still to praise and bless
With weak and watery kindliness.
Thou when thou the host did'st guide
For Helen—truth I will not hide—
In mine eyes had'st features grim,
Such as unskilled art doth limn,
Not guiding well the helm of thought,
And giving souls with grief o'erwrought
False courage from fresh victims brought,
But with nought of surface zeal,
Now full glad of heart I feel,
And hail thy acts as deeds well done:
Thou too in time shalt know each one,
And learn who wrongly, who aright
In house or city dwells in might.

VERSES 947—1001.

STROPH. I.

Why thus continually
Do ever-haunting phantoms hover nigh
My heart that bodeth ill?
Why doth the prophet's strain unbidden still,
Unbought, flow on and on?
Why on my mind's dear throne
Hath faith lost all her former power to fling
That terror from me as an idle thing?
Yet since the ropes were fastened in the sand
That moored the ships to land,
When the great naval host to Ilion went,
Time hath passed on to feeble age and spent.

ANTISTROPH. I.

And now as face to face,
Myself reporting to myself, I trace
Their safe return; and yet
My mind, taught by itself, cannot forget
Erinnys' dolorous cry,
That lyreless melody,

And hath no strength of wonted confidence.
Not vain these pulses of the inward sense,
As my heart beateth in its wild unrest,
 Within true-boding breast;
And hoping against hope, I yet will pray
My fears may all prove false and pass away.

Stroph. II.

Of high, o'erflowing health
There is no limit found that satisfies;
 For soon by force or stealth,
As foe 'gainst whom but one poor wall doth rise,
Disease upon it presses, and the lot
Of fair good fortune onward moves until
It strikes on unseen reef where help is not.
 But should fear move their will
 For safety of their freight,
With measured sling a part they sacrifice,
 And so avert their fate,
Lest the whole house should sink no more to rise,
 O'erwhelmed with misery;
Nor does the good ship perish utterly:
 So too abundant gift,
From Zeus in double plenty, from the earth,
Doth the worn soul from anxious care uplift,
And turns the famished wail to bounding joy and mirth.

Antistroph. II.

But blood that once is shed
In purple stream of death upon the ground,
 Who then, when life is fled,
A charm to call it back again hath found?
 Else against him who raised the dead to life
Zeus had not sternly warred, as warning given
 To all men; but if Fate were not at strife
 With fate that brings from Heaven
 Help from the Gods, my heart,

Out-stripping speech, had given thought free vent.
       But now in gloom apart
It sits and moans in sullen discontent,
       And hath no hope that e'er
It shall an issue seasonably fair
       From out the tangled skein
Of life's strange course unravel straight and clear,
While in the fever of continuing pain
My soul doth burden sore of troublous anguish bear.

THE LIBATION-POURERS.

VERSES 20—75.

STROPH. I.

Lo, from the palace door
We wend our way to pour
    Gifts on the dead;
And in our bitter woe,
Our hands with many a blow
    Smite breast and head.
On each fair cheek the nail
Has ploughed full many a trail,
And all to tatters torn
The garments we have worn;
The foldings of the vest
O'er maiden's swelling breast
    Are roughly rent;
For now on us the chance
That shuts out joy and dance
    Our fate hath sent.

ANTISTROPH. I.

A spectral vision clear
Thrills every hair with fear,
In haunted sleep,
Breathing of dire distress,
From innermost recess
Its watch doth keep,
Breaking with cry of fright
The still deep hush of night:
All through the queenly bower
Sharp cry was heard that hour.
And they to whom t'was given
To read decrees of Heaven,

In dream o'ertrue,
By solemn pledges bound,
Declared that underground
The dead were wrathful found
    'Gainst those that slew.

STROPH. II.

And so the godless queen
In eager-haste is seen,—
Sends me with gifts like this,
Full graceless grace, I wis,
As if, (O mother Earth,
To whom we owe our birth!)
    To banish dread.
And I would fain delay
This prayer of mine to pray:
What ransom can men pay
    For blood once shed?
Oh, hearth and home of woe!
Oh, utter overthrow!
Foul mists brood o'er our halls:
No ray of sunlight falls;
Thick darkness from the tomb
Of heroes makes the gloom
    Yet more intense.

ANTISTROPH. II.

And awe that once we knew,
Strong, mighty to subdue,
Falling on every ear,
Thrilling each soul with fear,
    Is gone far hence.
There be that well may bow
In craven terror now,
For lo! Success enthroned
As more than God is owned.
But Vengeance will not fail
Ere long to turn the scale.

On some her strokes alight,
While yet their day is bright;
Some, **as in** twilight's gloom,
O'erflow with gathering doom;
Some endless night doth **hold**
In realm of darkness old.

Stroph. III.

And for the blood which Earth,
To whom it owed its birth,
Hath drunk, there still doth wait
A stern avenging Fate;
The stain of blood doth stay,
And will not pass away,
And nerves are thrilled with pain
In soul that sets in train
The plague that **works amain**
        Its evil **great.**

Antistroph. III.

All help from him hath fled
Who with adulterous tread
Defiles another's bed.
Though many streams **should pour**
Their waters o'er and o'er,
Those waters evermore
        Are poured in vain;
They cannot cleanse the guilt
Of blood that once is spilt,
        Man's hand to stain.

Epode.

But since to me by Heaven
The exile's life is given,
  (Yea, far from home I know
The bond-slave's cup of woe,)
I needs must yield assent
        To good or ill intent,

Accepting their commands
Who rule with sceptred hands,—
Yea, I must hide my hate
In this my evil fate,
And under strong control
Keep my rebellious soul;
And now beneath my veil
I weep my woes' full tale;
For cares that vex and fret
My cheeks with tears are wet.

VERSES 576—639.

STROPH. I.

Many dread forms of woe and fear the Earth
  Doth breed; and Ocean's deep
Is full of foes men hate, of monstrous birth;
  And Air's high pathways keep
Their flashing meteors; birds that wing their flight,
  And things on earth that creep;
And one might tell the wrath of whirlwind's might,
  When tempests wildly sweep.

ANTISTROPH. I.

But who can tell man's purpose overbold?
  Or woman's, prompt to dare?
Or the strong loves that men in bondage hold,
  And bring woe everywhere?
Or strange conjunctions of the hearth and home?
  But still the palm they bear,
The loves unloved that women overcome,
  And hold dominion there.

STROPH. II.

And one whose thoughts are not o'erswift of wing,
  May learn and ponder well
What purpose Thestios' child to act did bring,
  Purpose most dire and fell,
Her burning thought who did her own child slay,
  Kindling the 'orch of death

That with her child's life kept its equal way,
Since coming from his mother's womb he cried,
To that predestined day on which at last he died.

ANTISTROPH. II.

And yet another must I in my song
    Devote to hate and scorn,
The murderess Skylla, who to deeds of wrong
    By Minos' gifts was borne,
And for her foes' sake slew a man she loved
    For Cretan chains gold-wrought;
She with dog's heart the deathless lock removed
From him, in deep sleep sunk; yet Hermes' power
She too was taught at last at her appointed hour.

STROPH. III.

But since I tell my tale of loathly crime,
And of ill-omened marriage out of time,
    Wedlock our house abhors,
The schemes and plots of women steeped in guile
Against a warrior chief, a chief erewhile
    The dread of foes in wars,
The foremost place I give to altar-hearth
Where no wrath burns and woman knows the worth
    Of mood from daring free.

ANTISTROPH. III.

Yet of all ills the Lemnian first may stand,
The cry of loathing rings through all the land,
    And still each crime of dread
A man will liken to the Lemnian ill;
And now by woe that comes from God's stern will
    The race is gone and fled,
Of all men scorned, for no man looks with love
On deeds that to the high Gods hateful prove;
    Is not this clear to see?

STROPH. IV.

And lo! the sword sharp-pointed pierces deep,
  E'en to the heart, the sword which Vengeance wields
B B

The lawless deed will not neglected sleep,
　　When men tread down what fear of high heaven shields;

Antistroph. IV.

But still the block of Vengeance firm doth stand,
　　And Fate, as swordsmith, hammers blow on blow;
And then with thoughts that none can understand,
　　Erinnys comes far known, though working slow,
And to the old house brings the youthful heir,
　　That deeds of blood wrought out of olden time
　　　　May the due judgment bear
　　　　For each polluting crime.

Verses 769—820.

Stroph. I.

Oh, hear me, hear my prayer, thou mighty Lord!
　　Sire of all Gods that on Olympos dwell,
Hear Thou, and grant my longing heart's desire,
　　That those who wise of heart would fain do well
　　　　May see each prayer for right
　　　　Fulfilled in holiest might;
　　　　That prayer, O Zeus, I pray.

Stroph. II.

Do Thou protect him, yea, O Zeus, and bring
　　Before his foes on yonder secret way;
For if thou raise him high, then Thou, O king,
　　　　Shalt to thy heart's content
Receive a twofold, threefold recompence,
　　　　For that thine anger bent
　　　　Against each old offence.

Antistroph. I.

Look on the son of one whom Thou did'st love,
　　Like orphan colt fast bound to car of woes;
Set Thou a mark that may as limit prove;
　　Ah, might one watch his footsteps as he goes,

In measured course and true,
This his own country through !

STROPH. III.

And ye who in our home
Stand in the shrine with plenteous wealth full stored,
Hear, O ye Gods, and come,
Yea, come with one accord,
Lead him on, wash away
With vengeance new the blood of crime of old ;
Let not the old guilt stay
To breed fresh offspring where our home we hold.

MESODE.

But grant him good success,
O Thou who dost within the great cave dwell !
With upward glance of joy our chief's house bless,
And that he too, full well,
Freely and brightly with the dear, loved eyes,
May look from out the veil of cloudy skies.

ANTISTROPH. III.

And then may Maia's son
Assist him, as is meet, in this his task !
Through Him success is won,
The boon that now we ask :
And many secret things will He make clear,
If that should be his will ;
But should He choose the truth should not appear,
Before men's eyes He still
Brings darkness and the blackness of the night,
Nor is He clearer in the day's full light.

STROPH. IV.

And then will we pour forth
All that our house contains of costliest worth,
Past evil to redeem,
And through the city we will raise the strain
Shrill-voiced of women's chant yet once again.
All this as good I deem ;

This, this my gain increaseth more and more,
And far from those I love is sorrow's bitter stour.

ANTISTROPH. II.

But thou, take courage when the time is come,
    The time to act indeed,
And when she calls thee " child," do thou strike home,
And let thy father's name for vengeance plead ;
Do thy dread taskwork to the uttermost.

ANTISTROPH. IV.

Let Perseus' heart within thy bosom dwell,
For thou dost work for each dear kindred ghost,
    And those on high, a bitter boon and fell,
      Completing there within
      The deed of blood and sin,
And utterly destroying him whose hand
      That crime of murder planned.

EUMENIDES.

COME then, and let us dance in solemn strain;
It is our will to chant our harsh refrain,
    And tell how this our band
Works among men the tasks we take in hand.
In righteous vengeance find we full delight;
On him who putteth forth clean hands and pure
    No wrath from us doth light;
Unhurt shall he through all his life endure;
But whoso, as this man, hath evil wrought,
    And hides hands stained with blood,
On him we come, with power prevailing fraught,
    True witnesses and good,
For those whom he has slain, and bent to win
Full forfeit-price for that his deed of sin.

STROPH. I.

    O Mother, Mother Night!
Who did'st bear me a penalty and curse
  To those who see and those who see not light,
Hear thou; for Leto's son, in mood perverse,
    Puts me to foulest shame,
In that he robs me of my trembling prey,
    The victim whom we claim,
That we his mother's blood may wash away;
    And over him as slain
Sing we this dolorous, frenzied, maddening strain,
The song that we, the Erinnyes, love so well,
That binds the soul as with enchanter's spell,
Without one note from out the sweet-voiced lyre,
Withering the strength of men as with a blast of fire.

ANTISTROPH. I.

For this our task hath Fate
  Spun without fail to last for ever sure,
That we on man weighed down with deeds of hate
  Should follow till the earth his life immure.
        Nor when he dies can he
        Boast of being truly free;
        And over him as slain
Sing we this dolorous, frenzied, maddening strain,
The song that we, the Erinnyes, love so well,
That binds the soul as with enchanter's spell,
Without one note from out the sweet-voiced lyre,
Withering the strength of men as with a blast of fire.

STROPH. II.

Yea, at our birth this lot to us was given,
And from the immortal Ones who dwell in Heaven
        We still must hold aloof;
None sits with us at banquets of delight,
        Or shares a common roof,
Nor part nor lot have I in garments white;
My choice was made a race to overthrow,
When murder, home-reared, lays a loved one low;
Strong though he be, upon his track we tread,
And drain his blood till all his strength is fled.

ANTISTROPH. II.

Yea, 'tis our work to set another free
  From tasks like this, and by my service due
To give the Gods their perfect liberty,
  Relieved from task of meting judgment true;
For this our tribe from out his fellowship
  Zeus hath cast out as worthy of all hate,
And from our limbs the purple blood-drops drip;
So with a mighty leap and grievous weight
        My foot I bring upon my quivering prey,
        With power to make the swift and strong give way,
An evil and intolerable fate.

And all the glory and the pride of men,
Though high exalted in the light of day,
Wither and fade away,
Of little honour then,
When in the darkness of the grave they stay,
By our attack brought low,
The loathèd dance through which in raiment black we go:

And through the ill that leaves him dazed and blind,
He still is all unconscious that he falls,
So thick a cloud enthrals
The vision of his mind:
And Rumour with a voice of wailing calls,
And tells of gathering gloom
That doth the ancient halls in darkness thick entomb.

So it abideth still;
Ready and prompt are we to work our will,
The dreaded Ones who bring
The dire remembrance of each deed of ill,
Whom mortals may not soothe with offering,
Working a task with little honour fraught,
Yea, all dishonoured, task the Gods detest,
In sunless midnight wrought,
By which alike are pressed
Those who yet live, and those who lie in gloom unblest.

What mortal man then will not crouch in fear,
As he my work shall hear,
The task to me by destiny from Heaven
As from the high Gods given?
Yea, a time-honoured lot is mine I trow,
No shame in it I see,
Though deep beneath the earth my station be,
In gloom that never feels the sunlight's quickening glow.

Verses 468—

Stroph. I.

Now is there utter fall and overthrow,
    Which new-made laws begin;
If he who struck the matricidal blow,
    His right —not so, his utter wrong shall win,
This baseness will the minds of all men lead
    To wanton, reckless thought,
And now for parents waits there woe, and deed
Of parricidal guilt by children wrought.

Antistroph. I.

For then no more shall wrath from this our band,
  The Mænad troop that watch the deeds of men,
Come for these crimes; but lo! on either hand
  I will let slip all evil fate, and then,
    Telling his neighbours' grief,
Shall this man seek from that, and seek in vain,
    Remission and relief,
Nor is there any certain cure for pain.
And lo! the wretched man all fruitlessly
    For grace and help shall cry.

Stroph. II.

Henceforth let no man in his anguish call,
When he sore-smitten by ill-chance shall fall,
    Uttering with groan and moan,
" O mighty Justice, O Erinnyes' throne!"
So may a father or a mother wail,
Struck by new woe, and tell their sorrow's tale;
    For low on earth doth lie
The home where Justice once her dwelling had on high.

Antistroph. II.

Yea, there are times when reverent Awe should stay
    As guardian of the soul;
It profits much to learn through suffering
    The bliss of self-control.

Who that within the heart's full daylight bears
    No touch of holy awe,
Be it or man or State that casts out fear,
Will still own reverence for the might of law ?

STROPH. III.

Nor life that will no sovran rule obey,
Nor one down-crushed beneath a despot's sway,
    Shalt thou approve ;
God still gives power and strength for victory
To all that in the golden mean doth lie.
All else, as they in diverse order move,
    He scans with watchful eye.
With this I speak a word in harmony,
    That of irreverence still
    Outrage is offspring ill,
    While from the soul's true health
Comes the much-loved, much-prayed-for joy and wealth.

ANTISTROPH. III.

    Yes, this I bid thee know ;
Bow thou before the altar of the Right,
    And let no wandering glance
    That looks at gain askance
Lead thee with godless foot to scorn or slight.
Know well the appointed penalty shall come ;
The doom remaineth sure and will at last strike home.
Wherefore let each man pay the reverence due
    To those who call him son ;
By each to thronging guests let honour true
    In loyal faith be done.

STROPH. IV.

But one who with no pressure of constraint
Of his free will draws back from evil taint,
    He shall not be unblest,
Nor ever sink by utter woe oppressed.
    But this I still aver,
That he whose daring leads him to transgress,

The chaos wild of evil deeds to stir,
　　In sharp and sore distress,
　　Against his will will slacken sail ere long,
When, as his timbers crash before the blast,
　　He feels the tempest strong.

ANTISTROPH IV.

Then in the midst of peril he at last
Shall call on those who then will hear him not.
　　Yea, God still laughs to scorn
The man by evil tide of passions borne,
　　Swayed by thoughts wild and hot,
When he beholdeth one whose boast was high
He ne'er should know it, sunk in misery,
And all unable round the point to steer;
　　And so his former pride of prosperous days
He wrecks upon the reefs of Vengeance drear.
　　And dies with none to weep him or to praise.

THE END.

PRINTED BY J. S. VIRTUE AND CO., LIMITED, CITY ROAD, LONDON.

THE LIFE AND LETTERS OF THOMAS KEN,

BISHOP OF BATH AND WELLS,

Author of the " Morning and Evening Hymns."

With Portrait, Fac-similes, and numerous Illustrations by Whymper.

Popular Edition.   Two vols. Demy 8vo, 12s.

" Everywhere lucid, accurate, and interesting."—*Guardian.*
"The Dean has devoted great labour to this life of 'the good bishop' and has
exhausted almost all that is to be said of Ken and his writings. The scheme of the
work is broadly comprehensive, embracing more than a mere biography, and he has
thoroughly imbued himself with the spirit of his subject."—*Times.*

THE DIVINA COMMEDIA, AND MINOR POEMS OF DANTE ALIGHIERI.

A New Translation, with Biographical Introduction, Notes and Essays, &c.

Two vols. medium 8vo, 21s. each.

" No book about Dante has been published in England that will stand comparison
with Dean Plumptre's. He deserves the gratitude of all true lovers of good literature
for writing it. . . . We have nothing further to say of it except that, take it for all in
all, the only fitting epithet we can find for it is 'noble'; and that we do most heartily
wish it all the success which it richly deserves."—*Spectator.*

SPIRITS IN PRISON,

AND OTHER STUDIES ON THE LIFE AFTER DEATH.

Fifth Thousand.   Large Post 8vo, 7s. 6d.

" Of very deep interest . . . . very clear, very candid, very learned . . . . a model
manual on the subject."—*Spectator.*

THE TRAGEDIES OF SOPHOCLES.

With a Biographical Essay and an Appendix of Rhymed Choruses.

New and Cheap Edition.   Crown 8vo, price 4s. 6d.

" Let us say at once that Dean Plumptre has not only surpassed the previous
translators of Sophocles, but has produced a work of singular merit, not less remarkable for its felicity than its fidelity. A really readable and enjoyable version of the
old plays."—*Pall Mall Gazette.*

THINGS NEW AND OLD.

A New Volume of Poems.   12mo, price 6s.

" The last volume, 'Things New and Old,' is quite worthy of Dean Plumptre's
reputation. 'Chalfont St. Giles,' a letter from Elwood, Milton's friend, describing his
intercourse with the old blind man, is a piece of true poetry. The Buddhist poems
have great sweetness and power. 'In Memoriam' is a section of the volume which
pays tribute to Maurice, Stanley, and other friends."—*London Quarterly Review.*

LAZARUS, AND OTHER POEMS.

Fourth Edition.   12mo, price 6s.

" Polished and often beautiful verse. . . . A scholar's reading of the religion of the
times, clothed in the rhythm and music of a poetical mind."—*Spectator.*

MASTER AND SCHOLAR, AND OTHER POEMS.

New Edition. With Notes. 12mo, price 6s.

" Worthy to be put on the same shelf with Heber and Keble."— *Westminster Review*.

" The exceedingly able article in the *Contemporary Review* for 1866, by the same author, on 'Friar Bacon,' should be read as a commentary and introduction to this poem ('Master and Scholar'). With exquisite delicacy the writer pours forth once more the pitiful wail of poor E'oïsa's broken heart over the idol of her passion, ... and weaves the traditions of the Magdalen into a charming poem."

British Quarterly Review.

MOVEMENTS IN RELIGIOUS THOUGHT.

CAMBRIDGE UNIVERSITY SERMONS.

I. ROMANISM.   II. PROTESTANTISM.   III. AGNOSTICISM.

Small 8vo, price 3s. 6d.

" Thoughtful lectures, conceived in a very large spirit, and set off by that sort of scholarship which adds so much of literary effect and vividness to the discussions of the religious thinker. The last lecture is one fuller of insight into the sources and roots of Agnosticism than any we have read for many years from a clergyman of our National Church."— *Spectator*.

CHRIST AND CHRISTENDOM.

THE BOYLE LECTURES FOR A.D. 1866. Demy 8vo, price 7s. 6d.

" It is long since the Church of England produced two more noble works of controversy than these ('Christ and Christendom' and Liddon's 'Bampton Lectures'), more likely by the blessing of God, to influence public opinion."— *Contemporary Review*.

" The Boyle Lectures for 1866 will stand not unworthily by the side of those produced by Dean Plumptre's most eminent predecessors. In them he displays with ease, force, and constant readiness, all the resources of a ripe scholar, a keen critic, and an eloquent writer."— *Athenæum*.

BIBLICAL STUDIES.

Post 8vo, price 5s.

" We have seen few books which will serve more efficiently to give life and body to ordinary people's conception of biblical characters, events, and narratives."

Literary Churchman.

THEOLOGY AND LIFE.

Small 8vo, price 3s. 6d.

" Vigorous in thought and unconventional in manner, faithful, earnest, and sound in the faith. . . . . At once scholarly, instructive and practical."

British Quarterly Review.

" It is long since we have read a volume of sermons which maintain so high a level of thought, feeling and expression."— *Theological Review*.

" Earnest, clear, eloquent,   adhering to the old formulæ."— *Spectator*.

SUNDAY.

8vo, price 3d.

" A learned, comprehensive, and singularly candid and valuable treatise."

Scotsman.

CONFESSION AND ABSOLUTION.

Price 1s.

THE LAW OF DEVELOPMENT IN THEOLOGY,

AND

RESPICE, ASPICE, PROSPICE.

TWO SERMONS. Price 6d.